ROK'S CAPTIVE

A FATED MATES ALIEN ROMANCE

BARBARIANS OF THE DUST
BOOK ONE

AG WILDE

PETRONIE
PUBLISHING

Because the universe provides—even when you didn't know you needed a glowing alien with a magic stick

CHAPTER 1
TOO LONG; DIDN'T READ THE FUCKING
FINE PRINT

JUSTINE

Hurrying down the street, my eyes flick up briefly to a holo-billboard overhead. The Xyma's iridescent eyes blink slowly above their stiff smile, their cream skin glowing like pearls in an oyster.

Nothing unusual—just another alien selling perfume with flowing silver-blue hair and that signature three-fingered gesture that went viral after first contact.

The Xyma looks so...perfect. Like something sculpted and not real. Not a hair out of place. Not a single blemish on their skin. While I...

I huff as I catch my and my sister's reflection in the window of a closed-down shop. If this job pays as well as it says it will, we might be able to get our hair done at an actual salon this week—maybe even get one of those Xyma serum treatments so each strand feels like silk. Just that alone, a bit of extra money for self-care, and this job will be worth it. Our hair hasn't seen professional attention since before Xyma ships became a common sight in our skies.

I check the address on my phone again. Three interviews this week, all rejections. This job *has* to pan out. The rent's due. We have nowhere else to go. And beggars can't be choosers.

I press another breath through my nose as we hurry down the sidewalk. Some douche bumps into me, causing my handbag to swing and almost fall off. I turn my head, scowling at him as my sister grips me and tugs me onward.

"Are you sure they said we can *both* come?" Jacqui is frowning underneath her shades, and I suddenly wish I'd worn mine, too. I'm in an airy blouse, loose brown pants, and heeled sandals. They're perfect for this ungodly heat, but I'm sweating, anyway. I'd rolled my blonde hair into a bun and put on my favorite butterfly earrings. I look presentable, I think. Hopefully, it's enough to land this job. God knows I'm putting my every hope on this.

"Yeah." I grip Jacqui's hand as we hurry on. "Lady on the phone said I could bring anyone interested."

Jacqui frowns and even with the dark shades, I can tell her blue eyes that look so much like mine are glaring at me. "*Justine*, are you sure? I didn't have to send a resume? For *alien research*?"

I shrug. "I didn't either. It was a post I saw on LinkedOut. I just filled out the questionnaire and they took my details. No experience necessary. The listing said they need healthy women for 'environmental adaptation research.' Something about testing how humans react in different conditions."

"And they're really paying *ten* grand for that?" Jacqui's frown deepens and I shrug again.

To be honest, I'm not completely sure why the pay is so high, but I don't care. "The Xyma could give two shits about money. That's the whole point of this integration between our species. They get to study us, we get their tech and funding. Win-win." I try to sound more confident than I feel. "Besides, government-funded research always pays well if you can get it. Remember when Anna from our old apartment did that drug trial? Paid her rent for like six months."

The explanation feels reasonable enough in my head. After all, the Xyma came and suddenly Earth evolved more than it ever could have in just two years. Makes sense them doing this research if we're to expand humanity across the stars.

Still, I can feel Jacqui's glare. For my younger sister, she's always acted like the mother we both lost.

"Alright, listen." I stop at the pedestrian crossing, taking a breath that feels just as hot as the air already in my lungs. As we wait for the light to turn green, people crowd at our backs and the humidity goes up by ten fucking degrees. "Look, we don't have a choice, do we? Unless you can fork up a month's rent in less than a day, we're both fucked hard in the ass with a big fat dick, Jaqs. Zero lube, baby."

An elderly woman scowls at me, probably because of my language, and I cringe, lowering my voice.

"We can turn back now if you're not sure about it." The anxiety that's been chasing me for weeks threatens to raise its head again. We'll be homeless, but I'll turn back if Jacqui really wants us to. I just hope she doesn't. "We can look for something else."

Jacqui stares at me for a moment before her shoulders sag. "No, you did good finding this. Better than good." She sighs. "We have to do it. You're right, we don't have a choice."

Swallowing down the lump in my throat, I nod. As the pedestrian light goes green, we turn and race across the road just before the little man turns red.

Jacqui grips my hand tighter as we hurry down the next street. "I just...look, I wore a *skirt*. Should I have worn pants like you? Jeans? Are we going to be doing physical tests or anything? If that's the case we're overdressed, Jus. What if they turn us away and—"

"You look great." I give her brown blouse a once over. Her low-heeled brown boots give it some flair. "Hey! Isn't that one of my blouses?"

She grins at me and I roll my eyes as we turn the corner.

"Better to be overdressed than underdressed," I whisper, echoing words our mother used to say. Back then, our hair was always done. Our clothes always barely worn. We were little girls who didn't know how cruel the world could be. Little girls who didn't expect to grow up in a world where aliens came to Earth and—poof—society just didn't function anymore.

I guess it could be worse. The aliens didn't enslave us. They just showed up and gave us tech that made our jobs obsolete.

Just a side effect of peaceful first contact.

Jacqui smiles, squeezing my hand. "You sound like mom." I don't miss the note of sadness in her voice. "All seriousness though, Jus, you did the checks, right? I mean, it's only been like, what, two years since the Xyma showed up? And now we're signing up to do *research* with them?"

Two years. It feels like two decades.

"Of course, I did the checks," I almost growl. To think she'd actually question if I did the checks! "I verified the number on the job post, Jaqs. It matched. It's the same one on the EXA website. And I researched the organization. EXA. Earth-Xyma Alliance. I mean, we see them on TV all the time. I even looked up their headquarters. It's that iconic white building in Washington. Not some tent in a sketchy back alley. The website said they've partnered with the government to keep humans productive."

"Productive." Jacqui says the word like it tastes like dirt as she dodges some man who is walking like he owns the entire sidewalk. She sighs again as we reach the next block and cross the street.

I know why she's questioning this so much. It's the Xyma. And even though they've turned out to be a peaceful race, it's still hard to trust them completely. They're aliens after all. Far more advanced than us. They could have crushed us like bugs when they arrived, but they didn't. Regardless of that they're still, well, *aliens*.

"They're paying how much again?" she asks after a few moments.

"Ten thousand. *If* we're accepted. Then a grand a day after that until the research ends." Jacqui's head snaps in my direction, eyebrows shooting above her shades. I hurry on. "I'm not too sure about that part. Maybe I didn't read it right. But even if it's a tenth of that it'll be more than enough for rent and food...if I can get them to give us an advance, that is." I bite my lower lip, thinking. "And if we make a good impression, maybe they'll keep us on. We could save until we find more stable jobs. Maybe in one of those new Xyma factories."

"Landing one of those jobs is rarer than a bitch with three clits."

I snort. "So two isn't rare enough?"

Jacqui releases a chuckle before shaking her head. "The Xyma have thousands of robots. Their factories don't need us. Heck, *they* don't need us. I'm surprised they're helping us at all."

I bite my lip. She's right, of course. But that's why we need this job. We need the money. Things are only going to get harder out here.

Jacqui groans, head tilting forward, and I know she's looking at her outfit again. No more questions come from her lips though; she's resigned to putting her best foot forward just like I am. Neither of us has been able to land a job despite constantly applying for over eight months. We have no savings. We've sold and pawned every single possession we could part with.

There's nothing left. Nothing apart from Mom's butterfly earrings attached to my ears and neither of us is selling those.

"I guess it won't be so bad, right?" Jacqui murmurs. "Who doesn't want to work with aliens and get paid to do it?"

I swallow down my emotions, knowing she's thinking about the same thing I am. That this is our last shot before our landlord demands payment in 'alternative means'. We'd rather die.

Shit. We really are fucked. In the ass. Zero lube.

My pace slows down as I scan the street. By my side, Jacqui sobers up and a heavy sigh weighs down her shoulders. Those mothering hormones kick in even though she's only a year younger than I am. I guess we've both learned to mother each other since Mom passed over a decade ago. "Cheer up, Jaqs. I'll buy you ice cream later."

She snorts and punches me in the side with her elbow. "I'm not a fucking child."

"Ah, so you *don't* want ice cream then? Strawberry with chocolate syrup? Hmm...guess I'll just have to eat it all on my lonesome."

"Hey, I never said I *didn't* want it!"

"Thought so." I chuckle as I frown, scanning the street ahead.

"What are you looking for, anyway? I thought you said we're going to the EXA."

I shake my head. "No, we're not going to the headquarters. There's supposed to be a shuttle taking us to the research facility."

Her eyebrows rise again. "Really...I guess that doesn't sound too bad for a ride to Washington."

"Not Washington. We're going to Arizona. They said we'd be transported there."

"Arizona?!"

I give Jacqui a tight-lipped grin. Arizona's like a death sentence in this heat but, well—again—we have no choice. It's either this or joining the growing number of people setting up tents along the curb.

"There it is!" I spot the white bus just as it pulls into the bus stop and I'm kind of glad when Jacqui turns her focus to the bus instead of me. "EXA" is emblazoned on the side in big dark letters over an alien script. I don't know, but it dispels some of my nerves seeing the text there.

"Damn, you're actually right. They really sent transportation," Jacqui mutters as I tug her along with me. We hurry together, my eyes widening when I realize all the people at the bus stop seem to be waiting for the same ride. Glancing back at Jacqui, her lifted brows tell me everything I need to know. We're thinking the same thing. This is a lot of people. But more than that, this is a nice, new, classy-ass bus. The exterior looks brand new, but what I can see of the interior looks even more impressive. Like some futuristic luxury limo or something.

I remind myself this is the Xyma we're dealing with, not our shitty government who would have made us take public transport and pay for it ourselves, too.

We're right in front of the wide double doors when they open with a swoosh. I push down the lump in my throat as we step on, but almost stumble at what I see before me. Glancing back at Jacqui, I squeeze her hand hard. Her sister-sister telepathy is fucking on because she gets the gist immediately. Her eyes open wide enough that I see them over the rim of her shades. Before us is the hottest guy I've ever seen. The bus driver is all sculpted cheekbones and piercing green eyes. He looks almost too perfect to be human, though I can't place exactly why. Maybe it's the way his skin seems to shimmer slightly under the fluorescent lights, or the unnaturally still way he holds himself. Almost inhuman if not for the expensive dark suit he's wearing. Even in the scorching heat, he's not sweating.

Xyma? No. He doesn't look anything like the ones I've seen on TV.

A shiver goes through me as his gaze slides from me to Jacqui. Only, it's not the type of shiver that should be there. Not the one that makes my blood tingle and butterflies swirl in my gut. This shiver makes me completely aware, as if there's a spider on my back and I shouldn't move as those green eyes focus back on me.

"I—uh—," I stutter. God, you'd think I haven't seen an attractive man in years. Have I? I've been too damn focused on the fact that we've been peacefully invaded. "Is this the bus for the EXA program?" Fuck, he must think I'm an idiot. The logo is on the side of the bus, but the neurotic part of me still has to double-check.

Without saying a thing, the driver simply gives me a stiff nod. That tingle of alertness goes through me again as I force my legs to move. Flipping out my cell phone as we take the two free seats directly behind the driver, I pull up my web browser and type in 'EXA' again.

The search results come up. The alliance is spearheaded by representatives from the New World government and the Xyma themselves. Formed soon after first contact, they've done a lot of work over the past two years as Earth shifted on the fact that we truly weren't alone.

Sliding my phone back into my bag, I shift closer to the window as Jacqui leans my way, giving space to the other people boarding the bus. I catch a few faces. A stream of women. There's one with a cane that comes in and sits in the accessibility bay. One with her hair hiding a birthmark that covers half her face. Another strawberry blonde who catches my eyes and grins. I smile back, some of the tension leaving my shoulders.

It's just regular people. Like me. Like Jaqs.

"Hey, you seeing this?" Jacqui whispers, her hand tightening on mine as her head tilts toward the stream of people filling the bus. "It's all women..."

"Yeah," I murmur. Her observation makes my spine tingle with unease. "I mean, I knew they wanted women, but..."

"Yeah? Only women? Don't you think that's weird?"

I squeeze her hand, but can't quite muster the reassurance I want to give. "The job post said something about biological differences in adaptation."

"Right...Of course." She shifts uncomfortably in her seat before adjusting her handbag with a defeated sigh. I place mine in my lap, clutching it a little too tightly. It's not long till the bus is full, every seat taken.

Slight nervousness makes me look over my shoulder from where we're seated and I catch the eyes of some of the passengers. Some of them are talking to each other, some are just looking out the windows. It seems like a varied bunch, but I guess that's what you'd get sourcing people from the city. There's nothing strange in that. Just a regular bunch of people looking for a quick paycheck like us.

None of them look overly worried or freaked out.

Ten grand if we get in. A grand a day after. If they keep us for the month, that's like forty a pop. With me and Jaqs that's like eighty. That's a good salary for a year. We wouldn't have to worry so much for a while.

Forcing the anxiety down, I settle into my seat, my gaze shifting to the rearview mirror so I can watch the driver.

When his gaze suddenly flicks up like some hawk, I get that

strange feeling again before I look away. Beautiful people are intimidating, but I never thought of myself as someone who was ever so easily frayed. I learned the hard way that life won't hesitate to pull you down if you let your nerves get in the way. It's why I'm taking this job. Why I have to try. But this dude... it's like his eyes are looking under my skin.

This close, I can see the shadow of silver-blue hair cropped close to his skull. So he *is* Xyma. How did he get his face to look so human? Probably another tech thing or maybe some other research they've been conducting. It's...creepy.

Gaze shifting to Jacqui, I elbow her in the side when I find her blatantly eating up the man candy, only her shades giving her any semblance of discretion.

"Stop!" I hiss.

She grins, running her tongue over her lips for effect. "What? He's hot."

"He's also obviously not human."

She grins wider, all her apparent worry from before seeming to disappear in the presence of alien dick. "I've seen some stuff on the internet..."

"God, you're gross."

"Says the girl who hasn't had a boyfriend in *four* years."

I elbow her again, a laugh choking in my throat. "Low blow."

Jacqui shrugs.

As the bus doors swoosh closed, my chest rises and falls in a sigh.

"WELCOME TO THE EARTH-XYMA ALLIANCE ENVIRON-MENTAL ADAPTATION RESEARCH PROGRAM." The auto-mated voice makes me jump. Jacqui lets out a surprised chuckle, head tilting as she looks around. Gaze shifting to the roof, I can't even see the speaker where the voice should be coming from. "PLEASE TAKE YOUR TRANSLATION DEVICE

AND THE PROVIDED LITERATURE. YOUR CONSENT IS REQUIRED FOR PARTICIPATION IN THIS PROGRAM."

My gaze flies to Jacqui's. So...we're in? We got into the program already? That's...fast and not how I'm used to things being done at all.

Sister telepathy buzzing, Jacqui shrugs. "Which translation device?" She whispers.

My eyes are wide as I shrug in an 'I don't know what the hell they mean either,' sort of way. "Maybe we'll be dealing with Xyma researchers who don't speak any Earth languages?"

Jacqui's brows lift higher. "Doubt it. They learned Mandarin and English even before they revealed themselves to us."

I tilt my head. She does have a point.

I glance around the seats and then in front of me, but I can't see anything that looks like a translation device or the supposed literature. This isn't like being on a plane and the seat before you has the safety information card in the pocket.

My mouth damn near falls open when a slot opens at my side, directly in the wall of the bus. Out slips two colorful flyers and a tray with two small circular discs.

"The fuck?" Jacqui breathes. It's like her murmur echoes through the bus, other people expressing the same wonder. "Those can't be the translators, can they? They look like earphones."

Reaching for the two little white things, I pass one to Jaqs as I turn the other over in my fingers.

"How do you turn it on?" Jaqs whispers before she puts it into her ear. I follow her lead and do the same, glancing over my shoulder to see some of the other women following suit, while others seem more hesitant.

"Maybe they'll tell us how it works when we get there," I mutter.

Grabbing the two flyers, my gaze shifts to the driver, who still has his gaze on me. Is there something on my face? I find myself self-consciously wiping my hand across my jaw as I give Jacqui her flyer, too.

Finally, he looks away, our bodies jostling as the bus pulls out and continues down the city street. Air conditioning suddenly kicks in and I almost release a groan.

Jacqui huffs a laugh through her nose and shifts her body so she's comfortable. "God, that feels good. I take it back, Jus. They don't even have to pay us. Just let us sit on this bus. Fuck the heat."

Someone chuckles behind us and I look over my shoulder to see a woman with long braided hair nodding in agreement. "She's right," the woman says, "it's like hell out there. At least we'll travel in comfort."

A little shiver of excitement goes through me. "You have any idea what we're in for?"

The woman shakes her head before shrugging. "Can't say I trust these Xyma, but at this point, everyone and their third cousin twice removed is looking for work. Been at it for months myself." She lets out a dry laugh. "This pays well and honestly sounds interesting. I mean, getting to work with Xyma tech has to be better than filing for unemployment again."

I smile at her and nod. It's a relief to know we're not the only ones here for the money. I'm about to turn back around when some sort of commotion occurs farther down in the bus. A young woman is speaking rapidly in what sounds like German to someone on her phone, and the woman beside her with strawberry blonde hair is all but beaming, even slightly jumping in her seat.

"I can understand her!" The giddy woman proclaims, and my gaze shifts to Jacqui. My first thought is to roll my eyes.

What's the big deal? But then it hits me. I punch Jacqui in the arm and she winces.

"What the fuck, Jus—"

"Talk to me."

"I *am* talking to you."

I shake her shoulder. "No, I mean in Japanese. You took classes. You must remember *something*."

Jacqui rolls her eyes. "It wasn't 'classes'. It was my *minor*."

"Jaaaqs..."

"Fine! Hello."

"No, I mean, talk to me in Japanese!"

"I *am* talking to you in Japanese! Right now, everything I'm saying."

"What?"

"Are you okay?"—I take the earbud out as she's speaking—"Kikoeru?"

My eyes widen into huge pools. "Oh...my...God. I could understand you!" I almost scream. "In *English*! Holy shit. Can this thing translate in real time?"

My exclamation spreads through the bus as everyone begins talking at once. "What, really?" Jacqui glances from me to the other women who are busy talking in languages they know. "Try it on me. Talk to me."

I go blank. "Do love languages count? You know I don't speak any other languages, Jaqs." But then, with a grin filled with mischief, I remember one thing. "Hasta la vista, baby."

Jacqui bursts out laughing. "I'm going to guess you just used the Terminator line, just from the way you smirked." She's laughing hard now as I nod. "I heard it in English."

"Wow." I reach up and touch the little earbud. "That's some technology. If the Xyma are sharing tech like this, no wonder everyone is scrambling to find something to pay the bills."

Jacqui shakes her head. "If this is any indication, maybe this won't be so bad after all."

I laugh then, some more tension leaving my shoulders.

"DISAGREEMENT WITH THE TERMS HIGHLIGHTED IN THE LITERATURE WILL RESULT IN REMOVAL FROM THE PROGRAM," the automated voice says again and I'm jolted back to reality. A hush goes through the bus as we're all reminded this isn't a holiday. We're here for work. Lifting the flyer, I start reading at the same time that Jacqui pushes her shades up to balance on her forehead.

"Let's see what we're actually signing up for," she whispers.

"The EXA Environmental Adaptation Research Program," I read out loud. "An out-of-this-world experience awaits." I scoff. Bet a human wrote that part.

The literature in my hand depicts planet Earth on the front of the flyer, facing what I assume is the planet the Xyma came from. It's tan and looks like it's filled with rocks and sand. Nothing like our little blue ball. When I open the flyer, I realize it isn't a regular flyer at all, but that it has several pages folded inside. More like a manual than anything else.

Jacqui chuckles. "Who the hell is going to read all this?"

The bus turns a corner, and we join the line of traffic heading out of the city. Whoo. We're really doing this.

"Says here participants will be placed in a controlled environment for the research period to test human adaptability," I murmur, brows furrowing as I read. I flip through more pages. "And then there seems to be a list of...rules..." My frown deepens as I try to read the fine print. "Rules for duration of the research." I read the title aloud. "No outside communication permitted during testing phases."

"Makes sense for a controlled experiment," Jacqui murmurs, her gaze skimming the manual. I see her eyebrow quirk. "Wait, are they saying we're starting today? Like, right now? I thought this was just orientation."

I'm staring at the manual, trying to skim fast to find where she saw this particular information. I see more rules as I go.

"Physiological monitors must remain adhered for emergency response protocols. All specimens, organic or otherwise, are property of EXA and will be reclaimed upon project completion. Voluntary withdrawal is only permitted prior to Phase 1 commencement. No unauthorized biological samples. No documenting procedures. No deviating from assigned schedules. No refusing medical examinations."

"Fuck me now," Jacqui utters and I'm sure I hear the bus driver growl. When my gaze shifts to him, his gaze flicks to us even though he should be watching the road. It's unnerving. "Look at this." Jacqui thrusts the last two pages of the manual into my face and a series of images greets my eyes. There are images of some harsh desert landscapes and what appears to be some kind of habitat dome.

"I get it now," Jacqui says. "They're taking us to the Arizona facility and they've probably set up some kind of habitat. We'll live there during the research period in some simulated biome thing. Kind of like those habitat zones they used to test how humans would endure life on Mars." I can almost hear her confidence increase the more she reasons out loud. "It says we're starting immediately upon arrival."

"Wait, what? We don't have any of our things!" I protest, flipping back through the pages. "There's gotta be some mistake."

"Damn," someone in the seat behind us mutters, and I glance over my shoulder to see a woman scowl at the lengthy fine print. With a roll of her eyes, she pulls a pen from her bag and simply signs. "Who the hell has time to read all this?" she mutters, glancing up at me. "But yeah, it definitely says immediate start. All necessary supplies will be provided."

I feel a wave of panic rise within me. We can't back out now; we need this job. But I'm wearing heeled sandals, for God's sake. How am I supposed to survive in a research facility in these?

I shrug, trying to calm myself. We're on the interstate now and moving fast.

"It says we're supposed to be pleasant in all interactions and there..." Jacqui's still reading. She brings the paper right up to her face, squinting at the fine print. "Hmm...there's a data privacy thing here, too. At the end of the document. It says that by signing, we're permitting the EXA as the only one dealing with our data."

"Well, that's a given. Why would we want them to share our data?" Scanning the flyer again, my gaze shifts to the road outside. What will we be losing? The few pieces of clothing left in our closet and the leftovers in the fridge? If we're lucky, this will be a month of free room and board.

Fuck it.

I shrug, taking my pen out. My signature looks huge on the tiny line, but the moment I lift my pen from the paper it feels like it's all settled. We're in it now. Gaze shifting to the window, I watch the traffic go by. Here, in the coolness of the bus, the heat outside almost looks unreal. Beside us is a family in a station wagon that probably looked new two years ago. Now it's packed with their belongings on top and what looks like three kids screaming at each other in the back. A lot of people have been starting over. Moving from the city to try living off grid so they can provide for themselves.

That would be me and Jacqui, too. But even that you need money to do.

As Jacqui signs and hands me back my pen, the automated voice sounds again.

"ALL CONSENTS SIGNED. THANK YOU FOR JOINING THE EARTH-XYMA ALLIANCE ENVIRONMENTAL ADAPTATION RESEARCH PROGRAM."

I turn to Jacqui, brows slightly raised, as I look around for the camera. But just like the speaker, I can't locate it.

"PLEASE SETTLE IN. IT WILL BE A LONG TRIP."

I give Jacqui one of those closed-mouthed smiles that say 'we're in it now' and settle back in my seat, eyes ahead as I watch the bus eat the road.

"They seem thorough," Jacqui whispers and I nod, though my mind is racing with panic. Maybe this won't be so bad after all, right?

For miles, the bus travels, till the city is far behind us and we're heading far into desert land where dusty gas pumps are miles apart. There's soft chatter in the bus that slowly reduces into low murmurs. Some people start dozing off. Others become content with staring out the window like I am.

I look at the view as we go by, wondering when was the last time Jacqui and I had a trip outside the city. Years. The last I can remember was long after mom died and we both had a dangerous streak, drinking and partying because we both wanted to die too. It's a time that's so painful I don't want to remember it, but I can't forget it either. And so I stare out the window now, remembering that time and also knowing that things have to get better for us. We can't keep living like this.

We're barely living. We're simply surviving.

With a sigh, I pull my gaze from the view.

The bus has been traveling for hours. The sun is setting now, casting long shadows across the landscape. I check my phone—no signal, not surprising this far out. What is surprising is that the GPS isn't working either. Just an error message on a blank screen.

"Weird," I mutter, showing Jacqui my phone. "GPS is down."

She shrugs, leaning her head against my shoulder, clearly fighting sleep. "Probably just no coverage out here."

"Yeah, maybe."

The bus makes a sudden turn off the main highway onto what looks like a maintenance road—barely more than a dirt path with tire tracks. The ride gets bumpier, jostling some of the dozing women awake.

"ATTENTION PARTICIPANTS," the automated voice returns, startling several of us. "PREPARING FOR TRANSIT PROTOCOL ADJUSTMENT. PLEASE REMAIN SEATED."

Jacqui sits up straighter, suddenly alert. "Transit protocol what now?"

The driver speaks for the first time, his voice melodic and strangely accent-free. "Earthlings. Due to unforeseen circumstances, we are implementing contingency route alpha. Please remain calm."

"Contingency route?" a woman a few rows back calls out. "What does that mean?"

No answer comes. The bus continues down the increasingly rough path, the windows reflecting the last rays of sunlight in a way that makes it hard to see outside clearly.

"Initiate secure transit mode," the driver says, seemingly to no one.

The windows suddenly darken, becoming completely opaque. Several women cry out in alarm.

"What the hell?" I stand up halfway, instinctively reaching for Jacqui's hand.

"PLEASE REMAIN SEATED," the automated voice insists, louder this time. "SECURITY PROTOCOLS ACTIVE."

The driver turns his head slightly, just enough that I can see his profile. Something about the way he moves is too smooth. That uncanny feeling I had earlier returns tenfold. I try to push it back.

This is the Xyma. We can trust them. Earth trusts them. Humans trust them. *We can trust them.*

"Emergency pressurization required," he announces. "Implementing atmospheric stabilization."

Atmospheric stabilization? Awesome. Love that for us. I'll just stabilize my own atmosphere while we're at it because panic is definitely setting in.

Before anyone can react, the air vents above us hiss open, and a fine mist begins filling the cabin. It has a faint greenish tint and smells vaguely metallic.

"Cover your mouth!" I hiss to Jacqui, pulling the collar of my blouse up over my nose. All around us, women are doing the same, some crying out in alarm.

"The atmospheric adjustment is for your safety," the driver says calmly. "Resistance will increase discomfort."

I glare at his disgustingly attractive face. "What do you mean atmospheric adjust—"

The bus lurches sideways, then seems to drop several feet all at once, like we've driven off a ledge. Women scream. Automatic restraints deploy from our seats, pulling me back down and strapping us in place.

Fear spikes. I try to free myself but I'm suddenly light-headed, my limbs growing heavy despite my efforts to hold my breath. Jacqui slumps against me, her eyes wide but unfocused.

"Jus," she slurs, "something's wrong."

The bus shudders violently. Through the fog filling my brain, I hear mechanical sounds—clicks and whirs and the hiss of what sounds like hydraulics.

"Transit anomaly detected," a new voice announces over the speakers. "Initiating emergency protocols."

The driver stands up—which shouldn't be possible with the bus still moving—and turns to face us. In the greenish mist, his eyes seem to glow with an inner light.

"Prepare for emergency suspension," he says, his voice resonating strangely through my earbud, which means he's probably not speaking fucking English anymore.

"What's...happening?" I manage to ask, my tongue feeling thick in my mouth.

"Sleep," he replies simply. "For your protection."

The mist grows thicker. My eyelids grow heavier. Jacqui's head falls onto my shoulder, her breathing slowing.

The last thing I hear before consciousness slips away is the driver's voice, oddly gentle.

"The journey will be longer than anticipated. But you will survive."

"Transit to orbital station commencing," says another voice over the speakers. "Estimated arrival: ten Earth hours."

Orbital what now?

Oh shit.

We should have read the fine print more carefully.

We're not going to a facility in Arizona.

We're leaving Earth.

CHAPTER 2
THIS WAS NOT IN THE JOB DESCRIPTION

JUSTINE

It's cold. That's the first thing I notice as soon as I come to. That means I'm not in my apartment and certainly nowhere in the city.

"What..." I groan as I lift my head, still a bit groggy. "What happened?"

Still on the bus, I'm slumped forward in my seat. Maybe it's what wakes me up. Pushes me to sit up too quickly. My head pounds and I sway, my shoulder hitting the side of the bus that's now so cold it feels like ice. "Jacqui?"

I turn to see my sister still in her seat beside me, her head thrown back against the headrest and her mouth open.

Panic surges in my veins as I reach for her. "Jacqui?! Jacqui, wake up! Jaqs?!" I touch her face and she winces slightly. But the relief I feel that she's still alive is quickly overpowered by rising fear.

There is groaning as more of the people regain consciousness and as my vision clears some more, I notice that so is the air, like a thick fog is lifting from around us.

The bus driver. The gas. My gaze shoots to where he's supposed to be, only to find the driver's seat empty.

"EMERGENCY PROTOCOL ENGAGED. WAKING ALL SUBJECTS FROM CRYOSLEEP."

Emergency protocol? Cryosleep? What? Jacqui groans again and my head pounds as I try to look around. Am I dreaming? The bus windows are all blocked out with gray metal. I can't see outside, not even through the windscreen, and the bus driver, whatever he is, is gone.

"PAYLOAD COMPROMISED."

Payload? What payload? My mind races as I try to piece everything together. It suddenly feels like nothing's making sense. I swallow hard, saliva soothing a very dry throat.

"What...what happened?" Jacqui groans, her brows furrowing as she presses her hands to her temples. "Where are we?"

More of the other women are waking up and asking the same questions. Some stumble from their seats. One woman, who is obviously more awake than everyone else, begins screaming. Her piercing cry seems to bounce off the metal walls around us.

"ENGINE FAILING. RELEASING CARGO TO REDUCE LOAD."

That...doesn't make sense. The Xyma bot isn't making sense.

It's all the thought I get to have before the whole bus jerks. Our limp bodies jostle in our seats before the movement suddenly stops. At first, it's not immediately obvious. Not until I see Jacqui's body rising right in front of me, held back only by the seatbelts still around her torso. It's only then that I realize I'm floating too, lifting off the seat without effort on my part.

Someone screams. "Ayy, dios mio!" Someone else is calling for help. I turn my head to see a few women who'd no doubt released their seatbelts floating up to the bus roof, their arms and legs flailing even though it's obvious they're still disoriented. They hit the metal top of the bus, wincing from the cold and the impact. But I'm starting to think this isn't a bus anymore, is it.

Gripping Jacqui's hand, I swallow hard. It's like moving saliva over cracked earth. My mouth feels slack and dry, like I haven't used it in a long, long time. "Don't unstrap yourself."

She's more awake now and her wide eyes find mine. "Jus, what the hell's happening?"

I wish I could answer. I don't like not having an answer.

"Gravity," the woman behind us suddenly says. Her head sways as we lock gazes. "This is zero gravity."

It feels like the floor opens up beneath me, but my feet are not even on the floor. I'm still floating slightly in my seat, only the seatbelts holding me stationary. Still, I try to dispel the fear clawing at my bones. "What could cause that?" I refuse to face the most obvious answer. "We were just on our way to Arizona. We can't be... *How* would we be in space?"

The woman's jaw tightens and I can tell she doesn't want to say it either.

"We're in fucking space?!" Jacqui exclaims and in the next second, there's a hum of voices raised in panic and distress like an echoing wave through the bus.

"I know I shouldn't have trusted that job ad. I knew it was too easy," the same woman behind us mutters.

I gulp. There must be a way out of this. We can find a way out. "Hey, what's your name?"

The woman doesn't answer immediately. Almost as if she's swallowing down a bout of the same fear swelling in my gut.

"Mikaela," she says after a few moments and I nod, swallowing hard to get rid of a wave of nausea that rises within me.

"And you?" I direct my gaze to the woman beside Mikaela.

"Erika."

"Okay. I'm Justine. This is my sister, Jacqui." I glance at Jaqs only to see her clenching her fists so hard her hands have gone white.

"I'm Hannah," the woman in the aisle seat across from Jacqui says, the fear in her eyes clear as she looks over at us. I nod, gaze shifting to the woman beside her. Her head's bowed, breaths coming heavy as she looks over at me sideways through her glasses, her eyes darting away the moment our gazes lock.

"Tina," she says. "I'm Tina."

The commotion in the bus increases even though outside is eerily quiet. There's no more Xyma bot, the driver has disappeared into thin air, and I don't hear anything except the panic echoing inside my chest.

"Alright. Erika, Mikaela, Tina, and Hannah, any of you know what the hell's going on?"

Unsurprisingly, they all shake their heads.

"No idea," Hannah gulps. "This was just supposed to be a side hustle."

"Same," Erika murmurs. "But it's clear this is something else now."

"My head feels funny," Jacqui groans.

"Mine too," I force back another wave of nausea. "But we can figure this out." We *have* to figure this out.

"Where's the driver?!" Someone from the back shouts. "Why's he left us here and what happened to the bus?"

The bus shudders again, and our bodies sway in their restraints.

"Don't take your seatbelts off!" Erika shouts, looking over

her shoulder. There are three women still just floating in the air, hindered only by the roof of the bus. At Erika's warning, other gazes shoot in our direction and the fear in their eyes is pronounced. "What now?" Erika turns her attention back to me.

She has an authoritative tone to her voice, as if she was a manager or something, and I get the sense she should be taking the leadership role here. Not me. Erika doesn't seem to be freaking out like the others and all I feel is pure panic in my blood. But when I glance at Jacqui and Hannah, they're looking at me with a flood of hope in their eyes, waiting for my answer.

And Jacqui. Poor Jacqui. If this goes to shit, I'm the one who took her along with me. I'm the one that put her in danger. The thought makes my heart wring underneath my ribs. I swallow hard. I have to find a way out of this. But I don't get the chance. The bus tilts. It's slow, like being on a fairground ride that's just starting up. It tilts till we're all upside down, held in place only by the seatbelts digging into our hips. More women scream and Jaqs and I both grip the seats themselves, hearts in our throats.

"What's happening? Why is it moving like this?" a woman cries out from the back.

"We're rotating," Tina says quietly, then pushes her glasses up with one finger as they start to float away from her face. "In space, without artificial gravity, objects tend to tumble unless stabilized. It's like…like when you toss a book in the air. It doesn't just go straight up and down—it spins." She pauses, then adds even more softly, "Though I have to say, my expertise was mainly in the Dewey Decimal System, n-not orbital mechanics."

Well. Fuck.

"Everyone just stay calm and keep your belts on!" I raise

my voice, trying to project confidence, but there's a betraying tremor underneath my tone.

I'm fucking terrified.

"Jus? I'm scared," Jacqui whispers. Her brows dive in a worried frown as if she's using willpower and thought to turn this all around.

I nod, pushing back my own fear. "I know, I know. Just breathe." Maybe I'm saying it more for myself than for my sister, because my lungs are burning as if I'm forgetting to fill them up. "We'll get through this."

Jacqui nods. "Remember that time we got stuck on the Ferris wheel at the county fair?" she says, her voice trembling only slightly. "We were what, eight and nine?"

A pang swells in my chest at the memory, but I nod, grateful for the distraction from the worried cries of the others. "Yeah...yeah I remember. The ride had gotten stuck at the top, and we were dangling up there for over an hour."

A shaky laugh escapes Jacqui's lips. "You were so scared. Crying and clutching that stupid teddy bear you'd won like it was a life raft."

I swallow hard, a chuckle that sounds more like a sob coming from my lips. "Mr Sparkles was supporting me while you were busy making jokes about how we'd have to eat each other to survive."

"I was a morbid little shit, wasn't I?" Jacqui says with a watery grin.

"The toughest little shit."

She grins at me, water falling from her eyes as she sniffles.

But the bus is still moving. Still rotating. Soon we're sideways. The only thing alleviating the strain on our bodies is the fact that gravity seems to be absent.

"What are we going to do?" I hear Tina whisper, and Hannah grabs her hand, squeezing it tight. At least, for now, no one else has released their seatbelts and one of the women who had floated up from her seat seems to be making her way back, grabbing on to other seats to push herself forward. Another of the floating women is watching and starting to make her way back, too.

I gulp hard, my hands shaking as I reach for my handbag. But it's not in my lap anymore. Must have floated up and away. I spot it floating near what would've been the windscreen, but is now just a wall of metal. My heart falls. I wanted to check my phone. See if there's a signal. I don't know. Call 911 from space? Stranger things have happened.

"It can't have been that long," I say out loud, pulling on the well of hope that has kept me surviving this long. "Maybe this is some kind of training thing? Some kind of hidden camera thing?" I'm grasping at straws. "This is an adaptation program, after all."

"A hidden camera thing?" Jacqui asks hopefully, and a murmur goes through the bus even as the speed of the rotation picks up. "Please make this a hidden camera thing. This is a survival test after all, right. That's what we signed up for. What if it started the moment we got into this bus?"

Yeah, that sounds plausible. Maybe this is a part of orientation. See? Nothing to freak out about, Justine.

"Wait wait wait. You could be right. We're still here. Still alive although the bus is..." The woman at the back who was beaming when the trip started forces a smile on her face again. She seems to blink away the dark cloud of fear that was encroaching on her brow. "Maybe we should all introduce ourselves and try to stay calm. Get to know each other if we're going to be working together." She grins, but even I can tell it's forced. "I'm Pam!"

Somebody curses at the back. "Who the fuck wants to know your name when *we're all about to die*!"

A commotion immediately rises and I feel my chest tighten. Pam might be overly positive, but she's right.

"Hey," I say. "Hey!" I raise my voice like a schoolteacher, but it seems to work. Everyone's looking my way as the bus continues to rotate, putting us right-side up. "Pam's right." Pam beams at me and I push past her sunshiny face. "We have to keep calm. Otherwise, it will simply be chaos and if this isn't a hidden camera thing, then..."

"Then we're really fucked in the ass," Jacqui murmurs. "Zero lube."

"Well, anal sex isn't bad if you do the right preparations." Tina doesn't seem so shy anymore as her head pops up, eyes meeting Jacqui's. The moment the words leave her mouth, she turns red. "I—I mean—"

Mikaela rolls her eyes. "God help us." She presses her head back against the seat as the woman beside her—what was her name again? Erika!—stifles a giggle.

"Not exactly where I was heading with this, Tina..." I murmur. Tina blushes harder. "But it's better than us screaming and freaking out." I watch as the two women who were making it back to their seats manage to do so. The other woman still floating seems to be trying to find a weak spot in the roof.

"This is a waste of time!" Someone shouts and the murmurs start again before one woman raises her hand.

"I'm Alex. I'm a nurse. I saw the job and thought, why not? It seemed like a not-so-stressful way to earn a few more bucks."

Some more murmurs, ones of agreement this time. We're on our sides again as the bus tilts and I try not to think about us going upside down once more. "Ok," I say loudly so everyone can hear. "That's good. Any other nurses here?"

A timid voice speaks up. "N-not a nurse but I'm in medical

school." I don't know who spoke and my belly threatens to expel everything as we go upside down. "Name's Mira."

"Okay!" I say, closing my eyes as the tilting happens again. It seems to be going faster as the minutes tick by. "That's good. Now, did anyone hear about an orientation for this job?"

If this is orientation then safe to say, I'm failing.

There are murmurs but the consensus is no. So this isn't an orientation of some sort. Probably not a secret camera thing. Even as the bus rotates, I can't pick up a camera anywhere on the metal walls. But I couldn't pick up the speaker either and we'd all clearly heard the Xyma bot before the zero-gravity kicked in.

The bus continues shifting, rotating almost lazily now. That feeling of being sick rises as my sense of up and down is completely thrown off. The cold metal presses against me as the side of the bus becomes the wall, then the ceiling.

"What are they doing to us?" someone sobs. "I just wanted to pay off a loan I have..."

As we turn again, Erika leans forward. "I get what you're doing," she whispers. "But you do know this isn't some test, right? Did you hear the recording when we just woke? Something about cryosleep? Payload? You know what that means, right?"

My gaze slides to hers and I see her lips tighten when they read what must be a myriad of emotions in my eyes.

"We're in space." Mikaela leans forward, too. "And we're fucked. In the ass, like your sister so eloquently said."

On the other side of the aisle, the woman sitting beside Tina—Hannah—is shaking her head in a nervous sort of way, her vision unfocused as she stares at the metal before us, and it's clear she's reaching the end of her tether. "Why would they put us in space without our permission? We're just normal people trying to make ends meet. We're not astronauts. At least, *I'm* not. How did we end up here?"

By her side, Tina shifts, pushing her glasses up on her nose as she takes out her flyer from a bag that's still strapped to her side. She brings it close to her face and it's obvious she's reading through it.

"You know what? Fuck this!" A woman who hasn't introduced herself yet unbuckles herself. She floats away immediately, sneakers connecting with someone's face before she hits the wall. "Ow! Watch where you're going!" The woman flails her arms like she's swimming and somewhat gets the gist before she heads straight to the back, pounding on the metal with her fists.

The dull echoes seem to amplify the more she does it, hurting our ears. But despite that, others start to do the same in their seats. Fists pound the walls and soon it's like being inside a steel drum.

Pressing my hands over my ears, I want to tell them to stop, but a part of me wants to pound on the walls too. I'm about to say fuck it and try to find a way out of this when a violent shudder rocks the bus. Screams echo through the metal chamber. The lights flicker and I only now notice the fluorescent strips lining the top of what is essentially just a metal rectangle. The woman who was floating loses her grip, her body flying through the air as the not-bus spins slightly faster. There's a sickening crack as her skull meets the floor. She lets out a cry of pain.

"Oh my god, are you okay?" Pam calls out, panic edging into her voice.

The woman just groans, blinking dazedly as a trickle of blood runs down her forehead. Someone else cries out at the sight of it and there are audible prayers and pleas for mercy.

The pounding on the walls increases, and I risk a glance at the front of the bus. Still sealed. No signs of an exit.

Not that we'd want to exit right here in the middle of space. But I guess a part of me is still hoping we're in a simulator.

"It's like we're trapped in a metal coffin," Jacqui murmurs.

Her words make my throat constrict with panic. Suddenly, I can't breathe. Can't think. Meanwhile, the other women are losing it—screaming, crying, praying. Jacqui is pale and shaking like a leaf.

Just as I feel I'm about to completely lose my grip on reality, the shuddering increases. So much, it feels like even the atoms in our bodies begin to vibrate.

The bus suddenly tilts, going vertical, our backs floating towards our seats.

"Jus?" Jacqui whimpers.

I grip her hand. I don't know how I can tell. Maybe some part of my body feels it before the rest of me does, but we're moving. Going down.

"Hold on!" I shout, just as the sensation of movement increases. Our backs are suddenly pressed into the seats and I hear piercing screams as gravity suddenly kicks in. Looking over my shoulder, I see the two women who were unstrapped suddenly fall to the front of the bus. There's another sickening thud as they land in a tangle of arms and limbs. One of them is screaming so loudly I know she must have broken something while the other with the head wound isn't moving at all.

"We're falling." Erika says from the seat behind me. "They brought us into space and now we're falling."

"Of. Course." Mikaela grunts. "Fucking Xyma." But despite her cynicism, I see the terror in her eyes.

Squeezing Jaqs' hand, I pull in a shaky breath.

"What now?!" Jacqui shouts over a deafening roar that sounds outside the shuddering metal cube. The movement increases so much, it would be an effort to rise from the force of the pull.

"Now...now we wait."

Jacqui nods, her chin meeting her chest a thousand times. "And we stick together." She squeezes my hand. "No matter what, Justine."

"No matter what."

CHAPTER 3
AND I THOUGHT THE JOB MARKET WAS TOUGH

JUSTINE

There's a deafening groan as metal tears. I whip my head around to see the back of the bus beginning to peel open like a frickin' sardine can. Air rushes in with a whoosh, and my hair flies around my head like I'm sitting in front of a fan.

"Oh god...we're falling! We're really falling!" I hear myself shouting, my voice shrill with panic.

"From space? How is this possible?" Jacqui's face is ashen as she braces against her seat.

All around us, the women react in varying degrees of terror. I swear one faints, her head rolling with each shudder of the bus.

"This can't be happening!" Hannah slaps herself in the face. "Wake up! Wake up! WAKE UP NOW!"

"We're all going to die, aren't we?" Mikaela mutters, her voice still holding that cynicism as if she really isn't surprised.

"I'm going to die wearing yellow sweatpants and granny panties."

"Dios mío, por favor, no me dejes morir!" Someone's praying from the back and I pray too. Because I can't breathe. We're in freefall, plummeting at terminal velocity through the thick atmosphere. The blistering heat of re-entry is already seeping in through the rupture, making the air scorching hot.

"The belts! Keep your belts on!" Erika shouts, and my gaze cuts to the two before us who aren't strapped in. In the chaos, their bodies have shifted and only the driver's seat is keeping them from moving.

She's right. As much as I want to succumb to the blind panic, a small part of my brain is still rational enough to realize the seat belts are our only chance. If this bus doesn't disintegrate from the friction, maybe we'll survive the impact.

It's a long shot, but I'll take any chance I can get.

"You heard her!" I shout as loud as I can, struggling to project over the cacophony. "Everyone, hold on!"

Jacqui is openly sobbing now, her face contorted in terror, but she nods jerkily and holds on to her restraints with shaking hands. Around us, the other women follow suit in a frenzy, wailing and babbling prayers.

The blistering heat intensifies as we continue to plummet. I screw my eyes shut, pulling Jacqui close and holding her trembling body against mine.

This is it. This is how it all ends. Guess this takes "falling for a job scam" to a whole new level. I didn't even get to file a W-2.

As the roar of re-entry becomes all-consuming, I open my mouth in a final, useless scream. Tears swell. My chest lurches with a sob. Oh God, we're going to die.

"DEPLOYING DRAG CHUTES."

We're suddenly tugged, like being in an elevator suspended

by a rubber band. And still, the crash shakes my teeth in my jaw. My whole body shudders, vibrations going through my entire frame even as I hold on to Jacqui. But then it stops.

Everything. Stops.

Breaths coming hard, I lift my head to look at Jacqui. Is it over? Is it done? Are we back now? Do I still get the ten grand if I admit I'm a pussy and quit on the first day?

"Fuck, Jus...FUCK!" It's a harsh whisper but I can feel my sister's relief.

I swallow hard, nodding at her. "We're back. It's done. It's over."

No sooner have I said that before there's another groan. One that makes my heart shudder as we move again. We're upside-down, the front of the bus being the thing that met the ground first and now the entire thing is tilting. With a groan like a creature wailing, the entire bus shifts to crash on its side. I hear cries of pain on the side it lands and as Jacqui and I dangle from what's now the roof, everything goes silent again.

"Fuck this job. Not even for ten thousand am I doing that again," Jacqui breathes.

For a moment, there is complete silence, and then whoops and cheers erupt from some of the women. But as I turn to look over my shoulder at the tear in the back of the bus, something strange skitters inside my chest.

Because what lies beyond is not the sunny Arizona sky I expected. It's yellow. The sky. Is yellow.

"Shit, how are we going to get out?" Jacqui looks down. It's not a far drop, but it will take some maneuvering.

"Oof!" Someone in the aisle seat behind Erika opens her restraints and promptly falls between the gap. "Ouch, that hurt," she murmurs, and I recognize her as the woman with the birthmark covering part of her face.

Other people release themselves and Jacqui does too,

angling her body so her feet hit Hannah's seat before she helps me down. Along with a few of the other women, we head toward the back where there's the tear.

"Where are you going?" A woman with light brown hair asks. She's in what would've been the window seat and she doesn't look like she has any intent on moving.

"Going to find out what the fuck just happened and who's responsible, of course." Mikaela's answer is exactly what comes to my mind first, but then I recall what I heard right as that green gas came down on us. That thing about transiting to some orbital station.

We stumble as we walk, legs feeling weaker than usual. But it's not only that. It feels harder to lift my legs. Everything feels a bit...heavier. It's even harder to breathe. Not too hard, but noticeable enough.

Must be the trauma from the crash.

The hole is just big enough for us to slip through one by one and when we finally do, I feel the heat immediately.

We're in an oven.

The air is so dry it sucks the moisture from my lips in seconds. Squinting against the harsh light, I raise a hand to shield my eyes and take in our surroundings.

"What the actual fuck..." Jacqui whispers beside me.

"This is definitely not Arizona," someone else whispers.

The landscape stretching before us is...different.

"What can you see?" someone shouts from inside the bus.

None of us on the outside speaks. I swallow down a lump in my throat.

"The ground is a tan, sandy color..." one of the other women that exited with us says.

"Probably because we're staring at actual sand," someone else says.

Sand.

Sand for as far as we can see.

Some parts of it are almost rust-like, some brown, but all sand. In the distance, rock formations rise like twisted fingers toward the pale yellow sky. No clouds. No blue. Just a vast expanse of yellow tinged with orange near the horizon.

And the sun.

Jacqui and I tilt our heads in unison as we look at the boiling star above us. I don't know how her shades managed to remain on her head, but once again I wish I'd carried mine. They slip over her eyes as I pull my gaze away from the star before it blinds me.

"The sun is closer..." Jacqui murmurs, frowning. "Whiter too. Frickin' blinding."

Or maybe that's not the sun at all...

But as I glance at the other women who'd exited the bus with us, I know not one of us wants to face that possibility just yet.

I turn in a slow circle, taking in the barren landscape. There are no plants. No shade. No animals. No road. No structures. Just miles of tan sand and those bizarre rock pillars in the distance.

"Jus..." Jacqui squints even as her brows furrow. She doesn't even have to say anything else. I know exactly what she's thinking. *Where the fuck are we?*

My mouth opens, but I can't form words. More women have climbed out after us, and one by one, they fall silent as they take in the sight before us.

"This isn't Arizona," Hannah states as she steps out into sunlight.

"No shit," Mikaela responds, arms crossed now as she turns in a slow circle. "Unless Arizona got a hell of a makeover while we were asleep."

Behind us stands what's left of our transport. The "bus" is

now a simple metal rectangle about the size of a shipping container, now dented and warped from impact. One end is completely crumpled, while the other—where we emerged—is torn open like a crushed soda can. Massive, partially melted drag chutes trail behind it like deflated balloons, their high-tech fabric still smoking from re-entry. Added to that, the exterior is scorched black in places and there are no windows, no wheels—just a plain metal box stamped with the EXA logo on the side.

"How—" I begin, but stop when I hear groaning from inside the container.

"We need help in here!" someone calls out. "There are people hurt!"

One woman, the young med-student, suddenly jerks to attention and hurries back inside the bus.

I turn to the others gathered outside. Shock is written across every face. Some are crying silently. Others look completely numb.

"Maybe we should wait inside until the Xyma come to pick us up." I swallow hard, pushing back my heart which has been steadily rising up my throat. "No use waiting out here in the heat. I'm sure this...orientation caught us all off guard and they'll be here to explain everything soon."

That doesn't even sound convincing to my ears. I catch Jacqui's single raised eyebrow and give her a look that says, "yea I know, but what else am I supposed to say?"

Luckily for me, these women actually listen and most begin filing back into the bus muttering about this being really messed up and out of the blue. The moment I step back inside, my shoulders sag with the relief from the shade. Some women who still have places to sit do so, but I head toward the front where there's a small huddled group.

As I get closer, I see the woman who said she was a nurse—

Alex—working on the woman who'd hit her head. The woman isn't moving, and for a moment, my breath stills in my chest.

"Is she…"

Alex glances my way. "I'm pretty sure she has a concussion." Her chest rises and falls, her hands moving with practiced ease as she checks the woman's pupils with her phone's flashlight, before feeling for the pulse at her neck. "She's responsive to pain stimuli but not fully conscious. I need something to stabilize her neck, and something to monitor her vitals. Does anyone have a first aid kit? Or at least some clean cloth we can use as bandages?"

Beside her, the med student is working on the other injured woman, who definitely has a broken arm.

I have to do something to help them. "First aid kit," I say. "I'll find you one."

Alex looks up and meets my gaze. She gives me an appreciative nod before placing her attention on the unconscious woman again.

Turning, I face the length of the not-really-a-bus again. I'm moving before I even give it proper thought, gaze scanning the gray interior.

"A first-aid kit?" I hear Jacqui hiss behind me. "Where the hell are you going to find that?"

I don't know. The walls of this thing are completely smooth. But when it was just a bus, the manuals and earbuds had come out of the walls themselves. Reaching between a woman who is leaning on the edge of a seat, I pound my fist against the side of the bus. Nothing. I continue moving down, doing the same thing.

"Anyone have any sort of first aid kit?" I say loudly as I make my way down. Behind me, Jacqui sighs and begins bracing herself up to reach the seats above us. She pounds on the other side of the bus, doing the same checks I am.

"Not first aid, but I have some wet wipes!" someone shouts.

"Great, anything can help. Bring it to Alex at the front, please." I'm almost at the back of what was our bus before I hit a panel with my fist and wince.

"Let me try," Mikaela says from behind me. Before I can react, she steps forward and slams her fist into the panel with enough force to knock a bitch out. There's a mechanical click and the panel slides open, revealing a compartment filled with emergency supplies.

I startle, eyes widening.

"Muay Thai," she smirks, shaking out her hand. "And that panel had a different sound when you knocked on it."

The panel falls to the floor with a dull clang.

"Damn—Nice punch," I tell Mikaela as I crouch.

She shrugs, but I catch the slight upturn of her lips. "Finally, something from my resume that's actually useful."

As if on cue, a mechanical whirring sound comes from the now-open section of the bus wall. A thin layer slides back, revealing several identical metal cases.

Jacqui crouches beside me, gaze flicking to mine. One metal case is about the size of a large suitcase, with the EXA logo emblazoned on top. With Jacqui's help, I tug the heavy thing out, placing it on the floor between us. My fingers hover over the latch.

"Should we open it?"

"What choice do we have?" Jacqui says. "Maybe it's emergency supplies. Better yet, a beacon."

With a deep breath, I kneel beside the case and flip the latches. The lid springs open automatically, revealing neatly packed contents: several sealed packets labeled "HYDRATION" in English beneath an alien script. There's also some clothing items in vacuum-sealed bags and what appears to be a small toolset.

"We should open the others. Take inventory," Erika says, already pulling out another one. "Maybe there's enough for all of us."

Some of the other women look on, peering but not seemingly interested in what we're doing. Others have drifted back outside, marveling at the landscape we've managed to find ourselves on.

That leaves just the four of us checking the cases—me, Jacqui, Mikaela and Erika.

"You're right," I tell her, already opening another one. "We need to take inventory. This one contains similar items, but also includes a small medical kit."

I hand the first aid kit to Mikaela, who grabs it and hurries back down the aisle to the nurse and the little infirmary at the front of the bus.

"Hydration packets, food packets, emergency blankets..." Erika trails off. "They planned for us to be here."

I stop searching the case before me to look at her. "Well... maybe not here exactly." I keep my voice low, not wanting to alarm the other women around us. "I think something went wrong."

Erika's throat moves, but she doesn't reply. The look in her eyes, though, it tells me I'm dead on.

"Search the cases," Jacqui whispers. "We need to find a beacon." Her gaze slides to mine and I can read the anxiety but also that quiet strength I've always admired in my sister. The same strength that kept me going after our mother died and Jacqui didn't speak a word out loud for months. I give her a silent nod, neither us nor Erika saying anything more on the subject until Tina appears, face buried in the manual. She almost falls over Jacqui in her intense concentration.

"Oof! Sorry!" She rights herself. "It says here that all research locations are equipped with 'basic human survival necessities, accessible once found.' Whatever that means." Her gaze then falls to the cases before us. "Oh. Guess...guess you found them. There's something else I found too."

Something curdles in my chest. "What?"

"It's—it's here. In the fine print." She points to a section of text so small I have to squint to see it.

"'The Earth-Xyma Alliance Environmental Adaptation Research Program includes off-world testing in controlled biospheres replicating Xyma habitation zones,'" she reads. "'Participants may be relocated via standard Xyma transportation protocols to other world testing sites for the duration of the research period.'"

"'Other world' testing sites?" Jacqui repeats. "Are you fucking kidding me?"

"Tina, let me see that," Erika says, taking the manual. She skims the text, her expression growing darker. "Oh my God. There's more. 'Relocation may include standard cryogenic suspension for interplanetary transit. All medical side effects of such procedures are covered under the EXA health protocol.'"

"We signed up for this?" The cheery lady, Pam, suddenly appears. Her smile seems frozen on her face; her perpetual optimism finally cracking. "I don't remember agreeing to leave Earth."

"That's because they buried it in the fine print," Mikaela returns, gaze shifting to the cases before us. "Classic corporate bullshit. Except instead of stealing our data, they stole our whole fucking bodies."

I run my hands through my hair—my bun is all but dislodged anyway. Turning from the group, my gaze travels over the vast expanse of sand I can see through the crack in the metal before us.

"But why? Why would they take us to…wherever this is? And then just drop us here?" someone else asks.

"Survival program, lady." Someone else says. "They never said *how* and as far as I see it, this is exactly what we signed up for."

That makes everyone go silent.

I hold Jacqui's gaze, not really sure *what* I'm supposed to feel.

"The recording," Jacqui whispers. "Before we landed. It said something about a payload being compromised. Engine failing."

"They dumped us," Erika whispers back. When my gaze shifts back at her, she's clenching her teeth. "Something went wrong with their transport, and they jettisoned us to save the main ship."

"Like fucking cargo," Jacqui spits.

I shake my head. It can't have been that. I refuse to believe. Closing my eyes, I try to keep my rising panic at bay. "Okay. Okay. Let's think this through. They wouldn't just abandon us completely."

"Maybe they're watching us. Who the fuck knows?" Jacqui throws her hands up.

"That would mean they planned for us to be here." Mikaela crouches, pushing a few of the items in the case before us.

Jacqui scoffs. "Are you kidding? You think they meant to crash-land us in a desert with a sun that's got a raging boner? This wasn't planned."

"Actually…" Tina adjusts her glasses, still studying the manual. "The pamphlet does mention 'simulated emergency scenarios' as part of the adaptation testing. It says, 'Participants will encounter various survival situations designed to test human adaptability in Xyma-compatible environments.'"

Some of the women exchange hopeful glances.

"See?" Pam claps her hands together, her optimism returning. "This is all part of the test! We're *supposed* to be here!"

"Then why did that automated voice say the payload was compromised?" Jacqui crosses her arms. "Why say the engine was failing? That sounded like a real emergency to me, not a simulation."

"I didn't hear that," someone else speaks up.

"I did." Erika stands. "And that crash wasn't controlled. People are seriously hurt."

"Maybe it's more extreme than we expected," one woman suggests. "You know, like those hardcore reality shows where they drop people in the wilderness?"

Erika shakes her head. "No reality show would risk killing contestants. That woman with the head injury could have died."

"Maybe the Xyma don't see it that way," Tina says quietly. She flips another page in the manual.

"What do you mean?" I ask, a chill running down my spine despite the oppressive heat.

Tina shrugs helplessly. "I don't know. They're aliens. Maybe the Xyma view risk differently than we do. They have longer lifespans, more advanced medicine. Maybe what seems dangerous to us is just...data collection to them."

"And that's exactly what we signed up for." Mikaela's shoulders rise and fall with a heavy sigh.

"Data collection." Jacqui gestures at the barren landscape. "There's nothing out here but sand and rocks."

"Which means we should stay with the transport," I stand, gaze shifting over the interior of the bus. "If this is a test, they'll be monitoring us, right? And if it's not—if something really did go wrong—then staying with the wreckage makes it easier for rescue to find us."

"If anybody's coming to rescue us," Mikaela mutters.

"The container still has shade," Erika points out. "And we don't know what's out there or how far we'd need to go to find shelter."

Several nods of agreement follow her words.

"We should check if there's a beacon or communication device in these cases," Jacqui says, returning to the supplies. "Something to contact the EXA, find out what's happening."

As we continue searching through the cases, a heated debate breaks out among the group. Some women, led by Pam, insist this is all part of the test—that we're exactly where we're supposed to be, and our response is being evaluated. Others, like Erika and Mikaela, are convinced we've been abandoned and need to focus solely on survival.

"Look at it logically," Tina says, pushing her glasses up her nose. "If this is a test, staying with the transport and using the supplies methodically makes sense. If it's a real emergency and we were jettisoned, then we still need to conserve energy and resources until we can signal for help."

"She's right," Erika says. "Either way, our first priority is to organize what we have and establish some kind of shelter."

I nod, grateful for their level-headedness. "We also need to take inventory of the supplies and ration them. We don't know how long we'll be here."

"What about that beacon?" Jacqui's voice rises a tad and I know that internally, she's absolutely freaking the hell out. "Shouldn't there be some kind of emergency signal we can activate?"

We all turn back to the cases with renewed purpose,

unpacking each one and cataloging the contents. The heat is oppressive. It's like the sun out there is alive and is focusing solely on us. Even inside the bus, it feels like I'm being cooked.

After nearly an hour of searching, Mikaela holds up a small device from one of the cases. "I think I found something!"

We gather around as she shows us a flat, rectangular object about the size of a paperback book. It has a screen on one side and several buttons marked with unfamiliar symbols.

"Is that it? A beacon?" Jacqui's hopefulness is catching.

"I don't know." Mikaela turns the device over in her hand. "It was in a compartment labeled 'EMERGENCY' in both English and what I'm guessing is Xyma script."

Tina takes it gently, examining the device. "There's no clear instruction for how to use it. Maybe it's in the manual some-where..." She begins flipping through the manual again.

"Try pressing the largest button," I suggest. "That's usually the power button, right?"

Mikaela hesitates, then presses the prominent red button in the center. The screen flickers to life, displaying a series of alien characters that scroll rapidly across the display.

"What does it say?" I ask, peering over her shoulder.

"I have no idea," she responds. "It's all in Xyma."

Suddenly, the device emits a series of high-pitched beeps and a small light on its top edge begins to pulse with a steady rhythm.

"I think you activated it," Erika says, watching the light blink. "That has to be a distress signal."

Jacqui grins, throws her hands up and releases a loud "Whoo!" Taking a deep breath, she places her hands on her hips. "Okay, so what now?"

Mikaela meets my gaze before shifting her focus to Erika. Erika shrugs. The fact is...we don't know. None of us do. When we all turn our attention to Tina, she pushes her glasses up her nose and shrugs.

"The manual doesn't say anything about that."

I release a breath as I stare out at the desert beyond. "What now?" My eyes narrow. "We wait."

CHAPTER 4
THE WORST ONBOARDING EXPERIENCE
EVER

JUSTINE

Three days.

Three whole days we've been stuck in this metal box.

Three days of trying not to think about how dirty I feel, my hair greasy and skin coated with a fine layer of gritty sand that seems to get everywhere despite us barely leaving the transport.

Three days. But at least we've started establishing our strange community. Settling into a mind-numbing routine that feels like some twisted parody of productivity.

Tina, with her encyclopedic memory of the manual, has become our technical advisor; Alex, the nurse, oversees our health with military precision; Erika manages our inventory; Mikaela has taken to scouting the immediate area. And Jacqui and I? We find ourselves functioning as unofficial morale officers.

Meanwhile, there's still no sign of rescue.

"I'd kill for a shower," I mutter, pulling my knees to my chest as I sit in what little shade the wreckage provides. The late afternoon sun—if you can even call it that—is slightly less blistering than midday, so a few of us have ventured outside for a brief respite from the claustrophobic interior.

Jacqui snorts beside me. "I'd settle for deodorant at this point."

"No joke." I wrinkle my nose. "I think we've officially reached the point where we all smell equally bad."

"Nature's equalizer," Mikaela says from where she sits nearby. I watch as she drops her cell phone into the sand. Dead. I don't think anyone still has charge. "Doesn't matter if you're in designer clothes or Malmart sweats when everyone stinks."

"Beacon still blinking?" Jacqui asks no one in particular.

"Yep." Erika emerges from the transport, the device in hand. "Same as yesterday and the day before. Blinking away, sending our little SOS to absolutely nobody."

She hands the beacon to me as she settles down in the sand. I turn it over in my hands, studying the rhythmic pulse of light for the hundredth time. Is anyone receiving this signal? Do they even care?

"Maybe we should try to find the instruction manual for that thing," Hannah suggests, joining our little gathering outside. "There could be different settings, signal strengths, something we're missing."

I shake my head. "Tina's been through that manual front to back. If there was anything about how to boost the signal, she would've found it."

Inside, supplies have been meticulously divided. Hydration packets, emergency rations that taste like cardboard dipped in artificial chicken flavor, heat-reflective blankets that we've rigged up as shade. We even designated an area about thirty yards behind the transport as our bathroom spot—though I try not to think about where exactly people are handling their more serious business in a landscape with absolutely no privacy.

"Someone should check on the woman with the head wound," I say, feeling a bit bad I still don't know her name. She'd regained consciousness on the first day, but has remained quiet and disoriented.

"Alex is with her," Erika replies. "Said she's improving, but still needs to stay still and quiet."

"And the one with the broken arm?" Jacqui asks.

"Pam's helping her with the sling," Hannah says. "That medical kit was pretty impressive, actually. Had everything Alex needed to set the bone."

"Almost like they anticipated injuries," Mikaela mutters.

No one responds to that. The implications are too unsettling.

"Anyone want to take a walk?" Pam steps out of the transport, her perpetual cheer only slightly dimmed as she gazes out across the sand. "I'm going stir-crazy in there."

"You made it exactly twelve minutes yesterday before you came running back saying you were melting," Jacqui points out.

Pam shrugs. "Today I'm going for fifteen."

Despite everything, I can't help but smile. Her optimism is both irritating and somehow comforting.

"I'll join you," I say, standing up and brushing sand from my pants. "Need to stretch my legs."

We don't venture far—nobody does. The merciless sun and the oppressive heat make anything beyond a short circuit around the transport unbearable. But it's still better than sitting inside, listening to the increasingly tense conversations about what we should do next.

"Those rock formations seem closer today," Pam stops walking, shielding her eyes as she gazes toward the horizon.

I follow her gaze to the strange pillars of stone jutting from the sand in the distance. "They're the same distance they've always been."

"Maybe." She doesn't sound convinced. "But they're the only landmark out here. If help doesn't come soon..."

She doesn't finish the thought. She doesn't need to.

We complete our brief circuit and return to the small patch of shade. Already, the sweat is pouring down my back, and my mouth feels like it's filled with cotton despite the hydration packet I consumed just an hour ago.

"Seven minutes," Jacqui announces when we return. "New record for shortest walk."

"Heat's worse today." I shrug before sinking back down beside her.

"Or we're just getting weaker." Mikaela braces back on her elbows. I don't reply, but I know she's right.

The evening brings marginally cooler temperatures and most of us gather outside the transport as the massive white asshole of a star begins its slow descent toward the horizon.

"I miss NewTube," someone sighs.

"I miss flush toilets," another adds.

"I miss not knowing what everyone's farts smell like," Mikaela says, earning a few tired laughs.

It's become our nightly ritual—this listing of what we miss. Wine. Air conditioning. Pizza. The sound of birds. Rain. Traffic. The annoying neighbor who played music too loud. All the things we never thought we'd long for.

One thing nobody misses though, is all the bills and debt we left behind. Nobody's mentioned that.

But despite this camaraderie, I don't...I don't know how much longer we can last like this.

Pam maintains her relentless optimism despite everything, suggesting silly games to pass the time. While Hannah's anxiety manifests as constant movement—pacing, fidgeting, rearranging supplies. Meanwhile, as I watch Mikaela tug and wrangle a piece of the torn ship (pretty sure she's planning on using it as a weapon), I realize her cynicism masks her survivalist mentality. And then there's Erika, whose natural authority sometimes clashes with Tina's intellectual approach to problems—Erika wants action while Tina insists on analyzing the manual for solutions. Alex remains professionally detached, though I've caught her crying silently when she thought no one was watching.

We're all sort of...stretched thin.

As the sun disappears and the three moons appear (that's right. Three), we retreat inside for the night. The temperature drops surprisingly quickly once darkness falls—another unpleasant discovery from our first night here.

"God, I'm bored to the tits," I mutter as we arrange ourselves in what has become our assigned sleeping spots. It's cramped and there's hardly any place to sit.

"I've been counting grains of sand to fall asleep," someone else whispers.

"I've been mentally redecorating my apartment," Pam says. "In my head, I've painted the kitchen three different colors."

As conversation dwindles and the transport grows quiet, I stare up at the ceiling. The metal creaks and pops as it cools in the night air. Outside, the wind picks up, whistling through the tear in the back and carrying fine particles of sand that settle on everything.

I don't know how or when I fall asleep. Dreams of water and trees and rain morph into something else. In my dream, the sand isn't just around us—it's alive. Microscopic creatures, glittering like tiny stars, swirl in the air. I watch in horror as they drift into the transport through every crack and crevice, seeking warmth, seeking life. They float toward us, drawn to our breath, our heat. I try to cover my face, but it's too late—they're entering through my nose, my mouth, my ears. I can feel them inside me, burrowing, multiplying, changing something fundamental in my cells.

I wake with a gasp, my hand flying to my throat. Just a dream.

Fuck, I'm going crazy. Lying back down, I promise myself it will get better, but dawn brings no relief—just another day of waiting, of scanning the yellow sky for any sign of rescue.

By midday on the fourth day, tensions are running high. I find myself staring at those rock formations in the distance, an idea forming that I know Jacqui won't like.

"We can't just keep sitting here," Hannah says, her words tumbling out rapidly as she paces. "We're going to run out of water soon. We'll dehydrate. We'll die. Has anyone even counted how many packets are left? What's our actual timeline here?" Her anxiety is infectious, making my own heart rate spike.

"The hydration packets will last exactly 8.3 more days at current consumption rates," Erika counters, consulting her meticulously organized inventory list. Her precision has become both reassuring and slightly intimidating. "We stick to the plan. That's final."

"And then what?" Mikaela crosses her arms, that familiar sardonic smile playing at her lips. "We just die of thirst on day 8.4 instead of today? Stellar fucking plan, Commander."

Erika bristles.

"Actually," Tina interjects, adjusting her glasses, "if we factor in the decreased metabolic needs as our bodies adjust to reduced caloric intake, we might extend that to 9.2 days, assuming the temperature remains consistent with what we've had so far."

"We stick to the plan." Erika stands to face Mikaela. "Stay with the transport. Maintain the beacon. Wait for rescue."

"It's been *four* days," Hannah points out. "If they were coming, wouldn't they be here by now?"

"Maybe they don't know exactly where we are." Tina shrugs. "The manual mentions something about 'variable location drops' for different simulation scenarios."

"This isn't a simulation anymore!" Hannah's voice rises. "This is real! We crashed! People got hurt!"

"Keep your voice down," Alex warns, glancing toward the woman with the head wound, who's dozing fitfully in her makeshift bed, which is really just two seats.

"She's right though," I find myself saying. All eyes turn to me. "We need to consider the possibility that no one is coming. Or at least, not coming soon enough."

"What are you suggesting?" Erika asks. Her expression is guarded and I wonder if it's wise to reveal my little plan.

I take a deep breath. "Those rock formations in the distance. They're the only feature in this landscape. If one of us could get there, maybe climb up high enough, we might be able to see something we can't from here. A settlement, an oasis, anything."

"That's *insane*," Jacqui says immediately. "It's got to be miles away. In this heat? They'd never make it."

"Not alone, maybe." I shrug. "But if a small group went, carrying most of the water..."

"And leaving the rest of us with less," Erika points out.

"If they find help, it wouldn't matter," Mikaela counters, surprising me by taking my side.

The debate escalates quickly. Voices rise and fall as different scenarios are proposed and shot down. Go as a group?

Too risky for the injured. Stay and wait longer? Supplies won't last forever. Send a signal party? Who would volunteer for what could be a suicide mission?

"Enough!" Surprisingly, it's Tina who finally silences the argument. "We're talking in circles. We need to make a decision."

"I think Justine's right," Mikaela says after a moment of tense silence. "Someone needs to check out those rocks. But it should just be one person. To conserve water. The rest stay with the transport."

"One person alone is even more dangerous," Erika objects.

"One person with most of the water," Mikaela clarifies. "Enough to make it there and back. The rest of us can ration even more carefully for a day or two."

More debate follows, but eventually, reluctantly, we come to a consensus of sorts. One person will go, leaving at first light tomorrow when it's coolest. They'll take a three day's worth of water and an emergency blanket that will double as a signal flag.

"So who goes?" Pam asks what we're all thinking.

Silence falls over the group.

"I'll go," I volunteer, surprising myself. "It was my idea."

"No. Way." Jacqui is immediately by my side, brows diving to her nose. "I'm not letting you—"

"We should draw for it," Erika interrupts. "That's the only fair way."

After some discussion, we agree. Those too injured to make the journey are exempt. Everyone else's name goes into the selection.

We have no straws to draw, no slips of paper to pull from a hat. Instead, Erika collects one used hydration packet and cuts it into strips of different lengths, keeping them hidden in her hand.

"Shortest straw goes," she says.

One by one, we step forward and select. Jacqui pulls a long one and visibly relaxes. Mikaela's is even longer. Hannah, Pam, Tina and all the other women—all draw straws longer than half the original length.

When my turn comes, I reach out with steady fingers and select my straw.

It's barely half an inch long.

"Shit," Jacqui breathes.

I stare at the tiny piece of plastic in my palm, my heart sinking to my feet even as a strange calm settles over me.

"No," Jacqui shakes her head vehemently. "No, this is bull-shit. I'm going instead."

"That's not how it works," Erika says gently, but her voice is firm.

"We all agreed to the draw," Mikaela adds.

"It's okay, Jaqs," I say, closing my fingers around the straw. "I'll be fine."

But I'm sure Jacqui isn't convinced. *I'm* not convinced. But someone has to go search for help, we all know that. Our water won't last forever, and we have injured people who need real medical care. Still, knowing all that doesn't make it any easier to be the one who drew the short straw.

Jacqui grabs my arm, her fingers digging in. "You don't have to do this. We can draw again—"

"And what if I draw it again?" I meet her eyes. "What if someone else does? We'd just be back here, having the same argument."

"Then we all go together!"

My throat tightens. My heart hurts. I don't want to go. But I have to. I shake my head. "You know we can't do that. We can't carry the injured ones, and the bus is the only shelter we can see for miles."

"Then I'll come with you—"

"No."

Jacqui looks stunned for a moment. Maybe it's my tone of voice. I rarely speak to her like this. As if my word is final. But if I don't know anything, I know I can't let her come with me.

I'm the reason she's on this survival "job" in the first place. If anything happens out there...I'd never forgive myself. I've already lost my mother...I can't...

"No." I say again, softer this time. The lump in my throat feels jagged as I swallow hard, watching the tears rise in Jacqui's eyes.

She shrugs me off and turns away, arms crossed, shoulders hunched, and I know she's fighting the urge to let those tears fall.

The other women have fallen silent, watching our exchange. I can see the relief in some of their faces—relief that it wasn't them who drew the short straw. Others look guilty, torn between volunteering to take my place and staying quiet.

Erika steps forward. "We'll take care of your sister, Justine. I promise."

I nod, grateful for her words even as Jacqui keeps her back turned to me.

The rest of the day passes in a blur. I'll take three hydration packets, three emergency rations, and a makeshift sun shield fashioned from the reflective emergency blanket. Alex gives me strict instructions about preventing heatstroke.

As night falls and the others settle in to sleep, I can't. Wrapping the sun-shield/emergency blanket over my shoulders, I crouch in the sand just outside the entrance to the bus. Someone exits behind me and I know it's her even before she speaks. I'll always recognize my sister.

"This is crazy," she whispers, settling beside me. "You don't have to do this."

"We drew straws," I remind her. "And someone has to go."

"Then I'll come with you."

"We've been over this. Two people means twice the water needed."

She falls silent, and in the dim light filtering through the tear in the transport, I can see tears shimmering in her eyes.

"Hey," I bump her shoulder with mine. "Remember when we got lost hiking in the San Juan Mountains? You freaked out, but we found our way back before they even organized a search party."

"That was different. We were sixteen, and there were trail markers."

"Still. I've always had a good sense of direction." It's a weak joke, but she manages a small smile.

"Just…" She swallows hard. "Just be careful, okay?"

"I promise." I squeeze her hand. "I'll be back before you know it."

Morning comes too quickly. As the first hints of light appear on the horizon, I stand outside the transport, equipped with my meager supplies.

"Keep the beacon active," I remind Erika. "If rescue comes while I'm gone…"

"We'll send them after you immediately," she promises.

Alex gives me a final once-over. "Remember, walk only during the coolest parts of the day. Find shade during peak heat, even if it means making less progress."

"I've got it." I nod.

"The formations look like they're about five miles out," Mikaela says, studying the horizon. "Should be able to make it there by tomorrow morning if you pace yourself."

"Here." Tina hands me a small object she's extracted from one of the cases—a compass-like device with Xyma markings.

"It seems to point consistently in one direction. Might help you keep your bearings."

Everyone has advice, last-minute suggestions, and words of encouragement. Everyone except Jacqui, who stands slightly apart. When my eyes land on her, that lump in my throat pulses. It's the same mask she wore during Mom's funeral. The one that reveals nothing, even when she didn't speak for months.

This is killing her. And I know it.

If she'd been the one to draw the short straw, I'd have felt the same way. Heck, I'd have taken her place instead.

Finally, it's time to go. I adjust my makeshift head covering, check my supplies one last time, and face the direction of the stone pillars.

"I'll be back in two days." I say it with more confidence than I feel. "Three at most."

Jacqui finally steps forward, and pulls me into a fierce hug. "You better be, or I swear to God, Justine…"

I pull away, give her a smile that I hope looks brave, and turn toward the desert. The bastard sun is just beginning to rise, casting the bus's long shadow across the sand. The rock formations stand silhouetted against the lightening sky, seeming both impossibly far and yet so close.

With a deep breath, I take my first step away from the safety of the transport.

I don't look back. I can't. If I see Jacqui's face again, I might lose my nerve. So I press on, shoulders straight, like I'm braver than I feel. I'm heading out to find some hope, because God knows we need it. There's nothing to worry about. All these days in the desert and we haven't seen one living thing. No predators. Nothing to suggest we're in danger. I'll be fine.

Nothing will go wrong.

CHAPTER 5
WHEN "REMOTE LOCATION" BECOMES LITERAL

JUSTINE

One step. Then another. And another.

The rhythm of my feet against the sand has become a mantra, the only thing keeping me moving forward as BS (Bullshit Sun? Bastard Sun? I haven't decided yet) climbs higher in the yellow sky. Left foot, right foot. Breathe in, breathe out. Keep the rock formation in sight and don't look back.

Actually, screw that. I glance over my shoulder for the hundredth time. The transport is still visible, though it's shrunk considerably—now just a speck against the endless tan landscape. At this distance, you'd never know it contained twenty-odd women from Earth arguing over sleep schedules and hoarding hydration packets like they're vintage Pokéboy cards.

"Keep moving, Jus," I mutter to myself, turning back toward my destination. "Ten miles. This is nothing. It's like a... a 5K race."

Except those races have water stations every mile, cheering spectators, and most importantly, take place on Earth where it didn't feel like gravity was constantly working against me and the air wasn't dry enough to turn my lungs into beef jerky.

I take a small sip from my first hydration packet, just enough to wet my mouth. Alex's warnings about rationing echo in my head. The packet tastes worse than I remember—like artificial berry flavor mixed with pennies—but it's wet, and that's all that matters right now.

The landscape offers nothing to distract me from the monotony of walking. No plants. No animals. Not even different colors of sand to break up the view. Just endless tan dunes stretching to the horizon, interrupted only by the occasional rocky outcropping too small to provide meaningful shade. It's like someone took the Sahara, removed anything remotely interesting, and then cranked up the heat.

Fuck them.

"This is fine," I say aloud, just to hear a voice, even if it's my own. "Totally normal survival adaptation activity. Deserted on a desert planet. The word 'desert' is right there in the name, Jus. You should have expected this."

I can't even laugh. The crushing reality of our situation weighs on me with each step. We're not on Earth. We're stranded on some alien planet with limited supplies and no guarantee of rescue.

And I'm walking alone through a wasteland that could kill me in a dozen different ways.

"But the pay was so good." I mimic the recruitment pitch that got us all into this mess. "Ten thousand dollars just for entering the program! What could possibly go wrong?"

I should have known it was too good to be true. Nothing pays that well for easy work. Nothing legitimate, anyway. Even if it's from aliens who probably have dollar bills in their bathrooms just for wiping their butts.

By midday, I'm forced to stop. The heat has become unbearable, BS is directly overhead turning the sand into a reflective oven. I find a small rocky outcropping that provides just enough shade for me to huddle beneath. It's barely better than being in direct sunlight, but it's something.

I check my supplies. Two and a half hydration packets left. The makeshift sun shield. And Tina's compass-like object, which continues to point stubbornly in one direction regardless of which way I turn it.

"Super helpful," I mutter, tucking it back into my pocket.

As I rest, my thoughts drift to the others back at the transport. Is Jacqui pacing anxiously, staring in the direction I disappeared? Is Mikaela maintaining her cool exterior while secretly worrying? Is the woman with the head wound improving, or is Alex struggling to care for her with limited resources?

And the biggest question of all: Is anyone actually looking for us?

If this is all part of the test, that would imply the Xyma are monitoring us. But if that were true, wouldn't they have intervened by now? At least for the injured women?

Unless the test is to see how long we can survive without assistance. To see what choices we make when pushed to our limits.

"If you're watching this," I say loudly to the empty air, "it's not funny anymore. You've made your point. We're adaptable. We're survivors. Now come get us before someone dies of heatstroke."

Only silence answers me. Not even a breeze disturbs the oppressive stillness.

After an hour of rest that doesn't feel restful at all, I force myself to continue. The rock formation looks closer now, but distance is deceptive in this featureless landscape. What seems like a mile could be three, or vice versa.

I focus on putting one foot in front of the other again, trying to ignore the growing ache in my calves and the way my skin feels tight and hot despite my makeshift covering. BS begins its slow descent, offering marginally less brutal conditions as the afternoon wears on.

And still, there's nothing. No sign of life. No hint of water. Just sand and rock and the increasingly large formation ahead of me—which is slowly growing larger the closer I get.

At one point I look up to see how much farther I have to go and stop short. A chill goes down my spine.

It's enormous. Far, far bigger than it appeared from the transport.

"Well, obviously," I scold myself. "Big things look small at a distance. That's basic math...or physics...whatever."

But the reality of its size becomes more apparent with each step. What looked like a cluster of stone pillars from afar is revealing itself to be a massive rock structure, easily hundreds of feet tall, with jagged spires reaching toward the yellow sky like this desert's version of icicles.

"All right," I mutter, trying to joke away my apprehension. "I know they say size doesn't matter, but that is seriously intimidating."

Nothing I say eases the flutter of anxiety in my chest. I'd been picturing something I could climb, something that would give me a vantage point to see beyond our immediate surroundings. But this...this is a sheer cliff face. There's no way I'm scaling that without proper equipment and a death wish.

By the time BS begins to dip below the horizon, I've reached the base of the formation. Up close, it's even more imposing—a wall of striated rock that towers above me, casting a long shadow across the sand. The stone is a darker tan than the surrounding desert, with veins of rust-red and burnt orange running through it.

I collapse in the blessed shade, allowing myself a slightly larger sip of water. My muscles ache from the unaccustomed exertion, and my skin feels tight and sensitive despite my precautions against the sun.

I know I have sunburn. I probably look like a roasted duck.

"Congratulations, Justine," I say to the empty air. "You've reached your destination. And it's completely useless."

There's no way up. No path, no handholds. Even if I somehow managed to start climbing, one slip would mean a fall that would leave me with far worse than that lady's broken arm.

I lean back against the cool stone, closing my eyes. The relative shade is heaven after hours in direct sunlight, but it doesn't change the fact that my mission has failed before it really began.

"So what now?" I ask myself, opening my eyes to stare up at the towering rock. "Go back with nothing to show for it? 'Hey guys, turns out it was just a really big rock! Sorry about the water I used up!' Ugh!"

I rest my head against the stone and close my eyes.

Fuck.

FUCK!

As darkness begins settling over the landscape, the reality of my situation crashes down on me as if it has a gravity of its own.

We're stranded on a desert planet.

The Xyma either can't find us or have no intention of rescuing us.

Our supplies will run out eventually.

And I just wasted precious water reaching a landmark that offers no help whatsoever.

"This is not how I planned to die," I whisper, my voice sounding small against the vastness surrounding me. "Starving on an alien planet because I needed money for rent. That's just..." I swallow hard, pushing back the tears that threaten to fall. "That's just pathetic."

I pull my knees to my chest, allowing myself a moment of pure, unfiltered despair. Not even the spectacular alien sunset —the yellow sky fading to deep orange, then a purple so intense it's almost painful to look at— can distract me from the hopelessness swelling inside.

Night falls completely, bringing with it a chill that seeps through my clothes and into my bones. I wrap the emergency blanket around myself, huddling against the rock for what little warmth it still holds from the day.

The stars emerge, constellations I don't recognize spread across a sky that's the wrong color. They should be beautiful, but all I can wonder is which one of them is my sun. Which one of them is shining down on Earth. On home.

MORNING ARRIVES WITH CRUEL ABRUPTNESS. HOW DO I KNOW? BS (Bitch Sun) tries to fry a part of my leg that was exposed beyond the shadow of the rock for too long.

"Fuck you." I give the sun the middle finger. It does nothing to make me feel better. "Fuck. Shit."

I ease up, mind a little groggy. Everything is stiff and sore, my mouth as dry as the sand surrounding me. I allow myself the smallest sip of water, barely enough to take the edge off my thirst.

Sitting up some more, I squint away the sleep and take in my surroundings. It's morning and nothing has changed. I'm still stuck here. In barren land.

Still the same towering rock that's inviting me to climb it, then fall and kill myself. Still the same tan smooth sand with—

Something catches my eye and I sit up some more.

A strange pattern in the sand, like straight lines but...not quite right. I pause, crouching down to look closer. For a moment, it almost looks like tracks of a rake. My heart rate kicks up—who would be raking sand in the middle of nowhere?—until I spot the culprit: a dried-up tumbleweed caught on a small rock, its brittle branches scraping back and forth in the wind.

I snort. Well, what do you know? There are plants here after all. Dead ones. Fantastic.

But wait...plants. Even dead ones mean something once grew here. Which means there has to be water somewhere. Maybe not on the surface, but underground...

I push myself to my feet with renewed determination. Where there's one plant, there might be more. Where there are plants, there might be life. And where there's life...

Rescue. Maybe.

It's time to make a decision.

I could head back to the transport. It would be the safe choice. I know the direction, I have enough water if I'm careful, and at least there would be other people there. We could try something else. Maybe send a larger group next time, or try a different direction.

Or...

I stand up, brushing sand from my clothes, and walk around the base of the rock formation. Maybe there's something I missed. A cave, a crevice, anything that might offer more information on where this plant came from.

There's nothing. Just more rock, more sand.

But as I complete my circuit and face outward from the formation, I notice something on the horizon. Another structure, similar to this one but different in shape. From this vantage point—which is higher than the area around the transport—I can see what might be a series of rock formations stretching into the distance.

I squint, trying to judge how far away the next one might be. Another day's walk? Maybe less?

"This is stupid," I tell myself. "You have limited water. The smart move is to go back."

But something tells me to keep going. Call it intuition, desperation, or just plain stubbornness, but I can't shake the feeling that turning back now would be giving up our best chance at survival.

I check my supplies again. If I'm extremely careful with my water, I might have enough to reach the next formation and still make it back to the transport. It's a risk, but at this point, what isn't?

"Sorry, Jacqui," I murmur, turning my back to the direction of the transport. "I need to see what's out there." But just for security, in case of anything, I leave a message.

Using tiny stones all around me, I create an arrow pointing to the other rock formation with a 'BRB'. If they come, Jacqui and any of the others will get what I mean.

But it won't get to that point.

I'll make my way back.

CHAPTER 6
TRESPASSERS WILL BE THOROUGHLY MISUNDERSTOOD

ROK

The male sleeps against my clan's boundary marker.

I crouch, watching from my position among the sandstone outcroppings. My skin ripples subtly, adjusting its amber-gold patterns to match the surrounding rocks.

This traveler has committed an outrageous offense.

In all my cycles, I have never witnessed such a blatant territorial challenge. The boundary markers are sacred to all Drakav—to rest against one is to claim it, to challenge the clan's right to the territory beyond. Even rival clans respect the protocol of proper challenges.

Yet this small, strange male simply collapsed against our marker as if it were nothing more than a convenient resting spot.

I extend my senses, attempting to catch his thoughts, but encounter only silence. No Drakav would shield their mind so completely unless they were hostile. Every attempt to establish a connection meets an impenetrable void.

Perhaps he is a youngling? His size suggests he might be, though something seems off. He lacks the proper markings of any clan I recognize. His skin is a strange pale color, and he wears coverings unlike anything I have seen.

A ripple of unease goes through me. What horror have the creatures this male killed endured for him to drape their hides as trophies across his body? Strange hides that cover his legs and chest. Worse yet is the reflective hide that catches Ain's light. It must have come from some creature I have yet to encounter in all my sols.

And the sounds he makes...Gods, my ear holes bleed. Constant, meaningless vocalizations expelled through his mouth. No proper mindspeak at all.

I shift, crouching lower, my complete focus on the male before me. I suppose it is good that he is so loud. If not for his constant vocalizations, I might not have found him.

Last dark, when I first spotted this intruder approaching our marker, I had hastily raked warning symbols into the sand. The pattern was haphazard, rushed, but any Drakav would recognize the meaning: **Turn back. Danger ahead. Territory claimed.**

The male ignored them completely.

Now he stirs, making more of those strange vocal sounds. He manipulates something to his mouth and I go still when a drop runs down the corner of his lips.

Water.

He is drinking water.

It is from a strange waterskin, though I am not sure I can call it a waterskin at all. I almost give away my position with the urge to move closer just to investigate, when, without thought or reverence, the male wipes away the drop that ran down his lips with the back of his hand.

My veins go cold. *Wasteful.* A being who would waste even a drop of the sacred life-giving liquid can be nothing but dangerous. A destroyer. A defiler. This confirms what I already suspected.

This male is a threat.

I tense as I watch him survey his surroundings, my muscles coiling with the instinctive readiness that makes my tribe such feared warriors. Has he detected me? Impossible. My camouflage is perfect. The male's gaze passes directly over my hiding place, lingers for a moment, then moves on.

His attention shifts toward another clan's territorial marker in the distance, and alarm pulses through me. That marker indicates the boundaries between my clan and theirs. They are our rivals. Males we have fought against and bled because of. If this male intends to take passage through our lands to go into theirs, I cannot allow it. We cannot appear to be weak. And we cannot appear to have helped this intruder. If he is as dangerous as I think he is...I should eliminate him here.

I must act. But how?

The male begins moving again, not back the way he came, but into our territory and toward the rival clan's.

I watch as he arranges small stones into a pattern before departing and I creep forward once he's a safe distance away, examining the creation.

It is a crude thing, but it has a point and an end. Even I can see it's a directional marker pointing toward our settlement, with strange symbols beside it. A message for others of its clan, perhaps? Reinforcements? This might be the beginning of some invasion.

The decision is made. I will follow this strange male. If he is scouting for an invasion force, I must know his purpose. If he is a lone intruder, I must prevent him from reaching the rival clan's territory and getting further into ours. Either way, I cannot let him wander freely.

I move in silence, my feet gliding over the hot sand without leaving even the slightest impression. The heat brings comfort to my foot pads. This is my element, my territory—where I am most powerful.

The male, in contrast, moves like a wounded sandfin dragging itself across the dunes. His footfalls are heavy, clumsy, leaving tracks so obvious that a blind nestling could follow them. Each step pushes deep into the sand, creating a trail that might as well be marked with signal fires.

"*Who are you?*" I project the thought toward him, focusing my mindspeak carefully. Nothing. The void remains.

But the male stops suddenly and turns around. I drop, my body flattening against the dust, skin shifting to match the exact shade and texture of my surroundings. My *dra-kir* hammers in my chest. Did he sense me? But no, he merely surveys the terrain before turning back and continuing his awkward trudge.

As Ain climbs higher in the sky, pouring its merciless heat onto the dust, I expect the male to seek shelter. He is obviously struggling. Instead, he continues, though his pace slows significantly. More vocalizations emerge from him—sharp, clipped sounds that carry a tone of... frustration? Pain? I cannot interpret the meaning.

He stops again and I freeze, this time behind a small rock outcropping barely large enough to conceal me. The male adjusts the shiny layer of his strange hide coverings, revealing more pale flesh beneath. He secures this covering over his head. I barely catch a glimpse of his dusty yellow fur.

What I do catch is a glimpse of his exposed arms. They are turning a deeper shade. A shade that often signals rage or warning in the dust. I don't move, my entire focus on him, waiting for him to lurch towards me in an attack. Instead, he turns, stumbles, and carries on.

Strange.

If he is not changing color as a warning, then... Is he unwell? Maybe he is no scout after all. Maybe he is heading to a Giving Stone—the place where all Drakav go to die. And the place where all Drakav emerge into this world.

Wrong. The nearest Giving Stone is in the opposite direction, and this male persists, continuing his determined march toward the rival clan's territory.

"Stop your advance. This territory is claimed." I try again with my mindspeak, pushing harder this time, but the void remains. Either he is deliberately blocking me, or—more disturbing— he is incapable of receiving mindspeak at all.

A being without the most basic form of communication? Impossible.

By the middle of the day, Ain blazes directly overhead, turning the dust into a pleasant warmth. Some creatures hide when Ain is at her highest point, but her rage does not affect me. The male, however, is clearly suffering. His movements have become erratic, his vocalizations more frequent and strained.

He finally collapses into the meager shadow of a small rock, consuming more of his precious water. That is twice now. Drinking so much in such a short time. It is wasteful. Unheard of.

He *must* carry some illness.

The next few solmarks pass with the male huddled in the diminishing shade while I maintain my vigil. When he finally rises to continue his journey, I notice his skin has changed color again—parts of it now an angry red. I know no clans that change color like this. All the Drakav I know are similar shades to me: amber-gold. Some lighter. Some darker. But never red.

It is a strange camouflage that appears to serve no purpose.

I am right about this male harboring some illness. It is even more important that I stop his trek through the dust. I watch as he winces before moving forward, still toward the rival clan's marker.

What a void-minded ka'vrakt.

His determination is both impressive and troubling. What could drive an ill runt of a male to push himself this way? What goal could be worth such suffering?

I can think of nothing good.

As Ain begins her descent, the light grows softer and the male's pace quickens slightly, as if renewed by the promise of coming darkness. The rival clan's marker is now clearly visible on the horizon, perhaps another solmark's journey at his current speed.

I cannot allow him to reach it. The truce between our clans is fragile at best. The tension between Kol (our leader) and Lucek (theirs) has been rising high since the water scarcity sols ago. A strange male crossing from our lands into theirs will be seen as either an attack or collusion—neither scenario ends well for my clan.

Each step brings him closer to the boundary, and my skin prickles.

I cannot let this happen.

I won't.

Surging forward, my body is a blur of motion against the darkening landscape. The male doesn't hear me approach— how could he when I move with the silence of wind over dust? At the last possible moment, he begins to turn, some instinct perhaps warning him of danger.

Too late.

I tackle him, angling my body sideways to take him off course, even as I'm careful to control my strength against his smaller frame. I expect an immediate onslaught against my mindspace, but there is nothing. What occurs is a shrill screech that comes from the male's throat. I'd cover my ear holes if I didn't have to grab his limbs as they suddenly kick out in every direction, trying but failing to land a blow on me.

We tumble across the dust, my momentum carrying us several lengths before coming to rest with the male pinned firmly beneath me, my hand covering his mouth to prevent more of that Ain-awful noise coming from his lips.

His eyes—the sight of them makes me freeze. They are a strange, single-colored blue without proper vertical pupils. Now they widen at me in shock and possibly fear. I can feel his dra-kir racing against my chest, his body radiating heat that speaks of exertion and stress.

His strange eyes dart wildly, searching for escape. Up close, I can see other disturbing details. His skin is even paler than I first realized, showing every pulse of his dra'kir beneath. Then there's the rounded flatness of his teeth visible through parted lips, the small pertness of his nose. Not to mention the complete absence of status markings on any visible skin.

He is the most beautiful male I have ever seen in all my existence...and yet, everything about this male is wrong.

The struggle intensifies as he thrashes beneath me, making those horrible sounds despite my attempt to muffle them. My concentration slips for a moment, thrown by his strange features and the complete absence of mindspeak. Clawless digits connect with my jaw. The impact is weak, but that single touch is enough. It sends a burst of information through my nervous system—temperature, texture, scent—all foreign, all wrong.

His screeching grows louder, and my blood runs cold.

Those sounds will carry across the dust. Every dust stalker within range will hear it, and the thought of those massive predators with their crystal-tipped claws makes my skin ripple with unease. Even a full hunting party approaches those beasts with caution. Alone, with this thrashing male drawing attention...

I must stop his racket.

I do not know how.

I release him and spring back, dropping into a defensive crouch, my body coiled and ready. The male scrambles away, falling twice before gaining his feet. He backs away but doesn't flee, watching me with those unnatural eyes. His chest heaves with exertion and my brow tightens. His chest is not flat like mine.

There are two rounded mounds. He must carry gourds strapped underneath the strange trophy hides he wears. What else does he hide? A blade? Some weapon I cannot see?

My gaze snaps up to his when more sounds suddenly spill from his mouth. This time in shorter bursts.

It hurts my ears.

I am not used to such constant noise-making. It has been many many moons since I had the need to use my own voice—and that had only been because I was in dire circumstances. With no Drakav close by, I could only shout to get someone's attention as the sandfin had tried to pull me under the dust to its den.

This male needs to be silent.

Ain touches the horizon. Soon the dust stalkers will begin their hunt.

My gaze travels over the male before me. To the wide blue eyes. The strangely soft face. The way he's looking at me, still making those vocalizations that I wish I could silence.

I've prevented him from reaching the rival clan's territory, but now I face an impossible choice. I cannot take him back to my tribe—bringing an unknown male to our sanctuary would be unforgivable. But I cannot leave him here, either to continue his mission or to become prey. If he dies in our territory, his clan—wherever they are—might seek vengeance.

Dust curse it.

A distant screech echoes across the dunes—not the male this time, but a hunting call. The male's head snaps toward the sound, and for the first time, I see real terror in those strange eyes.

What am I to do with this void-minded, water-wasting, marker-defiling creature?

The answer comes to me as another screech tears through the air, far across the dunes. The male's strange coverings will not protect him from what he has attracted here. His pale hide will be torn to shreds before Ain rises again.

I sniff the air, eyeing him as his chest rises and falls with heavy breaths.

I know what I will do.

CHAPTER 7
WHEN "FIRST CONTACT" MEANS EXACTLY WHAT THE FUCK IT SAYS

JUSTINE

It's a man. A *person*. The first living thing I've encountered apart from that ungodly screech I heard in the distance just now.

My heart hammers against my ribs as I stare at the figure before me. No, not a man—something else entirely. Humanoid, yes, but definitely not human.

"Holy shit," I whisper, backing away slowly. I've discovered an alien.

If this doesn't confirm we're on another planet far away from Earth, I don't know what will.

Unless the Xyma hired really committed cosplayers who got just as lost as we did, I'm going to go with door number one: definitely alien.

He's tall—at least seven or more feet of lean, sculpted muscle. His skin is the first thing that draws my attention—a golden amber that seems to shift and ripple like the very dunes around us. His face is angular, with high cheekbones and a strong jaw that could cut glass.

And he's completely, and utterly *NAKED*.

I avert my gaze then realize there's nothing particularly... obvious...to avoid looking at. Either his people have different anatomy or there's some kind of concealment I'm not seeing. I'm too disoriented to figure it out and frankly, being poked in the eye by D is the least of my concerns right now.

Oh shit, what did the Xyma do when they arrived on Earth again? I was so frickin' terrified I can hardly remember. Funny how the entire Earth population has just moved on and accepted them from those early days. But the being in front of me does *not* look accepting right now.

"Um, hello?" I try, raising my hands in what I hope is a universal gesture of non-aggression. "I come in peace? That's what you're supposed to say, right?"

The being winces at the sound of my voice, his strange eyes narrowing. They're amazing—vertical pupils like a cat's, with irises the color of true topaz flecked with bronze. His reaction makes me lower my voice to just above a whisper.

"Sorry. Too loud?"

He remains in a crouched position, perfectly balanced on the balls of his feet, looking ready to either flee or attack. His nostrils flare slightly as he...sniffs me? Great. I probably smell really *rich* right now.

"Look," I say, trying to keep my voice steady and quiet, "I'm lost. My people are back that way." I point in the direction of the transport. He doesn't even turn his head to look. Doesn't even glance at my arm. Those eyes remain locked on mine and it's hard to keep focus. I shake my head, clearing my thoughts. "We're stranded. Do you understand?"

Nothing. Not even a flicker of recognition in that predatory gaze. But he's watching me with an intensity that makes my skin prickle—not with fear exactly, but with the distinct feeling of being sized up. Like I'm a puzzle he's trying to solve, or worse—a threat he's deciding how to neutralize.

His lips pull back slightly, revealing teeth that are all pointed at the tips. Does this dude tear raw meat from the bone?

"Shit." *I'm* raw meat, currently on trembling bones.

The alien snarls again and the message is clear enough: back off.

I swallow hard. "Okay, so you're not the friendly welcoming committee. Got it." That's fine. This is fine.

Be brave, I tell myself. He's here, so there must be others. And after walking so long and seeing only sand, he's more than I hoped for. Much more. And I know this.

So I lift my chin a little higher and force down the lump rising in my throat.

Be brave.

"I need your help."

Despite the alien's obvious wariness, I can't help noticing details about him. The way his hair, a rich tan color like the sand around us, looks like it has metallic highlights and moves like liquid across his shoulders when he shifts. The strange markings on his chest that seem to have some purpose beyond decoration. The way he holds himself, coiled and ready, like something barely tethered and untamed.

I try a different approach, mimicking drinking water, then pointing to myself and making a walking motion with my fingers. "Water? Shelter? Do you know where I can find either of those things?"

His head tilts slightly. Is that curiosity or confusion?

But I'm encouraged by any reaction that isn't overtly hostile. I continue with my makeshift sign language. I point to the horizon, then make a crude house shape with my hands, followed by lifting my shoulders and arms in the "who/what/where/when" gesture.

"People? Settlement? Dare I say a city?" Yeah, that might be pushing it. "Anything that isn't endless desert?"

His eyes track my movements with laser focus. I'm desperate. As long as his people aren't cannibals, rapists, or both, I'll take anything. When I finish, he tenses even further, if that's possible. His gaze darts from my hands to my face, then to the dying light of the sun on the horizon.

Nothing in his posture suggests he's about to help. If anything, he seems more suspicious, like my simple question has confirmed something negative about me.

"Okay. Maybe appearing in your backyard and asking you to take me to your house doesn't really inspire trust." I sigh, running a hand through my hair. I barely get my fingers through. It's filled with sand. Great. "Look, I'm not a threat. I'm just lost, thirsty, and in need of your assistance."

The alien's nostrils flare again, and he makes a strange clicking sound in his throat. Is that communication? Annoyance? Gas? I have no way of knowing.

I decide to try one more time, using the most basic approach I can think of. I point to myself.

"Justine," I say clearly, tapping my chest. "Jus-tine."

Something shifts in his expression—a subtle change that suggests I might have finally broken through. He straightens slightly, rising to his full height in one fluid motion that reminds me of a wave rolling up a beach. It's unnervingly graceful.

My heart leaps. "Yes? You understand? I'm Justine."

Another wince at my voice, though less pronounced this time.

I reach up and touch my ear. The alien tracks the movement. The moment I feel the earbud the Xyma gave me still there, my heart leaps again. If he speaks, maybe I'll be able to understand him. I have no clue if this thing needs the Internet or some kind of connection to work. Don't even know if it translates all languages. I just have to hope.

But the alien before me has not said one word.

His expression doesn't change, but something in his posture shifts. He's still wary, but there's calculation there now.

It's a small victory, but a victory nonetheless. I try again with the settlement question, pointing to him first, then making the house gesture, then a gathering motion with my hands to indicate multiple people.

"Your people? Your home? Can you take me there?"

The effect is immediate and alarming. The alien's entire demeanor changes, his eyes literally darkening and those sharp teeth becoming fully visible as his lips pull back in a full-mouthed snarl. The raised markings on his chest seem to darken, too, and he takes a step toward me that is definitely not friendly.

"Whoa!" I raise my hands. "Sorry! Bad question! I take it back!"

Somehow, I've hit a nerve. Asking about his people was clearly the wrong move. Maybe they're territorial. Maybe they eat humans for breakfast. Maybe they just hate tourists.

Whatever the reason, I've screwed up, and now this golden-skinned warrior looks ready to do that meat-off-the-bones thing I feared earlier. If I could only get him to understand—

A blood-curdling screech tears through the air, much closer than before. The alien's head snaps toward the sound, his anger instantly replaced by something closer to alarm.

Another screech answers the first, this one from a different direction, and the alien makes a decision so quickly I barely register the change. One moment he's glaring at me, the next he's lunging forward.

"No, wait—" is all I manage before I'm upended, my world tilting as he throws me over his shoulder like I'm a sack of potatoes.

"Put me down!" The wind is knocked from my lungs as my stomach connects with his shoulder. "What the hell?"

He ignores me completely, breaking into a run that doesn't feel natural. It's too smooth, too fast. Each stride covers ground that would take me three steps, yet he moves with a silent grace that seems impossible for his size.

The blood rushes to my head as I hang upside down, my protests muffled against his back. The skin beneath my hands is warm to the touch and unexpectedly smooth, almost silky despite its appearance of toughness.

For a moment, I'm distracted by the little points of light that appear where my fingertips press into him.

Another screech tears through the air, closer now, and the alien picks up speed. My complaints die in my throat as I realize that whatever's making that sound is *hunting* us, and the alien—despite his obvious dislike of me—is trying to get us both away from it.

"What is that thing?" I gasp, though I know he can't understand me. "And where are you taking me?"

No response, of course, just the steady rhythm of his running and the increasingly frantic pounding of my heart. The desert blurs past in my inverted vision, darkness falling rapidly as BS (Batshit Sun) disappears completely.

Wait. He's running parallel to the rock formation I was heading for, not toward it! My carefully plotted course, my water calculations, my deliberately placed markers—all becoming useless with every step this alien takes.

"No, no, no—wrong way!" I smack his back again, which

accomplishes exactly nothing except probably annoying him further. "The big pointy rocks! That way!"

Nothing. It doesn't make a difference. He can hear me, I'm sure, but he can't understand me and even if he could, I'm not sure he'd listen. Fuck. Not only am I being kidnapped while something with murder-screech capabilities hunts us, but now I'm going to be completely lost.

The screeching grows louder, then multiplies—more than one of whatever nightmares is out there. The alien's pace somehow increases even further and I catch glimpses of rocky outcroppings passing by. We're no longer in the open desert but moving through more rugged terrain.

"Jacqui will never find me," I choke out, fighting back tears of panic. "None of them will. I'm supposed to be heading back with information, not getting abducted deeper into...wherever the hell this is."

My words are lost in the wind of our movement. The alien shows no sign of slowing or changing course. Every passing moment takes me farther from the crashed bus, farther from the women depending on me.

The others won't look for me. They'll think I succumbed to the unforgiving desert. But Jacqui...Jacqui will. She'll come after me. She'll follow my markers straight to where I was supposed to be, but I won't be there. She's going to think I'm dead, or worse—she'll keep searching until she runs out of water herself.

"Please," I try again, voice cracking. "My sister—I have to —" But the alien's grip only tightens as he changes direction, veering sharply toward what looks like a sheer cliff face in the deepening darkness.

It's pointless. What's worse, the screeching behind us has multiplied. Three, maybe four distinct screeching calls now, getting closer despite my captor's impressive speed. Whatever's chasing us, it hunts in packs.

The alien suddenly drops into a crouch. The movement is so abrupt I nearly lose the single biscuit I'd scarfed down for lunch. The emergency blanket gets loose and flies away.

"Wait!" Oh shit.

I reach for it, but he's moving again. Different this time. More stealth than speed, weaving between rock formations I can barely make out in the darkness.

The screeching stops.

Somehow, that's worse.

The alien freezes and I hold my breath, acutely aware that my racing heart might as well be a drumbeat announcing our location. His muscles coil beneath me, and I know with certainty that whatever's hunting us, it's close enough to taste our scent on the wind.

The alien moves. Not running now—climbing. The world tilts again as he scales what feels like a vertical surface with me still slung over his shoulder. How he's managing this with one arm, I have no idea. The rock face scrapes against my side as he maneuvers us into...a cave?

The absolute darkness is disorienting. I hear him moving, feel the shift as he finally sets me down. My legs wobble beneath me, and I reach out blindly, finding cold stone at my back.

"Where—"

His hand clamps over my mouth, callused palm pressing hard enough to hurt. There's nothing gentle about it. The message is clear: silence or death. Given the circumstances, I'm voting for silence.

The alien moves away, and for a terrifying moment, I think he's going to leave me here. But then I sense rather than see him positioning himself at what must be the cave entrance. His breathing is silent, but I can feel the coiled tension radiating from him. The cave isn't large—my outstretched hands can touch both walls, and the ceiling feels low enough that he must be crouching.

Outside, something moves. The sound is subtle. A whisper of movement across stone. Somewhere out there a pebble dislodges and clatters, echoing into the stillness. The alien's reaction is immediate. I sense him dropping lower. Pressing against the wall, I try to make myself as small as possible.

Then I hear it. A single click sound. Not from the alien this time, but from whatever's outside. It's answered by another set of clicks, then another, until the cave entrance is surrounded by what sounds like dozens of chittering, clicking monsters, the sound they make echoing off the stone like laughter.

I stare straight ahead, eyes wide in the darkness, barely breathing. They're communicating. Hunting. And we're trapped.

When the sounds rise to a crescendo, I squeeze my eyes shut tight, my lower lip bitten between my teeth so hard I taste blood.

No. Not going to die here.

I'm not going to die like this!

Minutes pass like hours. I don't dare move, barely dare to breathe. And the alien remains motionless. So silent that at one point I wonder if he left. Disappeared when there was a chance to do so, without me knowing.

Finally, my eyes adjust to spot his dark shape against the marginally lighter cave entrance. He's standing there, hands tipped with dangerously long claws. Looking like he's ready to tear apart anything that breaches the entrance.

When the sounds outside eventually fade, I hear him exhale. Those claws disappear, going back into his fingers like they were never there. And then something extraordinary happens. His skin begins to emit a soft, amber glow. It starts with raised markings across his chest, spreading outward like veins of light beneath his golden skin. The illumination is subtle, but it's enough to reveal the interior of the rocky chamber.

I forget to breathe for a moment. He's...magnificent. Savage and alien and dangerous, but magnificent. The light plays across the harsh planes of his face, those vertical pupils now reflecting his glow. His body is all lean muscle and scars, telling stories of survival I can only imagine.

The sight of those scars snaps me back to reality. Whatever he is, he's clearly dangerous—and I'm alone with him. The thought sends my mind racing to darker places. If creatures dangerous enough to mark him like that are out there, what chance do the others have?

Jacqui. My chest tightens. Instead of returning to her and the others with information, I'm trapped in a cave with a glowing alien who either saved me or kidnapped me—or both.

The worst part? I have no idea how to find my way back. Even if I could somehow slip past my alien captor, the twisting path we took to get here is already lost on me.

"I need to get back," I whisper, knowing he won't understand but needing to say it anyway. "My sister, the others— they need me. They're waiting."

The alien makes that clicking sound again, softer this time. Is it meant to be reassuring? Threatening? A warning to shut up? I have no way of knowing.

One thing is clear. From his stance at the entrance, he's not letting me pass.

I slide down the wall until I'm sitting, suddenly aware of how utterly exhausted I am. My muscles scream in protest, my throat burns with thirst, and every inch of exposed skin feels scorched.

At least I'm alive. For now. And not being eaten by whatever was making those sounds outside. Also a plus.

For a moment, I simply allow myself to breathe. Until the adrenaline dies down and my hands stop shaking enough to reach for my pack. One and a half water packets left. Each drop is precious, but after that run, and with my heart still racing, I need it.

I fumble with the packet in the darkness. When I finally get my fingers on the lid, a sharp movement makes me freeze.

His body goes rigid. The glow catches his eyes, fixed not on me—but on the packet in my hands. Before I can react, he moves, so fast I barely register it, snatching the packet from my grip with a swift motion that makes me gasp.

"Hey!" I protest, but he's already turning the plastic packet over in his hands, examining it with intense concentration, running his fingers along the sealed edges.

His nostrils flare as he brings it closer to his face, sniffing at it suspiciously. Those golden eyes narrow, darting from the packet to me, a strange accusation in his eyes that leaves me dumbfounded. Then he goes completely still, staring at me with such intensity it's almost physical. His focus is absolute, pupils contracting to thin slits as he continues to hold my gaze for what feels like an eternity.

I shift uncomfortably under his scrutiny. "What? Why are you looking at me like that? Like I'm supposed to read your mind or something."

He continues that unnerving stare, and I swear I can feel pressure building behind my eyes. It's probably just exhaustion and dehydration, but...weird. He tilts his head slightly, the stare never breaking. If anything, it intensifies, his brow furrowing with what looks like concentration or frustration.

"Sorry, buddy. Whatever you're trying to communicate

isn't working." I tap my temple. "No mind reading capabilities installed."

Something flickers across his face—surprise maybe, or confusion. He blinks rapidly, then returns his attention to the water packet, his fingers prod at it, trying to find an opening, but clearly unfamiliar with the technology.

I hold out my hand, palm up. "Give it back," I say, then realize he can't understand. "I'll show you."

After a moment's hesitation, he extends the packet toward me, but doesn't release it. We sit like that for a moment, both holding the packet, a strange standoff over the most basic of survival needs. My fingers graze his and his skin ripples in response, like something alive shifting beneath the surface. A slow wave rolls up his arm—like the desert itself just woke up inside him.

What the...

When my gaze shifts back to his, that lump rises in my throat again. He's not looking at me with that intensity he had a moment ago. This is different. As if he's struggling to process something, his pupils dilating and contracting rapidly.

I adjust my fingers so we're no longer touching. It reminds me of my cousin's shellfish allergy—that immediate physical reaction when his body encountered something it wasn't designed to handle. But this is different, more like the alien's skin is responding to me specifically. Like I'm the allergen.

"It's just water," I whisper, maybe to distract myself or him. It's a weak attempt. He still doesn't let go.

Slowly, carefully, I twist the cap with my free hand, my eyes never leaving his. The alien jerks in surprise when the cap pops off, but he still doesn't let go.

"See?" I say softly. "It's just water."

For a heartbeat, I forget where I am, forget the danger,

forget everything except those strange golden eyes locked on mine. They're...mesmerizing.

I'd be a dumbass to ignore the fact that this creature before me is by far the most wild and enchanting thing I have, and probably will ever, encounter. He's...beautiful. In the way a lightning storm is beautiful after calm. The air between us feels suddenly charged and I'm faced with the fact that he is as wild and strange as the desert around us, and I am at his mercy.

He blinks first, breaking whatever spell had fallen over us. His nostrils flare as he brings the packet closer to his face, sniffing at it suspiciously. The concentration on his face would be comical under different circumstances—like watching someone inspect fine wine instead of emergency rations.

Finally, he tips the packet ever so slightly, allowing the smallest drop to touch his tongue.

The moment the water touches his tongue, he jerks back like I just fed him acid. His lips peel back, exposing those sharp teeth, a growl vibrating through his chest. He wipes his mouth —again and again—his whole body shuddering in what can only be pure, unfiltered disgust.

He thrusts the packet back at me with such force I nearly drop it. "What—you don't like it?" I can't help the small laugh that escapes. "It's just water. Maybe a little stale, but—"

The alien makes another disgusted sound, and I stifle another laugh.

"Fine, more for me." I take a cautious sip, half-expecting it to taste terrible, but it's just water—slightly warm and with that faint metallic flavor all the emergency rations have, but nothing offensive.

The alien watches me drink with a mixture of disgust and horror, as if I'm downing poison by choice. When I finish, his gaze follows my hand as I carefully reseal the half-empty packet and return it to my bag.

"Different tastebuds, I guess." I shrug, settling back against the wall. "Or maybe your water's just better than ours."

The alien continues to stare at me for a long moment, then makes that clicking sound again—softer this time, almost thoughtful—before returning to his position at the cave entrance. He crouches there, perfectly balanced, a golden sentinel between me and whatever's outside.

I can't help but notice he keeps flexing the hand that touched mine, opening and closing his fingers as if testing them. And then he touches his jaw, trailing his fingers over the spot where I'd punched him earlier. The luminescence beneath his skin pulses irregularly along that arm, almost like after-shocks from when I touched him there.

I don't...I don't know what to think of that.

Did I hurt him? No—he's too solid for that. But then why does he keep touching where I did?

"Sorry..." I whisper, though I don't even know what I'm apologizing for.

Pulling my knees to my chest, I'm suddenly aware of how utterly exhausted I am. My muscles scream in protest. My throat feels better, at least. The initial panic has subsided into a dull, throbbing awareness of my situation.

I'm lost. Completely cut off from Jacqui and the others.

"What am I going to do?" I whisper, not expecting an answer.

The alien tilts his head slightly at the sound of my voice, but those luminous eyes remain focused on the darkness outside.

"Jacqui's going to kill me." A humorless laugh escapes before I swallow it down. "If those screaming things don't beat her to it."

The soft glow in the cave dims and I glance back at the alien's silhouette. His body language screams 'feral'—from the way he balances on the balls of his feet to the tilt of his head as he listens to sounds I can't detect. Those sharp teeth I glimpsed earlier weren't for show. This isn't some benevolent E.T. who's going to help me phone home. At least he seems to be standing guard and not coming after me.

Still, I'm double fucked.

In the ass.

Zero lube.

CHAPTER 8
WATER STORAGE: YOU'RE DOING IT WRONG

ROK

Night has deepened since I brought the male to this cave. The shadowmaws have moved on to easier prey, their clicking calls fading into the distance. Yet I remain vigilant, my senses alert for any threat that might return.

But the greatest puzzle is before me.

This male drinks foul water. Water that tastes of decay and artificial substances I cannot name. Water that should be rejected by any being with functioning senses. Yet he consumes this poison willingly, even eagerly.

It is no wonder he is so small. So weak. What other proper nourishment does he lack? No wonder he cannot perform mindspeak. He does not have the power to do so. The poor creature must have been surviving in these harsh conditions for many cycles.

The fact I found him breathing is a miracle in itself. He is not from this region. That is clear. A traveler then. From far away. One whose supplies probably dwindled and went stale as he made his way across the dust. His strange waterskin is proof enough.

I almost want to introduce him to one of our fresh pools, just so he can sate himself for possibly the first time in his existence, but I do not.

Instead, I watch as he settles against the cave wall, his eyes growing heavy. My instinct is to stay vigilant, to watch the cave entrance for shadowmaws, but I cannot help tracking his movements. The way he breathes. The strange hide on his body. The unusual dullness of his skin.

He is unlike any Drakav I have ever encountered. Too small, too soft, with strange rounded features and dull, flat teeth. How does he tear meat? How does he defend himself? If I had left him to the shadowmaws, he would have made an easy meal.

As the dark deepens, the shadowmaws' clicks grow fainter as they move away to hunt easier prey. Still, I remain alert. They are clever hunters. I've seen them feign retreat only to circle back when their quarry believes itself safe.

So...I will wait. With this traveler...

Staring out into the dark beyond, I weigh his discovery in my mind. Kol would have known what to do from the first moment. That is why he is our leader.

Solmarks pass. The male rests...even in my presence. His lack of caution is concerning. But this is the first time since being in his presence where my ears are not ringing from his constant vocalizations. The silence is like a balm, but his breathing is shallow and quick. Too quick, perhaps?

I turn my gaze from the cave entrance to study him more carefully.

Something is not right.

The male's skin has changed. Before, it was a pale color,

almost like the belly of a sand-skimmer. Now there is an unnatural flush spreading across his face. The skin there is hot, the warmth reaching me even from where I crouch at the cave entrance. This is not right. No Drakav would allow their temperature to rise so dangerously unless they were prepared for skin-shedding. And this creature is in no condition to shed anything.

I remain at my post. The shadowmaws are still too close. But my eyes continually stray back to the small being.

He makes a sound—not like his earlier vocalizations, but something raw and pained. The sound brings me to my feet before I can consider whether this is wise. I move silently across the cave, every sense alert for danger, both from without and from the male himself.

Lowering my head, I sniff the air around him. Sweet. A strange sweetness that assaulted my senses as I carried him here. But there is a new scent now. Something sharper. More acrid.

Then I see it.

The moisture.

I lower myself, moving on all fours, slow and careful. My hands and feet find purchase on either side of the male as I hover over him, studying. The color change is alarming, but there's something else wrong with his skin. There brim tiny droplets of...water?

I lean in closer, nostrils flaring. Yes. Salty like the east sands, but water nonetheless. It's seeping from his skin, collecting in small beads on his brow and trailing down his neck.

Water. Precious water. Leaking out as if his skin is filled with holes.

The sight is so strange I am transfixed by horror.

Either this male is dying or he is from a place far away, where water flows freely enough to waste from one's *skin*.

I growl low in my throat, disturbed by this offense against everything I know to be right. Water is life. Water is sacred. Water is never, ever wasted.

But as I stare at the male, something tells me this is not intentional. The rapid breathing, the flushed skin, the heat radiating from him—

He makes another sound, this one weaker than before, and something tugs at me. Something unfamiliar. A need to...help? Why would I help this creature? Why would I risk myself for a male that does not belong to our lands?

And yet...

I reach out, my hand hovering just above his face. Heat rises from his skin like the air above the dunes when Ain is at her highest. The warmth does not bother me, but then I recall how this male stumbled through the sands, obviously burdened by Ain's rage.

Before I can think twice, I touch his brow.

The rush of information is immediate, more intense than before. Temperature—far too high, even for a dust-dweller. Texture—so much softer than Drakav skin, with none of the protective layers we possess. Chemical composition—water, yes, salt...but also unfamiliar elements that sing across my senses in strange patterns.

And something else. Something that makes me want to press my palm flat against his skin, to maintain this connection that hums with an energy I have never felt before.

I jerk back, a wave of...*something*...going through me. What is this? Why does the touch of this male affect me? I have touched many injured Drakav before—my brothers, my tribe mates—and felt nothing like this strange pull.

The male twitches in his sleep, a small whimper escaping

his lips. The sound burrows into me, touching some part I did not know existed.

I flex my fingers before lowering myself again, this time pressing my palm flat against his brow. My skin glows brighter without my conscious command, responding to...what? Threat? Danger? No. Something else entirely.

The flood of sensation is stronger this time. The heat beneath my hand is alarming—hotter than the sands at Ain's highest point, hotter than the stone after a full day beneath Ain's brutal gaze.

Even our sacred sun does not burn with such intensity.

This creature—this male—is burning from within. The heat is unnatural—a wildfire burning beneath fragile skin. My kind does not suffer such betrayals of the body. We endure. We survive. We do not burn from within.

Fire, when uncontrolled, devours itself.

The male shivers, tremors rattling through his frame, and a sound leaves his lips—soft, needy. Not like any sound I have heard any Drakav make before. My chest tightens. It is the sound of a creature on the brink, the final plea before the void swallows it whole.

My claws extend. Fists clench. I should leave this male to his fate. The weak perish, the strong endure. That is law.

And yet.

I swallow, scowling at the clawing feeling inside me, the way my own body rebels against reason.

This male... He is not *completely* weak. He survived the dust long before I found him. If I leave him, it will not be because he lacks the will to live—but because I denied him the chance.

A growl rumbles in my chest. Unacceptable.

Water. He needs water to kill the fire. I have none to give. I had already consumed every drop I needed before leaving the tribe.

But...

There is one place. Deep within the cavern network, beyond the tunnels I call safe, there lies an underground spring. But the cave does not belong to us alone.

My jaw tenses. I do not hesitate often. I do not doubt. But this—

The male gasps, a fragile, broken sound. I do not allow myself another moment of thought.

I rise. And I run.

It takes me a short time to get there. A few moments out in the open sands before the caverns swallow me whole once more, darkness pressing against my senses as I navigate by memory and scent. The air thickens, damp with the promise of water, but so too does the scent of something else. Something old. Something that does not belong to us.

I bare my fangs. I have no time for a fight. Moving swiftly, silent like the dark winds, I trace the scent of the underground spring. When the first glimmer of water comes into view, I don't pause. I search the cave floor, finding what I need—a broad, thick leaf from the rare plants that grow only near the sacred waters. Their waxy surface holds water better than any hide.

I fold the leaf with care, creating a natural vessel. The leaves themselves are sacred—they grow nowhere else in the deep sands, surviving only on the pure waters and the dim light that filters through cracks in the cavern ceiling. This is to save a life. Ain will not punish me for this.

As I fill the makeshift vessel, I sense movement in the darkness behind me. The scent shifts. A presence.

I do not look. I do not falter.

I drink one swift mouthful—taking only what I need to return to my tribe safely—and secure the rest in the folded leaf. Then I am running once more, water sloshing inside the leaf. I steady my hand, not daring to lose a single drop to the dust.

I do not think I was gone for long. But when I return, the male is not where I left him.

I still, nostrils flaring. At first, I believe myself tricked. That the male feigned illness so he could slip away. But then my senses pick up one thing.

There is a scent, and it is *everywhere*. Saliva swells underneath my tongue as if I have just scented the most delicious meal.

Then I see it.

The male. He has moved to the far corner of the cave, thrashing weakly against the stone. But this is not what freezes my blood.

The coverings—those strange hides—they've been torn away, lying in scattered heaps on the cave floor. And the body revealed beneath them...

My breath turns to dust in my lungs. The leaf vessel nearly slips from my claws as my body locks in place. The male writhes on the ground, limbs twisting against the cool stone, seeking relief from the fire within. But all I can see are the curves. The softness. The undeniable shape of something that is *not* male.

Even the circular lumps I believed were gourds are instead fleshy mounds rising from his chest.

Every muscle in my being tenses. Every instinct roars to life. My skin flashes bright, probably alerting every shadowmaw in our vicinity, then dims, then flashes bright again—responding to a surge of...something I have no name for.

Slow steps carry me forward, the leaf clutched tight in my

claw, water forgotten for one breathless moment as I struggle to comprehend what my eyes tell me.

My nostrils flare as I inhale, and—

Something inside me cracks.

The scent hits me like a strike to the chest. Something rich, something designed to be *consumed*, to be *taken*. My vision darkens at the edges, my fangs lengthening, an unfamiliar snarl twisting in my throat.

My body moves before my mind can stop it.

I pin the creature down.

His skin is hot beneath my claws, moisture-slicked and trembling. A weak protest dies on his lips.

My breath ghosts over his throat, then lower, drinking in his scent like it's precious water in the dry season. I don't understand it. Don't know why my body reacts this way, why my gut clenches with a need so sudden, so absolute, it makes my muscles seize.

But then I reach his lower gut.

And the scent there—*gods*, the scent there.

A deep, primal growl tears from my chest, the sound surprising even me.

Something wakes inside me. Something old. Something lethals.

This is no male.

This is something else.

Something meant for *me*.

CHAPTER 9
FIRST AID ACROSS GALAXIES: RESULTS MAY VARY

JUSTINE

Everything hurts. Out of seemingly nowhere, my skin goes on fire, and the heat has somehow seeped into my bones. Every movement sends fresh waves of agony rolling through me, and my limbs feel like they've been replaced with lead.

My skin is burning, but not just from fever. It's as if something deeper pulses beneath the surface. A restless, gnawing heat. I twist, trying to rid myself of the sensation, my thighs pressing together as a familiar ache throbs between them. What the hell? I haven't been touched in months, years, but my body is reacting like I'm being teased by invisible hands. A whimper escapes my lips, and I bite down hard.

This isn't normal. This isn't me.

When I open my eyes, the cave is empty.

The alien? Gone.

He left.

A strange hollowness settles in my chest. Something I'd rather not think about too closely. I should be glad he's gone.

This is my chance. I can get out now. Head back to the bus.

But when I try to stand, my legs buckle. The world tilts, nausea clawing up my throat. It takes all my strength just to crawl to the cooler stone in the corner of the cave.

"Get up," I whisper to myself. "Come on, Justine. Get up. You've got this. You're not dying in a cave in the center of this fucking amped-up Sahara."

The rational part of my brain whispers about heat exhaustion, dehydration, and the dangers of overheating. But rational thought is becoming harder to hold on to because of this rising fever.

God, my clothes. They're sticking to my skin, making everything feel worse. With fumbling fingers, I tear off my top, then my shoes, then my pants—anything to cool down. The stone feels blissfully cool against my burning skin, but the relief is short-lived.

"Water," I croak, but there is no one to hear me. My last water packet is still in my bag, but I can't bring myself to touch it. If I use it now, I'll have nothing left for the trip back.

Oh fuck. Is this how I die? Curled in a ball in an alien cave, slow-cooked from the inside out while Jacqui waits for me to come back? She'll never know what happened to me. None of them will.

A sound at the cave entrance jerks me back to awareness.

At first, I think it's one of those creatures from earlier. But no.

Through fever-blurred vision, I see him—the alien. He's standing there, something clutched in his hand, his entire body gone rigid as he stares at me.

He came back.

I can't believe it. He came back for me.

I try to speak, to ask for help, but all that comes out is a weak moan. My eyes flutter shut, but I force them open again just in time to see the soft glow that had emanated from his skin before suddenly flare bright. I swear I see stars...and they're under his skin. His light flickers and dims, then flares again, like a heartbeat gone haywire. His eyes seem to change too—the pupils contracting to pinpoints before expanding to consume nearly the entire iris.

I should be afraid. Definitely afraid.

Instead, I'm transfixed.

The alien makes a sound—a low rumble that's somewhere between a growl and a purr. It vibrates deep in his chest, sending a strange shiver down my spine. He moves toward me slowly. Stalking rather than walking.

I should run.

Instead, I whisper, "Please."

I'm not even sure what I'm asking for. Help? Mercy? Water? All the above?

Before I can process what's happening, he's on me. One moment, he's across the cave, and the next, his much larger body is looming over mine, pinning me to the ground.

Panic flares through me, but I'm too weak to fight him off.

"W-what..." All the panic and my voice comes out as a whisper.

He's so close. Too close. His massive body cages mine, his weight pressing down on me, one of his hands pinning both of my wrists above my head. Through my delirium, I register the solid heat of him, the overwhelming presence of him, and the way his glowing skin seems to pulse with every ragged breath.

His face is so close to mine that I can feel his breath on my skin. Then he dips lower, his nose featherlight along my neck as he inhales, pulling air into his lungs so deeply that it sends a shiver through me.

Oh my god. He's scenting me.

Great. I survived an alien abduction only to die because I forgot deodorant!

"Okay," I mutter, but my voice shakes. "This…is fine. Totally normal alien behavior." But the words don't sound convincing, even to me.

He growls again, the sound vibrating through my chest. His nose continues its slow path down my collarbone, his breath warm against my fevered skin. Each place he touches sends conflicting signals through my body—part alarm, part something else I really don't want to focus on.

"Seriously," I croak, squirming weakly beneath him. "What are you doing?"

He freezes. His golden eyes meet mine, and for a moment, there's something almost…human in his expression. Confusion.

But then his gaze drops and I remember I'm only in my bra and panties. His growl returns, louder this time. The light beneath his skin concentrates along his chest and throat, forming intricate patterns that seem to flicker with his quickening heartbeat.

Oh no.

Oh no, no, no.

His pupils blow wide, swallowing the gold of his irises until only a thin ring remains.

"Wait," I try, my voice cracking. "Don't—"

But I don't get the chance to finish. His head dips lower, and I feel his nose trail down my stomach, leaving a burning path in its wake.

"You really don't want to," I whisper, but the words are weak, swallowed by the fever and the weight of him pressing me into the stone.

Then his face is there—between my thighs.

My entire body jerks in shock, every nerve firing at once.

"What the hell are you—" All the words disappear from my lips as he inhales deeply. The sound that comes from him is like an animal catching the scent of prey.

Heat floods my face, my chest, my entire body.

"Stop!" I twist beneath him, trying to close my legs. But his other massive hand clamps down on my leg, holding me open like I'm some kind of offering for him.

A sound tears from his throat—half growl, half groan—and it's so raw, so primal, that it freezes me in place.

I should be terrified. And I am. But what terrifies me even more is the way my body betrays me. The way heat pools low in my stomach, tangling with my fear and confusion in a way that makes me want to scream.

This isn't happening.

This can't be happening.

"Get off me!" I gasp, trying again to squirm free, but it's useless. He's too strong, his grip unyielding as his face remains buried between my thighs, his breath hot and steady against my skin.

The sound that comes from him next is almost violent, a deep, feral snarl that makes the hair on the back of my neck stand on end. His entire body goes rigid, his glow flaring bright enough to rival this planet's sun.

And then he freezes. His glow flickers like a flame in the wind.

The growling stops.

Slowly, his head lifts and his gaze meets mine. I freeze beneath him.

There's something in his eyes now—something wild and conflicted and utterly alien.

For a moment, we just stare at each other, my chest heaving as I try to catch my breath. Then, as if some invisible switch has been flipped, he lets out a low, frustrated sound and pulls back, releasing me as he retreats.

I scramble backward the moment he's off me, pressing myself against the cool stone wall, my heart hammering in my chest.

He doesn't look at me. His shoulders rise and fall as he takes a series of deep, shuddering breaths, his hands flexing at his sides. He looks like he's fighting something—like he's barely holding himself together. And the light underneath his skin, it flickers. Wildly. Stars. So many stars. All going on and off at once.

"What the hell is wrong with you?" I rasp. My voice trembles and I hate it.

When he turns back to me, there's something feral in his movement—a wild sort of grace that makes my heart slam against my ribs. He stalks toward me, and I press myself harder against the stone, certain he's about to...but instead, he reaches down beside me, retrieving a broad leaf I hadn't noticed before, braced carefully against the rock.

A cool drop of water lands on my chest.

I gasp at the shock of it.

Water.

"You brought water?" My voice is little more than a croak, but the words seem to register. His jaw clenches and he simply stares into my soul the same way he was before. That deep, probing gaze that makes me feel like he's trying to push thoughts directly into my mind. As if he could make me understand whatever he's thinking through sheer force of will alone.

His chest heaves with every breath as he reaches for me, slipping an arm beneath my shoulders and lifting me slightly. All the while, that storm of light erupts under his skin, worse now that he's close again—as if being close to me is setting off some kind of virus in him. The movement presses my body against his, and I gasp.

His temperature has changed. While my skin flares with heat, his is cool.

The contrast is shocking—his skin feels like smooth stone left in the shade, soothing against the fever burning beneath my own. The chill of him seeps into me, chasing away the dizziness for one fleeting moment, and I can't stop the involuntary sigh that escapes my lips.

He brings the leaf to my lips, and I drink greedily, the water cool and impossibly sweet. It's nothing like the stale, chemical taste of the emergency rations. Nothing like water back home, either. This is pure—perfect. Sent from the fountain of the gods.

"More," I whisper.

Before I know it, the last few drops disappear down my throat.

"Fuck."

The alien's eyes narrow slightly, his gaze flicking to my fevered body before he presses his palm against my forehead. His cool touch is electric, and my body reacts before I can stop it, a small sound of relief escaping my lips.

His expression shifts at the sound—something dark flickering across his face.

Then, just like that, he's gone again, moving toward the cave entrance with that strange, fluid grace.

"Wait..." I manage. "Don't leave me. Please."

But he doesn't leave. Instead, he gathers something from outside the cave—smooth stones, arranging them in a circle on the ground at my feet.

For a moment, my thoughts drift back to the transport. To Jacqui waiting for me, probably pacing and snapping at anyone who tells her to calm down. To Erika, meticulously rationing supplies, marking off how many hours I've been gone. To the others, watching the horizon for my return with dwindling hope. The guilt is almost as hot as the fever. I promised I'd come back with answers, with help. Instead, I'm dying in a cave with a creature I can't even communicate with.

The fever pulls me under again, my mind fogging as I collapse against the rock at my back. His scent wraps around me. It's earthy and metallic, like sun-baked stone, and my back arches instinctively. My nipples tighten to painful points, rubbing against my bra with every ragged breath. I should be terrified. I should be fighting. Instead, my hips rock faintly, seeking friction where there is none. Consciousness fades in and out. But one thought lingers, clear and sharp through the haze.

What the fuck is happening to him?

What the fuck is happening to *me*?

CHAPTER 10
CONFUSED DOESN'T START TO EXPLAIN IT
AT ALL

ROK

The air in the cave is heavy.

It clings to my skin, thick as the heat waves that roll off the dunes in the dry season, but this heat does not belong to the dust. It belongs to her.

The creature lies before me, trembling, fragile form pressed to the stone. Her breathing is erratic—too fast, too shallow—and the fire burning beneath her skin has not abated. Despite the water I brought her, despite the cooling stones, she remains on the edge of collapse.

And I am on the edge of madness.

I crouch a distance from her now, not for my protection. For hers. My claws dig into the stone floor, trying to focus on the rhythmic scrape of their sharp points instead of the chaos flooding my senses. Her scent is *everywhere*, saturating the air, worming its way into my lungs until I can taste it on the back of my tongue. Sweet and sharp and *maddening*.

Every breath pulls her deeper into my lungs. My skin prick-les, a slow *...something...*spreading beneath my flesh.

I do not understand what is happening to me.

This creature is not Drakav. I have known this from the moment I found her, wandering the dust like prey waiting to be taken. But now, as I stare at her, I know something else.

She is not from Xiraxis at all.

Her scent, her softness, the strange way her skin weeps water—none of it belongs to this world. She is...other.

And yet.

The curves of her body, the way her scent pulls at something deep inside me, the way my glow flares uncontrollably when I'm near her...

It is impossible.

The thought takes root in my mind, unbidden and unwel-come, but no matter how I try to bury it, it rises again, clawing its way up from the depths of memory.

The daughters of Ain.

A myth. A story passed down from times past. Of before the Drakav were hardened by the dust. Before we became the rulers of the sands.

The daughters were said to be soft, delicate creatures, unlike anything the Drakav had ever known. They were not male, like us. They were...

Female.

The word lodges in my mind like a sandfin's quill.

These *females* were said to be precious. Sacred. Gifts from Ain herself, sent to guide the Drakav when the world was still young and full of life. We worshiped them, but they were fragile, unable to endure the harshness of Xiraxis, and one by one, they disap-peared, until they were nothing more than echoes in the sands.

I bare my fangs, a growl rumbling low in my chest.

It cannot be. The daughters of Ain are a story. *Females* do not exist. They are not real.

And yet...

I look at her.

The rise and fall of her chest. The curve of her hips. The smoothness of her skin. I inhale deeply, the scent of her filling me again, and my claws curl against the stone.

Bare now, without those troublesome hides covering her scent, she smells like life. Like water. Like something I was never meant to touch.

The glow beneath my skin pulses erratically, my body betraying me with every moment I spend near her. My instincts are in chaos, torn between the urge to protect her, to keep her safe, and the darker, deeper urge to take her, to claim her, to make her mine.

I shake my head, as if the motion could dislodge the thoughts from my mind. This is madness.

And yet I cannot leave her.

The thought of her alone, vulnerable, defenseless against the shadowmaws, or worse, sends a surge of something primal through me.

I rise to my feet, pacing the length of the cave. The movement does little to calm me. My gaze keeps straying back to her, drawn to the sight of her trembling form.

She is still now, her eyes closed, her breathing shallow. The fire has taken hold of her completely. If I do nothing, it will burn her alive.

My claws flex at my sides.

With a frustrated snarl, I cross the cave and crouch beside her. Her skin is flushed, beads of water glistening on her brow and neck, and her scent is stronger now—richer, deeper, almost intoxicating.

I hesitate, my hand hovering above her face. The last time I touched her, I felt...

Too much.

But I have no choice. I press my palm to her brow. The moment my skin meets hers, a jolt rushes through me, a sensation so foreign, so violently *alive*, that I nearly recoil. My glow pulses like a struck gourd, answering her fire, responding to something in her blood, her bones. A thread pulls taut between us, unseen but unbreakable. The flood of sensation is immediate.

Heat. Softness. The strange, soft beat of her *dra-kir* beneath my hand.

She stirs at my touch, a weak sound escaping her lips, and my glow flares brighter, responding to her even as I fight to control it.

Her lips part, her voice barely a whisper. "Please..."

The word is small, fragile, and I do not understand it, but it strikes me like a blow.

Whatever we find in the dust, we keep. *And I found her.*

A daughter of Ain.

Here. On Xiraxis.

I do not know where she came from.

But I will not let her die.

So I lift her.

She is light, softer than anything I have ever held, her body molding against mine as if she belongs there. My glow flares as she settles against me, and something tightens deep in my chest, something raw and unknown.

Her skin is damp where it presses to mine. This water seeping must be how her kind cools themselves. But it is not enough.

I need to cool her.

I stride toward the cave entrance, stepping into the night

air. Xiraxis is a world of extremes—blistering heat during the day, bone-deep cold at night. The moment the night air touches her skin, she shudders, her body reacting to the sudden change.

Her lips part again, her head tilting toward my chest, and I feel the ghost of her breath against my skin.

Something stirs in me. A deep, primal thing.

I do not know what she is. Not fully. Not yet.

But she is female.

The first. The only.

And she is mine to protect.

She shifts slightly in my hold, her fingers curling weakly against my chest, and I look down at her face. Something shifts deep within me. A force I cannot name surges through my being, pushing me toward her in a way that defies reason. It is as if the very core of me recognizes her—something ancient, something buried—and refuses to let go. I am not meant to have this. I am not meant to feel this. And yet... I do.

She is not Drakav. Not of Xiraxis. But she is here. And I found her.

The dust takes.

But it also gives.

And I will not let it take her back.

CHAPTER 11
SOOOO...AWKWARD MORNING-AFTER VIBES CAN BE EXTRATERRESTRIAL. YOU LEARN SOMETHING NEW EVERY DAY

JUSTINE

Warmth.

That's the first thing I register as consciousness seeps back into my brain. Not the burning, feverish heat that had consumed me, but something else —something almost pleasant. A solid warmth against my side, cradling me like a cocoon.

My eyes flutter open, vision still blurry with sleep. Golden light fills the small cave, casting long shadows across the stone floor. It takes me a moment to realize that the light isn't just coming from the sun—it's also emanating from whatever I'm pressed against.

Then I feel it. The rhythmic rise and fall beneath my cheek. The solid mass of...something...I'm curled against.

Someone.

The memory of last night crashes back—the fever, the delirium, the alien—and I jerk upright so fast my vision swims.

"Holy shit!"

The alien—he's sitting propped against the cave wall, and I'm in his *lap*. I was sleeping in his freaking lap, my head on his chest like he's my personal body pillow. And he's just...staring at me, those golden eyes unblinking, his skin glowing softly in the early morning light.

I scramble backward, stumbling and rolling in my haste to put some distance between us. My body lands on stone, the sensation of them shooting through me, and that's when another realization hits me.

I'm still in my underwear. In my *underwear*, in an alien's lap.

"What the actual fuck," I mutter, crossing my arms over my chest, suddenly hyperaware of how exposed I am. "What... how...I mean..." I gesture vaguely between us, as if that explains anything.

He just watches me, head tilted slightly to one side, that same inscrutable expression on his face. The markings on his skin pulse gently. With the light streaming in, it's even more riveting.

"I was dying," I say, more to myself than to him. "I was literally burning up. And now I'm...fine?" I press a hand to my forehead. No fever. Not even a hint of it. It's like it never happened. "That's not how heat exhaustion works. That's not how anything works."

I look around the cave, trying to piece together what happened after I passed out. The smooth stones are still arranged in a circle where he placed them. My clothes are scattered across the floor where I'd discarded them in my fever-induced delirium.

"Did you...take care of me all night?" I ask, knowing he can't understand me but needing to fill the silence anyway.

He rises to his feet in one fluid motion, and I'm struck

again by how large he is—towering over me, all lean muscle and strange, alien grace. He crosses the cave in one stride, crouching in front of me, close enough that I can feel the coolness flowing off his skin. I honestly swore his skin was hot, warm at least, yesterday.

I swallow hard, fighting the urge to back away again. "Look, uh, thank you. For whatever you did. I was in pretty bad shape, and I...well, I'm clearly better now, so...thanks for the alien nursing service, I guess?"

His eyes narrow slightly, scanning my face with an intensity that makes my skin prickle. Then, slowly, he reaches out, one clawed finger hovering near my temple.

I freeze, breath catching in my throat. The claw gently brushes a strand of hair from my face, the touch so delicate it barely registers.

"Okay," I whisper, and I hate how breathy my voice sounds. "So that's...that's a thing that's happening."

The blazing sun streams in through the cave entrance, reminding me that time is passing. Jacqui and the others must be worried sick by now. I need to get back to them, explain what happened, figure out our next move.

"I've got to go," I say, gesturing toward the cave entrance. "People waiting for me. Probably thinking I'm dead in a ditch. Or whatever the alien desert equivalent of a ditch is."

I move to stand, and he rises with me, his massive form blocking the sunlight, casting me in shadow. For a moment, I think he's going to stop me, but he just stands there, watching with that same unreadable expression.

"Right. Clothes first." I spot my discarded outfit and make my way toward it, painfully aware of his eyes on me the entire time. "Don't suppose you have any privacy curtains in this five-star desert accommodation?"

I reach for my blouse, trying to ignore the way my cheeks

heat up. It's ridiculous to be embarrassed—he's already seen me in my underwear all night. Hell, he was holding me in my underwear all night. But something about being conscious for it makes it a thousand times more awkward.

As I grab my blouse, flashes of memory surface—his arms around me, the solid strength of his chest beneath my cheek, the strange, comforting rhythm of his heartbeat. Or whatever alien equivalent of a heart he has.

The memory sends a shiver down my spine, and I quickly look away, trying to ignore the warmth spreading through my belly. That's not supposed to be happening. Not now. Not to him.

I feel my face grow hotter, and I duck my head, hoping he can't see the fact I'm blushing, or that if he does, he won't know why I'm turning red.

No such luck.

He's suddenly there, moving with that soundless grace that still catches me off guard. His hand—so much larger than mine —cups the air between us before his fingertip barely grazes my cheek. The sensation is a whisper, a breath against my skin, cool and unfamiliar. My breath hitches, a jolt going through me that has nothing to do with fear.

"I'm fine," I stammer. Clearing my throat, I take a step back. "Just, uh, human stuff. You know, embarrassment? About being practically naked in the arms of a strange alien all night? Normal Tuesday for some people, I guess, but kind of a first for me."

His brow furrows, and for all his alienness, I can read concern in the expression as clearly as if he were human.

"Really, I'm okay," I say, softer now. "Just...a little weirded out by all this." And breathless, apparently. I gesture vaguely between us again. A flicker of something I don't recognize goes through me and I look away quickly, suddenly very interested in a random spot on the cave wall. It's as if something, some energy, has shifted in the air between us. Like static electricity before a storm. I don't like it. And then I remember the burning ache that had made me want to grind my hips on something during my delirium.

I don't know what the fuck is happening.

He makes a sound—a low rumble that I feel more than hear—and steps back, giving me space. It's such a considerate gesture that I find myself smiling despite everything.

"Thanks."

I turn back to my clothes, determined to get dressed and get moving. But first, maybe one more attempt at communication wouldn't hurt. He seems...more receptive today.

"Justine," I say, pointing to myself. "Jus-tine. That's my name."

He watches intently, and for a moment, I think he might try to repeat it. Instead, he just stares, his golden eyes fixed on my face with such focus it's like he's trying to memorize every detail.

"Right. Well, ditto, buddy," I mutter. "Can't wait to tell Jacqui about you. She's never going to believe any of this."

I turn my attention back to my clothes, pulling my blouse over my head. When I reach for my pants, though, they're suddenly gone.

I look up to find the alien holding them, examining the fabric with an expression of what I can only describe as distaste.

"Hey!" I lunge for them, but he steps back, holding them easily out of reach. "Give those back!"

He makes another one of those rumbling sounds, but this one seems almost...playful?

"I need those," I say, trying to sound stern, but I'm failing miserably. "I can't go walking around like a voyeur the way you do."

I make another grab for them, and he sidesteps me with insulting ease. His skin pulses brighter, and I swear there's a hint of amusement in those alien eyes.

"Oh my god, are you seriously playing keep-away with my pants right now? What are you, five?"

I chase him around the small cave, acutely aware of how ridiculous this must look—me in my blouse and underwear, hopping after a seven-foot alien who's holding my pants like they're some kind of prize.

"Give them back, you overgrown glow-stick!"

He dodges again, but this time I anticipate his movement and change direction, almost colliding with his chest. I reach up, stretching as far as I can, fingertips just brushing the fabric.

"Ha!" I jump, snatching them from his grasp. "Victory!"

The alien makes that rumbling sound again, and this time I'm almost certain it's laughter—or whatever passes for it among his kind. The thought makes something flutter in my chest, a strange warmth that has nothing to do with fever.

I shake it off, focusing on pulling my pants on as quickly as possible. "Very funny. Hilarious. You should take that act on the road."

Once dressed, I feel marginally more in control of the situation. I smooth my hands over my clothes, trying to look somewhat presentable despite having spent the night in a cave.

Meanwhile, the alien has moved away, crouching by the stones he'd arranged. He picks up a larger rock and begins crushing something—the leaf he'd used to bring me water, I realize. Why he's destroying it, I have no idea, but alien customs aren't exactly my area of expertise.

I shrug and finish getting ready, pushing my hair back from

my face and tucking it behind my ears. That's when I feel it—
or rather, *don't* feel it.

My hand freezes, fingers brushing against my bare earlobe.

"No. No, no, no," I whisper, my voice rising with panic as I
drop to my knees and scan the cave floor. "It has to be here. It
has to be."

The alien looks up from his work with the stones, watching
as I desperately crawl around the cave, running my hands over
every inch of stone.

"My earring," I say, touching my naked earlobe to demon-
strate even though I know he can't understand. "It's gone. It's
—" My voice catches, and to my horror, I feel tears pricking at
my eyes. "It was my mom's. She gave them to me right before
she—before she—"

I can't finish the sentence. I never can. Instead, I continue
searching, panic mounting with each passing second. It could
be anywhere—lodged in a tiny crevice, buried in the dust, lost
forever in this godforsaken alien wasteland.

"Please," I whisper, my voice cracking as I crawl toward
where I'd been lying during the fever. "Please be here. Please."

I dig my fingers through the sand settled there. Nothing.
My heart sinks further with each empty handful.

"This can't be happening," I mutter, crawling faster now,
more frantic. "Not the earrings. Anything but those." The tears
I hold back blur my vision as I search. "I've already lost everything else."

I'm so consumed by my search that I don't notice the alien
moving until a shadow falls across me. I'm about to look up
when a sound stops me cold.

"Jus-teen."

The voice is so rough, so guttural—like stone grinding
against stone—that for a moment I don't recognize it as

speech. When it registers, I freeze completely, my hands hovering above the ground.

Slowly, I look up.

The alien is standing over me, those golden eyes fixed on my face with an intensity that makes my breath catch. His mouth—that strange, alien mouth with its sharp teeth—is slightly open, as if he's surprised himself.

"You—" I stammer, momentarily forgetting about the earring. "You can *talk*?"

He doesn't respond, just continues staring at me with that same intense focus.

"Say something else," I urge, rising to my knees. "Anything."

He remains silent, but slowly crouches down to my level, bringing his face closer to mine.

The world seems to shrink around us, the cave walls fading away until all I can see is him—those topaz eyes flecked with gold, the strange patterns of light beneath his skin, the sharp angles of his face. He's so close now that I can feel his breath on my lips. My heart hammers against my ribs as he just stays there, studying me with such intensity that it feels like he's looking straight through to my soul.

I should move back. I should put some distance between us. But I don't. I can't. It's like I'm paralyzed, caught in the gravity of his presence. The rest of the universe has disappeared, and there's only this—only him—filling my entire field of vision, consuming every one of my senses.

Finally, his gaze slides from mine. Shifts to something to the side. To the crushed leaf he'd been working on, reduced to a paste, with some of it coating one long finger.

"So you can talk," I whisper, gaze traveling over his face. "You've understood me this whole time? Or just my name? Why haven't you—"

"Jus-teen."

I gulp.

That strange rasp is like he hasn't spoken in years, maybe never. It sends a shiver down my spine. I can't look away from him.

He leans in, even closer than before, his gaze sliding to my lips.

"What are you—"

Before I can react, he raises his finger—the one coated with the crushed leaf paste—and brings it to my lips.

That's all I manage before his finger slides between my lips. The paste is bitter and herbal, with an underlying sweetness that reminds me of molasses or licorice. I instinctively suck, trying to swallow the strange substance before I have time to think better of it.

The alien makes a sound the moment my lips enclose his finger—a low grunt that seems to come from deep in his chest —and his pupils dilate sharply, consuming the gold of his irises.

Something flutters low in my belly in response, a sensation so unexpected that I jerk back, his finger slipping from my mouth.

"What was that?" I ask, my voice embarrassingly breath-less. "What did you just give me?"

He doesn't answer, of course. Maybe "Jus-teen" is the only word he knows, or the only one he can pronounce with that alien mouth of his. But his eyes remain fixed on my lips, and there's something in his expression that makes heat rise to my cheeks.

"I need to find my earring," I say, trying to focus. "It's important. It's—"

"Jus-teen," he says again, softer this time, almost a caress.

And in that moment, with the desert sun streaming into

the cave and this alien creature saying my name like it's something precious, I realize with perfect clarity that I am in way,
way over my head.

CHAPTER 12
YOUR CAT ISN'T THE ONLY ONE THAT LIKES HIGH PLACES

JUSTINE

I don't find my earring. One more whole day has passed stuck in this cave and I've spent the time checking every grain of sand, every inch of this cave. It is nowhere to be found.

What's worse, I'm having nightmares. Or dreams, depending on how you want to look at it. Strange ones that crept into my mind in the night. Dreams where I'd seen those tiny particles again, swirling around me, inside me, changing something fundamental in my cells. Except, in this deam the alien was there, too. His hands, his touch, so gentle despite those deadly claws, had soothed the burning beneath my skin, chasing away the fear with a different kind of heat. A heat that lingers even now, a phantom ache that pulses between my legs with every beat of my racing heart.

I must be ovulating. It's not my fault it makes me a horny fiend.

It is with great effort that I push the thoughts away, focusing on combing through the last handful of sand.

"It's gone," I finally admit, sitting back on my heels. A hollow feeling spreads through my chest. "It's really gone."

My gaze shifts to the alien. Still crouched nearby, he'd helped me look. Somehow, he'd noted my distress and without a word, he'd kneeled beside me, methodically brushing through the sand even though he had no idea what I was searching for, only that it's obviously important to me. As if my distress alone was reason enough to help.

Now, still watching me with those unnerving golden eyes, he makes a low rumbling sound that almost feels sympathetic.

I brush angrily at the tears threatening to spill over. This is stupid. It's just an earring. A tiny piece of glass. It shouldn't matter so much, especially not here, where I'm stranded with much bigger problems to worry about.

But it *does* matter. And the loss of it feels like losing her all over again.

I take a deep breath and force myself to stand. Sitting here crying won't find the earring, and it won't get me back to Jacqui and the others.

"I have to go," I say, straightening my shoulders. "They'll be looking for me."

I move to my small pack—which is really just my handbag—checking the meager supplies inside. One water packet left. Two more emergency biscuits. Not much, but it'll have to do. I'd lost the emergency blanket somewhere in the desert, but there's nothing I can do about that now.

"Okay," I say, more to myself than to him. "That's it. Time to hit the road."

I sling the bag over my shoulder and turn toward the cave entrance. The alien is still watching me, his expression unreadable as I make my way past him.

I'm almost to the entrance when something large blocks my path. Him. He's moved with that unsettling speed again, positioning himself between me and the exit.

"Excuse me," I say, trying to step around him. "I need to go."

He doesn't budge.

"Look, I appreciate everything you've done. Really. You saved my life, and that's...well, that's a pretty big deal. But I have people waiting for me. People who are probably thinking I'm dead right now."

I try again to move past him, but he shifts, still blocking my way. His eyes have narrowed, and the glow beneath his skin has intensified—pulsing like a warning signal—and for a crazy moment, I want to reach out and touch him again, feel that strange ripple under my fingers. Then I mentally slap myself. No, not helpful.

"Seriously?" I throw up my hands in frustration. "What is your problem? I need to leave!"

He makes a low, rumbling sound—not quite a growl, but definitely not approval either.

"Move," I say, trying to make my voice firm despite the frustration and fear bubbling up inside me. "Please."

Nothing. He might as well be a statue, an immovable wall of muscle and stubbornness.

"Fine. If you won't move, I'll just..." I feint left, then dart right, trying to slip past him.

No luck. He's too fast, his reflexes too sharp. His arm shoots out, gently but firmly blocking my path.

"Okay, listen up, big guy," I snap. All patience has—poof— gone. "You can't keep me here! I don't belong to you. I don't belong here!"

My voice cracks on the last word, and to my horror, I feel tears welling up again. It's all too much—the lost earring, the unnervingly attractive alien refusing to let me leave, the growing fear that I might never see Jacqui or home again.

"Please," I say, the fight draining out of me. "Just let me go."

For a long moment, he stares at me, those golden eyes searching my face as if he's trying to decipher what I'm feeling. Then, with a sound that reminds me of a long-suffering sigh, he steps aside.

Relief floods through me. "Thank you," I breathe, hurrying past him before he can change his mind.

I step out of the cave, squinting in the bright morning sunlight, ready to begin the long trek back to where I last saw the others.

And that's when the world seems to fall away beneath my feet.

"Holy shit!"

I scramble backward, nearly colliding with the alien who's followed me out. My hands find the rough stone of the cave entrance, gripping it for support as I stare out at...nothing. Just open air and a drop that makes my stomach lurch.

We're not on the ground. Not even close. The cave is set into the side of a towering rock formation, a jagged spire that rises hundreds of feet above the desert floor. Below us stretches an endless sea of sand, rippling like water in the morning light. The sun is just cresting the horizon, painting the desert in shades of gold and amber, and from this height, I can see for miles in every direction.

It's breathtaking. And terrifying.

"We're on a cliff," I say, my voice barely above a whisper. "A really, really high cliff."

I turn to the alien, who's watching me with that intensity again.

"You carried me up here," I realize. "Last night. When we

were running from those things. I felt you climbing, but I didn't realize we were going up a freaking mountain."

He makes that rumbling sound again, and now I'm certain it's the alien equivalent of a chuckle.

"This isn't funny!" But even as I say it, a hysterical laugh bubbles up in my throat. "Oh my god, I was about to waltz right off a cliff."

I peer over the edge again, trying to see a path down. There's nothing but sheer rock face, with occasional ledges and outcroppings that might be handholds for someone with claws and superhuman strength, but certainly not for a clumsy human like me.

"Okay," I say, trying to keep the panic from my voice. "Okay. This is...this is a problem. A big problem. I need to get down from here, but unless you've got a parachute hidden somewhere—which, let's be honest, would look ridiculous on you—I'm going to need your help."

The alien tilts his head, watching me with that intense focus that still makes my skin prickle.

"Do you understand? I need to go." I point down at the desert floor, then at myself. "Me. Go. Down. To find my people."

He doesn't move, doesn't react. Just keeps staring at me with those unnerving golden eyes.

"Okay, let's try something else." I take a deep breath and resort to the universal language of desperate humans—charades. I point to myself, then down at the ground far below. When he doesn't react, I frown. "Fuck this." Crouching down, I resort to my less-than-stellar art skills and start drawing in the thin layer of sand near the cave entrance.

With my finger, I sketch out a crude landscape—a wavy line for the horizon, the spiry shape of the rock formation that I'd set out to reach first, and a stick figure with wild hair that's supposed to be me. I point to the stick figure, then to myself, then to the rock formations.

"I need to go there," I say slowly, tapping the drawing. "Back to where I came from. To my friends. You know, other people like me? Smaller than you, not glowy, probably sunburned and freaking out right now?"

The alien crouches beside me, studying my childlike drawing with such intense focus that I half expect him to critique my artistic skills. His expression shifts, his brow furrowing in what looks like confusion. Or is it disgust? Anger? It's hard to tell with a face that's not quite human.

"Please," I try again. "I need your help to get down from here."

He makes a sound—harsher than before, almost like a snarl—rises and turns away from me, heading back toward the cave entrance.

"Hey!" I follow after him. "Don't you walk away from me! You brought me up here. You're responsible for getting me down!"

He stops so suddenly I nearly run into his back. When he turns to face me, there's something new in his expression—something that makes me take an involuntary step backward.

"Okay," I say, holding up my hands in a placating gesture. "I'm sorry. I didn't mean to offend you or whatever alien cultural taboo I just stepped on. But you have to understand—I'm trapped up here. I can't climb down on my own. I'll die."

His expression softens slightly, but he makes no move to help.

"Fine," I mutter, running a hand through my tangled hair. "Just great. Saved from heat exhaustion only to die of starvation on a cliff with an alien who suddenly decides to be useless."

I pace along the narrow ledge outside the cave, frustration

building with each step. "This is ridiculous. I don't know why I thought this would work. 'Oh, let's try to reason with the seven-foot alien predator who can't understand a word I'm saying.' Brilliant plan, Justine. Really stellar work."

I'm freaking out and I know it.

Problem is, I can't stop.

Meanwhile, the alien watches my ranting with something that almost looks like awestruck amusement, and that just makes me angrier.

"You think this is funny? You—"

I don't get to finish the sentence because suddenly the world tilts around me. Strong arms scoop me up, and before I can process what's happening, I'm cradled against a broad chest, my feet dangling in the air.

"What are you—put me down!" I squirm in his grasp, but it's like trying to move a mountain. "I swear, if you don't—"

He turns, carrying me to the edge of the cliff, and I get a dizzying view of the drop below.

"No, no, no! What are you doing? Don't you dare—"

His grip tightens, securing me against his chest, and he looks down at me with what I swear is a mischievous glint in those golden eyes.

"If you throw me off this cliff, I swear I will come back and haunt you for the rest of your glowy alien existence!"

He makes that rumbling sound again—definitely laughter —and then, without warning, he just...steps off the edge.

I scream. I scream like I've never screamed before, a sound that tears from my throat as we plummet through open air. My arms lock around his neck in a death grip, my face buried against his chest.

This is it. This is how I die. Not from heat exhaustion or alien predators, but from being thrown off a cliff by a lunatic alien who thought it would be funny.

Except…we're not falling. Not really.

I risk opening one eye, then the other, and what I see doesn't make sense. We're moving down the cliff face, but in controlled bounds—leaping from one tiny outcropping to another with impossible grace. Each landing is smooth, barely a jolt, before he launches us toward the next foothold.

It's like watching a mountain goat navigate a sheer cliff, except this "goat" is carrying a terrified human. The inhuman strength of his grip is impossible to ignore—those powerful arms holding me against him with a pressure that's somehow both gentle and unyielding. His hands are firm, confident, effortlessly supporting my weight as if I'm nothing more than a child's doll. It's terrifying and yet…strangely reassuring.

"Oh my god," I breathe, my heart still pounding so hard I can feel it in my throat. "You're insane. You are actually insane."

He makes that rumbling sound again, and this time I can feel it vibrate through his chest where I'm pressed against him.

"This isn't funny!" But even as I say it, a hysterical laugh bubbles up inside me, too. "I don't know what I imagined when I asked you to take me down, but it wasn't this! "

We continue our descent in great, bounding leaps that somehow manage to be both terrifying and graceful. With each jump, my stomach lurches, but his arms hold me secure, his body absorbing the impact of each landing.

The ground rushes up to meet us faster than seems possible, and with one final, powerful leap, we're suddenly on the desert floor, standing in sand that's already warming in the morning sun.

He doesn't set me down immediately, and I don't ask him to. For a moment, we just stay like that—me cradled in his arms, my heart still racing, his golden eyes studying my face with that same intense focus. His arms tighten slightly, claws skimming lightly against my side in a way that sends unexpected shivers through me. There's a rumble deep in his chest —a sound of pure, unmistakable satisfaction, like he's thoroughly enjoying holding me this close.

"That was..." I struggle to find the right word. Terrifying? Exhilarating? Completely insane? "...something." Pushing past the heavy breaths wracking my chest, I force a grin.

The alien blinks, gaze shifting to my lips.

His mouth curves in what might be a smile—though with those sharp teeth, it's hard to tell if it's meant to be friendly or menacing.

Slowly, carefully, he lowers me to my feet. My legs feel wobbly, like I've just stepped off a roller coaster, and I have to steady myself against his arm.

"Thanks, I think," I say, looking up at him. "Although a little warning next time would be nice."

He tilts his head, that now-familiar gesture that seems to say he's trying to understand me but isn't quite there yet.

"So," I say, looking around at the vast desert stretching in all directions. "Where to now?"

CHAPTER 13
A NAME IS A MARK. SHE HAS MARKED ME

ROK

I cannot look away from her.

The realization comes slowly, settling into me like the dust settles after a storm. She stands before me, small and fragile against the vastness of the desert, and something in me has...changed. Shifted. As if the very foundation of my being has cracked, allowing something new to take root.

The wind tugs at the strange coverings she insists on wearing, and beneath them, I can sense the heat of her skin, the rhythm of her *dra-kir*—strong and steady now, no longer fighting against the heat that had threatened to consume her. She moves in a circle and I follow her movement with my eyes, tracking each gesture, each expression that crosses her face. The way her brow furrows as she studies the horizon. The way her lips press together in what looks like concentration. The way the sun catches in her hair, turning it to fire.

I want to move closer. I want to breathe in her scent again, that strange, sweet smell that is unlike anything on Xiraxis. I want to press my face to the curve of her neck, where her pulse beats visibly beneath her delicate skin.

I want to taste her.

The thought crashes into me with such force that my claws dig into my palms. This is not…I am not… These urges are foreign, and yet they burn through me with an intensity that I cannot ignore.

Female.

The word echoes in my mind, ancient and powerful. A myth. A legend. A gift from Ain herself.

And yet, here she stands. Flesh and blood and warm, strange scent. Not Drakav, not of Xiraxis, but undeniably, impossibly, female.

"Okay, so we're down from the cliff," she says, her voice quick and light. "That's good. Progress. But which way do we go now? I need to find my people."

I watch her turn in circles, scanning the horizon with those strange, fragile eyes. No secondary lid, as far as I can tell. How will she protect against the storms when they come?

No need. *I* will protect her.

I will not leave her side.

"I think it was that way," she says, pointing toward a distant ridge of stone. "Or maybe that way? I don't know. Everything looks different now."

The dust stretches endlessly in all directions, the same shifting sea it has always been. But she sees it differently. To her, it is a maze, a puzzle to be solved. She is lost.

Lost, and very far from home.

Perhaps Ain truly did send her. Perhaps there is purpose in her arrival, in our meeting.

Or perhaps the dust simply gives what it will, and takes what it will, and there is no greater meaning.

I try to mindspeak, focusing my thoughts into a clear image: *"Where did you come from?"*

But it is useless. She continues her restless movement, unaware of my question, her mind sealed away from mine.

She cannot perceive my thoughts. I have tried, again and again, to reach her mind, to share the images that would make her understand. Each time, I am met with silence—or rather, with the chaotic flurry of her own thoughts, sealed away behind a wall I cannot breach.

Yet somehow, she has given me her name.

"Jus-teen."

The sound still feels strange on my tongue, unfamiliar and awkward. But when she spoke it, pointed to herself and shaped those sounds, an image formed in my mind—a bloom in the dust, delicate and impossible, yet somehow existing. Bright. Beautiful.

Names are sacred. We do not own them. A name is something given, not in sound, but in thought—a mark left in the minds of others.

My name was given to me long ago, shaped by my brothers, my kin, my tribe. The image of me that exists in their minds is simple, unchanging: a stone, steadfast and unyielding, braced against the storm. Alone, but enduring.

Rok.

That is what I am. That is what they see.

But when I think of my name now, with her warmth still lingering against my skin, her scent still in my nose, the image shifts. The winds of the storm grow quieter. The stone is no longer solitary.

It...frightens me.

I am not meant to change. Stones do not bend, do not waver, do not soften. Yet something in me has. Her name lingers in my mind, as if it has carved itself into the stone, leaving a mark that I cannot erase.

"I think I might just have to pick a direction and pray," she vocalizes, eyes narrowing as she looks around. "Fuck. Shit. I can't make a mistake in this."

I do not understand her sounds, but her frustration is clear. It radiates from her in waves, as clear as if she were projecting her thoughts directly to me. She is afraid, though she hides it well behind her constant stream of sound.

She continues speaking, her voice rising and falling in patterns that have become almost familiar. I do not mind the sound as much as I did before. At first, her endless vocalizations grated against my senses, a constant, unnecessary noise. Now, there is something almost soothing about it, like the rhythm of the wind over the dunes.

"Hey," she says suddenly, turning to face me. Her eyes find mine, and for a moment, it feels as if she can see into me. "I just realized—I don't know what to call you. I've been thinking of you as 'the alien' this whole time, which is...well, accurate, I guess, but not very personal."

I tilt my head, trying to understand. She touches her chest, the way she did in the cave.

"I'm Justine," she says slowly. "Jus-tine."

And there it is again—the image that forms in my mind when she speaks her name. A bloom in the dust, delicate and impossible, yet somehow thriving.

Then she points to me, eyebrows raised in question.

She wants to know my name.

I hesitate. Names are sacred, private things. They are not meant to be spoken aloud, to be cheapened with sound. And yet...

I focus on the image that has been my name for as long as I

can remember: the stone, unyielding against the storm. I try to shape my lips around a sound that would capture it.

"Rok," I say. The sound is rough, clumsy, but it is the closest I can come to sharing my true name with her.

Her eyes widen, her mouth opening slightly in surprise. "You spoke again! You...was that your name? Are you telling me your name?" She touches her ear. Not the one with the strange creature trapped in crystal on it. But the other. The one with a stone lodged in it. "I swear I heard it in English. Is this translator thing working? Please, **please** be working."

I touch my chest, mimicking her gesture. "Rok."

"Rock?" she repeats, the sound slightly different from mine. "Your name is Rock?"

Something must shift in my expression, because she laughs —a bright, unexpected sound that sends a strange warmth through my chest. I am not even worried about the shadow-maws hearing. I will fight them all if she would make that sound again.

"I mean, it fits," she says, gesturing at me. "You're certainly built like a—wait, no. That can't be your name. Rock? Seriously? Like Dwayne 'The Rock' Johnson?"

I do not understand her words, but I understand that she has misheard my name. I touch my chest again.

"Rok," I say, letting the sound fall short, sharper than the noise she created.

She blinks, tilting her head at me. "Rok," she repeats, slower this time. Her brows furrow, and I can see her turning the word over in her mind. It is strange. I cannot sense her thoughts, but...I can almost see them through her eyes. "Not Rock. Rok. Same sound, I guess, but...sharper. It feels different."

Her brows furrow and I tilt my head, watching as she taps

her fingers against her thigh. "Yeah, okay. I'll spell it without the 'C.' That's better. Cleaner. It suits you."

Her words settle over me like a weight, and something deep inside shifts. She has taken my name—my true name, or as close as her kind can come to it—and made it her own. To hear it in her voice, to see her shape it into something she understands, feels strangely...good. As if she has reached into a part of me that no one else has ever touched.

"Rok," she says again, softer this time, as if testing it.

The glow beneath my skin flares faintly, betraying me. I have no words for what I feel, but it is enough to know that she has claimed my name in her own way.

She bares her teeth in that strange way I believe is non-threatening, and the sight of it does something to my insides. Her teeth are small, flat, nothing like the fangs of the Drakav, and yet there is something oddly appealing about the expression. I find myself mimicking it, baring my teeth in what I hope is a similar gesture.

Her teeth-baring falters for a moment, as if caught off guard, and then returns, wider than before. She shifts on her feet, a slight hesitation, that strange redness growing in her cheeks again. "Are you...smiling at me? Oh my god, you are. That's adorable. In a terrifying, wolfish way."

I wish I knew what her words mean, but the warmth in her voice suggests they are no insult. I continue the teeth-baring, and she laughs again.

"Okay, Rok," she says, and hearing my name in her voice sends another pulse of that strange warmth through me. "So we've established who we are. Now we just need to figure out where we're going."

She turns again, scanning the horizon, and I am struck by how small she seems against the vastness of the dust. So fragile. So alone.

Except she is not alone. She has me.

The thought comes uninvited, and with it, a fierce protectiveness that surprises me with its intensity. I found her in the dust. By the laws of Xiraxis, that makes her mine. Mine to protect. Mine to keep safe.

Mine.

The word settles into me with a weight that should be alarming, but instead feels right. Inevitable, even. There is no undoing this. It simply is. Like the sky. Like the dust. She does not know it yet, but she is no longer alone. She will never be alone again.

I move to her side, studying the terrain as she is. The dust offers little in the way of landmarks, but I know these lands well. I have hunted them since I was barely out of the Giving Stone.

She will need water soon. Food. Shelter from Ain, who is already climbing higher, its heat intensifying with each passing moment. The cave was safe, but she will not return there willingly. Not when she is so determined to head to the rival clan's territory.

I make a decision. If I cannot convince her to stay where it is safe, then I will go with her. I will guide her through the dust, keep her from the dangers she cannot see, cannot understand.

I will keep her alive, this strange, soft creature who has somehow spoken my name aloud and made it sound like something precious.

"Rok," she says, and I turn to find her watching me, her head tilted slightly to one side. There is something in her expression—uncertainty, perhaps, or vulnerability—that makes me want to reach for her, to draw her against me as I did when I held her all through the dark. To press my face to her and breathe in her scent. To taste the salt on her skin.

But I do not. I stand, unyielding as my name, and wait for her to show me where she wishes to go.

She points toward a distant ridge, the pale spire of stone barely visible against the hazy horizon. "I think that's where we need to go. That looks like the place where..." She hesitates, then waves her hand dismissively. "Well, it doesn't matter what I think it looks like. It's the only landmark I can see, so it's our best bet."

I follow her gaze, recognizing the formation. The Ridge of Shrieking Winds, we Drakav call it in our thoughts. A place where no living creature lingers long...and the last place I would take one I intend to keep alive.

It is a dangerous place, where the sand whips sharp enough to flay skin from bone, where the narrow passages between the stones amplify the howling of the wind until it can drive even the hardiest hunter to madness.

She starts walking toward it without hesitation, her stride determined despite the way her feet sink awkwardly into the sand, even with those strange shields she wears on them.

I do not move.

She takes several steps before noticing that I am not following. She turns, her face pinched as those piercing eyes find mine.

"Well, are you coming?" she calls, gesturing toward the ridge.

I remain where I stand, feeling the heat of the sand beneath my feet, sensing the danger that awaits in those distant ridges. No hunter would willingly approach the Shrieking Winds. Not alone. Not without preparation. And certainly not with a fragile, defenseless female in tow.

She must be protected at all cost. Not put in danger.

"Rok?" she says my name again and my glow reacts as if called, too. "Well?"

I tilt my head, trying to convey without words or shared thoughts that the path she has chosen leads only to death. But she cannot hear me, cannot feel the warning I am projecting with all my strength.

She looks back toward the deadly ridges, then to me again, a sigh escaping her lips. "I have to go, Rok. If you weren't here, that's where I'd be heading to."

Her expression hardens suddenly, eyes narrowing. "But wait, I wouldn't be here if you didn't trap me on a *cliff*. Granted, it was to save my life," she crosses her arms, pushing up those soft gourd-shaped protrusions on her chest, "so you get a pass for that."

I understand the frustration in her voice, if not her words. She is worried.

She turns again, taking a few determined steps toward the Shrieking Winds. Then she stops, her shoulders slumping slightly. She does not look back at me as she speaks, but something in her posture, in the sudden softness of her voice, makes my *dra-kir* ache.

"I guess this is goodbye then, Rok. And..." Her shoulders slump. "Thank you."

Her tone. The resignation. The disappointment. The touch of sadness. It all cuts deeper than any sandfin could. She intends to leave. To walk into death, alone.

I will not allow it.

She huffs and begins walking again, her stride stiff. I let her take three more steps before I move, closing the distance between us in just two strides.

I catch her easily, lifting her off her feet and into my arms. Her body is lighter than it should be, fragile bones wrapped in soft skin, nothing like the dense, armored forms of the Drakav. She fits against my chest as if made to be there.

Her vocalizations turn sharp, piercing. I do not need to

understand her words to know she is not happy with me. Her small hands push against my chest, ineffectual but insistent.

I ignore her protests. I will bear her anger, her resentment, her futile struggles. I will bear anything if it means keeping her alive.

I turn away from the deadly ridges, carrying her toward the safety of the eastern caves. She will not understand. She will fight me. But she will live.

And perhaps, in time, she will understand that I could not let her walk to her death simply because she could not hear the warnings in my mind.

CHAPTER 14
DESERT RAGE IS JUST HOTTER KIDNAPPING

JUSTINE

"Put me down! Right now! This is the second time you've kidnapped me, you giant glowy asshole!"

I'm pounding my fists against his chest, which is about as effective as hitting a brick wall with a marshmallow. My knuckles are going to be bruised, and he doesn't even seem to notice.

"I said put me DOWN!" I kick my legs, which just results in his arms tightening around me. "Don't you dare squeeze me like a tube of toothpaste—I swear I will bite you!"

Rok—because apparently that's his name—continues striding across the desert as if I weigh nothing at all. His face is set in that same impassive expression, golden eyes fixed on the horizon, completely ignoring my tantrum.

Because that's what this is, if I'm being honest. A full-blown, toddler-level tantrum. And it's getting me exactly nowhere.

"You know what?" I say, finally going limp in his arms.

"Fine. Take me wherever you want. I'm not wasting any more energy on this."

He glances down at me, one eyebrow raised in what might be surprise or skepticism.

"Don't look at me like that. I'm conserving my strength for when you finally put me down and I can run away properly."

He makes that rumbling sound again—definitely laughter—and continues his relentless march away from the direction I *think* I need to go in. Because let's face it. I'm lost. And Rok here, doesn't seem interested in helping me get back.

I let my head fall back against his arm, staring up at the yellow sky. It's starting to really sink in that I'm on another planet. Actually, legitimately on another planet.

"This is fine," I mutter. "Everything is going to be fine."

I'm just about to close my eyes and resign myself to my fate when I catch a glimpse of movement out of the corner of my eye. Not Rok's movement—something else. Something under the sand.

I jerk upright, suddenly alert. "Did you see that?"

Rok keeps walking, but his stride changes slightly, becomes more measured, more cautious. So he saw it too.

There it is again—a ripple beneath the surface of the sand, like something large moving just below. Like a shark, but without the fin.

"What the fuck is that?" I whisper, my fingers digging into Rok's arm without me even realizing it.

Another ripple appears, closer this time, and suddenly I'm very, very glad I'm not the one walking on the sand.

"Okay, so maybe you had a point about not wandering around out here alone," I admit. "But you still didn't have to kidnap me. Again."

He doesn't respond, of course, but something in his posture

relaxes slightly. It's as if he can sense when I've conceded a point, even if he can't understand my words.

With nothing else to do, I find myself studying him more closely. The way he moves across the sand is almost graceful—each step sure but light, barely leaving an impression. Unlike me, who would be sinking ankle-deep with every step.

His skin is fascinating up close. The subtle glow seems to come from within, and the markings across his chest were definitely carved there. I wince, just thinking about it. Almost without thinking, I flatten my palm against the raised bumps, feeling the texture of those markings.

He stiffens slightly at my touch, golden eyes darting down to meet mine.

"Sorry," I say, not removing my hand. "Just...curious."

What strikes me most, though, is that despite the heat—and it's getting hotter by the minute—there's not a drop of sweat on him. The sun isn't at its peak yet, but it's still hot enough that I can feel sweat beading at my hairline, trickling down my back.

"You're not sweating," I say, as if he can understand. "How are you not sweating? Are you even warm-blooded? Or is this some kind of...I don't know...alien temperature regulation thing?"

His chest rumbles beneath my palm, and I realize I'm still touching him. I should probably move my hand, but...I don't. The feel of his skin under my fingers is...not unpleasant.

Actually, it's kind of nice. Cool. Soothing. Firm but with a strange, smooth texture that reminds me a little of polished stone. Rok. Rock. I almost laugh at the aptness of it.

"Your skin feels like stone," I tell him. "Rok. Rock. Get it? Actually, that's probably why you're called that, isn't it? You're literally rock-solid."

I'm rambling now, but it's better than thinking about the

fact that I'm lost, being carried God knows where by an alien who may or may not understand a word I'm saying, while strange creatures swim through the sand around us.

Speaking of which...

His eyes are constantly moving, scanning the horizon, the dunes, the ripples in the sand. He seems to catch every movement, no matter how small. When something that looks like a beetle crawls across our path, he tracks it with those golden eyes before it even fully emerges from hiding.

This 'desert' is a lot more alive than I first thought. It's taken me too long to notice these things. Even about him.

My gaze drifts up to his ears—longer and more pointed than human ears, almost elf-like—and I notice they're actually moving slightly, twitching and turning as if catching sounds I can't hear.

"That's why you were wincing when I was yelling, isn't it?" I say with a sudden realization. "Those ears of yours—they're like satellite dishes. You can probably hear a pin drop from a mile away."

He glances down at me, his expression unreadable, but there's something in his eyes that makes me think I might be right.

"Great. So I've been basically screaming into megaphones the whole time. No wonder you looked like you wanted to drown me in sand half the time." I sigh. Oddly, I'm embarrassed. "Sorry about that. I'll try to keep it down."

Another thought occurs to me—if his hearing is that sensitive, maybe that's how he found me in the first place. Maybe he heard me talking, or screaming, or just generally making a human-sized racket out there in the desert.

Or maybe he saw me from miles away with those golden eyes. Either way, it raises another question.

"Are there more of you?" I ask, then realize how that

sounds. "I mean, you can't be the only one of your kind out here, right? You must have...I don't know...a family? A tribe or something?"

The moment the words leave my mouth, I remember how he reacted the last time I tried to ask about other people like him. His entire demeanor had changed. He'd nearly bit my head off. It wasn't an invitation to keep asking questions.

"Never mind," I say quickly. "We don't have to talk about that. It's just...it must get lonely out here, that's all."

Rok suddenly slows his pace, his entire body tensing around me. His ears twitch forward, and his gaze fixes on something in the distance that I can't see.

"What is it?" I ask, my voice dropping to a whisper without me even thinking about it. "What's wrong?"

He doesn't answer, but he stops completely, his head tilting slightly as he scents the air. It's such an animalistic gesture that it sends a shiver down my spine.

Then he's backing up, slowly, deliberately, each step careful and quiet.

I squint against the harsh sunlight, trying to see what he's seeing. There's nothing but more sand, more rocks, more of the same endless desert.

But then, my gaze snags on something.

At first, I think they're shadows in the distance. And then, almost immediately, I realize I'm wrong. Shadows don't move. Not like that.

They're moving like liquid across the sand, dark shapes that seem to flow rather than run. Five of them, spread out in what can only be described as a hunting formation.

"What the fuck are those?" I whisper, my voice catching in my throat.

And then I hear it—that same screeching sound I'd heard the night before. The sound that had preceded our mad dash through the desert, the sound that had sent us fleeing up the cliff to safety.

"Oh fuck," I breathe, my fingers digging into Rok's arm. "It's them. The things from last night."

Rok's entire body has gone rigid, and when I glance up at his face, what I see sends ice through my veins. His brow is furrowed, his eyes narrowed to slits of molten gold, and there's something like confusion—or maybe even surprise—in his expression.

Like he didn't expect to find them here. Like they shouldn't be here.

"We should turn back," I whisper, as if they might hear us. "Rok, we need to go back."

But it's too late. One of the creatures stops, its head—if you can call it that—swiveling in our direction. The others follow suit, and suddenly all five of those shadowy forms are facing us.

Rok snarls, a sound so feral and alien it makes the hair on the back of my neck stand up. Gone is the almost gentle giant who carried me down the cliff, who helped me search for my earring, who bared his teeth in an attempt to smile at me.

In his place is something wild, something dangerous, something that reminds me very sharply that he is not human.

And I realize with a jolt that the soft glow that seems to emanate from beneath his skin has dimmed, almost extinguished. He looks...darker. Harder. Like his name. Like stone. The opposite of the strange being I was starting to like.

Wait.

I am so not beginning to like him. That would be ridiculous. Stockholm syndrome takes longer than a day to kick in, right? Even if he did save my life. Even if he is breathtakingly beautiful in an alien, predatory way. Even if something about the way he says my name makes my stomach do backflips.

Nope. Not liking him at all.

But I'm definitely about to get eaten alongside him, which is more intimacy than I've had in years, so there's that.

The shadow creatures have begun to move again, slinking toward us with a fluid grace that's both beautiful and terrifying. They're too far away to make out details, but I can see now they're a lot like wolves. Or hyenas maybe. Except their bodies are sleek and low to the ground, and there's no fur—just scales or plates that catch the light as they move.

"Rok," I say, my voice barely more than a whisper as my fingers find his chest again. I can feel the rapid beating of his heart. "Run. We need to run."

But he's not looking at me. His eyes are fixed on the approaching creatures, and there's a look in them I haven't seen before. Not fear. Something darker, more primitive.

Rage.

Before I can say anything else, he's setting me down, too fast for it to be careful, too controlled for it to be careless. I stumble as my shoes hit the sand, momentarily disoriented after being carried for so long.

"Wait, what are you doing?" I sputter, grabbing at his arm. "Don't put me down *now*! This isn't the time to start listening to me! Pick me back up!"

The screeching of the creatures turns to clicking, a staccato rhythm that sounds almost like communication. They're closer now, close enough that I can see they have no eyes that I can discern—just smooth, elongated heads that end in what look like circular mouths ringed with teeth.

Yeah, hell to the fucking no.

"Rok, please," I say, real fear creeping into my voice. "We need to go up. High. Like before. They can't climb, right?"

He ignores me, pushing me behind him with one powerful arm. Then he drops into a crouch that looks disturbingly like he's about to run—not away from the creatures, but toward them.

On all fours.

"What are you doing?" I hiss, trying to move around to face him. "We need to run away, not toward them!"

He snarls again, using his arm to push me back with enough force that I stumble. His eyes dart to me, and the look in them chills me to the bone. It's not just a warning—it's a command.

Run.

He grunts, a deep sound from his throat, and pushes me again, harder this time.

And suddenly I understand what he's doing. He's going to fight them. All five of them. While I escape.

"No," I say, shaking my head. "No way. I'm not leaving you to—"

One of the shadow creatures suddenly darts forward, faster than seems possible, and the others follow in a wave of dark, scaled bodies.

Rok tenses, the air stills, and then he's moving, launching himself toward the creatures with a speed and power that takes my breath away.

Fear and adrenaline spike through me, and before I know what I'm doing, my legs are moving, carrying me away from the impending clash. The sand shifts beneath my feet, making running difficult, but terror is one hell of a motivator.

I glance over my shoulder. What I see stops me dead in my tracks.

"ROK!" I scream his name, watching in horror as he collides with the first of the shadow creatures, his body slamming into it with enough force that sand explodes around them.

I skid to a stop, my heart in my throat, unable to look away from the nightmare unfolding before me. Rok is a blur of motion, his claws slashing, his teeth bared in a snarl as he grapples with the creature.

The others circle, clicking and hissing, looking for an opening.

"ROK!" I scream again, my voice breaking with fear.

And then I feel it—a tremor beneath my feet, so slight I might have imagined it if I hadn't been standing perfectly still.

Another tremor, stronger this time. Breaths heavy in my throat, I only have a moment to look down. The sand around my feet shifts, as if something beneath it is moving.

I've just enough time to draw a single, terrified breath before the ground beneath me tilts and gives way, and I'm falling, tumbling, sliding down into darkness as the sand swallows me whole.

CHAPTER 15
SAND IN ALL THE WRONG PLACES

JUSTINE

I'm falling.

Sand pours in around me, over me, a suffocating avalanche that fills my screaming mouth, my nose, my eyes. It's in my ears, under my clothes, everywhere.

I try to scream again, but more sand rushes in, scratching my throat, choking me.

Close your mouth, idiot! Close your eyes!

The thought comes from some distant, rational part of my brain that isn't consumed by blind panic. I clamp my mouth shut, squeeze my eyes closed, but it's almost too late—I'm already half-suffocated, half-blinded by grit.

And still, I'm sliding down what feels like a shaft in the sand. My hands flail, trying to grab on to something, anything, but there's nothing solid, just more sand, endless sand.

Then, suddenly, I stop.

The impact knocks what little breath I have left out of my

lungs. For a terrifying moment, I can't move, can't breathe, can only lie there with sand pressing in from all sides.

I'm going to die here. I'm going to suffocate in a sand trap alone, and no one will ever find me.

But then I realize something—I'm not completely buried. There's space around me. I can feel it, a pocket of air. Half my body is stuck in sand, but I'm not entombed.

I force myself to be still, to calm the ragged gasping of my breath. Carefully, I wiggle my right arm, which seems to be the only limb not weighed down by sand. It moves freely. Good. That's good.

With trembling fingers, I brush the sand from my face—my eyes first, then my mouth and nose. I spit out what feels like half the desert, coughing and gagging at the gritty taste. And don't even get me started on my eyes.

It's like someone decided to shovel an entire beach into them and then stir it around for good measure. They're watering so much I'm probably crying mud at this point. I rub at them uselessly, only managing to smear the grit around. Perfect. Now I'm blind *and* exfoliated.

I squeeze my eyes shut, trying to will the burning away, and focus instead on what I can feel. That's when I notice it—the air is different here. Cooler.

Not cold, but a stark contrast to the blistering heat above. The sand I'm partially buried in is cool to the touch, untouched by the sun's relentless glare.

Finally, I crack my eyes open, blinking through the lingering grit.

I'm in darkness, but not complete darkness. Above me, maybe fifteen feet up, I can see a jagged hole where sunlight filters through—the surface I just fell through. The light is faint but enough to see that I'm in some kind of...tunnel?

"Rok?" I call, my voice hoarse from sand and fear. My throat burns, but I can't stop myself. "ROK!"

No answer, but then I hear the muffled sounds of growls and snarls from above. The shadow creatures. The battle. Rok, fighting them all.

For me.

I clamp my mouth shut, heart hammering. What am I doing? Calling his name isn't going to help him. If anything, it might distract him.

I bite back another shout, forcing myself to focus. The growls and sounds of combat seem to fade, or maybe it's just my imagination. Either way, I can't sit here waiting for him to save me.

I need to get out. I need to help him. I need to help myself.

I start clawing at the sand around me, trying to free my lower body. It's slow going—every handful I move seems to be replaced by two more sliding down from above. But gradually, I'm making progress.

That's when I notice that the tunnel doesn't just go up. It extends to the right and left as well, disappearing into darkness in both directions.

Something made this tunnel. Something dug through the sand, creating this network of...whatever this is. And whatever that something is, I really, really don't want to meet it.

I redouble my efforts, digging frantically now, fear giving my exhausted limbs new strength. Above me, the sounds of battle have gone quiet. Too quiet.

"Rok!" I call again, desperation making my voice crack.

The silence that answers me is deafening.

He's dead. He has to be dead. Nothing could take on five of those shadow monsters and survive.

To my horror, tears start streaming down my face, feeling thick as they meld with the sand and grime.

"No, no, no," I whisper, still digging. "He can't be dead. He can't be."

Why do I even care? I barely know him. He kidnapped me. *Twice*. He's an alien who doesn't understand a word I say. I shouldn't care if he's dead. I shouldn't be crying over him.

But I do. And I am.

"Stupid, glowy asshole," I mutter through my tears, still digging. "Getting yourself killed for me. Who asked you to do that? Who asked you to be a hero?"

I'm about a third of the way free when I notice something concerning—the more I dig, the more the sand from the sides of the tunnel starts to shift and slide. The walls aren't stable. One wrong move, and the whole thing could collapse, burying me alive.

"Perfect." I wipe angrily at the tears. "Just fucking perfect."

This fucking planet. This fucking desert. Those fucking shadow monsters. And those goddamn Xyma who dropped us here like pawns in some cosmic chess game. If I ever get off this sand-blasted hellhole and find out this was all just some inter-stellar reality show, I'm going to personally hunt down every single one of them and sue them from their weird, smooth heads to their—wait, do they even have tails?

Doesn't matter. I'll sue them anyway. No amount of money is worth this. Not even ten grand a day, if they'd offered.

I take a deep breath, forcing myself to calm down. Panic won't help. Neither will anger. I need to think.

Looking up at the hole again, I realize directly digging isn't going to work. The sand is too unstable, and I'm more likely to cause a cave-in than to free myself.

Instead, I start carefully packing sand beneath me, creating a little shelf, trying to build myself a platform to stand on. If I can get high enough, maybe I can reach the edge of the hole and pull myself up.

It's slow, painstaking work. Every movement has to be calculated, gentle, to avoid disturbing the precarious walls of sand around me. And all the while, my strength is waning. I'm tired. So tired. And thirsty—my throat feels like it's lined with sandpaper. And hungry. And filthy. And completely, utterly wrecked.

Part of me wants to just give up. To lie back in the sand and close my eyes and let whatever happens, happen.

But a stubborn little voice inside me—one that sounds suspiciously like Jacqui's—refuses to let me quit. So I keep going, packing sand, building my little platform inch by miserable inch.

Tears start flowing again—I fucking hate them. Tears not just for my situation, but for him. For Rok. For the alien who, for reasons I can't begin to understand, chose to sacrifice himself for me. Who said my name like it was something precious. Who tried to smile just because I was smiling.

"Jus-teen."

I freeze, my head snapping toward the hole above me.

That voice. That rough, gravelly voice that's only ever said one word to me.

"Rok?" I whisper, afraid to hope. "ROK!"

The faint light filtering in from above suddenly dims as something—*someone*—blocks the opening.

"Jus-teen!" Louder this time, more urgent.

Relief crashes through me, so powerful it makes me dizzy. "I'm here! I'm down here! Rok!"

He's alive. He's ALIVE.

And then, strangely, I hear something else. Not just my name, but words. Actual words, clear as day:

"Wait. I will not let you perish."

So the bastard *can* talk. And I mean really talk.

"I'll wait!" I call back, too giddy, too relieved to really care.

"I'm not going anywhere, trust me. Just...please be careful. The sand isn't stable."

But even as I say this, I realize the absurdity. There were no actual words. I saw an image of him digging for me in my head. An image of intense persistence and the sensation that he would get to me.

I didn't hear his voice say those things. It was my imagination. My yearning to understand him, to be understood.

The light shifts again, growing brighter. I hear the sound of digging, of sand being moved. He's trying to reach me.

Gratitude swells in my chest, so intense it feels like a physical ache. I've never been so happy to see anyone in my life.

I start digging upward again, more carefully this time, conscious of the unstable walls around me. But I can't not try to reach him. I need to see him, to touch him, to make sure he's really there and not just a hallucination born of fear and exhaustion.

After what feels like hours but is probably only minutes, I catch a glimpse of golden eyes peering down at me through the widening hole. Then a clawed hand reaches down, stretching toward me.

I've never seen anything so beautiful in my life.

I strain upward, extending my arm as far as it will go. Our fingers are inches apart, then centimeters, and then—

Contact.

His hand closes around mine with gentle strength, and then I'm being pulled upward, out of the sand trap in one smooth motion. The sunlight is blinding after the dimness below, and I squint against it as I'm suddenly pressed against a familiar chest.

We collapse backward onto the sand, me sprawled across him, his arms wrapped tightly around me. The warmth of the sun feels like a shock against my sand-chilled skin, but it's nothing compared to the heat of his body beneath mine. Warm this time, not cool like before.

Warm when I'm cold. Cool when I'm hot.

For a long moment, we just lie there, both of us breathing hard. I can feel his heart hammering against my cheek, almost as fast as my own.

"You're alive," I whisper, gripping the front of his chest like I'm afraid he might disappear if I let go. "You're actually alive."

He doesn't answer, not with words. Instead, his grip on me tightens, and his chest rises and falls beneath me in ragged, uneven gasps. I close my eyes, letting the sound of his breathing ground me, letting the steady thrum of his heartbeat convince me that this is real.

The adrenaline is still coursing through me, making my limbs tremble, but slowly—too slowly—it starts to ebb. My breathing slows to match his.

When the initial surge of adrenaline finally fades, I push myself up to look at him properly. My hands automatically move to his face, his chest, checking him over, making sure he's real, that he's whole.

"You did it," I say. The wonder in my voice is hard to hide. "You're okay."

But he's not okay. Not at all.

My relief turns to alarm as I take in the state of him. There are angry welts across his skin, deep gashes on his jaw, his chest, and especially his arms. He's bleeding from multiple wounds, and his blood is dark—almost black—but with a strange, shimmering quality to it, like it's infused with the same glow that lives beneath his skin.

"Oh gods," I breathe, my hands hovering uselessly over his injuries. "You're hurt. You're really hurt."

I reach for my bag, which miraculously is still strapped across my body, though now filled with about five pounds of sand. I dump it out, frantically searching for anything that might help. My cell phone (useless), an emergency sanitary pad (even more useless), my last two packets of emergency biscuits, my last water sachet, and a few crumpled dollar bills.

Nothing. Nothing that can help stop the bleeding, clean the wounds, nothing that can save him.

"Fuck," I say, tears welling up again. "I don't have anything. I don't know how to help you. At least back at the camp there's Alex. She's a nurse and…"

Fuck. It's not like I can even drag him back there. I have no idea which direction the bus is in and he's bleeding badly now, the dark, shimmering blood pooling beneath him, soaking into the sand. His eyes are still focused on me, but they seem dimmer somehow, the gold muted.

And I'm hit with the terrible realization that he might die right here, right now, in front of me. After surviving those shadow monsters, after saving my life again, he might bleed out on this godforsaken desert because I don't have so much as a bandaid to offer him.

"Please," I whisper. The uselessness, *my* uselessness, is pathetic. "Please don't die. Please."

To my surprise, he moves, gathering what seems like the last of his strength to push himself to his feet. Before I can protest, he's scooped me up against his chest again, holding me as if I weigh nothing, despite his injuries.

"What are you doing?" I gasp as he staggers forward. "Put me down! You're hurt, you can't—"

"Jus-teen," he says, his voice rough with pain, and I go silent.

Because in that one word—that single, solitary word that's all he can say to me—I somehow hear everything he's not saying. I hear. *Stop. Let me do what I need to do.*

I can't…there are no more words.

I stay quiet, pushing back the tears as he staggers forward, past what I only now notice are the bodies of the shadow creatures. All five of them, torn apart, their dark, scaled forms lifeless on the sand, their strange blood mixing with his.

He did that. He fought them all. For me.

"Why?" I whisper, reaching up to touch his face, careful to avoid the gash on his jaw. "Why would you do that for me?"

He doesn't answer, of course. Can't answer. But his golden eyes find mine, and in them, I see a determination, a protectiveness, a...something that makes my breath catch.

"Okay," I say, letting my head rest against his shoulder. "Okay. Whatever you need to do, I'm with you. Just...don't die, alright? Promise me you won't die."

He makes that rumbling sound in his chest—weaker than before, but still there—and keeps walking, each step seemingly more painful than the last. But he doesn't stop. Doesn't falter.

And I realize, with a clarity that cuts through my fear and exhaustion, that when he told me his name—Rok—he wasn't just telling me what to call him.

He was telling me who he is.

Unyielding. Steadfast. Unstoppable.

Even bleeding, even injured, even carrying me when he can barely walk himself, he keeps going. My fingers curl into the front of his chest, feeling the steady beat of his heart beneath my palm.

"You're going to be okay," I tell him, trying to put every ounce of certainty I can muster into my voice. "We're both going to be okay."

I don't know if I believe it. But right now, I need to say it. Need him to hear it. Need to believe that there's a chance, however small, that we might actually survive this place.

CHAPTER 16
THIS IS WHERE THE HERO USUALLY GETS A POWER BALLAD

JUSTINE

He staggers as he walks.

Each step seems to cost him more than the last, his movements jerky and uneven where before they were fluid and sure. But he doesn't stop. Doesn't falter. Just keeps pushing forward, one foot in front of the other, his arms still cradling me against his chest as if I'm something precious.

I can't take my eyes off him. Off the firm line of his jaw, clenched tight against pain. Off the unwavering focus in his gaze. This miraculous, impossible creature who found me in the sand and has somehow, against all logic, decided that I'm worth protecting.

Worth bleeding for.

And he *is* bleeding—his dark, shimmering blood has soaked into my clothes, staining the fabric in patterns that might be beautiful if they weren't so terrifying. But I don't care about the stains. I only care that each drop means he's losing more strength, moving closer to a threshold I don't want him to cross.

The gratitude and pain twisting in my chest is so intense it leaves me speechless. What do you say to someone who's willing to die for you? Especially when they can't understand a word you say?

"Thank you" feels woefully inadequate. "You're an idiot for carrying me when you're injured" seems ungrateful. "I don't know what I'll do if you leave me here" is too raw, too revealing of the fear clawing at my throat.

So I say nothing. Just watch his face, memorizing each alien feature, each mark, each line. Trying to capture the way his eyes had looked at me in the cave, the raw hunger in them mixed with something...softer. Something that made my breath catch and my heart pound even now, despite the exhaustion and fear dragging me down.

I have no idea where he's taking me, but I find I no longer have the urge to ask, to challenge, to question his decisions. All he's done since finding me is protect me. Apart from that one strange incident where he sniffed my underwear—which, in retrospect, was probably just him trying to understand what I was—he's been nothing but...good to me.

My fingers curl gently around the edge of his shoulder, careful to avoid the worst of his injuries. I hate that he's bleeding and still carrying me, but somehow I know with absolute certainty that he won't put me down. Won't let me walk beside him. It's there in the set of his shoulders, in the way his arms tighten almost imperceptibly whenever I shift my weight.

For whatever reason, carrying me is important to him. So I let him, even though it goes against every independent bone in my body.

We walk for what feels like hours. The sun climbs higher, its heat bearing down with an intensity that seems to press the very air from my lungs. I hadn't realized just how much protection the emergency blanket had offered. How much it had shielded me from the worst of the sun's wrath. Now, without it, the rays beat against my skin like a dom with a whip, drawing the moisture from my body, the strength from my limbs.

And I'm not even the one doing the walking.

"You need to rest," I murmur, knowing he won't understand but needing to say it anyway. "You're losing too much blood."

He doesn't respond, of course. Just keeps moving forward, his gaze fixed on the horizon, his breathing becoming more labored with each passing step.

Despite my exhaustion, I force myself to remain vigilant, scanning our surroundings for any signs of those shadow creatures. The memory of them is too fresh, too terrifying to allow even a moment of complacency. And there are other dangers here too—like whatever made that tunnel I fell into. This planet has things. Hidden things. Waiting things.

I wonder briefly if Jacqui and the others are facing similar horrors, or if they've somehow managed to avoid the worst of what this alien desert has to offer. I hope they're okay. I hope they're doing better than we are.

After what feels like an eternity, a dark shape appears on the horizon. As we draw closer, it solidifies into a rock formation—not the one I'd been aiming for when I first set out from that bus, and something that must be my heart drops. I push away the feeling, eyes cast on the formation ahead. It's a flat, mesa-like structure rising from the endless sand, its surface weathered and pitted by whatever passes for erosion on this planet.

Rok's pace changes slightly, becoming more determined, more focused, and I realize this must be our destination. This must be where he's been struggling to reach all this time.

For a moment, hope flares in my chest. Maybe this is where his people are. Maybe he's been taking me to his tribe, his family, others who can help him, heal him and also help me, Jacqui, all the others. My heart skips a beat. The thought of more beings like Rok is both thrilling and terrifying, but right now, I'd welcome any help we can get.

As we draw closer, though, I see it's not a settlement or village. Just a cave entrance, dark and forbidding against the brown stone.

My hope flickers but doesn't die. Maybe his people live inside, hidden from the sun's relentless glare. Maybe there's a whole community in there, just out of sight.

But a nagging doubt whispers otherwise. What if he *is* alone? But...he can't be. Where did he come from then? How has he survived out here, in this harsh, unforgiving landscape?

Rok carries me to the cave entrance, his steps becoming more unsteady the closer we get. By the time we cross the threshold, stepping from blinding sunlight into cool shadow, he's trembling with exertion, his breathing ragged and shallow.

The entrance reveals nothing but sand and stone, no signs of habitation, no indications that anything has ever lived here. My heart sinks further. But Rok continues deeper, past a curve in the rock wall that hides whatever lies beyond from immediate view.

And then the world opens up.

The narrow passage widens suddenly into a chamber that takes my breath away. It's enormous, far larger than it appeared possible from outside, with walls that curve upward to form a dome. Directly above, a circular opening in the rock reveals a perfect circle of yellow sky, letting in just enough light to illuminate the space without the harshness of direct sun.

And there's foliage. Sparse, but foliage nonetheless in tiny patches scattered across the otherwise barren floor. Small plants, nothing like the lush vegetation of Earth, but vegetation nonetheless—spiky, resilient-looking things with thick leaves and stems that seem designed to conserve every drop of moisture.

There's no visible water source, at least none that I can see, but the air feels different in here. Cooler, yes, but also somehow...damper. As if the very rock exhales moisture into the chamber.

The relief of being out of the sun, in this small oasis of relative comfort, is so intense it makes me dizzy. Or maybe that's the exhaustion, the dehydration, the emotional toll of everything that's happened in the past twenty-four hours.

Rok's arms relax, and for a moment I think he's going to keep holding me, but then he carefully, gently, sets me on my feet. His hands linger at my waist, steadying me, making sure I'm stable before he lets go completely.

I turn to thank him, words finally forming on my lips, but they never make it out. Because the moment his hands leave my waist, Rok crumples to the ground.

"No!" I drop to my knees beside him, hands hovering over his body, afraid to touch him, afraid to make his injuries worse. "Rok? ROK!"

His eyes are closed, his breathing shallow and rapid. And there is no glow beneath his skin. I've come to think of it as normal, that the fact it's not there has anxiety spiking within me.

"No." I finally reach out to touch his face. "Don't you dare die on me. Not after all this. Not after everything."

He doesn't respond. Doesn't move. Just lies there, each breath a visible struggle.

Panic rises in my throat, threatening to choke me, but I force it down. Panic won't help him. Nothing will help him if I can't figure out what to do.

I look up, gaze flicking around the chamber, searching for something—anything—that might help. There's...nothing. Plants, yes, but I'm no herbalist. All that's here is, well, me...my handbag.

With trembling hands, I dump its contents out again, eyes shifting over my cell phone, the emergency biscuits, the crumpled dollar bills, my water sachet, and the sanitary napkin.

I stare at the pad for a long moment. It's not much, but it's the only absorbent material I have. And Rok is still bleeding.

"Better than nothing," I mutter, tearing open the plastic wrapper.

My breaths come hard and fast as I work, my gaze shifting to Rok every few seconds. He's still lying there, unmoving, only his chest rising and falling with pressured breaths.

"Come on, Justine. Come on."

Swallowing hard, I peel back the adhesive strips and separate the pad into its layers, exposing the ultra-absorbent core. It's not sterile, not by a long shot, but it's the best I can do.

I shift closer to Rok, getting a better look at his wounds in the soft, diffused light of the cave. What I see gives me a small measure of hope—the smaller cuts and gashes have already started clotting, the bleeding slowing to a trickle. His physiology must be different from humans, his blood clotting faster, his healing more efficient.

But the deeper wounds—particularly a nasty gash across his ribs and another on his upper arm—are still oozing that strange, dark, shimmering blood.

I tear the absorbent pad into strips and press the first one against the worst of the wounds, watching his face for a reaction.

"Does it hurt?" No reaction. No response.

Swallowing down the lump in my throat once more, I apply gentle but firm pressure. The material turns dark almost immediately, soaking up the blood with an efficiency that would be impressive if my heart wasn't beating so hard.

"Hold on," I murmur, not sure if he can hear me but needing to fill the silence anyway. "Just hold on. You're going to be okay."

After a few minutes, I carefully lift one corner of the makeshift bandage to check underneath. The bleeding seems to have slowed, but not stopped entirely. I press the strip back down, wishing I had more, wishing I had actual medical supplies, wishing I had any idea what I was doing.

My gaze shifts to the water sachet lying on the floor beside me. It's small—probably like 500 ml—and it's the last one I have. My last source of hydration in this alien desert.

I stare at it for a long time, biting my lip so hard it hurts. I should save it. I know I should save it. For myself, at the very least—I'm already dehydrated, and without water, I'll die out here.

But Rok is dying in front of me. Right now. *Because* he saved me. Because he chose to fight those monsters rather than run.

And he could have run. He's done it before. He's fast enough. He could have left me and run.

He didn't.

And maybe I shouldn't run now either.

"Fuck it," I whisper, snatching up the water sachet. "You're not dying on my watch."

I pop the little cap off and carefully, gently, tilt Rok's head back. His lips are surprisingly supple, fuller than I'd noticed before, with a tempting curve that makes me pause for a heartbeat too long—definitely not the thoughts I should be having while he's literally bleeding out. I dribble a tiny amount of water between them, watching anxiously to see if he'll swallow.

For a moment, nothing happens. Then his throat works, and the water disappears. Encouraged, I pour a little more, and then a little more.

Suddenly, his whole body convulses. His eyes fly open, golden irises blazing in the dim light, and he chokes, water spraying from his mouth as he gasps and heaves.

"No!" I cry, but it's too late. In one violent movement, his arm lashes out, knocking the water sachet from my hand. It flies across the cave, its precious contents spilling onto the stone floor, soaking into the cracks, disappearing forever.

"Noooo!" I scramble after it, hands scraping at the stone, as if I can somehow take it back, force it back into the sachet. But there's nothing to salvage. Not a drop left.

"Shit," I whisper, pressing my hands against my face, trying to keep my panic in check. That was it. The last of the water.

And now it's gone. My chest rises and falls in uneven gasps. No water. No way forward.

I should be angry. Furious, even. But all I feel is fear.

I turn back to Rok, just in time to see him collapse back onto the floor, his brief moment of consciousness already gone. His breathing is still labored, but now there's a wet, rattling quality to it that terrifies me.

I crawl back to his side, tears streaming down my face. "I'm sorry," I whisper, brushing my fingertips across his forehead. "I was trying to help. I didn't think..."

Gone. Our only water, gone. And for what? For a few seconds of consciousness that seemed to hurt him more than help?

Hopelessness crashes over me like a wave, dragging me under. I've done everything I can think of, and none of it seems to be working. I have no more supplies, no more ideas, no more hope to offer.

I curl up beside him, pressing my forehead against his shoulder, feeling the faint warmth of his skin against mine.

"Please," I whisper, the word barely audible even to my own ears. "Please don't leave me alone here. Please live."

But there's no response. Just the shallow rise and fall of his chest, the soft, pained sound of his breathing, and the crushing weight of my own helplessness.

CHAPTER 17
THE DESERT GIVES. THE DESERT TAKES.
I KEEP

ROK

I wake to a weight against my side and the scent of her in my nose.

Sweet. Strange. Unfamiliar and yet, somehow, more familiar to me than my own breath.

For a moment, I do not move, letting my senses catalog my surroundings. The cool stone beneath me. The faint rustling of the fire bloom plants that grow in the cracks of the stone.

And her. Jus-teen. Curled against me like a young hunter during his first stormy season, seeking warmth.

She stayed.

The realization settles into me slowly, like dust after the winds. She could have left when I collapsed. Could have fled into the dust. She had no obligation to remain at my side.

Yet here she is. Her small, strange body pressed against mine, her breath soft and even in sleep.

I test my strength, flexing my arm, and wince at the sharp pain that lances through me. The shadowmaws took their toll.

More than they should have. But I am alive, and so is she, and that is what matters.

The shadowmaws. They should not have been hunting in the open dust while Ain still shone. They are creatures of darkness, of shadow, emerging from their dens only when Ain sleeps and the three moons rise. To find them stalking the dust while there is light...

It is not right. It is not the way of things.

If I had known they were skulking about the open sands, I would not have taken the female that way. Would have risked the Ridge of Shrieking Winds as she wished, despite the dangers there. Better the known peril than the unexpected ambush.

Instead, I almost lost her. This female, first of her kind, sent by Ain herself. Mine that I found. Mine to protect. Mine to keep safe.

I stretch carefully, assessing the damage. The worst of the wounds have already begun to heal, my body doing what it has always done—mending itself, erasing weakness, returning to strength. I have not been unconscious for long. Ain has yet to reach her zenith in the sky. It is still early in the sol, which is good. We have time and many solmarks of light.

My gaze drifts back to her sleeping form. So small. So fragile. Her hide-coverings are torn and stained with my blood, yet even in sleep, there is something fierce about her. Something unyielding.

I reach out, carefully brushing a strand of her strange head-fur from her face. It is softer than anything I have ever touched, softer even than the belly fur of a newborn sand pup. The color of it reminds me of fire blooms in their fullest glory, when they burst open under the light of all three moons.

She stirs slightly at my touch, but does not wake. Her skin is cool now. The dangerous fire that had threatened to consume her has not returned. Perhaps the poison in her was only temporary.

Speaking of poison.

My gaze falls to the strange waterskin lying empty on the stone nearby. Not a waterskin. The shape is all wrong. It is more like a pouch. Her water pouch. Filled with poison water. She had tried to give me her poison—her water. I stare at the pouch, turning the fact over in my head.

In the dust, there is no greater gift, no deeper sign of care, than to offer one's water to another. It is life itself, precious beyond measure, never to be wasted or given lightly. Even among kin, among clan, water is shared only in the direst need, only to save a life that would otherwise be lost.

She gave me hers freely, desperately, despite her own need. Despite knowing, surely, that she had no way to replace it.

Her poison burned in my throat, seared my lungs, but her intent was clear: this female did not want me to perish. Just as I had told her—or tried to tell her, through the barrier between our minds—that I would not let her perish when she fell into the sand serpent's tunnel.

The memory of that moment—of seeing her disappear beneath the sand, swallowed by the dust as if she had never been—strikes me anew with a fear so profound it feels like physical pain. It was more than fear for her safety, more than concern for a creature under my protection. It was as if I was about to lose an essential part of myself I hadn't known existed until that moment.

As if, should she die, some part of me would perish with her.

The feeling is unfamiliar, unsettling. I am a hunter, a protector. I have guarded my tribe, my brothers, my territory. I have fought for them, bled for them, would die for them if needed. But this...this is different. Deeper.

Somehow, so much deeper. I can feel it. Feel it in my very bones. But explain it, I cannot.

It reminds me of the ancient stories, the legends told around the warming stones when the cold season comes and the dust storms are too fierce to hunt. Tales of how the first Drakav came to Xiraxis, of how Ain chose our people to guard her daughters, to protect them from the dangers of the dust.

I need to return to the clan. By now, Kol will have noticed my absence. As clan leader, my older brother is not one to let even a minor deviation from routine go unquestioned. They will likely send a hunting party to search for me soon, if they have not already.

I should go back. Kol and the other older brothers would know more about the ancient legends of the daughters of Ain. They would better understand what is happening here, where Jus-teen has come from, why I feel this way toward her. This strange, overwhelming sense of...possession. Of connection I cannot explain.

A connection that grows stronger with each passing moment, like now, as I find myself reluctant to untangle from her grasp despite knowing I should rise, should gather the fire bloom plants to speed my healing and to refresh her when she wakes.

These are not sensations I have known before. Not urges I have felt. Even in the hunting season, when the call of blood grows strong, I have never felt this...fixation. This need to keep one specific being safe above all others.

I need to understand. Need to know why my people worshipped the daughters of Ain. Need to know why I feel this urgent, overwhelming drive to worship her. Not with words or offerings, as we worship Ain herself, but with protection, with care, with my very life, if needed.

What I did in the dust—facing a pack of shadowmaws

alone—is not something even the most foolhardy hunter would attempt. I knew they would follow wherever I fled, knew they would hunt her down, and the thought of her in one of their jaws...

I couldn't allow it. Had to face them. Had to end them.

She shifts against me again, a small sound escaping her throat, and I know she is close to waking. As carefully as I can, I disentangle myself from her and rise to my feet.

The movement sends fresh pain through my wounds, but I grit my teeth against it. I do not want to rouse her. She needs rest. Despite being a daughter of Ain, she is clearly not adapted to the harsh conditions of the dust. While carrying her, I noticed how she tucked her face against my chest, how she tried to shield her eyes from Ain's glare.

I understand now that the hides she wears—the strange coverings I initially thought might be trophies from her kills—are not decorative. They are protective, meant to shield her delicate skin from Ain's light and heat. And I made her lose one of them. The one that shone in the light. The one she seems to need the most.

So I will protect her now. Will find a way to keep her safe from Ain's heat until we can return to the clan, where the deep caverns offer cool respite even in the hottest part of the sol cycle.

"Rok?"

Her voice, still thick with sleep, draws my attention back to her. She's sitting up, rubbing at her eyes, her gaze darting around the cave before settling on me.

"You're awake," she says, the relief in her voice unmistakable even if her words are beyond my understanding.

Then her eyes widen. I almost reach for her, fearing they will pop out of her skull. She scrambles to her feet so quickly she nearly stumbles, rushing toward me with such urgent concern that something warm unfurls in my chest. Her hands hover over my wounds, not quite touching, but close enough that I can feel the heat of her skin.

"What are you doing standing? You shouldn't be up!" Her voice rises with worry, her hands gesturing for me to sit. "You were practically dead a few hours ago. Please, sit down. Rest. Tell me what you need, and I'll—" She stops abruptly, pressing her lips together and shaking her head. "God, I'm an idiot. You can't tell me anything, can you?"

Her meaning is clear in every line of her body—the creased brow, the gentle hands that want to help but don't know how, the frustrated care in her eyes. She's concerned. For me.

Her gaze shifts to the small patches of orange, the fire blooms growing from the cracks in the stone.

"Are these plants medicinal?" she asks, miming something with her hands, rubbing them together as if grinding something. "Herbal remedies? Is that how you healed so fast?"

I watch her gestures, tilting my head slightly. Her meaning eludes me, though I can tell she's asking about something. Her attention keeps darting between me and the fire blooms. She points to her wounds, then to mine, then to the plants. Is she asking if they hurt me? If they're dangerous?

I move to the nearest fire bloom, a small but healthy specimen growing from a deep crack in the stone. The plant's thick, fleshy leaves are a deep blue-orange, tapering to sharp points tipped with tiny spines that glow faintly in the dim light of the cave. Its roots reach deep, seeking the hidden water that flows beneath this part of the dust, kept secret from all but those who know where to look.

Carefully, I pluck several of the largest leaves, making sure to leave the roots and the smaller growth intact so the plant can regenerate. The fire blooms are resilient, adapted to survive in the harsh conditions of the dust, but they are not inexhaustible. A hunter must always ensure the continuation of what sustains him.

"Are you going to crush that?" Jus-teen asks, making a grinding motion with her hands again. "Like you did with the other plant before?"

I understand her meaning, but that is not what fire blooms are for. At least, not immediately.

Instead, I pop one of the leaves into my mouth and begin to chew, feeling the familiar, bitter juice coat my tongue. The taste is harsh, astringent, but the healing properties are worth the discomfort.

Jus-teen stares at me, her eyes widening again as I take another leaf and do the same. The juice of the fire bloom will speed my healing from within, will cleanse the shadowmaw venom from my blood, and will restore the strength I lost in the battle.

When I've chewed several leaves, I offer one to her, extending my hand toward her mouth. She hesitates, her gaze darting between the leaf and my face, uncertainty clear in her expression.

"You want me to eat that?" she asks, pointing to the leaf and then to her mouth. "Is it safe for humans? I mean...for me? Will it make me sick?" She looks at the leaf again. "Fuck, how are you even supposed to know that?"

I continue to hold the leaf out to her, waiting patiently. I cannot explain in vocalizations she would understand, but the fire bloom will help her as well, will renew her, will provide some of the moisture her kind seems to need so desperately.

She reaches toward it cautiously, then pulls her hand back with a small sound when one of the tiny spines pricks her fingertip. A bead of red appears—so different from my own blood—and she puts the finger to her mouth.

I freeze, suddenly aware of my oversight. Her skin is so

much softer than mine, more vulnerable to the fire bloom's defenses. How could I have missed something so obvious? The thought of causing her pain, even accidentally, sends an uncomfortable ripple through my chest.

Quickly, I withdraw the leaf and use my claws to carefully strip away the spines from its edges, working meticulously until it's completely safe for her. Only then do I offer it again, holding it flat on my palm to show her it won't harm her now.

She studies my actions, a strange look in her eyes. Finally, she takes the leaf, her fingers brushing against mine in a touch that sends an unexpected jolt through my skin. She examines it for a moment, turning it over in her hands, before cautiously placing it in her mouth. She does a single chew.

"Ugh. That is *awful*." She glares at me as if I've personally offended her. "Are you sure this won't kill me?"

I do not need mindspeak to know she is pouting at the leaf.

I huff a soft breath, amusement curling in my chest. She is strange. So very strange.

And yet, I do not think I could let her go.

I do not think I want to.

To my surprise, she puts the leaf in her mouth again. I watch her reaction, my eyes traveling over her face as she begins to chew. The juice from the plant turns her mouth a deep, rich brown, almost red—a concerning color against her pale skin, but one I know is temporary. She chews slowly, her brow furrowed, before swallowing with a slight grimace.

"That's...bitter," she says, making a face. "But not terrible. Kind of like really strong, unsweetened tea. Is it medicine? Food? Both?"

I tilt my head. She does not seem irritated by it. The fire bloom is sustenance in times of need, medicine for the wounded, a source of moisture when water cannot be found. It is one of the dust's few gifts, one of the treasures known only to the Drakav and a few other dust-dwelling creatures.

With the remaining leaves, I begin to prepare poultices for my wounds. I crush them between my palms, releasing more of the bitter juice, then press the resulting paste directly onto the deepest gashes—the one across my ribs, another on my upper arm, and several smaller but still significant wounds on my legs and torso.

The paste stings on contact, a burning sensation that quickly gives way to numbness as the fire bloom's properties begin to work. The bleeding, already slowed by my body's natural healing, stops completely. Soon, the edges of the wounds will draw together, the skin knitting itself closed with the fire blooms' help.

I continue methodically treating each wound, even the minor scrapes and scratches, not wanting to waste any of the healing properties of the precious plant. There are a few injuries in other places as well—a nasty gash on my inner thigh, dangerously close to more vulnerable areas, where one of the shadowmaws managed to rake me with its claw before I tore its head from its body.

As I tend to this particular wound, I become aware of Justeen's gaze, fixed on a point between my legs. When her eyes lift to meet mine, her face suddenly blooms with color, a deep, rich red spreading across her cheeks and down her neck.

For a moment, I'm alarmed. Is it the fire starting beneath her skin again? That cursed burning that nearly consumed her before? I drop the remains of the fire bloom and lunge toward her, pressing her back into the cool sand of the cave floor, my face close to hers as I inhale deeply, trying to detect the scent of this dust-cursed sickness.

She sputters in surprise, her hands coming up to push against my chest, but her efforts are weak, uncoordinated.

"What are you doing?" she gasps, her voice higher than usual. "Rok, what—"

But I'm focused on my task, sniffing at her face, her neck, trying to determine if the fire has returned to consume her from within. Her skin isn't unnaturally hot, though, not like before. And the scent is different—still her unique, sweet smell, but with an undertone of something new. Something I haven't detected from her before.

I pause, confused, and look down at her. She's gone completely still beneath me, her eyes wide and fixed on mine, her breathing rapid but not labored. There's a strange look in those eyes, something I haven't seen before—a mixture of what looks like fear, but isn't quite fear, and something else entirely. Something that makes the glow beneath my skin suddenly pulse to life with no input from me at all.

A rumble vibrates low in my chest as I try to understand what is happening, why she's reacting this way. My eyes travel over her more carefully now, noticing for the first time the small cuts and scrapes across her body—not bleeding, but evident on her soft skin, nonetheless. Harm from when she fell in the dust serpent's tunnel.

I remain positioned over her, keeping her between my thighs as I crouch above her. Her eyes follow my movements as I reach for another fire bloom leaf, crushing it between my palms until the healing paste forms.

I try to send mind-speech to her again, projecting the concepts of healing and protection as clearly as I can. Nothing. No recognition in her eyes, no response. After so many attempts, I am certain now—she cannot hear the thoughts I send.

I must resort to using my tongue, an organ I have used more times since meeting her than I have ever used in my life.

It feels like a hunter trying to kill a dust stalker with a muted blade—clumsy, inefficient, painful for the hunter.

Carefully, I begin applying the paste to a scrape on her arm. The moment my fingertips touch her skin, something unexpected happens. The glow beneath my skin erupts, pulsing brighter, and it's not the only thing going haywire. It's as if the nerves in my hands are shooting tingles from where I touch her straight through my frame, bypassing every defense I've built.

I have no choice but to pause for a moment. I cannot move.

"Rok?"

So soft, that vocalization. I have never felt my name so softly.

My gaze shifts to her.

She doesn't move, just watches me with wide eyes, her mouth slightly open as I force myself to continue treating her wounds. That strange new scent grows stronger, filling the space around us, clouding my thoughts. I try to ignore it, focus on the task, but it calls to something...else within me.

A sensation builds at the apex of my thighs where my member rests. It has never responded before. Not like this. I stiffen, staring down at her, confused by my body's reaction. Perhaps the shadowmaw's venom has done more to me than I thought.

How can I protect this strange creature if I am compromised? At the very least, I must survive long enough to ensure her safety. I cannot allow the rival clan to find her—they would not be gentle with something so soft, so different.

I know then...that I must try to speak. To protect her properly, to figure out how she came to be wandering the dust alone, I must communicate with her.

I focus, trying to remember how to shape sounds with my mouth rather than thoughts with my mind. Trying to remember how to use a language only vocalized at death, when the Giving Stone opens to take you back within itself.

It has been so long. The muscles in my throat feel stiff, unwilling.

Finally, I manage to push air through vocal cords rarely used, forming sounds that feel alien on my tongue.

"You do not...burn," I say, the words rough and grating, not even sure if she will understand. Her vocalizations are nothing like I have heard before. "The fire...from within...is gone. That is...good."

If it's even possible, Jus-teen stiffens beneath me, her eyes widening like polished flat stones.

For a pulsebeat, neither of us moves. Then slowly, her hands rise toward my face, hovering just a breath from my mouth, fingers trembling slightly. Her gaze searches mine, and my gaze shifts to her hand.

I wish...I wish she would put her touch upon my lips.

"Your language," she whispers, "it's beautiful." Her eyes flick between mine, studying me with new intensity. "I wish I could understand you."

Ain. She does not comprehend my words. Does she? I try again, preparing to force more sounds from my unused vocal cords, when suddenly I hear another voice—not Jus-teen's, but similar in cadence, with a strange quality that sends a shiver down my spine.

"ARCHAIC LANGUAGE DETECTED. DRAKAVIAN. CALI-BRATING."

I leap backward with a snarl, dropping into a defensive crouch, my claws extending instinctively. My eyes dart around the cave, searching for the source of the disembodied voice. The glow beneath my skin suddenly dies and I sniff. All I can scent is her. Jus-teen.

Confused, my gaze shifts back to her. That's when I notice

the same hand that had reached toward me now reaches to her ear. To the stone she has lodged within it.

Jus-teen's eyes widen. Her mouth falls open.

"You heard that?" she vocalizes.

I'd noticed it before but hadn't given it much thought. Discovering her presence was shocking enough. Her wearing a stone inside her ear was the least strange thing about her. Now it glints unnaturally, and I realize the voice came from there. Some kind of magic? A trapped spirit? Is she possessed by something?

I bare my teeth, claws scraping against stone, ready to defend us against whatever unseen threat has revealed itself.

"Oh my God," she breathes.

I wish I could understand, but I am no fool. She does not appear to be alarmed. *Why?*

Because she knew of this intruder all along. How long has this spirit been watching us? Listening to us?

My nostrils flare. My spine curving as I get ready to pounce. I will rip it from her ear and smash it till it turns to dust. I cannot trust this female's instincts when she has left such a thing so close to her skull.

This is an unknown. Danger.

Danger she was aware of.

The tribe. My clan. I cannot take her there. Not yet. Not until I understand what she is, and why Ain has sent her.

Seeing my stance, she rises slowly, arms stretched out toward me, palms pointing down. "Wait!" She's standing now, approaching me like I would a creature of the dust that I do not want to startle. "It's not dangerous—it's helping us!"

Useless words.

Useless words mean nothing.

"Rok...Rok...It's okay, it's okay. It's just my translator. It's not dangerous."

The stone in her ear speaks again. "CALIBRATION AT 10%."

The sound seems to come from nowhere and everywhere at once.

I do not trust it. I do not trust anything that speaks words without a mouth, that hides inside her skull like a parasite.

This is...unnatural.

I stare at her outstretched hands, at the hope blazing in her eyes, at the stone that whispers with voices that should not exist. My muscles remain coiled, ready to strike. To protect. To destroy.

CHAPTER 18
VIOLENCE: NOT THE BEST
COMMUNICATION STRATEGY

JUSTINE

It happens so fast I can barely process it.

One moment, I'm watching Rok crouch defensively, his golden eyes fixed on my translator earpiece, his body coiled like a spring about to release.

The next, there's a blur of movement— so quick I can't even track it—and then his clawed hand is at my ear, a sharp pain flares across my skin, and he's leaping back with my earpiece clutched between his fingers.

"NO!" I scream, lunging forward. My hands wrap around his forearm, but it's like hugging the branch of a tree. He doesn't even seem to notice my grip, my strength completely negligible against his.

With one swift, savage motion, he slams the earpiece down and crushes it with a rock. I would laugh at the pun if a scream didn't lodge itself in my throat instead. Over and over he slams the rock down until only fragments remain—bits of crystal, twisted metal, and tiny components I can't even identify.

The world stops.

I stare at the destroyed remains of the translator as they fall like dust from the stone.

My last connection to understanding. My only chance of communication. Gone.

The sound that escapes my throat doesn't even sound human—it's raw, primal, a keening wail of loss and fury and disbelief.

"What have you done?" My voice rises, breaking. "WHAT HAVE YOU DONE?"

Rok stands motionless, watching me with those unreadable alien eyes, his posture still tense but no longer poised to attack. His claws are still visible, though, and the set of his jaw is still tight.

"You had no right!" I scream, my hands balling into fists at my sides. "No right! That was *mine*! Do you have any idea what you just destroyed? Any idea at all?"

He tilts his head slightly, and the gesture—that same goddamn head tilt he's done since we met, like I'm some curious specimen he's trying to catalog—only enrages me further.

"Stop looking at me like that!" I shout, taking a step toward him. "Like you're so superior, like you know what's best for me! You don't know anything about me! You don't know where I'm from, what I need, who I am!"

My emotions are a hurricane, tearing through me with such force I can barely stay upright. I'm shaking, my whole body trembling with a cocktail of rage, helplessness, and a soul-deep despair that threatens to drown me.

"That was my only chance to understand you!" I yell, gesturing at the destroyed earpiece. "My only chance to tell you what I need, to ask for help finding my people! And you just...crushed it! Like it was nothing!"

Rok remains still, his expression unreadable. Is he even capable of regret? Of understanding what he's done? Or am I just a pet to him, some strange creature to be managed and controlled?

"You primitive, controlling, arrogant alien!" My voice breaks on the last word, and I hate it—hate the weakness, hate the tears that are now threatening to stream down my face, hate how utterly, completely powerless I feel.

My only hope. Crushed by a fist that could just as easily crush me.

"I don't even know why I'm screaming at you," I say, my voice dropping to a bitter, choked whisper. "You can't understand a word I'm saying, can you? And I can't understand you. You made sure of that."

I turn away from him, unable to bear the weight of his gaze anymore. My eyes fall on the remains of the translator, scattered like stardust across the stone floor. With trembling fingers, I kneel and begin to gather the pieces, though I know it's futile. The technology is far beyond anything we have on Earth—I couldn't repair it even if I had all the tools and knowledge in the world.

But I can't just leave it there, these fragments of my last hope.

"You don't get it," I whisper, not looking at him as I collect the tiny pieces. "I'm lost. I'm stranded on an alien planet with no way to contact my people, no way to get home. That translator was my only link to understanding anything about this place. About you."

My hand closes around the last shard, a jagged piece of crystal that cuts into my palm. I barely feel it. The physical pain is nothing compared to the hollowness spreading through my chest.

"I was starting to trust you," I whisper, still not turning to face him. "I thought...I don't know what I thought. That maybe we could figure this out together. That maybe you weren't just some mindless brute who found me in the desert."

I stand slowly, the pieces of the translator clutched in my hand, blood from the cut mixing with the broken technology. When I finally turn to look at him again, my anger has crystallized into something colder, more bitter.

"I was wrong," I say flatly. "You're just like every other man I've ever met. Thinking you know best. Thinking you have the right to control everything. Making decisions for me without even asking what I want."

I know he can't understand the words. But he understands the tone—I can see it in the way his posture shifts, in the subtle movement at his throat, the clenching of his jaw.

"I survived before I met you," I tell him, raising my chin. "I survived the crash, the desert, the heat. I can survive without you, too."

But even as I say it, a small, traitorous voice in the back of my mind whispers: *Can you, really?*

Can I really survive alone in this desert, with no water, no shelter, no protection against those shadow creatures? Without Rok, who fought them all to save me? Who carried me for miles, covering ground I couldn't possibly cover on my own? Who's treated my wounds and shared his water and shelter?

The thought sends a cold ripple of fear through me, momentarily dampening the heat of my anger. But I push it aside. I can't afford to think like that right now. Can't afford to acknowledge how much I've come to rely on this alien in such a short time.

"Just...stay away from me," I say, the fight suddenly draining out of me. I'm exhausted and I feel like a headache is coming on. Probably more heat exhaustion. "I need to think."

I move to the far side of the cave, as far from him as I can get while still remaining in the shelter's relative safety. My back against the cool stone wall, I slide down until I'm sitting, knees drawn up to my chest, the broken translator still clutched in my hand.

Rok makes no move to follow me. He remains where he is, watching me with those unnervingly perceptive eyes, his face a mask I can't read.

The silence between us stretches. I close my eyes, too drained to maintain the glaring contest, and let my head fall back against the stone.

My head is starting to pound.

What now? What the hell am I supposed to do now?

We're back to square one, but somehow it feels worse than before. Before, I had nothing, knew nothing—there was no loss because there was no expectation. Now I've had a tantalizing glimpse of communication, only to have it ripped away before it could truly begin.

And the worst part is, I'm still stuck with him. Still dependent on him for survival in this hostile world.

A sob builds in my throat, but I choke it back, unwilling to show any more weakness than I already have. My free hand moves automatically to my ear, feeling the spot where the translator had been. There's a small cut there, where his claw must have caught my skin when he tore it away, but it's not deep. Just another minor injury in a catalog that's growing longer by the hour.

I become aware of movement and open my eyes to see Rok approaching, his steps slow, as if trying not to startle me. In his hand, he holds one of those bitter leaves, its orange-blue hue vibrant even in the cave's subdued light.

My first instinct is to lash out, to tell him to get away from me, but I'm too tired. Too defeated. And my headache is fully on now. I just want to lie down.

I watch as he crouches beside me, his massive form somehow managing to look less threatening despite his proximity.

He extends the leaf toward me, his golden eyes meeting mine with an intensity that makes me actually feel...regretful for my outburst. There's something in that gaze—not an apology, exactly, but...a plea? A request for understanding? Or am I just projecting again? Like that time under the sand when I thought he spoke to me?

"I don't want your stupid plant," I mutter, looking away. "I want my translator back."

But he persists, gently pressing the leaf into my hand—the one still clutching the broken pieces of technology. When I reflexively close my fingers around it, the sharp edges of the translator fragments dig deeper into my palm, and I wince.

Rok notices immediately. His hand moves to mine, carefully uncurling my fingers to reveal the bloodied mess of my palm—cut not just from the crystal shard but from how tightly I've been gripping the broken pieces.

Before I can pull away, he takes my hand in his, his touch surprisingly gentle for a creature with such strength. With his other hand, he begins removing the translator fragments, setting them aside one by one until my palm is empty except for the blood welling from the cuts.

I watch, too stunned by the gentleness of his actions to resist, as he crushes the fire bloom leaf between his fingers, then applies the resulting paste to my injured palm. The liquid stings at first, then numbs, just as it did when he used it on my arms earlier.

"Why?" I ask softly, not pulling my hand away. "Why help me if you won't let me understand you?"

He doesn't answer, of course. But his eyes never leave mine as he finishes treating my palm, his thumb brushing once, lightly, across my wrist before he finally releases me.

The gesture is so unexpectedly tender that it breaks something in me—some final barrier holding back the flood of emotions I've been trying to contain since I first woke up on this fucking batshit planet.

"I'm scared, Rok," I whisper, my voice barely audible even to my own ears. "I'm so fucking scared. I don't know where I am, or how to get home, or if I'll ever see my sister again. I don't know what's happening or why, and now I can't even ask you about any of it."

Tears flow freely now, streaming down my face without restraint. I don't bother trying to wipe them away.

Rok makes a sudden, alarmed sound—something between a hiss and a growl—and before I can react, he's kneeling in front of me, his large hands gripping my shoulders. His eyes, wide with concern, fix on the moisture tracking down my cheeks.

With a gentleness that seems impossible for hands so powerful, he reaches up, trying to push my tears back into my eyes with the pads of his thumbs. The gesture is so unexpected, so bizarrely tender in its misunderstanding, that for a moment I just stare at him.

He makes another distressed sound when more tears immediately replace the ones he's wiped away, his movements becoming more urgent, as if he thinks I'm literally leaking vital fluid.

Despite everything, a choked laugh escapes me. "I guess you don't cry, huh?" I say through my tears. "This is normal for me. Just like being able to communicate with others around me was normal."

My voice breaks again, and fresh tears well up. Rok's

distress visibly increases. He pulls me against his chest, cradling me as if I'm made of glass, still trying desperately to stem the flow of my tears as if he thinks I'm melting. I can feel his heart pounding against his chest, almost as if he's panicking inside.

"Stop," I whisper, pulling back slightly to look at him. "Rok, it's okay. I'm not dying. This is just...how humans express sadness. Pain."

He's still trying to wipe my eyes. Still trying to push the tears back, a wild look in his gaze. One very different from the look he had when he fought those shadow creatures. Very different from the one he had when he took the translator and smashed it.

"Oh, Rok." I reach up and grip his hand, squeezing it gently as I lean forward and press my forehead against his. That's the only thing that makes him stop. Golden eyes just inches from my own, I try to tell him through my eyes that I'm okay. Just... well...sad.

I'm sad.

"Jus-teen," he says softly, and our gazes lock.

"Rok," I whisper. This close, the bronze flecks in his eyes look like art. Like looking at a painting of the stars in gold.

"I'm trying so hard to be strong," I whisper. "But the truth is...I need you. I hate that I need you, but I do. You're literally all I have in this entire world right now, and I don't even know if I can trust you."

My voice breaks on the last word, and I close my eyes, unable to bear the intensity of his gaze as I fall apart. It's all too much—the fear, the confusion, the loss, the pain, the sheer overwhelming alienness of everything around me. I've been running on adrenaline and determination for so long, and now, with this final blow, I have nothing left.

I've completely forgotten that Rok can't understand a word

I'm saying. At this moment, I'm not talking to him, anyway. I'm talking to myself, to the universe, to whatever twisted cosmic joke has landed me in this situation.

And then, impossibly, I hear it—not with my ears, but somehow within my mind itself:

"I am...sorry."

My eyes fly open. With tear-blurred vision, I search his face. His lips haven't moved. There's no way he could have spoken those words. And yet, I heard them as clearly as if he'd whispered them aloud.

I let out a shaky laugh, wiping at my tears. "And now I'm hallucinating again. Like the time I thought I heard you speaking to me. When I was trapped in the sand."

But there's something in his eyes, something deep, something unspoken, that makes me wonder if I imagined it after all.

For the first time, I feel like I'm really seeing him—not as an alien, not as a savior or a threat, but as a being with thoughts and feelings as complex as my own.

And...I understand something: we may never share words, but that doesn't mean we can't communicate.

I don't know what possesses me to do it. Maybe it's the pure emotion of the moment, or the vulnerability in his eyes, or just the desperate need to connect with someone—anyone —in this alien world.

Before I can overthink it, I lean forward the few inches separating us and press my lips against his.

Rok goes completely rigid, his entire body freezing as if struck by lightning. His lips are unlike anything I've ever felt before—warmer than human lips, with a texture like fine suede but firmer, more unyielding. For a terrible, suspended moment, I'm certain I've just made the worst possible mistake, violating some sacred taboo of his species.

Then, slowly, minutely, I feel his tension ease. His lips remain motionless, but the glow beneath his skin erupts into pulsing waves, illuminating the shadows around us with surges of golden light that match the pounding of my heart.

My lips move, my tongue licking at the seam of his lips, the taste of him sending a shiver through me. When Rok opens his mouth, a rumble vibrating in his chest, sudden awareness of what I've done comes crashing over me.

I pull away, cheeks no doubt flaming red. I can feel the heat.

What was I thinking? He's an alien—an actual extraterrestrial being—and I just kissed him as if we're in some ridiculous sci-fi romance.

I take a deep, shuddering breath, trying to steady myself. "Okay," I say quietly, desperate to move past the moment. "Okay. I'm still mad at you. I still think you had no right to do what you did. But...I get that you probably thought you were protecting me. From what, I have no idea, but I get that was your intention."

His forehead remains against mine, but I can't look at him. The knowledge of that intense stare alone has my cheeks flaming hotter.

"So let's...try again," I continue, straightening my spine and forcing him to pull back slightly. "We need to figure out how to communicate without the translator. I need to find my people, and you need to...well, I don't know what you need. But I'm guessing you don't want to stay in this cave forever, either."

I gesture between us, then out toward the cave entrance, trying to convey the concept of leaving, of traveling together. His eyes follow my movements, only to come back to my lips.

"And next time," I add, my voice firmer now, "before you destroy something of mine, maybe try asking first? I know you can't exactly say 'Hey, is that device dangerous?' but there has to be a better way than just…smashing it."

I mime crushing something in my hand, then shake my head emphatically. His head tilts, but this time the gesture doesn't infuriate me. It just reminds me how much work we have ahead of us if we're going to build any kind of understanding.

But maybe that's not impossible. Maybe we can find a way to communicate that doesn't rely on technology or shared language. After all, humans managed to communicate across language barriers for thousands of years before the invention of universal translators.

It won't be easy. Nothing about this situation is easy. But as I look into Rok's eyes and see the intelligence, the concern, the complexity there, I feel something I thought I'd lost: hope.

"Alright," I say, sitting up straighter, wiping the last of my tears away with the back of my hand. "Let's start over. My name is Justine Parker." I touch my chest, then point to him. "You are Rok."

Basic. Childish, even. But it's a beginning.

And right now, that's all I can ask for.

CHAPTER 19
THAT WAS WEIRD. WANT TO DO IT AGAIN

ROK

She is in pain.

Not the obvious agony of a claw wound or the burning torture of shadowmaw venom, but something quieter, deeper, more insidious. I can see it in the way she winces when she opens her eyes, in how she presses her fingertips to her temples, in the tight lines around her mouth.

Jus-teen has retreated to the far side of the cave, where the shadows are thickest, away from the shaft of Ain's light that pierces through the cave's opening. She leans against the cool stone wall, eyes closed more often than open, her breathing shallow but controlled.

A daughter of Ain, hiding from Ain's gaze. It makes no sense, yet I have learned to accept that little about this strange female follows the patterns I understand.

I remain near the cave entrance, keeping watch for dangers that might approach. The shadowmaws will not return—not after I left their pack decimated in the dust—but there are other threats. Dust serpents that can sense movement from beneath the sand. Sandfins that follow the scent of blood. And always, the rival clans, who would see a lone Drakav and his... companion...as easy targets.

My gaze shifts to her again.

Her vocalizations are soft, strained, the tone revealing her discomfort. "This is ridiculous," she says, pressing the heels of her hands against her eyes. "Just a stupid headache. I should be stronger than this."

I watch her struggle to sit up straighter, wincing again as the motion seems to intensify whatever pain grips her.

"We should be moving," she continues, gesturing weakly toward the cave entrance. "Finding water. Finding my sister. Not...sitting here because my head feels like it's going to explode."

She sighs, her shoulders slumping. "I'm sorry, Rok. I'm slowing us down. Just...give me a little longer, okay? Then we can go."

I move toward her, plucking another fire bloom leaf from the crevice where they grow. These particular blooms are nearly depleted—we have taken much from them for our healing—but they will recover in time. The dust provides for those who respect its ways.

Carefully, I use a claw to strip away the tiny spines that line the leaf's edges, removing anything that might harm her delicate skin. When it is safe, I offer it to her, crouching beside her with the leaf extended on my palm.

She looks at it, then at me, a small baring of her teeth despite her obvious discomfort. I bare mine back in this custom we've developed.

"More of your wonder plant?" she vocalizes, taking it from my hand. "I guess it can't hurt."

She takes a few bites, chewing slowly, grimacing at the

bitter taste but forcing herself to swallow. After several mouth-fuls, she sets the remainder aside and lies down, curling on her side, one arm braced beneath her head.

"Just for a moment," she murmurs, her eyes already clos-ing. "Just...need to rest..."

I watch her as she drifts into a light sleep, her breathing evening out, some of the tension easing from her face. The fire bloom will help, though perhaps not as quickly as it does for a Drakav. Her body is different, processes things differently. But it should provide some relief, some restoration.

And yet, as I watch over her, I become aware of something strange within myself. A sensation I cannot name, cannot identify from all my cycles of experience in the dust. Despite having consumed many fire bloom leaves to speed my own healing, there is something...off. Something altered in my system.

I do not know what.

My gaze returns to Jus-teen, drawn to her, as it has been since the moment I found her in the dust.

Everything has changed since finding her. Xiraxis has shifted, rearranged itself around her presence. And now that she has shared water with me...

Dust.

She shared water with me in the most peculiar way. Her lips against mine, a touch I had never felt before, soft yet firm, warm yet unlike any warmth I have known.

My claw rises to my lips, tracing the outline where she touched me. A shadow memory of contact that my body refuses to forget. Her tongue touching my mouth with just a taste of her water from within—but it was enough to send my systems into disarray. The glow beneath my skin had pulsed wildly, uncontrollably, lighting the cave as if all three moons shone at once. Even now, solmarks later, the memory causes the glow to flicker and surge.

I do not know why I can no longer control my glow. Worse, I do not know why she decided to share water in such a manner. It is not a thing we Drakav do.

I only know that I want her to do it again.

I want to feel it again.

But I worry for her, for how much water she has left to spare. She lost so much from her eyes—those strange, clear drops that fell like precious moisture wasted. I still do not understand why her body does these things, why it doesn't perform the most basic function of any desert creature: conserve water at all costs.

Either way, it does not matter. I will find more water for her. That is what a hunter does—provides for those under his protection. And that means I will have to leave the safety of the cave, venture out into the dust where the water-bearing plants grow deep.

I rise from my crouch, moving toward the cave entrance. Ain is past her zenith now, beginning her slow descent toward the horizon. I can move quickly, gather what we need, and return before the worst dangers of dusk begin to stir.

I glance back at Jus-teen, still resting in the shadows. She should be safe here. This was once a resting cave. One me and my brothers used. We smeared the scent of sandfins near the entrance. A scent that still lingers. No other creatures will come near.

But...

As I step toward the entrance, preparing to leave, I stop short. Like a hook embedded in my chest pulling me backward, I return to Jus-teen's side.

Strange.

I try again, but this time, with each step away from her, the feeling intensifies, a growing pain that has no source I can identify. I check my chest, but there is no wound.

"*Must be the beginnings of mind sickness.*" I should not make such a joke. Mind sickness is truly debilitating.

I cannot imagine not being able to communicate with my clan. To be shut out. To lose the single thing that would keep me connected to—

I freeze, understanding flooding through me like fresh water.

Jus-teen. The strange stone in her ear. The one I destroyed.

I did not understand her words when I crushed it, but I understood her eyes. The hurt. The despair. The fury. A storm of emotions raged across her face, all because of what I did.

The stone spoke in vocalizations like hers. Was that stone her connection? Was it communicating with her? And did I... destroy her hopes of this communication?

The thought settles like a boulder in my gut. I have lived my entire life connected to my clan through mind-speak, never truly alone, even when physically separated. But she—she is utterly isolated. The lone daughter of Ain. Dropped on a world with creatures she cannot speak to.

And I made it worse.

I still do not trust that ear stone. Still believe it was dangerous, unnatural. But I regret the pain I saw in her eyes. I regret causing her more suffering when she has already endured so much.

The memory of the water flowing freely from her eyes...I do not want to see such a sight again. Anything to prevent that.

I must make amends. Must hunt for her, bring her better nourishment than fire blooms, find water to replace what she has lost. Show her through actions what I cannot tell her through vocalizations or mind speak.

I turn back to the cave entrance, determined now, but the

pain in my chest immediately flares again—sharper, more insistent, demanding I return to her side.

Cursed dust.

I pause at the cave entrance and look back again. She has not moved, has not awakened. But the pain grows more intense with each beat of my *dra-kir*.

This is...not normal. Not right. I am a scout and a hunter. I leave the clan caves for sols, sometimes several at a time, tracking prey across the vast dust. I have never felt this...tether before. This invisible vine binding me to another being. Not even to my brothers.

I try again, forcing myself to take another step into the dust. The pain sears, white-hot now, making my nostrils flare, and the glow beneath my skin rises and flickers erratically.

I try to dim it. My skin does not listen to me.

My gaze shifts back to the female. I...cannot leave her.

I return to the cave, moving silently to her side, and without conscious decision, I find myself sinking down beside her. Carefully, mindful of her delicate form, I gather her into my arms, cradling her against my chest as I did when carrying her through the dust.

The moment she is against me, the pain vanishes. Just... gone, as if it never existed, replaced by a sense of rightness, of completion, that I have never known before.

She stirs slightly, her face pressing against my chest, but does not wake. Her breath is warm against my skin, her *dra-kir* beating a quick, light rhythm I can feel through the thin hide she wears.

What is this? What is happening to me?

I have no answers, only questions that pile like dust in a storm, swirling and obscuring any clarity I might find. All I know with certainty is that I cannot leave her, cannot be separated from her without experiencing that strange, pulling pain.

She shifts in my arms, murmuring something in her sleep, her hand coming up to rest against my chest, directly over the place where that strange pain had centered. The glow beneath my skin pulses gently beneath her palm, responding to her touch again without my input.

I sit with her like this for what feels like an eternity, watching her breathe, feeling the warmth of her against me, trying to understand this new reality in which I find myself bound.

The light in the cave shifts as Ain continues her journey across the sky. Soon, it will be dusk. The most dangerous time in the dust, when the day hunters return to their dens and the night predators emerge, hungry for the first meal of their waking hours.

We cannot stay here. The fire blooms are nearly gone, and without water, neither of us will survive much longer. I must hunt. Must find sustenance. But I cannot leave her.

There is only one solution.

With a gentle motion, I adjust my hold on her, lifting her against my chest as I stand. She murmurs something, nestling closer, but does not fully wake.

I move toward the cave entrance, pausing only to scan the horizon for immediate threats. The dust stretches out before me, golden and deceptively peaceful in Ain's fading light. In the distance, a whirlwind spins lazily, picking up dust and carrying it skyward.

I step out of the cave's protection, Jus-teen cradled securely in my arms. The pain in my chest remains blissfully absent as long as she is with me. Carrying her like this will make hunting more difficult—impossible to move with my usual speed and stealth—but there is no choice.

We will find water together or perish together in the attempt.

As I begin the long trek toward the distant hidden spring, a flicker of movement catches my eye—something on the horizon, fast-moving, kicking up dust in its wake.

Not a whirlwind. Not a natural phenomenon.

Hunters. Coming this way.

And from their trajectory, I know with grim certainty—they are not of my clan.

CHAPTER 20
IS IT TOO LATE TO FILE A WORKER'S COMP CLAIM?

JUSTINE

The headache hits me like a sledgehammer.

One moment I'm talking to Rok, trying to convince myself (and him) that I'm strong enough to travel, and the next I'm curled against the cave wall, my skull feeling like it might split open. Light becomes my enemy, sound an assault, and all I want to do is curl into nothingness until the pain subsides. I press my forehead to the cool stone, willing the pain to recede.

Then the world tilts.

Heat pools low in my belly. Sudden and damn near impossible to ignore. Rok's hands are everywhere, leaving trails of fire across my skin. "Mine," he snarls against my throat, and my back arches, offering myself. His mouth seals over my nipple, sucking hard, and I cry out—

I jolt awake, gasping. My thighs are clenched, my pulse hammering in places it shouldn't be. The cave is silent except for Rok's steady breathing nearby.

Fuck.

Did I just...? I squeeze my eyes shut, mortified. The dream clings like sweat, too vivid to dismiss. Rok's hands. His teeth. The way he'd looked at me before I was jolted from the dream...

And now here I am, throbbing because of him, while he stands guard like some unshakable sentinel.

This planet is messing with me.

The headache must be doing something worse than I thought. Or maybe it's the alien plants. Or the way Rok's bare chest gleams in the light, muscles shifting as he—

Nope. Not going there.

I've had migraines before—who hasn't?—but this is different. More intense. More...consuming. I have no other logical choice but to attribute it to heat exhaustion, dehydration, the trauma of the crash, and the stress of being stranded, my only company a glowing alien guy *that I kissed*! I mean, really, what's one more physical malfunction at this point?

I try not to fall asleep again. Having wet dreams when in dire circumstances isn't in any survival manual I've ever read. All I can do is clench my teeth and fight the pain in my skull.

I'm vaguely aware of Rok giving me something to eat—one of those strange plants that taste like lettuce soaked in lemon juice and pepper—before I rest some more, promising myself it will just be for a minute or two.

The next thing I know, I'm moving.

Not under my own power, but cradled against something warm and solid. Rok. He's carrying me again.

I crack an eye open, immediately regretting it as harsh light stabs into my retina like a needle. I snap it shut again, burying my face against his chest to escape the brightness.

"Where—?" My voice is a raspy whisper. "What's happening?"

No answer, of course. Not that I expected one.

I try opening my eyes again, this time more gradually, squinting through my lashes. We're moving—Rok carrying me in his arms—but not quickly. Not with his usual efficient stride that eats up the desert terrain. He's being...cautious. That's the only way I can describe it. Tense. Cautious. Slinking along what looks like the shadow of the massive stone formation, his back pressed against the rock face.

And then I notice something extraordinary: his skin, which normally glows with that unearthly golden light, has changed. It's taken on the exact color and texture of the stone behind him—a perfect camouflage that would make him nearly invisible to anyone not being carried in his arms.

Despite my throbbing head, I can't help but stare. How many other abilities has he been hiding? What else can he do?

The thought 'full of surprises' has barely formed in my mind when he glances down, meets my gaze, and his hand clamps over my mouth—firmly but not painfully. I've been here before. The gesture is clear: be silent.

My eyes widen, adrenaline instantly cutting through the fog of pain. My body tenses, every sense suddenly on high alert despite my pounding head. I scan the landscape, searching for whatever threat has triggered his response.

Nothing. Just rock and sand and the vast, empty desert stretching toward the horizon.

I look up at Rok, a question in my eyes, and what I see sends a chill through me. His expression is tight, focused, deadly—the same look he wore when facing down those shadow creatures. His nostrils flare slightly, scenting the air, and his eyes never stop moving, tracking...something.

And then I hear it. Not with my ears, but inside my head, clear as crystal. Clearer than ever before:

"Danger."

His lips haven't moved. Not a single sound has escaped him. But I *heard* it—*felt* it rather—it's weird...hard to describe.

Or maybe it's just my instincts kicking in. My subconscious?

Danger. But where?

I want to ask. Want to ask what kind, how many—but I know better than to make a sound. If it's more of those shadow creatures, we're in serious trouble. Rok is still injured from our last encounter, and I'm...well, I'm a liability at best. I can barely lift my head without wincing, let alone run or fight.

Rok continues his slow backward creep, pressing us deeper into the shadow of the rock formation. His muscles are coiled tight, ready to spring, but there's something else in his posture—something I haven't seen before. Uncertainty? Fear? No, not quite fear, but...caution. Extreme caution.

Suddenly he crouches, pulling me tight against his chest as he turns me to the stone and goes completely still. Not just still—frozen, like he's become part of the stone itself. And he's blocking me. Hiding me with his body since I have no camouflage of my own.

His breathing slows to almost nothing, and the camouflage effect intensifies until I can barely distinguish where his skin ends and the rock begins.

I'm curled awkwardly in his arms, my face pressed against his shoulder, but I manage to twist just enough to peer under his arm at whatever has him so alarmed.

At first, I see nothing. Just a ridge of stone maybe a hundred feet away, its surface rippling with heat waves in the desert sun.

I think maybe I'm looking in the wrong direction, but I have no choice, so I keep staring, hoping that whatever's got Rok so tense will leave. For minutes, he holds me like that, barely breathing when suddenly, there's movement.

A figure vaults atop the ridge with fluid grace, landing in a half-crouch before straightening to its full height.

My breath catches in my throat.

It's...like Rok. But not Rok, obviously. Male, tall, powerfully built, with the same general physiology—the elongated limbs, the distinctive facial structure, the claws. But where Rok's coloring is golden, this one's skin is a deeper, darker bronze. His hair is shorter, too, a shade closer to copper than gold.

Staring at this newcomer, I'm struck by a sudden, uncomfortable realization: Rok is terrifying. Or he should be. He's massive, powerful, decidedly non-human, with claws that could disembowel me without effort and strength that makes my own feel laughably insignificant. Yet somehow, I've...never seen him that way. Not even at the start. Somewhere between him saving me from the sand and me kissing him in the cave, he stopped being "alien" and started being just...Rok.

But this one—this stranger staring out across the desert with chilling intensity—he radiates danger in a way that makes my instincts scream. There's nothing I can point to specifically, nothing I can articulate, but something about him feels...wrong. Hostile. The hair on the back of my neck stands up, and my heart hammers against my ribs with such force I'm certain it must be audible.

Is this another member of Rok's tribe? His clan? I don't think so. Not with the way Rok is hiding from him, concealing both of us in the shadow of the rock, his body positioned to shield me completely.

The stranger moves along the ridge, his movements fluid and powerful, scanning the terrain. Like Rok, he is silent and I think he is alone when another of his kind launches themselves up on the rock, too. This newcomer is just as large. Just as powerful.

They're not alone. From my limited vantage point, I can

make out at least another moving on the far side of the ridge—similar in build and coloring, all with the same predatory alertness. Hunting. They're hunting something.

Or someone.

I stare at the first alien, unable to look away despite the fear coiling in my gut. And then, as if he can feel my gaze—feel my *thoughts*—his head snaps in our direction.

I stop breathing. My heart seems to stutter and freeze in my chest. His eyes—darker than Rok's—feel like those of a lion as he stares directly at our hiding spot.

Does he see us? Can he sense us somehow?

Slowly, so slowly it feels like time has stretched to breaking, I tuck my head behind Rok's shoulder, breaking the line of sight. I don't dare move. Don't dare breathe. The pounding in my head fades to background noise, drowned out by the roaring of blood in my ears and the single, terrifying thought looping through my mind:

Rok isn't alone on this planet. His species—whatever they are—aren't a single unified group. And the ones out there right now aren't friendly.

I thought I'd be happy to see more signs of life. But this... this is a problem.

A very, very big problem.

CHAPTER 21
THE DUST PROVIDES. (SOMETIMES)

ROK

The dust is silent now, but I do not trust it.

The hunters are close. Too close.

I hold still, my body pressed against the stone, my skin blending seamlessly with the rock face. The female is curled against me, her breaths shallow, her body trembling ever so slightly in my arms. I can feel her confusion, her fear—emotions that radiate from her like heat waves rising from the dunes.

But she does not make a sound. She trusts me to keep her safe, even if she does not realize it yet.

I cannot fail her.

Above us, more hunters move with the precision of a stalking shadowmaw, their footsteps light but deliberate. I can feel the vibrations through the stone, each one a reminder of the danger we are in. They are searching, their senses sharp and attuned to the smallest disturbance. Their presence is wrong here—out of place.

This is not their territory.

Their scent is unfamiliar, but the markings on their skin... Those, I recognize. The rival clan. One that roams the dust, taking what they need from those too weak to defend it. They are drifters, scavengers, raiders. And they are deadly.

The one on the ridge—bronze-skinned, his hair like copper fire—turns his head, scanning the horizon with eyes fierce like a beast. His nostrils flare, scenting the air, and for a moment, I am certain he has found us.

I shift my grip on Jus-teen, pulling her closer against me, shielding her entirely with my body. Her soft form presses against my chest and I am once again reminded that she is so small. So fragile.

The thought sends a surge of protectiveness through me, so fierce it borders on pain. I clench my jaw, forcing myself to stay still, to focus. If they find us, I will not survive this fight. Not in my current state. Not with her to protect.

I close my eyes, drawing in a measured breath. The scent of her fills my senses—sweet and strange, not found anywhere else on Xiraxis. It grounds me, sharpens my thoughts. The hunters may be stronger, faster, and uninjured, but I have something they do not.

A purpose.

I will not let them take her.

The vibrations of their footsteps grow fainter. They are moving away, their search carrying them farther along the ridge. I do not relax. Not yet. The dust is patient, and so am I.

Jus-teen shifts slightly in my arms, her head tilting as if trying to see past me. I tighten my hold on her, a silent command to stay still. She freezes, her small hands gripping my chest.

Good. She understands.

The hunters remain in view for several more moments

before they disappear over the far side of the ridge. I wait, counting beats of my *dra-kir,* my claws flexing against the stone. One hundred beats. Then two hundred. Only when I am certain they are gone do I allow myself to exhale.

"*Safe,*" I push toward her.

Jus-teen looks up at me, her blue eyes wide and filled with questions. She speaks, her voice soft and hesitant, but the meaning is lost to me.

I wish I could answer her. I wish I could tell her what the hunters are, why they are here, why they cannot find us. But the words will not come. My tongue is clumsy, my throat unpracticed in shaping sounds. Either way, I do not believe she would understand. And I...I have destroyed her chance to communicate.

Instead, I set her down and gesture for her to stay low, pressing my hand flat against the rock to emphasize the need for caution. Her brow furrows, but she presses her chin to her chest twice before following my lead as I begin to move.

The shadows are our ally now. Ain is low in the sky, her light dimming and the stone formations casting long, jagged shadows across the dust. I keep to them, my movements slow, my senses alert for any sign of the hunters' return.

Jus-teen stays close behind me, her footsteps light but clumsy compared to mine. She is untrained, her movements unrefined, but she is quiet. Her instincts are good.

We reach the base of the ridge, where the shadows are deepest, and I pause to scan the terrain ahead. The dust stretches endlessly before us, broken only by the distant rise of another stone formation. It is far, but that is where we are headed. We cannot stay here.

I turn to Jus-teen and incline my head toward the formation in the distance. Her gaze follows, and I can see the exhaustion in her posture. The strain in her movements. She is not built for this.

I will carry her.

I crouch before her, gesturing for her to climb onto my back. She hesitates, her expression uncertain, but then she steps forward, wrapping her arms around my neck as I rise to my full height, securing her legs with my hands.

Her weight is nothing to me, even in my weakened state. She clings to me, her cheek pressed against my shoulder, her breath warm against my neck. Something about the sensation sends a strange flutter through my chest, different from the pain of separation I felt earlier. This is...pleasant.

I move swiftly now, keeping to the shadows before we're in the open dust, my strides eating up the distance between us and the distant formation. Jus-teen remains silent, her grip firm but not restrictive, trusting me to carry her safely.

But as the journey continues, I can feel Jus-teen's discomfort in the way she shifts against me, seeking relief even from Ain's dying gaze. She was not made for the dust, for this harsh, unforgiving landscape.

But I was. And I will be her shield.

We reach the new formation when Ain has almost completed her descent. This structure is different from the one we left—taller, more jagged, with deeper crevices carved by wind and time. Perfect for hiding.

I scan the perimeter, searching for any sign of the hunters or other predators. Nothing. The dust is still.

For now.

Setting Jus-teen down in the shade, I gesture for her to wait as I assess our temporary sanctuary. She does that movement with her head—the quick lowering of her chin that I've come to recognize as agreement—before she sinks to the ground, her back against the stone.

The entrance narrows quickly, forcing even smaller Drakav to turn sideways. A natural defense I've relied on before. Beyond lies the main chamber with its high ceiling where sound travels strangely, echoing in ways that confuse those unfamiliar with its patterns. Then the passage to the left that leads to the small sleeping chamber, and the one to the right that descends sharply to what I seek.

I move through the familiar passages with practiced silence, confirming nothing has changed since I last took shelter here during the great dust storms two seasons past. No signs of recent visitors. No disturbance of the stone dust that accumulates near the unused chambers. Good.

I make my way to the hidden heart of the formation—a chamber accessible only through a crevice that requires turning one's body at an awkward angle to pass through. Inside, the air grows noticeably cooler, the temperature dropping to a comfortable chill that will help ease Jus-teen's discomfort.

And there, in the center of the chamber, is the greatest treasure this formation holds: the sacred pool. Not large—perhaps the span of three bodies across—but deep and clear, the water clean and pure, reflecting the stone ceiling above like a mirror. Fed by underground springs that run beneath the desert, it remains even during the most terrible droughts.

Water. Life. Healing.

The sight fills me with relief. This is what Jus-teen needs most now—cool water to drink and soothe her burning skin. Perhaps its properties will help slow whatever poison has taken hold in her foreign body once more.

I return to Jus-teen quickly, finding her where I left her, though her eyes are closed now, her breathing shallow. When I approach, she startles, then relaxes upon seeing me.

I gesture for her to follow, and she rises slowly, her movements stiff and pained. The journey has taken its toll on her already weakened body.

Without thinking, I sweep her into my arms once more, cradling her against my chest. She makes a small sound of surprise but does not protest. Instead, she rests her head against my shoulder, her eyes drifting closed again.

The passage to the hidden chamber is narrow, requiring me to turn sideways with her in my arms at points, but I navigate it carefully, protecting her from the jagged edges of stone. When we emerge into the chamber, her eyes open, widening at the sight of the water.

"Water," she whispers.

"Wah-ter," I mumble, forcing my throat to work. Her gaze flies to mine and she bares her teeth at me in delight. I bare my teeth back. I have made her happy. This is good.

I set her down gently at the edge of the pool, and she reaches out, trailing her fingers through the clear liquid with a reverence I understand all too well. Water is life in the dust. Water is everything.

I crouch beside her, cupping my hands to gather some of the precious liquid, then offer it to her. She looks at me, then at the water in my palms, before leaning forward to drink from my hands. The trust in this simple act sends another of those strange flutters through my chest.

She drinks deeply, her eyes closing in pleasure, and I find myself watching the movement of her throat, the curve of her neck, the way her lashes rest against her cheeks. She is unlike anything I have ever seen before—alien, yes, but also...beautiful, in a way I cannot fully comprehend.

When she has drunk her fill, she sits back, exhaling deeply, some of the tension leaving her body. "Thank you," she says.

Gratitude perhaps. Or maybe she is saying she simply wishes to rest now.

I do her chin jerk motion then gesture to the pool and back to her, hoping she understands my meaning: Rest. Drink. I will return.

Her brow furrows, and I see the question in her eyes: *Where are you going?*

I mime hunting, making a gesture with my claws that I hope conveys the concept of bringing back food. Her expression clears, and she chin jerks again, though there is uncertainty in her eyes.

I hesitate. The chamber is safe, hidden, defensible. She will be protected here. But the thought of leaving her, even for a short time, sends a twist of discomfort through me.

Yet I must. She needs nourishment beyond what the fire blooms can provide, and the creatures that make their homes near these rocks will sustain us both.

With a final glance at her, I turn and make my way back through the passage, emerging once more into the harsh light of late afternoon.

The pain begins the moment I step away from the formation.

It is different this time—not the sharp, pulling sensation I felt in the cave, but a spreading warmth that builds in intensity with each step I take. Like fire in my veins, flowing outward from my chest to every extremity.

I press on, fighting against it, determined to fulfill my purpose. The dust is alive with small life for those who know where to look—creatures that burrow beneath the dust, serpents that bask on the rocks, and larger prey I will not hunt this sol.

I focus on the hunt, on the familiar rhythm of tracking, stalking, capturing. But the pain persists, growing stronger, more insistent. It is not debilitating, not yet, but it is...distracting. Each successful capture is followed by an overwhelming urge to return to the formation, to Jus-teen.

I resist, gathering more prey than I initially intended, as if to justify the time spent away from her. By the time Ain touches the horizon, painting the dust in shades of amber and gold, I have enough to sustain us for at least two sols.

The return journey is swift, driven by the increasing discomfort in my chest. It is not pain, exactly, but a burning need, a compulsion that grows stronger with each beat of my dra-kir.

I reach the formation just as the first lights appear in the darkening sky, slipping through the narrow passages with ease despite my burden of fresh-caught prey.

As I approach the chamber, I slow, sensing a change in the air—a shift in humidity, the gentle sound of movement in water. I pause at the entrance, my free hand resting against the cool stone.

Jus-teen is in the pool.

She floats on her back, eyes closed, her strange coverings set aside on the stone edge. The water embraces her, supporting her in a way that seems to ease her pain. Even from here, I can see the tension has left her body, replaced by a calm serenity I have not witnessed since we met.

She is...revealed. Completely. Exposed in a way I have not seen before.

Water sluices down the mounds on her chest, her hips, the dark curls between her thighs. My *mouth* waters. Within my pouch, my stem jerks so hard it hurts. If I touched her now, I would ruin her. If I tasted her, I would forget mercy.

I should turn away. Should retreat to allow her privacy.

I do none of these things.

Instead, I watch, transfixed, as she moves through the water with slow movements, careful not to splash, to waste a single precious drop. Her skin gleams in the fading light that filters through cracks in the ceiling, droplets clinging to her like tiny stars.

I have always thought water was the most beautiful thing in the dust—clear, vital, sacred. But I was wrong.

It is her.

The hunt slips from my grasp, forgotten, as I step forward. The sound alerts her, and she turns, startled, her eyes finding mine across the chamber.

She does not scream. Does not try to hide. Instead, she watches me with those impossibly blue eyes, her chin lifted slightly, a challenge or an invitation—I cannot tell which.

I move closer, crouching at the edge of the pool, my gaze never leaving hers. Beautiful. She is...beautiful. The water on her. I have never seen a sight more entrancing.

Her eyes lock with mine—steady, unflinching. There's a challenge there, a daring glint that holds me captive.

I draw in a breath, catching her scent—clean water, and something uniquely hers. Something wild. It stirs a beast deep inside me, a pull I can't fight, even if I wanted to.

"Rok," she says, my name soft on her lips, but the sound of it strikes me like a thunderclap. I feel it in my chest, in my blood, a jolt that robs me of sense and reason.

I lean closer, too close. My balance shifts, my weight tipping forward as if I can't bear the distance between us any longer.

The world tilts.

The cool shock of water engulfs me as I plunge into the pool, the heat of my skin extinguished in an instant. Everything is muffled—except for her laugh. Low, surprised, and undeniably amused.

I break the surface, gasping for air, my hair plastered to my face. She's there, treading the water beside me, light in her eyes.

"You fell," she says.

I reach for her, my hands finding her waist, steadying her as the water shifts around us. She is soft beneath my touch, yielding yet strong, a contradiction that fascinates me.

Her hands come to rest against my chest, directly over the place where that strange fire has burned since I left her. At her touch, it transforms, changing from pain to a different kind of heat—intense but pleasant, consuming but welcome.

She looks up at me, water clinging to her face, her lips parted slightly. I remember the sharing of water, the press of her mouth against mine, and suddenly I want nothing more than to experience that again.

I lean down, drawn by a force as inexorable as the pull of Ain's light. She stiffens for just a moment, surprised perhaps by my boldness, but then she rises to meet me, her lips finding mine in a gesture that is becoming familiar yet remains thrillingly new.

The contact sends a surge through me, the glow beneath my skin brightening until it illuminates the water around us, casting everything in golden light. Her mouth moves against mine, teaching me this strange, intimate language, and I respond eagerly, learning with each passing moment.

This is more than sharing water. This is...connection. Understanding. A bridge across the vast gulf that separates our worlds.

When we finally part, both breathless, the look in her eyes tells me she feels it too—this inexplicable bond, this tether that binds us, that brings me pain when she is not near, that pulls us together across all barriers of language and species.

"Rok," she whispers again, and in that single syllable, I hear everything I need to know.

The hunt can wait. The danger can wait. The dust and all its threats can wait.

For now, there is only this—her in my arms, her eyes reflecting my glow, her breath mingling with mine in the cool darkness of our sanctuary.

And for the first time since I found her in the dust, I feel truly, completely alive.

CHAPTER 22
FIVE STARS. WOULD GET KIDNAPPED AGAIN
(MAYBE)

JUSTINE

His hands find my waist in the water, strong and sure, and before I can process what's happening, Rok lifts me. Water streams from my body, cascading back into the pool as he carries me to the edge and sets me down on the cool stone.

The contrast between the stone's chill and my heated skin sends a shiver through me. Or maybe it's the way he's looking at me—eyes luminous in the dim light, pupils dilated, focused on me with an intensity that steals my breath.

"Rok," I whisper, suddenly aware of my nakedness, of my vulnerability. I should feel embarrassed, exposed. I should reach for my clothes.

I do none of those things.

Instead, I watch, mesmerized, as he pulls himself from the pool in one fluid motion, water sluicing off his golden skin. He crouches before me, his face inches from mine, studying me with that predatory focus that should terrify me but instead sends a thrill of anticipation through my body.

My headache is gone. Completely gone. As if it never existed. The water—there must be something in the water. The same way my fever disappeared when he brought me water before. But instead of relief, I feel...something else. A different kind of heat building inside me, a restlessness that makes me shift on the stone.

Oh no. I *cannot* be getting horny.

Rok inches closer, his nostrils flaring slightly as if he's catching my scent. His glow suddenly flares and pulses brighter in the dimness, highlighting the sharp angles of his face, the broad expanse of his chest. He reaches for me, one clawed hand hovering just above my shoulder, before he stops.

I should shift away. I should remember all the reasons why this is a terrible idea. I should—

A lump forms in my throat. I swallow it down...and I don't move.

His hand descends, his touch feather-light as his fingers trace the curve of my shoulder, down my arm, leaving trails of fire in their wake. His expression is one of wonder, of discovery, as if he's mapping uncharted territory.

"This is insane," I whisper, more to myself than to him. "You're an alien and I—"

He silences me with his lips on mine, soft at first, questioning, then more insistent as I respond. His mouth is hot, demanding, the kiss deeper than before, exploring rather than just connecting. I gasp against him, and he takes the opportunity to tilt his head, changing the angle, deepening the kiss further.

My hands find his shoulders, his skin warm and smooth beneath my palms. I dig my fingers in, holding on as the world spins around me. He growls into my mouth, and the vibration sends shockwaves through my body, igniting nerve endings I didn't know existed.

When he pulls away, I'm panting, my lips tingling. *Oh God. He shouldn't taste so good. This shouldn't feel that good.*

I think he's done, but he doesn't go far. His forehead rests against mine, our breaths mingling in the small space between us. His glow has intensified, casting golden light across the stone around us, turning the water into rippling amber.

"We should slow down," I say weakly, but my body betrays me, arching toward him.

He doesn't understand my words, but maybe he senses my hesitation. He pulls back slightly, head tilted, studying my face. Then he reaches up, one finger tracing the outline of my lips with exquisite gentleness.

I should be afraid. Those claws could tear me apart. But I'm not. Not at all. I'm pretty sure this wild, wild thing would never harm me. I know that for certain now.

His first touch is hesitant—clumsy, even—like he's mapping foreign terrain. The brush of his lips against my jaw is featherlight, uncertain, as if he expects me to vanish under his hands. But then his breath hitches, his nose dragging along my pulse like he's memorizing my scent, and something shifts. The moment his tongue flicks out to taste my skin, restraint snaps. His mouth grows bolder, hot and open against my throat, his teeth scraping in a way that makes my back arch. It's like he's discovering hunger for the first time, and now that he's had a bite, he can't stop.

"Rok," I gasp, my head falling back, giving him better access. Why does it feel so good?

He takes full advantage, his mouth moving down to my collarbone, his hands coming to rest on my waist, steadying me. Every touch, every brush of his lips, sends sparks shooting across my skin. It's too much and not enough. I should stop this. I should—

His mouth finds my breast, and all rational thought evaporates.

He freezes, his breath hot against my sensitive skin. I feel him inhale deeply, as if memorizing my scent. Then, cautiously, experimentally, his tongue darts out, tasting the water droplets still clinging to my skin.

"Oh god," I whisper, my hands flying to his shoulders, nails digging in.

My cry seems to embolden him. His tongue flattens against my nipple, sending a jolt of pleasure so intense it borders on pain through my body. I arch into him, a moan escaping my lips.

Rok growls again, the sound vibrating through me. He's enjoying this—enjoying my reactions, my responsiveness. He circles my nipple with his tongue, then takes it gently between his lips, the careful pressure making me squirm beneath him.

I reach for him, needing something to hold on to, but he catches my wrists in one large hand, pinning them above my head against the stone. The restraint should feel threatening, but instead, it sends another wave of heat through me.

And that burning intensity is rising beneath my skin.

His free hand slides down my side, mapping the curve of my waist, the flare of my hip, and he shudders again even as his mouth continues its sweet torture on my breast. He's licking it like it's a fruit. When he switches to the other side, giving it the same thorough attention, I'm writhing beneath him, panting his name like a prayer.

"Rok...please...I can't..."

I don't even know what I'm begging for. More? Less? My body is a riot of sensation, every nerve ending alive and singing. The burning need under my skin has intensified, concentrated into a throbbing ache between my legs that's becoming impossible to ignore.

And I should ignore it. I bite my bottom lip as images, those dreams of him and how perfect—oh fuck—just how perfect it was, rise back into my mind. My core clenches even as I fight hard to push back against the feeling.

Rok lifts his head, his eyes meeting mine. The glow beneath his skin pulses in time with his breathing, which has grown rapid, uneven. He's affected too—I can feel the tremors running through his powerful frame, the slight tremble in the hand still pinning my wrists.

His gaze drops to my body, traveling slowly downward, taking in every detail. He might not be able to talk my ears off, but the look in his eyes is undeniable. Like a man starved, he's looking at me like I'm a bountiful buffet. When his gaze reaches my stomach, he releases my wrists, both hands now moving to my hips, holding me in place as he lowers his head again.

The moment his tongue brushes my skin, my breath stutters. He traces my navel, circling it before dipping briefly inside, as if he doesn't want to leave an inch of me untouched. I gasp, arching against his hold. He freezes, his face inches from my belly, nostrils flaring as he inhales deeply. Whatever he scents there makes him growl, a deeper, primal sound that only makes a throb go through my center.

"Rok," I whisper, half-warning, half-plea.

He shifts lower, positioning himself between my legs, his hands moving to my thighs, gently urging them wider. I should stop him. This is too fast, too much, too—

His breath ghosts over my center, and my objections dissolve into a moan that sounds wanton even to my own ears. There's no tentative exploration, no cautious first taste. He devours me with a primal hunger that takes my breath away, his tongue parting me in one broad, possessive stroke that has me crying out, my back arching off the stone.

"God—Rok—" The words fracture as pleasure spikes through me, sharp and overwhelming.

His hands tighten on my thighs, pinning me in place as I try to squirm away from the intensity. But it's clear he's not stopping, not slowing down, not until he's had his fill. My fingers find his hair, trying to anchor myself as he unleashes his hunger against me, his tongue relentless, his growls vibrating through my core.

There's nothing gentle in the way he claims me. This is pure, raw need—a barbarian feasting after famine, caring only for his own savage pleasure in the taking. Yet somehow, impossibly, it's exactly what my body craves. Each ruthless stroke of his tongue sends me higher, each possessive grip of his hands makes me wetter, each rumbling growl against my sensitive flesh pushes me closer to the edge.

"Yes—there—don't stop—"

My pleas turn to mindless sounds as he finds the perfect rhythm, the perfect pressure. And I'm helpless.

My body trembles beneath him, tension building to an almost unbearable peak. His hands grip my thighs with bruising force, holding me open, keeping me exactly where he wants me as I come apart under his lips. The moment it happens, it's like the sun explodes. The glow under Rok's skin is blinding, the growls against my pussy like a crazed animal. I try to close my legs as the sensation becomes too much, but he snarls against me, the vibration only heightening my pleasure as he forces them wider.

Through the haze of my own ecstasy, I feel the tremors running through him, see the intensity of his glow pulsing brighter with each sound I make, sense the way his muscles bunch and flex with his own rising need. Is he...is he getting pleasure from consuming mine? His body responding to my surrender without being touched?

It's that realization that pushes me over the edge. I shatter with his name on my lips, my body convulsing in waves of pleasure that crash over me like a tsunami, my vision narrowing to pinpoints of golden light. Even as I peak, he doesn't relent, driving me higher, extending my climax until I'm sobbing with the intensity of it, my hands pushing at his shoulders, trying to escape the overwhelming sensation.

And then he stops.

Abruptly.

The absence of his touch is a shock to my system. My body collapses back against the cool stone, trembling, my breaths coming in ragged gasps as the echoes of my release ripple through me. I feel wrecked—utterly, completely wrecked. My skin burns, my limbs shake, my heart pounds so hard I can feel it in my throat.

But before I can even process what's happening to me, before I can catch my breath, I feel the shift in him.

It's immediate. Violent.

I lift my head, my still-blurry vision locking onto him, and what I see sends a jolt of fear straight through me.

Rok is on his knees, his body hunched, his claws digging into the stone beneath him. His glow is wild—erratic—flickering in sharp bursts that cast jagged shadows across the chamber walls. His breaths come in harsh, guttural snarls, and when he lifts his head to look at me, his eyes are...

Wrong.

The brilliant gold I've come to know is gone, swallowed by black, his pupils blown so wide they look endless. His lips curl back, revealing those sharp fangs, and a sound rumbles out of him—a growl low and guttural, but layered with something else.

Pain.

His growl deepens, reverberating through me, but something about it changes. It's not just hunger or need—it's... strained. Like he's holding himself back. Then he freezes. His head lifts, his gaze locking on mine, and for a moment, he looks almost...terrified.

"Rok?" I breathe, reaching for him, but he jerks back, his entire body trembling. Whatever's happening to him, it's too much. Too overwhelming. And I'm not sure if it's me he's trying to protect—or himself.

"Rok?"

He doesn't respond. Or maybe he can't. His gaze locks on me, piercing through me, and the intensity in it makes my breath hitch.

And then it hits me.

Did *I* do this?

My chest tightens, my mind racing as I take in the way he trembles, the way his claws flex and scrape against the stone. Did I hurt him somehow? I look down at myself, to the wetness still coating the inside of my thighs...

I've heard of people being allergic to semen, but never... Oh shit.

"Rok..." My voice cracks.

He doesn't move, his entire body taut and shaking with tension, his claws curling deeper into the stone. His glow pulses erratically, brighter and brighter, until it's almost blinding.

And that's when I feel it.

The heat.

It starts low in my belly, a strange, simmering warmth that spreads outward, seeping into my veins like molten fire. At first, I think it's just the aftereffects of what he did to me—my body still reeling from the intensity of it all. But then it builds.

Hotter.

Brighter.

Wrong.

I gasp, pressing a trembling hand to my stomach as the heat surges through me, making my skin prickle and my head spin. It's not just heat. It's need.

A need I don't understand.

And yet, somehow, I *know* it's connected to him.

"Rok...something's happening..." I manage.

He reacts then—not to my words, but to the sound of my voice. His growl deepens, his claws slashing out, raking the stone wall beside him in a violent, uncontrolled movement. The screech of it makes me flinch, and the gouges he leaves behind are deep enough to make my stomach clench.

He's fighting something.

But what?

I push myself upright, every muscle in my body trembling from the effort. My legs feel useless, my skin feverish, but I force myself to move toward him.

He jerks back, his growl cutting off sharply as if my presence physically hurts him. His claws scrape against the stone as he staggers to his feet, his movements jerky and uncoordinated, like he's running on instinct alone.

"Wait—don't go!" I reach for him, my hand outstretched, but he stumbles away from me, his glow flaring in sharp, erratic bursts.

His gaze meets mine, and the look in his eyes sends a fresh wave of fear crashing over me.

He's not just in pain.

He's afraid.

Of *me*.

He looks...lost. His breathing is ragged, his chest heaving like he's struggling just to stay here, just to keep looking at me.

For a split second, I see something in his eyes that makes my stomach twist. Not just fear. Not just pain. Guilt. Like he thinks he's done something wrong. Like he's afraid of what he's capable of.

"Rok," I whisper, but he jerks back as if my voice physically hurts him.

"Rok," I whisper, my voice breaking.

But he's already moving.

He bolts for the entrance of the chamber, his claws slashing at the walls as he runs, leaving deep gouges in the stone. His growls echo through the narrow passages, a sound so raw and feral it sends a chill racing down my spine.

I try to follow, but my legs buckle beneath me, my body too weak, too overwhelmed. I collapse back against the stone, gasping for breath, my skin damp with sweat and burning with that strange, alien heat.

The glow of his body fades as he disappears into the darkness, leaving me alone in the silent chamber, trembling and... well...terrified.

I press a shaking hand to my chest, trying to calm the frantic beating of my heart, but it's no use. The heat inside me flares again, making me gasp, and I curl into myself, trying to fight the sensation.

It's not about *what* is happening to me anymore. Something is happening.

And that something is happening to him, too.

CHAPTER 23
IS IT HOT IN HERE, OR IS IT JUST MY ALIEN-INDUCED FEVER?

JUSTINE

The heat won't go away.

Even naked, my clothes washed and drying on the stone, the fever underneath my skin persists still.

Hours have passed since Rok fled—hours of me curled on the cold stone beside the pool, shivering despite the fire burning under my skin. I've tried drinking water, splashing it over my face, even submerging myself completely in the cool pool.

Nothing helps.

The fever (if that's what this is) ebbs and flows like a tide, sometimes receding enough that I can almost think clearly, other times surging with such intensity that I can only lie still and wait for it to pass.

During one of the calmer moments, I manage to explore the chamber more thoroughly. It's larger than I initially thought, with high, smooth walls worn by centuries of what must have been water flow. It's hard to imagine this vast surface of dust having any water at all.

When I return to the chamber with the pool, I find the remains of what might have been a fire pit—ash and charred stone suggesting that someone, or something, once used this place as shelter.

I also find what Rok left behind in his frantic exit—the animals he'd hunted. Three strange, lizard-like creatures with spiny ridges along their backs and scales that shimmer with an iridescent blue-green sheen. They're about the size of rabbits, but with longer, more sinuous bodies and no visible eyes that I can see.

Despite what they are, my stomach clenches. A sharp reminder that I haven't eaten anything substantial in days. The leaves Rok gave me were better than nothing, but barely. My body is running on fumes, and I can feel my strength ebbing with each passing hour.

"Shit," I mutter, prodding one of the dead creatures with my foot. "I don't suppose you come with cooking instructions?"

I have no idea if they're edible, let alone how to prepare them. Do I skin them? Gut them? Cook them whole? Are there poisonous parts I need to avoid?

With a sigh, I slump back against the wall. Then another realization hits me like a punch to the gut.

My bag. My supplies. They're all back in the first cave, abandoned in our hasty escape from those other aliens.

"Perfect. Just perfect." My voice echoes off the stone walls, mockingly hollow. "I have post-sex fever and I don't even have my emergency protein biscuits."

I close my eyes, exhaustion washing over me in a wave that threatens to pull me under. I should stay awake, should try to figure out what to do about food, about the fever, about Rok...

I don't even know if he's coming back...

The thought makes me curl into myself, and I close my eyes against the sudden pain that possibility creates.

I don't know how long I sit there like that, trying to remain alert, all the while exhaustion pulls me under.

The moment sleep claims me, it drags me down into a dream that burns brighter than the fever in my veins.

—

HIS HANDS ARE EVERYWHERE, LEAVING TRAILS OF GOLDEN LIGHT across my skin. I arch into his touch, desperate for more, for relief from the burning need consuming me from within.

"Rok," I gasp, his name a plea on my lips.

He growls, the sound vibrating through me where our bodies touch. His mouth finds mine, and I yield to him, opening beneath his assault like I was made for this, for him.

"More," I beg, my nails raking down his back, feeling his skin grow hotter beneath my touch. "Please..."

He pulls back, his eyes blazing gold, his glow so bright it hurts to look at him directly. But I can't look away. Won't look away.

I gasp at the sensation of him pressed against me. The hardness of him. How perfect he is. Perfect for me. As if the universe looked into my deepest thoughts and carved a cock that was made just for me.

"Yes," I breathe, tilting my head back, exposing my throat to him. "Please, Rok. I need—"

—

THE MOMENT HE PIERCES ME, THAT WIDE THICK GIRTHY THING spreading me wide is the moment the dream shatters.

I jolt awake, my body drenched in sweat, the echo of dream-pleasure still pulsing between my legs. For a moment, I'm disoriented, unsure where I am or what woke me.

Then I hear it—a soft sound at the entrance to the chamber.

I push myself up, wincing at the way my muscles protest even that small movement. How long have I been asleep? Hours? Days? The light filtering through the cracks in the ceiling has changed, grown slightly brighter, suggesting it's already early morning.

There is no sound now, and I hold my breath, straining to see through the shadows at the chamber entrance.

When a figure emerges, silhouetted against the darkness of the passage, my heart leaps into my throat. But then they move closer and I see the tall, broad-shouldered outline of the intruder.

Powerful. Alien. Unmistakably Rok.

Relief hits me with such force that I nearly collapse back onto the stone. He came back. Despite whatever happened between us, despite the pain or fear that drove him away, he came back.

But almost immediately, the relief twists into something sharper. Anger? Frustration? I don't even know. All I know is that he left me here—alone, confused, burning with whatever the hell this is—and now he's standing there like nothing happened.

He doesn't say anything, doesn't even move, just stares at

me with those glowing eyes, his body tense like a coiled spring. And I realize...he's still fighting it. Whatever had him bolting from the cave in the first place, it's still inside him, clawing at him.

The glow beneath his skin flickers unevenly, and his claws twitch at his sides, flexing and clenching as if he doesn't trust himself to stay still. He looks like he's barely holding himself together, and the sight sends a shiver crawling up my spine.

"Rok," I whisper. My voice cracks on the word, and I hate how small it sounds. "You...you came back."

His glow pulses once, twice, before dimming slightly, and I realize he's not just watching me—he's watching my reaction. Like he's bracing himself for something. Like he's not sure if I'm going to scream or run or...what?

I take a shaky breath, trying to steady myself. "You scared me." The words tumble out before I can stop them. "When you left like that. I didn't know if—"

I stop myself, swallowing the rest of the sentence. *I didn't know if you were coming back. I didn't know if I'd survive if you didn't.*

He freezes at the sound of my voice, his entire body tensing. The glow beneath his skin flickers once, twice, before settling into a steady, controlled pulse—brighter than normal, but not the erratic flare I saw before he fled.

He takes a step forward, then stops again, as if uncertain. No, not uncertain—cautious. Like he's approaching something dangerous.

Like he's approaching me.

The realization stings more than it should. I've been worried about him, terrified that whatever happened had hurt him, and he's looking at me like I'm the threat.

"I'm not going to bite," I snap, unable to keep the hurt from my voice. "Though apparently that's not a guarantee, because

I've been dealing with a lady boner and I'm feeling fucking feral."

Rok tilts his head, studying me from a distance. The air shifts as he inhales, and I'm pretty sure he can smell my arousal. The thought makes me press my thighs together, which doesn't help. Rok's expression is guarded, his posture tense. Nothing like the passionate, uninhibited alien who devoured me so thoroughly just hours ago.

After what feels like an eternity, he approaches, each step careful and slow. He crouches a few feet away, close enough to reach out but maintaining some space between us. His eyes never leave mine, watching for...what? Signs of the fever? Signs that I might trigger whatever happened to him again? Signs that I might tackle him and hump him the way a little voice in the back of my head is telling me to? I don't know.

His glow flickers again, brighter for a moment, then dims. He's being careful, like he's afraid one wrong move will shatter whatever fragile balance he's trying to maintain. And maybe it will. Maybe *I* will.

Every instinct in me is telling me to throw myself into his arms. To close the space between us. To touch him again.

Trying to ignore the heat burning beneath my skin, I force myself to stay still. To let him come to me, if that's what he's going to do.

Slowly, he extends a hand toward me, and I force myself to stay still, to let him decide how close he wants to get. His fingers brush my forehead, testing my temperature, I guess, then trace the line of my jaw, feather-light and clinical. Nothing like the hungry, possessive touches from before.

I don't know why that hurts, too.

I swallow hard, fighting the urge to lean into his hand, to close the distance between us. Whatever's happening here, it's clear he's struggling with it as much as I am.

"I'm okay," I say softly. "Are you...Are you okay?"

His gaze drops to my mouth, then down to my breasts. Goosebumps rise along my skin at his attention at the same moment that his glow seems to pulse. I hadn't gotten dressed yet. My clothes are still wet and—

Rok seems to lean in before catching himself. In the next moment, he rises to his full height and turns toward the center of the chamber, where the fire pit lies.

I wrap my arms around myself, now very aware of my nudity.

Not fair. He's been naked all along.

Within minutes, he has a small fire burning, its warm glow filling the chamber with dancing shadows. I stare at it, having no clue how he got a fire started. There's no kindling. Just those strange dark stones in the center. The ones I'd thought were charred.

I'm frowning at the fire when Rok moves. My gaze shifts to him as he retrieves the lizard creatures, carrying them to the fire. He selects one, positioning it over the flames using a long, straight stick as a makeshift spit. It is only when he pulls it back that I realize it's not a stick at all. Just a crude length of bone that looks like it came from the quill of some great creature. The lizard's scales hiss and pop as they heat, the iridescent colors dulling to a matte gray.

After a few minutes, he removes it from the fire. The meat is barely warmed through. With practiced motions, he uses a claw to slice off specific parts—the ridge of spines along the back, something that might be a gland near what I assume is the creature's throat—tossing these into the fire where they emit a noxious-smelling smoke. Next to go are the shiny scales. All plucked off like they were nothing but feathers.

Then, apparently satisfied that he's removed anything

dangerous, he sets the lizard before me, those golden eyes meeting mine.

"Uh...thank you."

With a satisfied grunt, he moves to the fire again. Reaching for another of the creatures, he prepares it the same way—a brief pass over the fire, removal of what I assume are poisonous or inedible parts, and the scales. In the next second, he tears into what remains, his sharp teeth easily ripping through flesh that still looks mostly raw to my eyes.

My stomach growls loudly, a painful reminder of how long it's been since I've eaten anything substantial, and my gaze slides to my meal in front of me. Raw alien lizard isn't exactly at the top of my culinary wishlist, but at this point, I'm not sure I can afford to be picky.

Rok pauses mid-bite, his eyes flicking to me. I give him a smile, taking up the lizard in my hand. The meat is warm but definitely not cooked, blood oozing from where his claws pierced the flesh. My stomach churns in a conflicted mix of hunger and revulsion.

I watch him eat for a moment, trying to gather my courage. He tears into the meat with efficient movements, his focus entirely on his meal. No table manners necessary in the apocalypse, I guess. Or on alien planets.

Looking down at my portion, I make a decision. Moving closer to the fire, I find a flat stone and place the creature on it, positioning it directly in the flames. Rok watches with curiosity as I cook it properly, using his bone stick to turn it occasionally until the flesh turns from translucent to opaque, the blood congealing, and the meat firming.

When it seems done enough not to give me alien-lizard salmonella (if that's even a thing), I tear off a small piece and cautiously take a bite.

It's...not terrible. Sort of like chicken that spent too much time marinating in fish sauce, with an aftertaste that reminds me vaguely of rosemary. The texture is chewy but not unpleasantly so, and my body's desperate need for protein overrides any lingering concerns about the taste.

I eat slowly, savoring each bite, knowing I need to be careful after going so long without proper food. As I eat, I can't help glancing at Rok, noting the way he studiously avoids looking at me, focusing instead on his own meal or the fire or the walls of the chamber—anywhere but at me.

The silence between us stretches. It's tense. Uncomfortable. So different from the easy companionship we'd somehow managed to build despite the language barrier. Before...well, before whatever happened happened.

I set down my half-eaten food, suddenly losing interest in eating. My eyes drift to Rok's profile, illuminated by the dancing firelight. The strong line of his jaw, the slight furrow between his brows as he concentrates on his meal, the way the glow beneath his skin pulses with his heartbeat—steady, controlled, alive.

For a moment, everything else fades away—the hunger, the fear, the confusion, the alien world around us. There's just him, just this moment, just us.

"I wish I could understand you," I whisper, the words hardly more than a breath. "It would make all of this so much easier."

He freezes, the chunk of meat in his hand forgotten. Slowly, with a deliberateness that makes me hold my breath, he turns to face me.

His eyes are wide, intent, fixed on mine with an intensity that makes my heart stutter in my chest. Before I can react, he's moving—not with the careful restraint from earlier, but with purpose, closing the distance between us in a swift, fluid motion.

I instinctively pull back, raising my hands. "Whoa, hold on—"

But he's not grabbing for me, not pinning me down or trying to resume what we started earlier. Instead, he crouches before me, his chest heaving with rapid breaths, his eyes searching mine with a desperate kind of hope I don't understand.

"Rok?" I whisper, confused by the sudden change.

He reaches out, cupping my face in his hands with exquisite gentleness, and presses his forehead to mine. His eyes close, his breath warm against my lips, and I'm struck by the ritual feel of the gesture.

"I don't...I don't know what you want," I whisper. It almost feels sacred, what he's doing right now.

He stays like that, forehead pressed to mine, eyes closed, utterly still but for the rise and fall of his chest. Waiting. Expecting something from me I can't even begin to guess at.

And in that moment of complete confusion, I think: *Fuck it.*

What do I have to lose? My dignity? Left that behind when I started having wet dreams about an alien. My sanity? Questionable at best since I crash-landed on this dust ball. My heart?

Well. That might be a concern.

I close my eyes, letting my forehead rest more firmly against his, giving myself over to whatever this is. Maybe it's just an alien version of kissing. Maybe it's some kind of apology. Maybe—

"I heard—my light."

I jerk back, my eyes flying open in shock. That voice—in my head, not my ears, but clear as a bell—wasn't mine. It was deeper, richer, with an accent I can't place, lilting and musical yet somehow harsh at the edges. And so much like Rok's... only...clearer.

Rok is staring at me, his eyes blazing with intensity, his hands still cradling my face.

Oh...

Oh my God...

"Did you..." I swallow hard, my throat suddenly dry. "Was that you?"

CHAPTER 24
NOT SAFE FOR HUMANS

ROK

She is entering the mindspace.

I can feel it.

Xiraxis has allowed her in. Ain has allowed her in. I am certain of it.

Her expression tells me I am not wrong.

The way her eyes widened, the sharp gasp of her breath when she heard me—truly heard me—her mind brushing mine for the briefest moment before it disappeared again. The look she gives me now is one of awe, of disbelief, as if something impossible has just happened.

But it is not impossible.

It is her.

It is us.

She stares at me with those strange, water-like eyes—the same ones that had blurred with heat and desire when I tasted her—and I close my own, pressing my forehead to hers, willing my thoughts to reach her again.

"Speak to me."

Nothing.

Her mind remains blank to me, a frustrating void, though I hold her there, trembling with the effort. I growl low in my throat, and the sound vibrates between us before I pull back, my chest heaving. Frustration coils tighter within me, and I can feel my claws twitching, needing to release the mounting pressure, aching to sink into something. But not her.

I cannot risk hurting her.

My body, so disciplined, so controlled, is betraying me in ways I cannot comprehend. The glow beneath my skin—once a tool like my eyes, my ears, my hands—now flares beyond my control, responding to her like a storm answering the call of the wind. My *dra-kir* pounds erratically, my breathing labored, and the heat coursing through my veins feels foreign, invasive.

But the worst part isn't the confusion. It's the fear. The fear that this unstoppable pull toward her will consume me entirely. That I will lose myself. And if that happens, I will lose *her*.

She is so small, so fragile, and the beast clawing at me—this wild, relentless need—does not care for such things. My claws, my strength, my very being could tear her apart, even if all I want is to protect her. The thought of harming her sends a deep, guttural panic through me. I cannot risk it. I cannot risk her. Not like this.

And so I fight.

I stalk away from her, pacing the chamber like a trapped shadowmaw. My claws clench and unclench, my muscles feeling tight, too tight, with the effort it's taking to maintain control.

She is watching me. I can feel her gaze following my every move.

I cannot look her way.

"Rok!" she says, her voice higher than usual. There's something in her tone—something between awe and panic—that makes me stop for a moment, my head snapping toward her.

She is vocalizing to me, her words flowing in that strange, lilting melody I do not understand. Softly, urgently. Repeating herself, as if saying it enough times will make the meaning clear.

But it doesn't.

It doesn't, and it *enrages* me.

I hiss low in my throat, and her eyes widen. I hear her breath hitch, but she doesn't retreat. She doesn't flinch.

Instead, she steps closer.

Her hand—small, delicate, and trembling—reaches out toward me, brushing against my arm. The contact sends a shockwave through me, a surge of heat that flares in my chest and spreads outward, burning through every nerve.

I jerk back, snarling, but she doesn't let go.

"Rok," she says again, her voice softer now, her tone soothing. Her touch lingers, and I stare down at her, my chest heaving, my claws curling into fists at my sides.

I cannot look at her.

I cannot *think* with her so close.

Taste.

The memory of her taste rises in my mind. Her scent, her heat, the way her body had yielded to my mouth like water yields to the stone—it all crashes over me, overwhelming my senses.

Her *slit.*

It was nothing like I'd expected it to be. Not a simple pouch for storing a member as I had assumed, but something else entirely. Something soft and sweet and *wet.* Something made solely for *me.*

The fire that burned under her skin has transferred to

mine, and it is taking everything I have not to pull her to me again. To spread her open and taste her until the fire consumes us both.

I stagger away from her, growling low in my throat as I fight for control. My claws leave deep indents in my palms as I pace, unable to stand still, my body alight with sensations I have never felt before.

I feel as though I am being remade—every bone in my body breaking and reforming, every nerve reawakening to a new and unbearable intensity.

This is why I left.

To keep her safe. From *me*.

I had fled the chamber, my body screaming in protest with every step I took away from her. But I hadn't gone far. Couldn't.

The pain in my chest had flared the moment I crossed the threshold, a sharp and relentless pull that would not let me go farther. I had paced outside the cave, camouflaged and restless, my instincts warring with themselves.

And now, being close to her again is worse.

Much worse.

I feel feral. Dangerous.

Every shadow in the chamber feels like a threat. Every sound, every shift in the air sends my claws twitching, my senses heightened to a point that borderlines pain.

And...she notices.

I can see it in the way her eyes follow me, wary but curious. She is vocalizing again, her words soft and insistent, but I cannot focus on them.

I need to move.

I need to *do* something before I lose myself completely.

The fire under my skin burns hotter with every passing moment, every breath that fills my lungs with her scent. The glow beneath my skin pulses faster than my *dra-kir*, brighter than it should be.

Something is happening to me—something I don't understand—and before it consumes me completely, I need to take her to safety. To my clan. Despite what I thought before, about the danger, I have to take her there. Kol will know what to do. My brothers will protect her if I...

If I lose control.

I clench my fists at the thought, my claws digging into my palms as I pace some more. My body demands that I stay close, but my mind knows better. I can't trust myself. Not now.

Jus-teen suddenly grasps my hand again.

I hiss sharply, but again, she doesn't let go.

Her touch is fire. Pure, searing fire that spreads through my veins, making my muscles tighten and my vision blur.

"Rok," she breathes. Her voice trembles, but it is insistent.

Her lips move again, shaping sounds I don't understand, but the tone—the tone is clear. She's pleading with me. For what, I don't know, but the desperation in her voice cuts through the haze clouding my mind.

My gaze drops to her hand, small and fragile against mine, and something inside me snaps.

I can't resist her.

I can't resist the sight of her, all soft curves and bare skin, her body still flushed from sleep—or from the fire that now burns inside me. This is why she wore those hideous hides. The sight of her bare flesh is undoing me.

With a single, sharp motion, I pull her to me, catching her around the hips and pulling her against my chest. She gasps, her hands flying up to my shoulders, her breath hitching as my claws curl possessively against her back.

Her scent surrounds me, intoxicating and maddening, and I lower my head to press my forehead to hers.

Speak to her.

I close my eyes, concentrating with everything I have, willing the words to form in the mindspace.

"We must go. It is not safe here."

Her breath catches, her lips parting slightly, and I know she understands.

But she doesn't agree.

Her hands tighten on my shoulders, and she speaks again, her voice low and urgent. Her forehead presses against mine, an unspoken gesture of connection, of effort, as if she's trying to push her thoughts into my mind.

Nothing.

The silence in the mindspace is deafening, and frustration surges through me like a storm.

I growl low in my throat, pulling back sharply, and her gaze locks on mine. There's water in her eyes now, glistening like tiny stars, and the sight of it sends a jolt of alarm through me.

She cannot leak again. I will not allow it. I must fix this.

"Jus-teen," I growl. She blinks rapidly, the water pooling in her eyes spilling over her cheeks.

Her voice softens, trembling, and she nods slowly, as if accepting something. Then she wriggles, forcing me to set her down though I do not want to, and turns toward her hide coverings.

I watch her as she moves, my body tense, my claws twitching at my sides.

Her clothes are still damp, clinging to her fingers as she pulls them on one piece at a time. My gaze follows every movement. The curve of her back, the line of her legs, the way her hair falls over her shoulders.

Hunger coils in my chest as if I have not just consumed something, and I clench my fists, forcing myself to look away.

But I can't.

Her scent fills the chamber, her every movement drawing my attention like a shadowmaw tracking prey. Every sound, every shift in the air sharpens to a painful degree.

Her eyes flick to me as she dresses, as if she knows something inside me is unraveling. She doesn't vocalize, but the way she watches me—alert, cautious—makes it clear she senses the change.

I can't stay still.

So, I pace the chamber.

She finishes dressing, pulling on her strange foot coverings before turning back to me.

Her gaze is steady, her expression unreadable, and for a moment, we simply stare at each other, the tension between us thick and suffocating.

Then she crouches.

I stop pacing, my head tilting as I watch her. She picks up the sandfin bone, using it to carve into the dust at her feet.

"This is me," she says, pointing to the figure she draws, then to herself. "Justine."

I nod, giving her the chin jerk she recognizes as understanding.

She draws another figure, larger and broader, and points to me.

My chest tightens.

She's trying to communicate.

I crouch beside her, studying the marks in the dust as she continues to draw.

The next shape is a stone formation. Familiar.

The place where I found her.

She points to it, then to herself, then to other figures she draws—many grouped together.

I lean forward, touching my brow to hers. With a breath, I close my eyes. "*My clan.*"

"No." She shakes her head, her hair tousling on her shoulders. "Not your clan." She points at the figures again. "Not Rok's." Shaking her head again. "*Mine*." She touches her chest. "*Justine's* clan."

Her words flow again, faster now, her tone rising with urgency.

My brow furrows, trying to piece it together. She repeats the motion—pointing to the stone formation, then to herself, then to the others. She vocalizes the same sounds over and over, pointing at each figure.

I tilt my head, my brow furrowing.

She draws something else—a new shape, a circle with radiating lines.

Ain.

My chest tightens.

Justine gestures toward Ain, then picks up a small stone from the ground. She holds it high, above the figures, and then lets it fall, the rock landing in the dust with a soft thud.

My glow flares brighter, but she doesn't notice. She's already moving, drawing more figures around the fallen stone. Tiny, crude shapes that surround it like a gathering.

She points to the stone formation again, then back to the figures, vocalizing softly, her tone urgent and pleading.

My claws curl into the stone floor as I try to make sense of her meaning.

The stone. The figures. Ain.

She pauses, glancing at me with wide, expectant eyes, as though willing me to understand. But I don't.

Her lips press together in what looks like frustration. She draws more figures, pointing to them as she speaks, her voice trembling with emotion. The same vocalizations again. Over and over.

"Jah-kee. Mih-kay-la. Eh-rihka."

Then it clicks. She names them. She *names* them.

The sound of her voice, the way her hands move, the desperation in her tone—it all clicks into place. As she draws two more lines—one leading from her figure to the fallen stone, the other from my figure to the same point, I understand.

There are more of her.

And she wants to go back for them.

Her people.

Daughters of Ain.

The realization hits me like a blow, and my chest heaves with the weight of it.

She is not alone. *Was* not alone. She wants to return to the place where I found her, near the Silent Valley, where danger lingers.

She wants to go back.

And I have no choice but to take her.

CHAPTER 25
THIS IS FINE. EVERYTHING IS FINE. I'M TOTALLY FINE

JUSTINE

Rok won't look at me.

He's been pacing for hours, his movements growing increasingly agitated with each pass across the cave floor. Every few minutes, he pauses to stare at the entrance, nostrils flaring, head tilted as if listening for something I can't hear.

"Are they still out there?" I ask, even though I know he can't understand me. "The other aliens?"

No response. Just more pacing, his claws scraping against stone with each turn.

I watch him from where I'm sitting by the small fire, the remains of the last lizard-thing long since picked clean. The cave has grown darker as the day progresses, shadows lengthening as the light filtering through the ceiling cracks changes from harsh white to a softer gold.

Rok's behavior is...concerning. He's always been a bit wild—I mean, I knew that from the moment I met him—but this is different. There's a frantic quality to his movements, a tension in his shoulders I haven't seen before. His glow pulses erratically beneath his skin, flaring brighter whenever he glances my way.

Which isn't often.

In fact, he seems to be going out of his way to avoid looking at me. Like making eye contact might somehow hurt him.

"You know, the silent treatment is getting a little old," I say, mostly to fill the uncomfortable silence. "Especially now that I know you can actually talk. Sort of."

I still can't wrap my head around it. His voice in my mind —clear as day, rich and deep with that strange accent I can't place. Not some hallucination or fever dream, but actual communication.

Telepathy. Actual honest-to-God telepathy.

"The longer I stay on this hellscape of a planet, the weirder things get," I mutter, poking at the fire with the bone stick. "Next thing you know, I'll be growing a third eye or developing the ability to shoot laser beams from my fingertips."

I glance up, half hoping for a reaction, but Rok is focused intently on the cave entrance again, his body tense and alert.

"You said there was danger," I say, my tone more serious now. "Is it those other aliens? The ones who were hunting you?"

Nothing. Not even a twitch to suggest he's heard me.

I sigh, setting the bone aside and drawing my knees up to my chest. "If we could just talk properly, this would be so much easier. All those times you've been staring at me—were you trying to communicate? Was I just too dense to hear you?"

The thought makes something sour swell in my chest. How frustrating must it have been for him, trying to reach me while I remained oblivious?

"Maybe it's this place," I say, gesturing vaguely around us.

"Maybe the longer I'm stuck under Bitch Sun, the more I'm adapting. Developing new skills. Like hearing voices in my head."

I laugh, but there's no mirth in it.

"That's it. I'm officially going crazy. Next, I'll be naming the rocks and having deep conversations with that pool over there."

But I know I'm not imagining it. His voice was real—as real as anything can be on this strange, impossible world.

Through the corner of my eye, I catch Rok watching me, his gaze intense and burning. He looks away the moment I turn toward him, but not before I see something in his expression that sends a delicious shiver down my spine.

Hunger.

The memory of what happened between us rushes back, almost overwhelming. His mouth on me. The way my body responded to him, as if he knew exactly what I needed before I did. The pleasure that had crashed over me. It was unlike anything I'd ever experienced before.

I press my thighs together, trying to ignore the heat building low in my belly. *Not the time, Justine. Not the time.*

But apparently my body hasn't gotten that memo. Because even now, with Rok clearly struggling with...whatever he's struggling with, I can't stop thinking about his hands on my skin, his tongue on my...the way he licked my...Fuck.

"Focus," I mutter to myself, pressing the heels of my hands against my eyes. "We need to get out of here, find the others, and figure out how to get off this planet. No time for inter-species hookups, no matter how mind-blowing they might be."

When I look up again, the cave has grown noticeably darker. The light filtering through the cracks has faded to a deep amber, signaling the approach of night. Rok has stopped pacing, his attention now fixed on me, his expression unreadable in the growing shadows.

For several long moments, neither of us moves. The only sounds are the occasional pop of the fire stones and the distant, eerie howl of wind through the stone formations outside.

Then, without warning, Rok moves toward me.

"Rok?" I whisper.

He doesn't respond. Doesn't even acknowledge that I've spoken. His eyes are locked on mine, and just the look in those eyes has my thoughts shooting back to what happened between us earlier. I swallow hard.

The closer he gets, the more I notice the tremors running through his body. His claws curl and flex at his sides, as if he's fighting to keep himself grounded.

Oh God.

Something's wrong—something worse than I thought.

I swallow again, my stomach filling with dread. He's always been strange to me—he's an alien, after all—but this is different. The careful control he's always maintained, even in his most primal moments, is gone. Ever since...

Oh fuck.

The realization makes the cave go cold.

The Xyma water.

What if I poisoned him? What if something in the water—something I didn't even realize was dangerous—did this to him?

"Rok?" I say again, louder this time, my voice rising with panic.

Still, he doesn't respond.

When he finally reaches me, he sinks into a crouch, his broad shoulders trembling with the effort. Each inhalation shudders through him like it hurts to draw breath.

"Rok, look at me," I whisper. "Please, tell me. Are you okay? Did I—did I hurt you?"

His head lifts at my words, his molten gold eyes locking onto mine with a force that steals the air from my lungs.

Despite the tremors wracking his powerful frame, despite the tension coiling through every muscle in his body, his touch, when it comes, is exquisitely gentle.

His hands come up to cradle my face. The warmth of his palms seeps into my skin, and I almost release a moan.

I freeze, my breath hitching.

"Rok..." I whisper.

His thumbs brush along my jaw, and for a moment, I forget everything—the fear, the uncertainty. There's only him, his touch, his eyes burning into mine with a desperation I don't understand.

And yet...

I can see that this is costing him.

His glow flickers, dimming and brightening, dimming and brightening, as if the effort of touching me is too much. His claws twitch against my skin, as if he's struggling to hold himself back.

"Why are you doing this?" I murmur, my voice barely audible. "If it hurts you, why—"

He leans forward then, slowly, pressing his forehead to mine.

I gasp softly at the contact, my heart pounding in my chest as his warmth surrounds me. His breath fans against my lips, ragged and strained, as his body trembles against mine.

For a moment, neither of us moves.

We just stay like that, forehead to forehead, his hands cradling my face, my fingers clutching at his wrists.

His eyes flutter closed, and I can't help but stare at him, at the way his features soften even as his body remains tense.

"This is almost more intense than French kissing," I whisper, but the joke falls flat even to my ears.

I close my eyes as Rok's fingers tighten slightly against my jaw, and then—

His voice fills my mind.

Urgent. Strained.

"Leave. We must hurry."

A lump forms in my throat as I open my eyes. He's already staring at me, his molten gold gaze piercing through the darkening shadows of the cave. His eyes are wild, desperate, and for a moment, I can't breathe.

"Yes," I whisper, the sound barely audible. "We should."

His gaze flickers down to my lips, lingering there, and my heart stutters in my chest. Without thinking, my tongue runs over them like an invitation.

Kiss him.

"We can't." The words leave my lips, but they lack conviction.

I know what he wants.

I know it in the way his glow pulses erratically beneath his skin, the way his hands tremble as they cradle my face.

The air between us crackles like a live wire, coiling tighter, brighter, until it feels like the cave itself might ignite.

And then I think: *Why not?*

Before I can second-guess myself, I close the small distance between us, pressing my lips to his.

It's soft at first, tentative. His lips are warm, and they mold to mine perfectly.

But then something shifts.

A low growl rumbles from his chest, and his hands tighten against my jaw, pulling me closer. The kiss deepens, his mouth claiming mine with a hunger that steals the breath from my lungs.

I gasp into him, my fingers tangling in his hair—soft, surprisingly soft—and he groans, the sound vibrating through me.

His lips part mine, his tongue sweeping inside, and I'm lost.

Completely and utterly lost.

Rok kisses me as if he's starving. As if he wants every part of me.

It's overwhelming, intense, unlike anything I've ever felt before. His kiss is wild and consuming, a force of nature that sets every nerve in my body ablaze.

I don't even realize I've wrapped my legs around his waist until he lifts me, his strong arms cradling me as if I weigh nothing.

My thighs tighten around him instinctively, and he staggers forward, pressing me against the cool stone wall.

The contrast between the cold rock and his fiery warmth sends a shiver racing down my spine.

"Oh fuck," I gasp and he growls again, his lips trailing down my jaw to my neck, his teeth grazing the sensitive skin there. My head tilts back, a moan escaping me as his mouth finds the hollow of my throat.

I've never been this turned on in my life.

Wait—didn't I say that before? Well, I mean it even more now. FUCK.

Every touch, every kiss, every possessive growl makes me burn hotter, my body arching into his as if begging for more.

In the back of my mind, I notice how quickly he's learned to kiss—how perfectly he's attuned to my reactions, how he seems to know exactly what I need, what I want.

But then something changes.

He freezes.

At first, I think he's just catching his breath, but it's just like before. When he had me quivering after giving me the best orgasm of my life. His entire body stiffens, his hands twitching against my skin.

"Rok?" I whisper, my eyes flying open.

He pulls back slightly, his head tilting as he inhales deeply. His nostrils flare, his glow pulsing brighter for a moment before dimming again.

And then he releases me.

Just like that.

I barely have time to catch myself before he staggers back, his hands flying to his head as he lets out a guttural snarl.

"Rok!" I cry, stumbling forward, but he holds up a hand, stopping me in my tracks.

His glow goes haywire, flickering and pulsing erratically beneath his skin. It doesn't look natural—it's chaotic, unstable, like a storm raging beneath the surface.

He falls to his knees, his body shaking violently. His claws rake against the stone floor, leaving deep gouges as his breaths come in harsh, ragged gasps.

"Rok, what's happening?" I whisper, dropping to the floor beside him.

I reach out, my hand trembling, but the moment my fingers brush his arm, he flinches like he's been hit by a truck, a sharp hiss escaping him.

My touch makes it worse.

I pull back, my heart pounding as I watch him, helpless and terrified.

And then...his glow changes.

It happens so suddenly, so drastically, that I fall back in shock.

The soft amber light beneath his skin darkens, shifting to something deeper, something...*different.* It looks like smoke, like shadows writhing under the surface, swirling and coiling in unnatural patterns until they consume him from within.

His skin has gone pitch black.

"Oh, shit," I whisper, chest heaving.

His body convulses, his head tilting back as a guttural, animalistic growl tears from his throat. The darkness beneath his skin grows thicker, consuming him, and for a moment, I think he might explode.

And then—

Stars.

The darkness is suddenly filled with stars.

Tiny, glimmering points of light swirl beneath his skin, like entire galaxies trapped within the confines of his body.

It's beautiful and terrifying all at once, like staring into the heart of the universe.

He collapses forward, catching himself on his hands, his head hanging low as his body trembles.

I scramble toward him, my fear overridden by the need to help him, to do *something*.

"Rok, talk to me." I plead, intent on pressing my forehead to his so he can tell me what's going on. Is he dying? He can't be dying. My heart lurches at the thought, tears filling my eyes. I push them back.

He can't be dying. Because I refuse it.

When my fingers brush his shoulder, he flinches again, but this time he doesn't pull away.

Instead, he lifts his head, his glowing, star-filled eyes locking onto mine.

The look in his eyes...

I cannot explain it.

I see *myself*. All my dreams. All I've ever wanted.

And in that moment, I know.

Whatever's happening to him, it's because of me.

And there's no going back.

CHAPTER 26
THIS SOFT CREATURE IS MINE

ROK

I am burning from the inside out.

The fire that began when she touched me, when I tasted her essence, has spread through every part of me until I am nothing but flame. My body has become alien to me —shifting, changing, reforming itself according to some ancient pattern I can't begin to comprehend.

I collapse to the stone floor as waves of sensation crash over me. Pain, yes, but more than pain—awareness, heightened to a point that borders on agony. I can feel every current of air against my skin, hear the rapid beating of Jus-teen's *drakir*, smell the fear and concern radiating from her like a dust cloud.

And beneath it all, something else. Something new. Something becoming.

"Rok, talk to me." Her voice cuts through the storm raging within me.

I try to respond, try to push thoughts toward her, but my

mind seems incapable. My vision blurs, darkens, then expands beyond anything I have ever experienced. I can see *everything* —the dust in the air, the subtle patterns in the stone, the aura of warmth surrounding her body.

When her fingers brush my shoulder, the contact sends a jolt through me that is both torture and relief. Her touch soothes the fire even as it feeds it? It's a contradiction that makes no sense. But it feels utterly right.

I lift my head, struggling to focus on her face through the chaos of sensations. Her eyes widen as she looks at me, her lips parting in shock, and I realize something has changed—something fundamental.

I look down at my arms, at my chest, and freeze.

My skin...has transformed. Darkness flows beneath the surface, not the absence of light but something deeper, richer —like the dark sky above the dust plains. And within that darkness, stars. Countless stars, swirling and shifting like the great dance of the celestial bodies we use to track paths through the dust.

What is happening to me?

Justine's hand reaches toward me again, tentative but determined, and when her fingers make contact with my skin, the stars beneath the surface surge toward her touch, clustering beneath the point of connection like they are drawn to her.

"What's happening to you?" she whispers. "What can I do?"

I want to tell her to run. To flee. That I am dangerous in this state, unpredictable, a threat even to myself. But I cannot speak, cannot form the words, and even if I could, I know the truth—I *need* her. Need her presence, her touch, her essence to survive whatever transformation is consuming me.

The fire surges again and I cry out, a raw, animalistic sound that echoes through the chamber. Jus-teen flinches, her beautiful, water-like eyes going wide, but she doesn't back away. Doesn't retreat.

Instead, she moves closer.

"I'm here," she says, her voice low but steady, resolved. "I'm not going anywhere."

Time becomes fluid, elastic.

Moments stretch into what feels like solmarks, each beat of my *dra-kir* dragging out endlessly as the fire rages beneath my skin. Then, just as suddenly, time compresses, everything blurring together in flashes of sensation. Pain. Heat. Her voice.

Solmarks pass. Sols. The light, then the dark. Light, then dark. Cycles. I am dimly aware of my Jus-teen moving around me.

She brings water from the pool, the cool liquid soothing my burning skin as she drapes something damp across my forehead. Her touch lingers, and I feel the faint tremor in her hands.

She's afraid.

And yet she stays.

Her voice washes over me, vocalizations soft and insistent, lost in the roaring that fills my ears.

"...never seen anything like this..."

"...please be okay..."

"...don't you dare die on me, Rok. I mean it."

Her words are a balm, even when I cannot make sense of them.

But then, something shifts.

At first, it's faint. Barely noticeable through the haze of pain and heat.

A whisper.

Not her voice—not the one I hear with my ears—but something deeper, softer, resonating within my mind.

Thoughts in the mindspace. Thoughts that are not mine. Images that transform into words. Understanding.

"*What if he's dying?*"

The thought is fleeting, like a ripple across the still water, and for a moment, I think I've imagined it. But then another comes, clearer this time.

"*What if I did this to him?*"

It's Jus-teen.

I can hear her.

In the mindspace.

I can hear her directly.

The barrier between our minds has thinned, becoming so fragile it's nearly transparent. For a moment, I am distracted from the pain.

Her thoughts come in fragments, disjointed yet vivid, each one cutting through the chaos like a blade.

"*I need to...him to cool down. His skin...burning up.*"

"*Stupid Xyma water. Stupid Xyma themselves.*"

"*What am I going to do if...doesn't recover, huh? What the fuck are...going to do, Justine?*"

Humor rises inside me. Her thoughts are just as many as her vocalizations. A constant stream of commentary.

I hold them close to my *dra-kir* as the darkness takes me.

For solmarks more, the fire rages.

Time passes. Jus-teen remains by my side, sometimes speaking, sometimes silent, but always touching me in some way—a hand on my arm, fingers brushing my face, her shoulder pressed against mine. Each contact soothes the fire within me, brings me closer to some equilibrium I cannot name.

When exhaustion finally claims her, she curls up beside me, her body a warm, steady presence against my side, her head resting on my shoulder. Her breathing deepens, evens out, and I know when she succumbs to rest.

I watch her, marveling at the trust this small, fragile being places in me. Even after witnessing my transformation, even knowing what I am capable of, she rests beside me without fear.

The thought fills me with a protectiveness so fierce it borders on violence. I would tear apart anything that threatened her, would face down the rival clan and shadowmaws and the dust itself to keep her safe.

Perhaps it's the thought. For, without warning, the fire within me surges again—different this time, focused, concentrated in a way it wasn't before. The heat pools in my gut, then lower, in the pouch that houses my member, and panic flares alongside it.

No. Not this. Not now.

But my body responds to some call I cannot resist, some transformation that has been building since I first tasted her essence. No...since I first *touched* her. My member, normally sleeping within its protective pouch, begins to swell, to change, to push outward.

The pain is excruciating—not like the burn of the transformation, but sharper, more localized. I bite back a cry, not wanting to wake Justine, but the agony of it tears through me like a dust-stalker's claw.

It feels as though my member is being reshaped, remolded —which is impossible. The sensation is wrong, terrifying. But it is true.

My claws dig into the stone as I brace against the pain, a surprised grunt going through me as I see myself emerge. It breaks free of the protective pouch, the pouch itself reshaping as it escapes, fully extended for the first time in my life. I stare down at it in shock and confusion.

This is...not what I expected.

My stem...it has changed—transformed as completely as the rest of me. It is larger, thicker, the dark skin shot through with the same starlight that flows beneath the rest of my skin. The shape is different too—no longer the simple rod I emerged from the Giving Stone with, but something more complex, curved slightly, with a broad head and ridges along the underside.

And beneath it, where there was once only smooth skin, hang two heavy sacs, tight and full, their purpose a mystery to me.

My breath comes in harsh pants as I try to make sense of what I'm seeing, of what I'm feeling. The fire has localized here, concentrated in these new appendages, and the sensation is...intense. Not pain, not pleasure, but something in between, something that makes my claws flex against the stone and a growl rumble in my throat.

The movement, the sound, is enough to wake Jus-teen. She stirs against me, her eyes fluttering open, still heavy with sleep. For a moment, she seems disoriented, confused by the starlight emanating from my skin. Then her gaze drops to my lap, to the transformed member jutting proudly from between my thighs, and her eyes widen, all traces of sleep vanishing in an instant.

"Oh," she whispers, the sound barely audible even to my enhanced hearing. "Well, that's...made an appearance."

Her face flushes a deep red, but there is no fire there. It is... blood. I can sense it...though I do not know how. Blood rushing to the surface of her skin in a way that fascinates me. She looks away quickly, then back, as if she can't help herself, then away again, a nervous laugh escaping her.

"I, um...that's...wow."

There's something in her voice, something that comes

through in her thoughts. Embarrassment, certainly, but also… interest? Fascination? I don't understand the complexity of her reaction, but I can smell the change in her scent, the subtle shift that makes my fangs ache.

The realization sends another pulse of heat through my new stem, making it twitch. Visibly. Jus-teen's eyes widen further.

"*Oh my God,*" Justine projects into the mindspace.

She calls to Ain. I would have asked her more about this if the stars beneath my skin didn't suddenly begin to fade.

One by one, they extinguish themselves like dying lights. The darkness that had consumed me recedes, retreating into some unseen place, leaving my skin bare—normal. That rich amber-gold. Like it was before.

I even test my glow. Brightening, then dimming myself. It follows my commands.

The fire is gone.

The transformation is complete, and yet…I am not the same.

I glance down at myself, at the new appendages between my legs, still throbbing with heat. My stem still juts forward.

I close my hand around it, trying to ease the ache there, but the touch only intensifies it. A low, rumbling groan escapes me before I can stop it, the sound reverberating through the chamber.

Jus-teen, who had been gazing at me with those wide, cautious eyes, flushes bright red. Her gaze flickers downward —toward the source of the sound—and her face somehow turns an even deeper shade of crimson. She quickly averts her eyes, looking anywhere but at me.

"Well," she says, her voice unsteady, "I guess you're better?"

Her gaze darts back to my stem, then away again just as

quickly. When I clench it tighter, she takes a step backward, holding her hands up as if in surrender. "I'm just...gonna give you some privacy."

She turns and moves to the other side of the chamber, her back to me, but I can still feel her presence like a flame in the dark.

I should stop.

I should release myself. Force my new stem away. Do something to regain control. But I can't. For one, I no longer have a pouch to put it away.

My claw remains fisted around it, twitching as I watch her. The sight of her—her bare arms, her hair falling loose around her shoulders, the curve of her hips even beneath her strange coverings—fuels the fire in me.

I don't understand these sensations, this hunger. All I know is that I cannot shift her from my mind. Cannot shift the memory of her wet slit, soft and glistening, the taste of her essence still haunting me.

She turns slightly, glancing back at me over her shoulder. Her eyes widen as she realizes I'm still watching her—still holding myself.

"Um..." She clears her throat, her voice rising with nervous energy. "Is there...any chance you can, uh, put that back?" She gestures vaguely toward my crotch, her cheeks blazing.

The question confuses me at first, but her thoughts—completely unfiltered—reach me, projecting an image of my pouch from before. The image is faint, fuzzy, but clear enough for me to understand her meaning.

It makes me laugh.

The sound is low and rough, rumbling from deep within my chest, and her eyes snap to mine, startled.

She blinks, her brows furrowing, and I watch as realization

dawns. "Oh my God," she says, her voice barely above a whisper. "You're laughing at me."

I rise to my feet, towering over her, and her gaze drops instinctively.

Her breath catches as her eyes land on my stem once more, jutting forward like a weapon, and her face flames red again. She quickly looks away, but not before I catch the way her pupils dilate, the subtle quickening of her breath. Not before I catch the *thought*.

Dust.

An image of my stem sliding through her wet slit.

The image is so sudden, so startling, I almost fall to my knees. Another pulse of heat goes through me, making my stem twitch *hard*. Is that how we are to join? I'd never considered using my stem in such a way with my brothers. But then again, I've never had these urges before. Not until her.

And now that I know this new purpose...what she needs...

Oh, the thought.

A grunt escapes my throat as I fist my new stem harder.

"Rok," she says, her voice sharp, but there's a tremor in it that betrays her. She makes a sound in her throat, forcing her gaze back to my face. "Focus, okay? Can you...can you put it away or not?"

I shake my head the way she does. "No," I say simply. One of her words. Awkward but clear.

Her hands fly into the air. "Of course not. Suddenly grow a big fat raging cock after scaring me to death that you're dying, and *then* tell me that weapon of pussy destruction cannot be disarmed."

Pussy?

What is a pussy?

The images are coming too fast. I can hardly make sense of what these vocalizations mean. But then there's the image of her slit again, warm and wet and dripping. Sheathed over my stem.

I groan.

Her pussy. Yes.

She plants her hands on her hips, glaring at me. "Okay, fine. I'll fix this. Just...stay there."

She turns in a slow circle, scanning the chamber, her expression thoughtful. I tilt my head, curious despite the need coursing through me and culminating in my rigid shaft.

"Right," she mutters to herself, as if coming to a decision. "I know what to do."

Before I can ask—or think—what she means, she reaches for her leg coverings.

She strips them off in one quick motion, leaving her legs bare, and I feel my body react instantly.

The sight of her exposed skin, the smooth curves of her thighs, the way the light catches on her soft flesh—it's almost too much.

My stem...my *cock*—as she called it—hardens further, the ache intensifying, and I let out a low growl, unable to suppress the sound.

She doesn't notice.

Or if she does, she ignores it.

Instead, she picks up a jagged-edged stone and uses it to tear the hide of her coverings into two flat panels. Soon, she's only wearing half of it, her legs deliciously bare.

"These might..." She pauses, glancing at me nervously. "These might help."

She approaches slowly, the makeshift hide in hand, her gaze determinedly fixed on my face.

When she reaches me, her hands tremble slightly as she presses the fabric against my lap, tying it in place with quick, efficient movements.

Her nearness is electric.

Her touch is even more so.

I can feel the heat of her hands through the thin fabric, can smell the faint, intoxicating scent of her skin.

Her fingers brush against me accidentally—light, fleeting—and it takes everything in me not to groan aloud.

"Okay," she says, stepping back to admire her handiwork. "That should—" She stops abruptly, her gaze flickering downward, and her face reddens again.

The fabric is tented obscenely, the outline of my *cock* clearly visible. Cock. A much better word than stem. I like it. I shall call it my cock from now on and teach my brothers, too.

My gaze shifts to hers when I get an image that almost brings me to the ground. An image of Jus-teen on her knees beneath me. Her mouth over the new bulbous head of my cock.

It is enough to make my claws dig into my palms.

But these aren't my thoughts in the mindspace. They're *hers.*

"Yeah, that's...not really helping," she mutters, dragging a hand down her face.

I chuckle again, the sound low and rumbling, and she glares at me.

"Don't laugh," she says, pointing a finger at me. "This is your fault."

Her words are sharp, but there's no real anger in them. If anything, there's a flicker of amusement in her tone, and for a moment, the tension between us eases.

Then she sighs, gesturing toward the floor. "Do you need to...rest or something? Recover?"

I get images of my own form resting on the stone. Of her resting beside me.

Jus-teen blinks at me before she mimes lying down, her movements exaggerated, and I realize she still doesn't know I am getting imprints of her thoughts. She is not doing it on purpose then.

And I...do not want to tell her. Not yet.

Something tells me that if I do, all these delicious images she's sending my way will stop.

So, instead, I lower my head and press my forehead to hers, letting the soft, trembling warmth of her skin connect with mine.

The moment our foreheads touch, it's as if the ground beneath me shifts.

A jolt of energy surges through me and I hear her gasp, feel the slight tremor in her body as it passes through her, too.

Her hands fly to my arms, clutching at me for balance as her knees buckle slightly. A soft, breathless moan escapes her lips, and the sound strikes me like lightning, sinking deep into my chest.

"*No rest,*" I project, my thoughts flowing into hers like dust melding with dust. My voice in her mind is steady, but the words carry the weight of my urgency, the fire that still burns within me. "*No time. We have already delayed too long.*"

Her breath hitches again, her trembling growing more pronounced as my thoughts wrap around hers. I can feel the heat of her emotions—confusion, fear, curiosity—all inter-woven with something else. Something warmer.

"Rok..." she whispers, the sound of my name soft but filled with trust.

My name in her mouth does things to me. Makes my claws curl. Makes my cock twitch and throb. And the thoughts bleeding from her mind—dust.

She sees me all wrong.

I know what I am. Scar tissue and survival. Claws made for gutting prey, not...whatever soft things she imagines when I touch her. But her mind keeps throwing these broken reflections at me:

—My battle-worn hands *gentle* on her hips

—My fangs (which have ripped out throats) making her shiver when I bite

—Some golden-eyed being she's built from dust and hope

Worst part? I *want* to be that for her.

The realization tastes like blood in my mouth. I've spent cycles proving I'm the sharpest blade in the clan, and now this soft-skinned female has me aching to sheathe myself in her fantasies.

Her breath hitches when I step closer. I can *smell* her pulse jump—hear the wet catch in her throat. She thinks I don't notice how her thighs press together when I loom over her. Like she's *trying* to drown in my shadow.

And then, under all that, a burning need. A fire growing. A sensation that rises and culminates in a single spot between her thighs.

She cuts herself off, but I've already felt it. That fire. The pull between us that neither of us can deny.

The stars beneath my skin pulse faintly, responding to her, but they don't return. My transformation is complete, I suppose. This is not the chaos from before. This is something new.

Is this mind sickness?

I should walk away. Should let her see the real me—the one who left her people to rot in that valley. But then her fingers brush my chest, and the lie does not manifest to thought.

I pull back slightly, just enough to meet her gaze. Her pupils are blown wide, her cheeks flushed a deep red, and her lips are parted slightly, as if she's struggling to catch her breath.

She doesn't move away.

She doesn't pull back.

I can sense her every breath. Every beat of her *dra-kir*. As if Xiraxis has formed around her and she is the world in its entirety.

The fire within me still burns, but it's no longer a chaotic blaze. It's a controlled heat now, simmering just beneath the surface, focused and ready.

And at the center of it all is her.

The small, fragile being who has placed her trust in me despite everything.

I will not fail her.

I put my forehead to hers. *"I will take you to your clan. But first we must go to mine."*

CHAPTER 27

HELP ME, OBI-WAN KENOBI. YOU'RE MY ONLY HOPE (OF ESCAPING THIS SEXUAL TENSION)

JUSTINE

We don't leave the cave once night falls.

"*Too dangerous,*" Rok says—or rather, thinks at me, his forehead pressed briefly against mine. "*Predators hunt in darkness.*"

I nod, pretending this makes perfect sense, like receiving telepathic warnings about alien predators is just part of my daily routine now. No big deal. Just another day on Planet Dust.

"Sure, sure," I reply, as if we're discussing whether to grab takeout or cook dinner. "Wouldn't want to be someone's midnight snack."

The tension between us is thick enough to cut with a knife. Or one of those wicked claws of his. We've both been carefully avoiding discussing what happened earlier—his cosmic transformation, the stars beneath his skin, and especially that new... addition to his anatomy.

Which is now mercifully covered by my sacrificed pants legs, though the makeshift loincloth does little to disguise the impressive outline beneath.

Not that I'm looking. Much.

And Rok, Rok seems tense. Not tense like he was before when he was in pain. This is different. He's watching me like a hawk, and the look in his eyes is making me feel all sorts of things. He ventures out briefly—just outside the cave entrance —to hunt, returning with more of those strange lizard creatures. He prepares them the same way as before, removing the dangerous parts and cooking them just enough to make the meat safe.

My observant alien even cooks mine a little longer, his nostrils flaring as if he thinks he's doing a disservice, but he does it anyway.

It's still a little rarer than I'd like, but I eat without complaint, too hungry to be fussy. The protein feels good, strengthening, and I know I'll need my energy for tomorrow's journey.

After eating, I deliberately position myself on the opposite side of the cave from Rok. It seems like the sensible thing to do, given...everything. Distance. That's what we need. Distance and time to process whatever is happening between us.

Except I can't sleep.

I lie on my side, facing the wall, acutely aware of every sound he makes across the chamber. The soft sounds of him moving. The steady rhythm of his breathing. The occasional low rumble that might be a sigh or might be something else entirely.

I can hear every slight shift when I hadn't been able to before. Rok has always been so silent to me. Just another of those new skills I've developed, I guess.

When I finally give up and roll over, I find him watching

me, his eyes reflecting the dim glow from the stones that are still burning. How? Alien magic, maybe.

He doesn't look away when I catch him staring. If anything, his gaze intensifies, his lips parting slightly to reveal those sharp teeth in what's his version of a smile.

Bastard.

It should be terrifying—those fangs, those predatory eyes—but somehow it just looks...rakish. Almost charming, in a dangerous, alien sort of way.

I notice something else, too. His skin, which has always emitted that warm, golden glow, is now completely dark. Not the star-filled darkness from earlier, just...normal. Like human skin, but with that strange amber-gold tone.

Is this new? Another change along with his newly acquired anatomy? Or is this how he's always been? Able to control his luminosity at will.

There's so much I don't know about him. So much I can't ask without pressing my forehead to his and entering that strange mental space where our thoughts intermingle.

I'm not ready for that. Not yet. Not with the memory of his transformation still so fresh, and certainly not with the current state of his...lower half.

I mean, where did it even come from? There's no way he hid that thing in some lower cavity I didn't notice. It's just... too big!

After another hour of pretending to sleep while secretly watching him watch me, I give up and sit up.

"I need some water," I announce to the darkness, not sure if he understands the words but needing to say something to break the silence.

I make my way to the pool, grateful for the cool, clear water that seems perpetually fresh, as if being constantly replenished from some underground source. I cup my hands and drink deeply, knowing how precious this liquid will be once we're back in the desert tomorrow.

"Drink it all, Justine," I mutter to myself. "Who knows when you'll see water again once we're out in the sand with only Bitch Sun for company."

The thought of tomorrow's journey makes my stomach clench with anxiety. Not just the physical challenges—the heat, the terrain, the dangers Rok warned me about—but the fact that I'll be doing it with only half my pants.

"A miniskirt," I say with a disbelieving laugh. "I'm going to trek across an alien desert in a makeshift miniskirt and heels. Because apparently, that's where my life choices have led me."

Still, it was worth it. The alternative—Rok walking around with his new appendage swinging free—was simply not an option. Not if I wanted to maintain any semblance of focus or dignity.

And yet, despite my best efforts, my mind keeps returning to the image of it. To him. To how that perfect, thick head would feel—

"Nope," I say aloud, splashing water on my face to cool my suddenly burning cheeks. "Not going there. Not thinking about alien anatomy. Absolutely not."

Except...it wasn't truly alien, was it? At least, not in the way I would have expected. It looked surprisingly...uh...attractive, if exceptionally well-proportioned. Almost as if designed specifically to appeal to human—to *my*—preferences.

Did this planet just custom-order a dick for me? What kind of five-star resort bullshit is this?

"Right," I snort softly. "Because the universe conspired to create the perfect alien penis just for me. That makes total sense."

The absurdity of it all hits me suddenly, and I have to stifle a hysterical laugh. Here I am, on God knows which planet, hiding in a cave with a golden-skinned, occasionally glowing alien, concerned about his newly manifested genitalia while we prepare to trek across a desert to find my sister and the others.

If I woke up tomorrow and discovered this had all been some elaborate fever dream while I was passed out on that bus, I'd be...relieved?

No. That's not quite right. Confused, certainly. Bewildered, absolutely. But also, strangely...disappointed?

"You're losing it, Justine," I mutter, pushing myself up from the pool's edge. "Complete mental breakdown imminent."

I turn to head back to my designated sleeping area, but my eyes catch on Rok again. He's sitting by the fire, his body angled so that the makeshift covering does little to hide the still-prominent outline beneath. How is he still...like that? Doesn't he get uncomfortable?

Obviously, he could just...take care of it. I mean, I'm not a prude. Everyone does it. I certainly wouldn't judge him for needing some relief after whatever transformation he went through.

But he doesn't. Instead, he's focused intently on something in his hands—a small, round object that looks vaguely like a miniature pumpkin. He's using one of those sharp bone tools to carve into it, his movements precise and delicate despite his massive claws.

I'm so distracted by the unexpected sight that I don't immediately notice when his attention shifts from his project to me. But when I do, the intensity of his gaze makes my breath catch.

Heat creeps up my neck and into my cheeks, and I look away quickly, suddenly very interested in a random spot on the cave wall.

But the damage is done. The thought is there, firmly lodged

in my mind—Rok, alone in the darkness, those strong hands wrapped around himself, those starlit eyes closing in pleasure...

I shuffle awkwardly back to my spot, keeping my eyes firmly on the ground. The heat that started in my face has migrated lower, settling in my core like a banked ember, ready to flare at the slightest provocation.

This is worse than those dreams.

A pulse goes through my core, and I clench my thighs. No. I can't—not here, not like this, with him watching. But my body doesn't care. Every breath I take drags his scent deeper into my lungs, my muscles clenching around nothing. I squeeze my eyes shut. Was it the air? The water? Or just him?

I swallow hard, my nails biting into my palms. I need to touch him. Need him to touch me. Need—

No.

This is ridiculous. I've never been this sexually frustrated in my life. Not even during that four-year dry spell after breaking up with my ex. Not even during the pandemic lockdowns.

It has to be this planet. The air, maybe, or something in the water. Some alien aphrodisiac that's affecting my normally very reasonable libido.

Because the alternative—that I'm genuinely, intensely attracted to Rok, who until recently didn't even have the appropriate equipment—is too bizarre to contemplate.

I curl up on my side again, squeezing my eyes shut and willing myself to sleep. "Just rest," I mutter. "Tomorrow's going to be a long day of not dying in the desert. Focus on that."

Eventually, exhaustion wins out over my racing thoughts. I guess I fall asleep because in the next moment...

—

His hands are everywhere at once—too much, not enough. Calluses scrape my ribs as his mouth hits that spot under my ear that makes my hips jerk. I'm panting before we even really start, nails digging into his shoulders hard enough that I smell copper.

"Fuck, Rok—" The words get strangled when he growls against my throat. Not some romantic purr—a real fucking growl, all vibration and teeth that I feel in *my* teeth.

His knee shoves my legs apart like he's staking a claim. No sweet nothings, just ragged breathing and the slick sound of his mouth on my skin. When his fingers dig into my thighs, I know there'll be bruises tomorrow.

I don't care.

I can feel him, all of him, pressing where I'm already soaked through. No poetry here. Just sweat and spit and the animalistic need to get closer. My heel rams into the small of his back, pulling him in hard enough to knock the air from my lungs.

"Oh fu— You're huge—" I'm not thinking in complete sentences anymore. Just heat and pressure and the single-minded drive to take everything this golden bastard can give me.

His claws catch the light as they trail down my stomach. He's holding himself back by a thread and we both know it. I can see his control fraying in the twitch of his jaw, the way his hips stutter when I rock up against him.

"Stop being so fucking careful," I snarl, biting his shoulder hard enough to taste him. Salt and something electric, like licking a battery.

His answering snarl shakes the cave walls.

—

I JOLT AWAKE, MY BODY FLUSHED AND TREMBLING, THE ECHO OF dream-pleasure still pulsing between my legs. For a moment, I'm disoriented, unsure where I am or what woke me.

Then reality crashes back—the cave, the pool, Rok...

Rok, who is watching me from across the chamber, his eyes gleaming in the darkness, his expression unreadable.

How long has he been staring? Did I make noise in my sleep? Did I say his name out loud?

The thought makes my face burn, and I quickly look away, pretending to stretch as if I've just woken from a perfectly normal, not-at-all-erotic dream about the alien sitting ten feet away.

"Morning," I say, wincing at how rough my voice sounds. "Or...whatever time it is."

The light filtering through the cracks in the ceiling has changed, growing brighter, suggesting it's early morning. Time to leave, to venture back into the desert, to face whatever dangers lie between us and my sister.

To go back to a place where there are no pools for bathing, no privacy, no barrier between me and the object of my increasingly inappropriate dreams.

And what the hell was that? That dream. I'm convinced this planet wants me to fuck him. What else could it be?

It's slowly driving me crazy. Like a hum under my skin. A literal itch only he can scratch.

Fuck.

I push myself up, running a hand through my hair, trying to gather my composure. I don't have anything to take with me on the journey to Rok's people. My handbag was useless anyway and there was nothing in it except for those two biscuits. I have nothing. And going out into a killer desert with nothing in hand sounds like suicide.

All I have is Rok.

As I move around the cave, preparing for our journey (by basically drinking as much water as my belly can hold and tying up my hair so it's not hanging on my neck), I'm acutely aware of Rok's gaze following me. There's something different about him this morning—a new focus, a clarity in his eyes that wasn't there before.

He seems to have settled, his body appearing normal—well, normal for him—the stars no longer visible beneath his skin. But there's still a change, a shift in his presence that sends a little shiver down my spine.

When I finally work up the courage to look directly at him, he meets my gaze steadily, unblinking. Then, slowly, he bares his teeth in that not-quite-smile that today manages to be even more charming than the day before.

I narrow my eyes at him. How's he getting better at that so quickly?

"Ready?" I ask, gesturing toward the cave entrance, hoping he understands the question.

He nods once, then rises to his full height. The makeshift covering around his waist has shifted during the night, and I quickly avert my eyes before I can see whether his...situation... has resolved itself.

Some questions are better left unanswered.

But then I notice him moving toward the pool, a tent still pitched before him and the small pumpkin-like object still in his hands. He crouches at the water's edge, and I see now it's not a pumpkin at all, but some kind of gourd. He dips it into the water, filling it completely, then carefully pushes the carved top back in, creating what looks like a surprisingly effective water bottle.

"Smart," I murmur, impressed despite myself.

But what he does next catches me completely off guard.

With a single motion, Rok reaches up and grasps a few strands of his hair. Before I can process what he's doing, he gives a sharp tug, pulling several long, gleaming filaments free from his scalp.

"What are you—" My eyes widen in shock.

He ignores my half-formed question, focused intently on his task. With those dexterous claws, he twists the strands around the end of the bone stick he's been using, securing them like a makeshift handle. Then he threads the bone through a hole in the gourd, creating a carrying strap.

When he's finished, he rises and approaches me, extending the water vessel with an expectant look.

I stare at it, then at him, understanding slowly dawning. He made this. For me. Spent hours carving it while I slept, and even sacrificed his own hair to make it functional.

"For me?" My voice goes embarrassingly small.

He nods once.

I reach out and take it, my fingers brushing against his in the exchange. "Thank you," I whisper, hoping he can hear the gratitude in my tone.

The air between us seems to crackle with unspoken tension as we stand barely a foot apart. As I take my new water bottle, his gaze drops to my lips, lingering there with an intensity that makes my face flush hot the moment I notice. My pulse hammers in my throat and I push it back with a swallow.

Is he going to kiss me again? Part of me—a growing, insistent part—hopes so.

He leans forward, and I unconsciously tilt my face up toward his, but instead of capturing my lips, he presses his forehead to mine in that now-familiar gesture.

"*Let us go. My clan awaits.*" The images are more vivid than before—the two of us crossing the desert, approaching a series of stone structures nestled against a cliff face, beings similar to Rok emerging to greet us.

"Oh. Of course," I breathe, trying to hide my embarrassment at where my thoughts had wandered. "Right. Going. To your clan. Got it."

I step back, clutching the gourd to my chest like it's some precious artifact rather than a practical tool. My heart is still racing, and I'm painfully aware of the blush staining my cheeks.

This is ridiculous. I'm behaving like a teenager with her first crush, not a grown woman who should be desperate to get back to her sister and off this dusty rock!

Yet as I nod my agreement and follow him toward the cave entrance, I can't shake the growing certainty that I'm in serious trouble here. As we step out into the morning light, I give myself a stern internal lecture about priorities and survival and the extreme inadvisability of interspecies romance.

But as Rok turns back to make sure I'm following, that not-quite-smile tugging at the corner of his mouth, I know it's already too late.

I am so, so screwed.

And not in the fun way. Yet.

CHAPTER 28
THIS NEW BODY: INSTRUCTIONS NOT INCLUDED

ROK

The dust stretches endlessly before us, vast and unforgiving under Ain's harsh gaze. Our journey will be long—longer than I initially planned.

I must take Jus-teen on a winding path to avoid the rival clan's territory. Their scent lingers in the air, faint but unmistakable, carried on the wind like a warning. They are restless, their movements concerning. It is as if they are searching for something—or someone.

Perhaps they sensed Jus-teen's arrival. Perhaps they simply expand their reach, emboldened by the changing cycles. The calm season is upon us. A perfect time for exploration and travel. But whatever the reason they move, we cannot risk an encounter. Not with Jus-teen so vulnerable.

Not with me in this...condition.

Everything feels different. There is a hum beneath my surface now, a ceaseless vibration that I cannot suppress. An awareness that sharpens every sense, pulls every thought toward her.

Toward Jus-teen.

I lead us in Ain's rising direction, away from the direct route to my clan's settlement. The path is harder, winding through broken stone ridges and stretches of loose sand, but it offers safety. I keep to the shadows of the ridges where Ain's light cannot reach us fully, though even here the heat is unrelenting for the female at my back.

She follows without complaint, her smaller form moving steadily behind me, though I can sense her fatigue growing with each passing solmark.

She is strong for one so small, so soft. Her resilience impresses me, even as I worry for her safety.

And yet, her presence is a torment.

The new appendages between my legs have not returned to their former state. My cock remains fully extended, pressed uncomfortably against the hide covering she fashioned for me. The sacs beneath it feel heavy, tight with some purpose I do not understand but cannot ignore.

I find myself acutely aware of her every movement.

The swing of her arms as she walks. The way her chest rises and falls with each breath. The occasional brush of her hand against mine when the terrain forces us closer together. Each point of contact sends a pulse of heat through me that settles in my stem, making it twitch with renewed interest.

It is...distracting.

During the darkness, as she rested in the cave last dark, I found myself unable to look away from her.

She had curled near the fire, her small body folded into itself like the fragile creatures that burrow beneath the dust. Her breathing was soft, steady, her lips slightly parted. Occasionally, she murmured in her rest, the sound too faint for me to distinguish but enough to make my claws flex against the stone.

Without conscious decision, my claw had wrapped around my stem. My new appendage, so unfamiliar, so sensitive, throbbed at the memory of her taste, the feel of her essence on my tongue.

At first, I moved slowly, testing the sensation, unsure of what my body demanded. The pleasure was sharp, like the sting of cold water on Ain-heated skin, but it pulled me deeper, made me grip harder.

And then the images came.

Not from my mind, but from *hers* as she slept.

Jus-teen beneath me, her soft body yielding to mine.

Jus-teen, her thighs wrapped around my waist, her head thrown back in pleasure.

Jus-teen, her hands clutching at my shoulders, her breathless voice calling my name.

The projections were vivid, unguarded, pouring into the mindspace between us like a flood. I could feel her softness, taste her on my tongue again, hear the sounds she would make as I claimed her.

My claw moved faster, gripping tighter, the pleasure building until it consumed me completely. When the release came, it was unlike anything I'd ever known—a pulse of wetness spilling over my claw, my body trembling with the force of it.

For the first time in my existence, my body wasted water, and I was too far gone to care about it.

But the relief was temporary. By dawn, the tension had returned, sharper than before, the need building like pressure in a dust geyser.

I cannot allow myself to lose control again, not while she depends on me for protection.

———

AIN IS AT HER HIGHEST WHEN I NOTICE JUS-TEEN FALTERING.

She has fallen behind me, her steps slow and uneven, her breathing labored. The red tint spreading across her exposed skin concerns me—it is the warning sign I have come to recognize as her body struggling with Ain's heat.

I stop and move back to her side, assessing her condition. The gourd is nearly empty. Even though she has already consumed what would have served me and five of my brothers for sols, I know that for her needs, she has been conserving it well. But the journey is taxing her small form more than I anticipated.

"*Rest*," I project, as I gesture to a shaded alcove beneath a nearby ridge.

She hesitates, her brow furrowing as if to argue, but when I press my forehead to hers, the thought passes between us clearly.

"*Rest. You cannot continue like this.*"

She releases a breath, her shoulders slumping in defeat. "Fine. But only for a little while."

I steady her as she moves toward the shade, my hand brushing against her arm. Even that brief contact sends a surge of heat through me, and I release her quickly, retreating a step to regain control. Her scent lingers in the air, warm and sweet, mingling with the heat of the dust, and the tension beneath my skin coils tighter as I fight the urge to touch her again, to press my forehead to hers and feel the flood of her thoughts.

She leans against the rock, her breathing slowing as her body relaxes.

We rest through the height of Ain's passage, when the dust is hottest and most treacherous. Jus-teen dozes, her back against the stone, while I keep watch for dangers. Shadow

287

stalkers rarely hunt during peak light, but small serpents emerge from their burrows to warm themselves, and rival clan scouts sometimes use this time to traverse open territory, knowing few predators will challenge them.

When Ain begins her descent, we resume our journey. Jus-teen moves more slowly now, her stride shortened. She does not complain, but I can see the toll the journey is taking on her.

By the third solmark, I make a decision.

"Jus-teen," I say, moving to stand before her. I crouch, indicating my back, then mime lifting something.

Her brows furrow in what looks like confusion, but then her expression clears.

"Oh no," she says, shaking her head. "I can walk."

Her protest is weak, unconvincing. I make the gesture again, more insistent this time, and after a moment, she relents with a small nod.

Carefully, I lift her onto my back, her arms wrapping around my neck, her legs encircling my waist. The position brings her body flush against mine, her softness pressing into my hardness in a way that makes my stem throb painfully.

I nearly stumble at the sensation, momentarily blinded by the surge of heat that courses through me. But I steady myself, focusing on the path ahead rather than the feel of her against me.

Her breath is warm against my neck, her scent surrounding me, her small fingers occasionally brushing against my skin. Each touch is a spark to the fire already burning within me.

It is both relief and torture, carrying her this way.

By the time we reach the second shelter, I am nearly crazed with need.

The constant pressure of her body against mine, the soft sounds she makes when the terrain jostles us, the heat of her skin seeping into mine—it all combines into a torment I can barely endure.

I set her down carefully at the cave entrance, forcing myself to release her even as my claws linger at her waist.

"Thank you," she says, her voice soft, paired with a small baring of her teeth that makes my chest tighten.

Once I check the interior to ensure no creatures linger there, I do a chin jerk, then gesture for her to enter the cave while I secure the area. She hesitates, glancing at me with a question in her eyes, but then complies, disappearing into the shadowed interior.

The moment she is out of sight, I lean against the stone wall, my chest heaving with the effort of restraint. My stem is painfully hard, straining against the hide covering, demanding attention I cannot give it. Not here. Not now. Not with Jus-teen so close, so vulnerable, depending on me for protection.

I force myself to focus on practical matters. Sustenance. Water. Shelter. These are the priorities, not the insistent throbbing between my legs.

With determined strides, I move away from the cave, scanning the surrounding terrain for signs of prey. It doesn't take long to spot a colony of dust crabs—small, six-legged creatures that burrow just beneath the surface of the dust. They aren't as substantial as our previous meals, but they're plentiful and easy to catch.

I harvest a dozen of them, pinning each with a quick strike of my claw before adding them to the collection. Their flesh is bitter but nutritious, and properly prepared, they will provide enough sustenance for both of us until dawn.

When I return to the cave, I find Jus-teen sitting cross-legged on the floor. She looks up as I enter, her expression brightening at the sight of food, though that hope quickly fades when she realizes what I've brought.

I settle across from her, setting my catch between us. Unlike our previous shelter, this barren cave offers no fuel for kindling. We will have to consume the dust crabs raw—a prospect I know will not please her.

She watches intently as I begin to prepare the small creatures, my claws working to remove the poisonous glands and bitter organs. Her brow furrows slightly, and I catch her glancing around the cave, perhaps searching for something to burn.

"No fire," I project, though I do not think she receives the message. I mimic creating a flame with my claws, then spread them wide—the gesture for absence among my people.

For a moment, she blinks at me and then understanding dawns in her eyes, followed by poorly concealed dismay as she looks back at the pale, glistening flesh of the dust crabs. To her credit, she doesn't recoil, merely takes a deep breath as if steeling herself for an unpleasant task.

When I offer her a portion—the best parts, with the least bitterness—she accepts it with a grateful nod, though her expression suggests she's preparing for battle rather than a meal.

Her first bite is cautious, tentative. She chews slowly, her face contorting briefly before she forces herself to swallow. But she doesn't complain, merely continues eating with determined efficiency, washing down each bite with small sips from what's left in her gourd.

I will need to carve her a better one, I think as I watch her eat. It is hard not to admire her resilience, her adaptability. She is stronger than she appears, this soft creature from beyond the dust.

But as she eats, my gaze shifts to the movement of her throat as she swallows, the way her lips press together between bites, the occasional dart of her tongue to catch a stray morsel. Each small action sends a fresh pulse of heat through me, stoking the fire that has been building all day.

I cannot continue like this. The pressure is becoming unbearable, the need too insistent to ignore. If I remain here, watching her, I fear what I might do—what primal impulse might override my reason and honor.

"*Rest*," I lean forward, touching my forehead to hers briefly before rising to my feet more abruptly than I intended.

She looks up at me, confusion clear in her expression. "Where are you going?" she vocalizes, her tone making the question clear even if I don't understand her words.

I gesture vaguely toward the cave entrance, then mimic the motion of scanning the horizon.

I don't wait for her response, striding quickly from the cave before my resolve can weaken. The cool evening air is a relief against my heated skin, but it does nothing to dampen the insistent throbbing between my thighs.

I move a short distance from the cave, just far enough that she won't hear or see me, but close enough that I can reach her quickly if danger approaches. Finding a secluded spot behind a large boulder, I lean against the cooling stone and finally allow myself to address the need that has been tormenting me all day.

With swift, decisive movements, I unfasten the hide covering, freeing my stem from its confines. It springs forth eagerly, fully extended and aching with need. The sacs beneath it feel heavier than before, tight and full of something I instinctively know must be released.

I wrap my claw around the length of it, flinching slightly at even that light touch. The sensitivity is almost painful, but the pleasure that follows the pain is immediate and intense.

As I begin to move my claw, stroking from base to tip and back again, I close my eyes and let the sensation wash over me.

Images of Jus-teen fill my mind—her perfection, her laugh, the way she looked at me when I transformed, fear and wonder mingling in her expression.

I think of her body pressed against mine as I carried her across the dust, the feel of her soft curves, the scent of her skin. I remember the taste of her essence, sweet and tangy on my tongue, and the sounds she made when pleasure overtook her.

The memory alone is enough to make my movements quicken, my breath coming in harsh pants as the pressure builds. I should feel shame for using thoughts of her this way, but I cannot bring myself to care. Not when the release is so close, so desperately needed.

When it comes, it is even more powerful than before—a surge of pleasure so intense it nearly brings me to my knees, my claw squeezing rhythmically as wetness spills over my fingers in pulsing waves. For moments afterward, I can only lean against the stone, trembling, as my body slowly calms.

The relief is immediate but incomplete. Like a thirst only partially quenched, it leaves me satisfied for the moment but aware that the need will return. And with it, the knowledge that what my body truly craves cannot be satisfied by my own touch.

I clean myself as best I can, brief guilt as I bury the moisture beneath the dust and refasten the hide covering. I make a quick circuit of our shelter to ensure no threats have approached while I was...distracted. Finding nothing concerning, I return to the cave, composed once more, ready to face Jus-teen without the overwhelming desperation that drove me away.

She looks up as I enter, her expression questioning but not suspicious. "Everything okay out there?" she asks, gesturing toward the entrance.

I nod, moving to sit across from her against the opposite

wall of the cave. The distance between us is necessary, I tell myself. Safe.

But even as I think it, I find my gaze drawn to her again and again. To the curve of her neck where it meets her shoulder. To the soft swell of her chest beneath her coverings. To her hands, small and delicate, yet capable of such strength.

This soft creature is mine to protect, I remind myself. Mine to guide safely to my clan. Nothing more.

But as she settles back against the cave wall, her eyes drifting closed in exhaustion, I cannot help but wonder if that is truly all she is to me. If that is all she can ever be.

The stars that appeared beneath my skin, the transformation of my body, the constant pull I feel toward her—surely these things mean something. Surely the ancestors would not have remade me so completely without purpose.

I watch her as she slips into sleep, her breathing deep and even, her face peaceful in the firelight. And in that moment, I make a silent vow to the ancestors, to Ain herself.

I will discover what this connection between us means. I will understand why I have been transformed. And I will honor whatever purpose the ancestors have set before me, even if it means embracing feelings I cannot yet name.

Until then, I will protect her with every breath in my body. I will guide her safely through the dust. I will reunite her with her clan and bring her into mine.

And I will control this fire within me, no matter the cost.

CHAPTER 29
PROOF THAT ALIENS HAVE EXCELLENT TASTE (IN EVERYTHING)

JUSTINE

I wake with a start, my heart pounding and my skin flushed. The dream clings to me like damned desert dust—vivid and embarrassingly real. Rok's hands were everywhere, leaving trails of lightning. I'd gasped as his claws scored my ribs, pleasure so sharp it bordered on agony. *'Mine,'* he'd snarled against my throat as my back arched, offering myself. His mouth had sealed over my nipple, sucking hard, and I'd cried out—only to wake panting...and with my fingers already buried between my thighs.

I freeze. Oh. Oh no. My clit throbs.

I've never woken up like this, fingers wet, hips grinding into my own hand. A broken sound escapes me. Another alien fantasy to add to my growing collection. What is this planet doing to me?

I press my thighs together, trying to quiet the persistent ache there, and take a deep breath to steady myself. The cave is dark, just faint starlight filtering through the narrow entrance, but something feels off. Something woke me.

A sound. Movement.

As my eyes adjust to the darkness, I make out Rok's silhouette near the cave entrance. He's pacing—three steps one way, pivot, three steps back—his movements jagged and tense. His breathing sounds labored, almost pained, and alarm shoots through me.

"Rok?" I whisper, sitting up. "Are you okay?"

He freezes at the sound of my voice, his massive form going completely still. When he turns, I can just make out the gleam of his eyes, the tight set of his jaw. His teeth are bared in what looks like a grimace of pain.

My first thought is danger—maybe something attacked him while I slept. My second thought is that he's undergoing another transformation, like the one that brought those stars beneath his skin and his new magic stick.

But as I look closer, I catch a glimpse of movement at his waist. His hand is moving rhythmically, gripping something beneath the makeshift loincloth.

Oh my god. He's masturbating. Right here in the cave while I sleep.

My brain short-circuits, embarrassment and something else—something hotter, sweeter—flooding through me. I should look away. I should absolutely, definitely look away.

I don't.

And as I watch, I realize this isn't what I thought at all. His movements aren't the smooth, practiced motion of self-plea-sure. He's gripping himself hard, almost painfully, his posture rigid with what looks like agony rather than ecstasy.

He's not masturbating—he's suffering. As I watch, he seems to lose whatever battle he's fighting with himself and collapses against the cave wall, sliding down until he's sitting, legs splayed, one hand still clutching himself so tightly I wince in sympathy.

I should look away. I should pretend to be asleep. I should do anything but stare at an alien in the throes of what appears to be the universe's worst case of blue balls.

But I can't tear my eyes away, especially when he lets out a sound—low, pained, almost a whimper—that cracks something open in my chest.

He's tormented. Genuinely suffering. And suddenly it hits me that he's been this way since his transformation—constantly aroused, with no release, no relief, not even during the brief private moment I thought he took outside the cave earlier.

For some reason, he's denying himself. Controlling himself. Even when it causes him pain.

I hesitate, torn between embarrassment and an unexpected wave of tenderness. He's not what I expected when I first saw him—this fierce, golden predator. He's thoughtful. Considerate. Protective.

When's the last time a man sacrificed his comfort for mine? Made sure I had water, food, safety? Carried me when I couldn't go on?

The answer comes quickly: never.

Something shifts inside me, a decision forming before I'm fully aware of it. Why not? Why cling to prudishness on a planet where I might die tomorrow? Why deny both of us something we clearly want?

I rise to my feet, and Rok's head snaps up at the movement. Even in the dim light, I can see him trying to straighten, to hide his state, to compose himself despite the obvious pain. His hand moves away from his groin, and he tries to adjust the loincloth to hide his predicament.

My heart cracks a little at the gesture. He's embarrassed—trying to spare me discomfort even while suffering himself.

"I thought you were a wild thing when I first saw you," I say softly, moving toward him with more confidence than I feel. "But you're more thoughtful than most men I knew back on Earth."

His head tilts slightly. That gesture I've come to recognize as confusion. Of course, he doesn't understand my words, but something in my tone or expression must communicate my meaning because his posture relaxes slightly.

The way he's looking at me now makes my breath catch. His eyes roam over me with naked hunger. As if I'm the most beautiful thing he's ever seen, despite my torn clothes, dust-caked hair, and sunburned skin.

No one has ever looked at me like that. Like I'm precious. Like I'm perfect exactly as I am.

I reach him and lower myself to my knees between his outstretched legs. He stiffens, a low growl in his throat.

"Let me help you," I say, a bit surprised my voice is actually steady. "It's okay."

I reach for the loincloth, and he tenses but doesn't stop me as I unwrap it, revealing his fully erect cock. Fuck. It's even more impressive up close—long and thick, the skin a slightly darker shade of that amber-gold, with that broader head that makes my mouth water.

I hesitate, suddenly nervous despite my bravado. What if his anatomy works differently? What if I hurt him somehow? What if—

His hand comes up to touch my face, so gently it's barely a whisper against my skin. There's no recognition of my intent in his eyes—just concern mixed with his own barely contained need. He's checking if I'm alright, even now.

"You have no idea what I'm about to do...do you."

His slightly furrowed brow makes a soft chuckle leave my lips. He tilts his head, his hand brushing against my jaw more firmly now.

With only a moment's further hesitation, I wrap my hand around his length. His reaction is immediate and dramatic—he hisses through his teeth, his head falling back against the cave wall, his entire body going taut like a bowstring.

It's the reaction of someone experiencing a completely new sensation. The realization hits me like a thunderbolt: he's never been touched like this before. This might be his first sexual experience of any kind. I don't know why that makes a pleased laugh brush through my nose.

With the cold that seeps in the night, he's hot—right now warmer than human body temperature—and harder than seems possible, yet the skin is velvet-soft. Perfect, my mind supplies. He's absolutely perfect.

I stroke him slowly, marveling at how my hand barely wraps around his girth. He responds with a full-body shudder, his hips jerking involuntarily, a sound escaping him that's half shock, half pleasure.

And then I can't help myself—I imagine how he would feel inside me, stretching me, filling me completely. The thought alone makes me clench with want.

Rok's reaction is immediate and startling. His cock pulses in my hand, and a bead of clear fluid forms at the tip—slightly golden, catching the faint light. He makes a sound that's half growl, half moan, his eyes locked on mine with such intensity a delicious shiver goes down my spine.

It's as if he knew what I was thinking. As if he could read my mind, see those dirty things I'm thinking about, and react to it. Which...isn't impossible.

That should probably concern me more than it does, but I'm too far gone to care. Encouraged by his response, I lean forward and, before I can second-guess myself, take him into my mouth.

His entire body jerks in shock, a strangled sound escaping him that's somewhere between a gasp and a roar. His hands clutch at the stone floor beside him, claws scraping against rock as if he's desperately trying to anchor himself.

The taste hits me immediately—sweet and rich, like warm honey. Nothing like a human man. It's delicious, addictive, and I find myself wanting more.

I glance up to find him staring at me with an expression of absolute wonder, as if I'm performing some kind of miracle. It dawns on me that even though he licked me, this, *me* doing this to *him*, might be completely foreign to his species. The thought sends a thrill through me—I'm introducing him to oral sex. I'm his first.

I take him deeper, working him with my hand and mouth together, finding a rhythm that has him panting and trembling beneath me. His restraint is impressive—he's holding himself back, his hands still pressed flat against the stone rather than touching me, his hips rigid as if he's afraid to move.

"You can touch me," I murmur, pulling back just long enough to say the words before taking him in again.

He doesn't understand the words, but after a moment's hesitation, one trembling hand comes up to rest lightly on my shoulder, then slides into my hair. The touch is so careful, so restrained, that it makes my heart ache. Even now, lost in what must be overwhelming sensation, he's afraid of hurting me.

It doesn't take long. Soon his breathing changes, becomes more ragged, and his cock swells impossibly larger. He makes a desperate sound, trying to pull back, to warn me of what's coming next.

I hold firm, determined to finish what I started. When he comes, it's with a force that catches me by surprise. Hot, thick pulses fill my mouth—sweet like the pre-cum, but richer, more complex. It should be strange, alien, but instead, it's the most natural thing in the world to swallow it down, to lap up every drop as his body shudders beneath me.

As the final tremors subside, I sit back on my heels, wiping my mouth with the back of my hand and feeling oddly proud of myself. Rok stares at me, his expression a mix of awe, gratitude, and complete bewilderment, as if I've just shown him a new color he never knew existed.

"Better?" I ask, a small smile tugging at my lips.

He reaches for me with hands that still tremble slightly, pulling me gently up and into his lap. His forehead presses against mine, and suddenly his thoughts are flowing into me, clear and strong but tumbling over each other in their urgency.

"*Jus-teen. What...how...never felt...beautiful Jus-teen. No words. No words.*"

The raw emotion behind the jumbled thoughts makes my chest tight. I hadn't expected such vulnerability from him, hadn't expected the wave of gratitude and wonder that accompanied his words in my mind.

"You're welcome," I murmur, relaxing against him. "Though I'm pretty sure I enjoyed that as much as you did."

I feel his confusion, then there's a low rumble that vibrates through his chest.

"*You taste like water in the desert,*" he thinks at me, the thoughts clearer now. "*Sweet. Necessary.*"

I freeze, suddenly realizing what just happened. He responded directly to what I said. To words I spoke aloud in English.

"Wait," I say, pulling back slightly to look at his face. "Can you...understand me? Not just when we're touching foreheads?"

His eyes meet mine, and he tilts his head slightly before pressing his forehead back against mine.

"*Your thoughts. They come to me. Images. Even when you speak with sound-words.*"

A shiver runs through me—equal parts wonder and alarm. "Since when? How long have you been able to understand what I'm saying?"

He tilts his head again, and I get the sense it's not as straightforward as I think. There are still kinks.

"*Since stars,*" he replies, and an image flashes between us—his skin illuminated from within, his body changing. "*Growing stronger. At first, just feelings. Now, more.*"

I can't help the laugh that escapes me. "So all this time I've been talking to myself, you were getting the gist of it? That's... actually kind of embarrassing."

There's a pause as he seems to process my words, a slight furrow appearing between his brows. Then his thoughts flow into mine again.

"*Nothing about you is small,*" he thinks at me. "*Your courage. Your kindness. Your spirit. All vast like the endless dust, but beautiful.*"

Whoa, to think I thought this dude had no semblance of communication. How dumb was I?

I can't help the laugh that escapes me. "That's a new one," I whisper. I can feel my cheeks warming. I can't even hide it. "Usually, guys just say 'you're hot' or something equally profound."

His head tilts against mine. "*You are warm, yes. But more than warm. You are...*" He struggles to find the concept, then gives up and sends me a feeling instead—a rush of wonder, desire, and protectiveness all wrapped together.

"Oh," I breathe. The intensity of it is almost overwhelming.

This... this communication is more than words could ever tell me.

We sit like that for a long moment, my body cradled against his, his thoughts gently washing over me. It should be strange—this connection, this intimacy with a being so different from myself. Instead, it feels like the most natural thing in the world.

His thoughts shift, and suddenly I'm seeing images—golden beings like him, but with subtle differences. Some taller, some broader, all with the same amber skin and fierce eyes. A settlement carved into stone cliffs. Weapons made of bone and stone. Rituals around a fire.

"*My clan,*" he explains. "*Strong warriors. Have lived in the dust since before my memory began. Will help find your clan.*"

The communication is still imperfect, thoughts fragmenting as they transfer between us, but I understand enough. These people—his people—have survived in this harsh desert for generations beyond count. And now they'll help me find Jacqui.

Eventually, I pull back slightly, suddenly aware of how tired I still am, how far we still have to travel tomorrow.

"We should sleep," I say, making a pillow gesture with my hands.

He nods, understanding, but when I move to return to my spot across the cave, his arms tighten around me.

"*Stay,*" comes the thought. "*Safer together.*"

I hesitate only briefly before nodding. "Okay. But just sleeping, right? I mean, that was fun, but I'm exhausted, and—"

He cuts off my rambling with a gentle press of his forehead to mine again. "*Rest, Jus-teen. I will guard.*"

I settle against him, his arms wrapping around me to provide a barrier between my softer body and the hard stone floor. His warmth envelops me, comforting in the cool night air of the cave.

As I drift toward sleep, a thought occurs to me that should probably terrify me but somehow doesn't.

I'm falling for an alien.

A golden-skinned, occasionally starlit alien with fangs and claws who, until recently, didn't even have the appropriate equipment for the decidedly non-platonic feelings I'm developing.

If someone had told me a week ago that this would be my life, I'd have laughed in their face. But now, curled against Rok's solid warmth, I can't imagine being anywhere else.

The universe, it seems, has a strange sense of humor. And apparently, excellent taste in cock design.

I'm almost asleep when his thought drifts into my consciousness, so soft it might be a dream.

"Daughter of Ain, sent from the sky to bring change. I will protect you till my last breath."

My eyes snap open in the darkness, my heart suddenly pounding. Daughter of whom? What exactly does he think I am?

But his breathing has deepened, his arm heavy around me, and I'm left alone with the chilling realization that the being I'm falling for may believe I'm something I'm not.

And that kind of misunderstanding could be dangerous for us both.

CHAPTER 30
THERE MUST BE SOMETHING IN THE WATER

JUSTINE

I'm dying.

Or at least, that's what it feels like as I stumble through the sand behind Rok, trying to keep my gaze fixed firmly on the horizon and not on the obscene tent in his loincloth.

It started this morning, the moment I woke up, curled against him.

I'd opened my eyes to find myself practically plastered to his chest, my thighs draped over his hips, my panties soaked through and my swollen, aching...self grinding against his massive, hard cock.

My first thought had been, *Oh my God, I'm humping him in my sleep.*

My second thought had been, *Oh my God, I'm still humping him.*

The moment I realized what I was doing, I'd scrambled off him so fast I nearly fell. Rok had stayed where he was, his jaw clenched tight, his fangs bared slightly as if in pain. And that's when I noticed the way he was holding himself—his hands gripping his thighs, his whole body rigid, his cock straining against the loincloth like it was trying to break free.

I hadn't said anything. What could I even say? Sorry I dry-humped you all night like a sleep-deprived dog in heat?

Instead, I'd muttered something about needing water and bolted for the gourd.

And now here we are, hours later, trekking through the desert while I try to ignore the fact that my panties are still damp, my skin feels like it's on fire, and every time Rok so much as glances in my direction, I feel a pulse between my legs that makes me want to scream.

It's like a fever, but not the kind that comes with chills and body aches. This is something else entirely. My skin feels too tight, like there's energy trapped beneath the surface, begging for release. My thoughts are a mess, spiraling back again and again to the way he tasted, the way he looked at me last night, the way his body had felt against mine.

I need something.

Water. Food. Anything to ease this restless, gnawing ache taking over my body. Every time I've ingested something from this planet—its water, its strange, bitter foods—it's soothed the mystery ailments that have plagued me since I woke up here. Maybe this is the same. Maybe I just need to drink or eat something to feel normal again.

But as my gaze drops to the impressive tent beneath Rok's loincloth, another thought flickers in my mind. A memory.

The taste of him. Sweet and warm, like honey—but richer. And before I can stop myself, I wonder: Does he count as part of the menu?

The moment the thought crosses my mind, a pulse of heat flares low in my belly. My thighs clench, almost causing me to stumble, a fresh wave of need making my breath hitch. I force my gaze away, ashamed of the direction my thoughts have taken, but it's too late.

The memory of his taste lingers. It's maddening, and I can't shake the idea that maybe—just maybe—what I need isn't water or food at all.

This planet is messing with me. That's the only explanation. It has to be something I ate or drank, some chemical reaction that's turning me into a horny, insatiable mess.

I take a deep breath, trying to steady myself, but it's no use. The heat, the tension, the constant ache between my legs—it's all-consuming, making it impossible to focus on anything else.

And then Rok stops.

I nearly run into him, too busy berating myself for my inappropriate thoughts to notice his sudden stillness. He sniffs the air, his nostrils flaring, and a low growl rumbles in his chest.

My heart skips a beat, and for a brief, mortifying moment, I wonder if he can smell me. The heat pooling between my thighs, the tension thrumming under my skin—can he sense it?

But then I notice the way his shoulders tense. The way he's not focused on me.

It's not me.

It's something else.

Danger.

I don't dare say a word. I don't even breathe too loudly as I watch him scan the horizon, his golden eyes narrowing to slits.

The next, his hand shoots out, grabbing my arm so tightly I nearly yelp.

"Rok—" I start, but he's already moving, tugging me forward, his pace relentless.

I stumble after him, my pulse spiking as I try to keep up with his long strides. His head is tilted slightly, his nostrils flaring as he sniffs the air. A low, guttural growl rumbles from deep in his chest, and the sound is enough to make my stomach drop.

"What is it?" I whisper, my voice barely audible.

He doesn't answer. His grip tightens on my arm, and without warning, he takes off at a dead sprint, dragging me with him.

My shoes slip and skid in the loose sand as we weave through the jagged rock formations. My heart pounds in my chest, adrenaline surging as I hear it—a sound behind us.

Like a whisper at first, soft and eerie. But then it grows louder, a low, rumbling hiss that sends a shiver down my spine.

I glance over my shoulder and nearly keel over.

The sand is moving.

It shifts and churns like a living thing, a massive wave rolling toward us like it was water and not tiny specks of rock.

"Oh my God," I breathe, my legs suddenly feeling like jelly.

Rok yanks me forward, his claws digging gently into my arm to keep me upright while forcing me to run.

I don't need to be urged twice.

We dart through the rocks, the path twisting and turning in a way that makes my head spin. The sound behind us grows louder, closer, and I can feel the vibrations in the ground beneath my feet. My breaths come hard and fast, my lungs burning, my legs screaming in protest, but I don't stop.

Rok leads me with single-minded purpose, his movements quick as he pulls me deeper into the maze of stone.

The sand wave surges higher, nearly licking at our heels. I stumble on a hidden rock, my ankle twisting, and I let out a cry of pain. Before I can even register what's happening, Rok scoops me up against his chest and continues running, his pace barely slowing under my weight.

Ahead, the rock formations grow denser, creating a natural barrier against the advancing sand. I close my eyes, praying hard that we make it. There are many ways I've imagined dying since waking up on this planet. This wasn't one of them.

Finally, the rumbling grows fainter as the rocks force the sand to split and flow around rather than through. The terror doesn't leave. Instead, it remains in my veins.

When I glance up at Rok, his gaze meets mine, and he leans in for a brief moment, pressing his forehead to mine.

"*Safe soon*," he projects into my mind.

I cling to him, watching over his shoulder as the wave of sand crashes against the rocks behind us, spraying fine particles into the air. For a moment, I think we've escaped.

Then I see it—a thin tendril of sand, weaving through the rocks like a sentient thing, following our path with unnerving precision.

"Rok," I whisper, tightening my grip on him. "It's still coming."

He doesn't look back, just increases his pace, his muscles bunching and releasing with each powerful stride. The landscape blurs around us as he races through a series of increasingly narrow passages, taking turns that seem random but must be calculated.

Finally, we reach the entrance of a cave. Rok practically shoves me inside, his massive body blocking the opening, as he turns to face the desert.

I collapse against the wall, my chest heaving as I struggle to catch my breath. My heart is pounding so hard it feels like it might burst.

Rok remains completely still, his shoulders rising and falling as he scans the sand. His claws flex at his sides, his posture tense, ready for a fight.

I watch him in silence, my mind racing.

I'd be dead without him. The thought pounds in time with my heartbeat as I press my back against the cool stone wall of the cave, struggling to catch my breath.

Not just this time—but every time.

The shadow creatures. The rival clan. The unrelenting heat of this brutal planet.

I'd be dead a dozen times over if it weren't for Rok.

I can still feel his grip on my arm, the way his claws held me firm but never hurt me as he pulled me through the labyrinth of jagged rock formations. The way his body had shielded me as that *thing* in the sand chased us, relentless and terrifying.

He saved me. Again.

And now, I watch him as he crouches at the mouth of the cave, his golden eyes scanning, his massive body coiled with tension. He looks like a warrior carved from stone, every muscle prepared to strike, his claws flexing slightly as he listens for any sign of pursuit.

I should be looking out too, but I can't tear my eyes away from him.

My heart pounds for an entirely different reason now.

The longer I watch him, the more my chest tightens, the more my breath comes faster. Gratitude swells inside me, so big and overwhelming it almost hurts. But it's not just gratitude. It's something deeper. Hotter.

He turns to face me, his sharp features softening just slightly as his gaze sweeps over me, checking for injuries.

"*Safe,*" he projects as he approaches, forehead touching mine. The word sends a shiver through me. His *touch* sends a shiver through me. My breaths are still coming fast, my chest rising and falling as I stare up at him.

He reaches for me, his hand cupping my jaw, his thumb

brushing lightly over my cheek. His touch is so careful, so gentle, it makes my chest ache.

And then I lose it.

Before I can think, before I can stop myself, I grab the back of his neck and pull him down into a kiss.

It's desperate. Raw.

I pour everything into that kiss—every ounce of fear, gratitude, and need that's been building inside me since the moment he snatched me on this godforsaken planet.

Rok freezes, his body going rigid beneath my hands. For a split second, I think I've made a mistake. But then he growls—a low, deep sound that vibrates through my chest—and kisses me back.

It's clumsy at first. His lips are rough, his movements hesitant, but the sheer hunger behind them makes my knees weak. His claws slide down to my hips, gripping me tightly, and I gasp into his mouth as he pulls me against him.

"Jus-teen." Fuck. The way he says my name. Like he's hungry. Starving. Desperate. Like he can't believe this is happening.

I pull back, gasping for air, the realization of what I've done hitting me like a freight train.

"What am I doing?" I whisper, my fingers pressing into his chest as I keep myself back.

But he's looking at me with those golden eyes, so full of wonder and longing, and I can't stop myself.

Before I can think too hard about it, I throw myself against him again, kissing him harder this time.

This time, he doesn't hesitate.

His hands slide down to my thighs, lifting me off the ground as he presses me back against the cave wall. The heat of his body is overwhelming, his scent surrounding me—earthy, metallic, and entirely him.

When he pulls back, his gaze is dark, his lips parted as he struggles to catch his breath.

"Jus-teen," he rasps.

I reach for him, sliding my hands down the hard planes of his chest to the knot holding his loincloth in place.

"Let me," I whisper, my fingers trembling as I untie it.

Rok is forced to set me down as the cloth falls away, and my breath hitches.

He's so fucking perfect. Thick and long, the darker color of his shaft deepening slightly around the broad head.

He shifts under my gaze, his claws flexing against me. When he leans in, forehead against mine, a rush of images greets me so intensely that my knees almost buckle. Images of me and him.

Images of me underneath him.

Writhing. Pulsing. Needy.

There is no doubt what he wants to do right now. And no doubt I'm too weak to resist it.

"*Is...good?*" he projects.

I let out a shaky laugh, the sound catching in my throat. "Good doesn't even begin to cover it," I murmur, reaching out to wrap my hand around him.

Rok's entire body jerks at the contact, his head falling back as a strangled growl escapes his throat. His hands fly to the stone walls of the cave, claws flexing as he braces himself against the sensation.

"Jus-teen," he groans, drawing out my name like it's the only word he's ever known. Just hearing him like that—his voice low and guttural, tinged with desperation—sends a thrill racing through me.

I watch him carefully as I stroke him, my fingers sliding up and down his length. Every touch seems to unravel him. His hips jerk slightly, as if his body is moving on instinct, and his breath comes in ragged gasps, his chest heaving.

God, he's beautiful. The perfect build, the strength in those arms, those legs, every muscle taut and trembling as he struggles to hold himself together.

But it's not just his body that makes my heart race—it's the way he looks at me. Like I'm something fragile and precious, something he's afraid to touch but can't bear to stay away from.

He's so careful, so hesitant, and the realization starts to creep in—the way his hands have never wandered too far, the way he's frozen when I've kissed him, the way he's looking at me now, like he's never done this before.

My hand pauses on his length, and I meet his gaze, my heart pounding.

"Oh my God," I whisper, my voice barely audible. "You're a virgin, aren't you?"

Rok's eyes are heavy-lidded, as if he's in a dream. But he focuses on me. I don't think he understands what I asked.

I close my eyes, focusing, and bring images to my mind. Images of him, alone. The absence of women in his memories. The way he's looked at me, touched me, like I'm something new and entirely unknown.

He leans in, pressing his forehead to mine, and I see it—another fleeting glimpse into his world. His clan, all males. Their harsh, barren home. The constant battles for survival, the brutal hunts, the unrelenting heat of the desert.

There are no women. No softness. No love.

"Jus-teen," he rasps, his breath warm on my face. "*First. You...only.*"

His words steal the breath from my lungs.

First. Only.

The gravity of it sinks in. I'm the first woman he's ever touched, ever been close to.

For a moment, I don't know how to respond. But then a possessiveness I've never felt before suddenly flares to life inside my chest. I want to claim him, to teach him, to show him everything. *I* want to.

I release him, my hands trembling as they reach up to cup his face. He leans into my touch, his eyes never leaving mine, and I see the wonder there—the awe, the hunger, the need.

"I need to show you something," I say softly, pushing the thought toward him. His brow furrows in concentration as he tries to understand, but I can feel his eagerness, his excitement.

Taking his hand, I guide it to my chest, pressing his palm against my breast. "This," I murmur, "is a woman's body. My body." I guide his fingers down, tracing the curve of my waist, the flare of my hip. His eyes darken, his breath growing ragged as he watches his hand moving over me.

"And this," I whisper, trailing his hand even lower, until his fingers brush against the fabric of my panties. I guide his fingers beneath the hem, pressing them against my wetness. "This is my pussy."

A strangled growl escapes his throat, his fingers flexing involuntarily as he feels the heat of me. His eyes lock with mine, a question burning in them. I nod, giving him silent permission to explore.

His fingers delve deeper, parting my folds with a tentative touch that sends shivers down my spine. He's clumsy at first, his movements uncertain, but the raw hunger in his eyes is unmistakable. He wants this. Wants me.

I guide his thumb to my clit, showing him the sensitive bundle of nerves that sends sparks through my body when touched. His eyes seem to glow as he feels the reaction, a low vibration in his chest as he starts rubbing in slow circles.

"Wah-ter," he groans, his forehead pressed against mine. The images in his mind are a whirlwind—flashes of my body, my face, the feelings coursing through him. It's overwhelming. Intense.

He lifts me again, bracing me against the stone as I reach for him, wrapping my hand around his length, stroking him in time with the movements of his fingers. He growls, his hips bucking into my touch, his breath coming in ragged gasps.

"I want you inside me," I whisper, guiding the head of his cock to my entrance. His eyes flick up to mine, a mix of fear and anticipation swirling in their golden depths.

His forehead presses to mine, and I shove the images at him—*his hips snapping into me, my nails raking his back, the obscene stretch of him filling me completely.*

The second he understands, he *moves.*

No gentle easing in. One hand fists in my hair, tilting my head back as he drives into me with a single brutal thrust. The stretch burns—*fuck*, he's *huge*—and I scream, my spine arching off the stone. Claws dig into my thighs hard enough to draw blood, but I don't give a shit because yes, *yes*, finally—

Rok freezes. His whole body locks up like he's been speared, muscles trembling.

"Jus-teen." His voice is shredded, rough like he's been screaming. His pupils are blown black, but he's holding himself still, even though I can feel him twitching inside me. "*Hurts?*"

I choke out a laugh. "Yes. *No.* Don't stop."

When I clench around him, his snarl shakes the cave walls.

His jaw clenches, his muscles taut as he holds himself still, every inch of him trembling beneath my touch. He's fighting himself, barely holding back, and the sight of him—this massive, powerful warrior brought to the edge by me—is enough to make my core clench around him.

He groans, his head falling forward to rest against my shoulder, his breath hot against my neck. His teeth graze the tender skin there, and my eyes roll over as I groan.

My nails drag down his back as I shift slightly, adjusting to his size. The movement sends a jolt of pleasure through me, and I gasp, my hips instinctively rocking against him.

"Move," I whisper, my voice trembling. "Rok, please. I need you to move."

He growls again, his hands tightening on my hips as he pulls back slowly, the thick length of him dragging against my inner walls in a way that makes my toes curl. And then he thrusts back in, harder this time, and the force of it knocks the breath from my lungs.

"Jus-teen," he groans, his voice desperate as he starts moving, his hips rolling in a slow, earth-shattering rhythm. Each thrust is deep, powerful, pulling me apart and putting me back together again.

His forehead is against mine again, our breaths mingling as his golden eyes burn into me, full of awe and hunger and something deeper—something that shatters everything I thought I knew.

"*You feel...perfect.*" His lips brush against mine. "*You **are** perfect.*"

I shudder at his words, my body tightening around him as pleasure coils low in my belly. "No, *you're* perfect," I whisper back.

His hands slide down to my thighs, gripping them tightly as he lifts me higher against the wall. The new angle has him hitting deeper, harder, and I cry out, my head falling back as my legs tighten around his waist.

"Rok," I gasp, my voice a broken plea.

He growls low in his throat, his hips snapping harder now, his rhythm growing more urgent. His claws dig lightly into the soft flesh of my thighs, and the slight sting only heightens the pleasure coursing through me.

"*You're...mine.*" His golden eyes blaze as they lock onto mine. "*My Jus-teen. **My** female.*"

I should tell him absolutely not. That there's no way this would work out between us. But the words don't come. Instead, all that leaves my lips, my thoughts, is a broken, surrendering, "Yes."

The word seems to snap something inside him. He lifts me higher, his hands gripping my ass as he pulls me away from the wall, holding me in the air like I weigh nothing. He thrusts up into me, deeper than before, and I scream his name, my nails digging into him.

"*Feel you.*" Even in his thoughts, his voice is tight with desperation. "*So good. So...wet.*"

I can't think, can't breathe, can't do anything but hold on as he fucks me, his pace relentless now. Each thrust sends shockwaves of pleasure through me, and I can feel the tension coiling tighter and tighter in my belly, ready to snap.

I don't think it will happen. Unfortunately, I've never been one of those girls who could come with only penetration. But this is different. Rok is different. And his cock. It really is like it was made just for me.

"Rok," I gasp, my voice breaking. "I'm gonna—I'm—"

My orgasm crashes over me and I scream his name as my body tightens around him, gripping him like a vice. Pleasure pulses through me in wave after wave, leaving me trembling in his arms.

Rok groans, his thrusts growing erratic. His golden eyes lock onto mine, his gaze blazing with intensity. "*Mine.*"

"Yes," I gasp, my voice barely audible. "Yours."

He grunts, his head falling back as his body tenses beneath me. I feel him throb inside me, his cock pulsing as he comes, filling me with his release. The sensation is overwhelming, and a delicious shiver runs through me as I pant, gasping as I cling to him.

For a long moment, neither of us moves. Our breaths mingle in the quiet of the cave, our bodies trembling as the aftershocks of pleasure roll through us. His forehead presses against mine again, his golden eyes softening as they meet mine.

"You...are a miracle."

I smile, my heart swelling at the possessiveness in his tone. I cup his face, brushing my thumb over his jaw. And as I rest my head against his chest, his strong arms still wrapped around me, I know one thing is certain. There's no turning back from this. Not now. Not ever.

CHAPTER 31
WHAT JUST HAPPENED? (AND CAN WE DO IT AGAIN?)

ROK

The universe has shifted.

In all my cycles, I have hunted the great beasts of the dust. I have fought rival clans and survived the black winds. I have shed blood and suffered wounds that would have killed lesser beings. But nothing—nothing—has prepared me for this.

For her.

I watch her now as she sleeps, curled on the smooth stones of the dust stalker's abandoned nest. Her breathing is soft, her face peaceful in a way it rarely is when she's awake. The fire I've built casts golden light across her skin, highlighting the strange paleness that first made me think she was something other than flesh.

My Jus-teen.

My female.

The claiming still pulses through my blood, a satisfaction

so deep it feels carved into my bones. The memory of being inside her makes my stem harden yet again, an urgency I never knew before she fell from the sky.

When I first coupled with her against the cave wall, it was like the universe clicked into place. Like every breath before had been shallow, and suddenly I could fill my lungs completely. Her body welcomed mine, tight and wet and perfect, as if the great Ain had crafted her specifically for me.

She'd taken me again after we rested, guiding me to taste the sweet water between her legs. The sounds she made—soft cries that built to desperate screams—are branded in my memory. And when she'd mounted me afterward, her soft body sliding down over my hardness, her watery eyes locked with mine...I'd nearly lost myself completely.

I shift closer to the fire, adding more fuel to keep her warm. She shivers even in sleep, her small form vulnerable to the cold of the cave. My Jus-teen is delicate in ways I never expected. Strong in spirit but fragile in body. She needs protection. Nourishment. Warmth.

She needs me.

The possessiveness that floods through me is like nothing I've ever felt. Mine to protect. Mine to feed. Mine to please. The thought of her living with me in the clan cave shoots through my mind, and my chest rumbles with satisfaction.

My clan will welcome her—a blessing from the sky, a gift from Ain herself. They will see her value, just as I have. They will help me protect her and find the others of her kind.

I have already gathered water while she slept, filling the gourd from a small spring deeper in the cave system. And now I will hunt. My female needs meat to strengthen her, especially after our coupling.

I touch her face gently, careful not to wake her with my

claws, and ease away toward the cave entrance. I slip out into the twilight, my vision sharpening as I adjust to the dimness. The pesky dust serpent that had been after us is now gone, leaving the sands peacefully still.

The hunt is quick. A rock-jumper has made its burrow nearby, foolishly close to the cave. I catch it easily, snapping its neck with one clean motion. It's not much—barely a mouthful for a warrior of my size—but it will nourish my Jus-teen.

When I return, she's still sleeping. I set about preparing the meat, using my claw to skin and clean it before spearing it on a sharpened rock to warm over the fire. Because my female likes her food this way. So I will do it for her. The scent fills the small chamber as I turn the meat, and Jus-teen stirs, her eyelids fluttering. When she opens them fully, her gaze finds mine immediately, and the smile that spreads across her face makes my chest tighten in the strangest way.

"You made food," she says, her soft voice still heavy with sleep. She sits up, drawing her legs beneath her, and I notice her wince slightly.

I move to her side immediately, concern flooding through me. *"Hurt?"* I push through mindspeak. I reach for her, my hand hovering over her thigh, uncertain where the pain is.

Her cheeks darken in that fascinating way, and she shakes her head. "I'm fine, just a little sore. From, um, you know." She glances down at my stem, which responds immediately to her attention, hardening once more.

If she will have me, I will sink deep inside her once more. But not before she has eaten.

Her eyes widen, and she laughs—a sound that makes my blood heat. "Already? Seriously?"

I don't understand her words, but the images flashing through her mind are clear enough. She's thinking of our coupling, of my size inside her, of the slight discomfort and overwhelming pleasure.

My stem jerks at the intensity of those thoughts.

"*For you*," I project, gesturing to the roasting creature. "*Eat. Strength.*"

She shifts toward the fire, reaching for the gourd of water I've placed nearby. "Thank you." She drinks deeply, then turns her attention to the meat. "This smells amazing. I'm starving."

I watch with satisfaction as she tears into the meat, making small sounds of pleasure that have my stem twitching beneath my hide coverings. Loincloth, that is what she calls it, though I do not know why she wants me to hide myself. She seems quite happy when it is on display and I would rather she not hide herself, either. I would put all these hide coverings into the fire to burn, but I do not.

This is a gift from my female. I will treasure it forever.

She eats with an appetite that pleases me, licking the juices from her fingers in a way that makes me want to claim her again immediately.

"This is so good," she says between bites. She pauses, looking up at me with her head tilted in that way I've come to recognize means she's curious about something. "Do you want some?"

I shake my head. "*For you*," I project. "*I hunt more later.*"

She smiles at me, and then her expression shifts to something more mischievous. "Thank God you don't understand everything I say or you'd know I'm thinking about jumping your bones again."

I can't suppress the grunt of laughter that escapes me. The image in her mind is clear—her body pressed against mine, her mouth on my stem, her legs wrapped around my waist as I thrust into her.

Her eyes widen, the meat forgotten in her hand. "Wait. Did you just...understand what I said?"

"*Yes*," I reply, both with my voice and my thoughts. And then, in the old tongue: "*I see your thoughts. Clear. Like when we touch heads, but...no touching needed now.*"

"*Stop eavesdropping on my thoughts*," she projects, her mental voice stronger than her spoken one.

"*I am not dropping anything*," I respond.

She freezes, blinking rapidly. "Say that again. I mean, *think* it again."

"*I am not dropping anything*," I repeat in my mind, focusing on sending the thought clearly to her.

"Holy shit," she whispers, setting the meat aside. "We can hear each other now? Without touching foreheads?"

She is right. I'd been too caught up in the aftermath of her glow that it did not fully occur to me.

I nod, though I cannot hide the disappointment. "*I enjoyed being close.*" The words echo in the mindspace. "*Looking into your water-eyes when we share thoughts.*"

Her expression softens, and she moves toward me, the meat forgotten as she climbs into my lap, her legs straddling mine. The position brings her core directly against my hard stem, and I grip her hips to steady her.

"We can still be close," she whispers, leaning forward to press her lips to mine. The water sharing is slow, deep, a claiming of her own. Her hands frame my face, her thumbs tracing the angles of my jaw with a tenderness that makes heat pool low in my gut.

"This is madness," she whispers against my mouth. "What if I'm imagining all this?"

I grunt. "*I am real.*"

"But you're reading my thoughts. And this planet. Everything about it. Everything about you. And your *cock*. It's like..."

"*It is real, too.*" My hands tighten on her hips, keeping her anchored to me as I slide my hips upward, rubbing her along my length. "*As real as the pain I feel whenever you are not near. As if part of me is missing.*"

She blinks. "Pain?"

My gaze searches hers. "*I cannot be far from you, my light. It is impossible for me.*"

Her throat moves, and I see confusion in her eyes. I sense it in her mind.

"Last night…" she whispers.

I pull back just enough to meet her gaze, my hands sliding up her sides to cup her small, perfect mounds through the thin fabric of her top. "*You showed me the universe,*" I finish for her, "*and now I will show you mine.*"

Her eyes darken, her lips parting as her breath quickens. The scent of her arousal fills my nostrils, and it's driving me to near madness.

"How soon will we reach your clan?" she asks, even as her hips continue their maddening rhythm against me. "Are you sure they'll help the others? There are many of us."

"*Many daughters of Ain,*" I agree, my hands moving to the band of her strange coverings. I want to feel her skin, all of it, pressed against mine.

She goes still beneath my touch, a strange tension entering her body. Before I know what I did wrong, she looks away, her thoughts suddenly guarded.

"*My clan will do anything to keep such treasures safe,*" I continue, confused by her reaction. I pull at the thin fabric, revealing more of her pale skin to my hungry gaze. "*You are precious to us. To **me**.*"

She shifts off my lap, turning her back to me as she pulls her coverings back into place. Her shoulders slump, and I sense a heaviness in her that wasn't there before.

I approach her carefully, uncertain what has changed. Have I offended her somehow? Misunderstood a signal? The intricacies of female behavior are unknown to me.

When she turns to face me, there is water in her eyes. Alarm shoots through me. She's leaking again, as she did when she told me of her missing kin.

"*Jus-teen?*" I reach for her, my hand hovering uncertainly. "*Why leak water? Pain?*"

"It's normal," she vocalizes, wiping at her eyes. "They're called tears. It happens when we're sad or scared or...overwhelmed."

I cup her face gently, my thumb trying to rub the tear back into her skin. I do not like seeing her body waste water so. Even after so many times, it is alarming. "*What makes you sad? Tell me, and I will fix it.*"

She laughs, but the sound is hollow, lacking the warmth I've come to crave. "You can't fix this, Rok. Because you think I'm something I'm not."

I tilt my head, confused. "*What do you mean?*"

"This planet is filled with danger," she vocalizes, her voice quiet but steady. "If you're going to risk your life to take me to my sister, you should at least know the truth." She takes a deep breath, her hands coming up to rest against my chest. "I'm not a daughter of Ain."

I am still as I wait for her to explain. Not a daughter of Ain? But she fell from Ain and she is unlike any being I have ever encountered.

Soft. To be worshipped. Just like the beings in those stories of old. The daughters we Drakav cherished.

"*I don't...understand.*"

She sighs, moving away to settle near the fire again. "I don't even know who Ain is, Rok. I'm just...a human woman." Human? I blink, still struggling to understand. I have never heard of such a tribe or clan before. "I'm from a planet called Earth. I was on a bus—I guess it was a ship—and something went wrong. We crashed here. I'm not special or magical or whatever you think I am. I'm just lost."

Lost?

No.

She is exactly where she is supposed to be. I know this with every fiber of my being.

I watch her, studying the way the firelight plays across her features. Her strange, rounded ears. Her oddly colored eyes, the soft curve of her mouth. Everything about her is foreign, yes, but also...right. Perfect.

"*Ain,*" I begin, trying to explain what every youngling in my clan learns from their first conscious moments. "*Ain is creator of the dust and sky. Ain is the light that gives us all life. And you...you fell from her. A daughter—*"

She shakes her head. "I'm not some special mythical being, Rok. I'm as confused and scared as anyone would be, waking up on a strange planet."

"*But you are,*" I insist, moving closer to her. "*If not, I would have made the mistake of killing you in the dust. You are mine now. And I am yours. Entangled. Forever.*"

Her brow furrows. "What?"

"*I cannot exist without you,*" I explain, touching her arm gently. "*Being away brings pain.*"

She stares at me, her expression unreadable. "That's impossible."

I take her hand, turning it over in my claw. "*This...you...are not like my people. There is something in you, Jus-teen, that is not of the dust. But if you did not come...my existence would have meant nothing.*"

"Rok..." she begins, but trails off, uncertainty clear in her voice.

"It does not matter what you call yourself," I shift, pulling her against my chest. *"Daughter of Ain or human female. You are Jus-teen. My Jus-teen."* I press my forehead to hers, wanting her to feel the truth in my thoughts. *"And I will protect you. Find your kin. Keep you safe."*

Her thoughts finally open to me again. A tangled web of confusion, fear, and something else—something that makes my chest warm. She's afraid I'll reject her now that I know she's not what I thought. She's afraid I'll abandon her in this hostile world.

"Never." I push the thought hard. *"You are mine now. Nothing changes that."*

I feel the moment the tension leaves her body, the way she melts against me, her arms coming up to wrap around my neck.

"I don't know what's happening to me," she whispers against my skin. "I don't understand any of this. But I know I need you. And that scares me more than anything on this planet."

I cradle her against me, my hand stroking down her back. *"Fear is wise in the dust,"* I tell her. *"Fear keeps you alive. But fear of me?"* I shake my head. *"This you do not need. I would die before I let harm come to you."*

She pulls back just enough to look into my eyes, her hands framing my face. "That's exactly what scares me," she whispers. "How much I already care about you. How much I don't want anything to happen to you."

The admission sends a rush of warmth through my chest. She cares for me. This strange, beautiful creature cares for me.

"We will be careful," I promise her. *"We will reach my clan safely. Find your others. All will be well."*

She nods, but I can sense she doesn't fully believe me.

There's something else she's not telling me, some fear she's holding back.

"*What else troubles you?*" I ask, brushing her strange, soft fur back from her face.

She hesitates, her lower lip caught between her teeth. "What if...what if your clan doesn't believe I'm just a human? What if they think I'm this daughter of Ain? What will they expect from me?"

I consider this, knowing the reverence with which my people view the tale. "*They will be curious,*" I admit. "*They will want to see your light, hear your knowledge. But they will not harm you.*"

"And when they realize I don't have any special knowledge or powers? When I can't do whatever it is they expect from a daughter of Ain?"

I stroke her cheek, marveling at its softness. "*We expect nothing from the daughters. Nothing but their favor. When I bring you to my clan, they will see you as I do. As Jus-teen. Strong. Beautiful. Worthy of protection.*"

She leans into my touch, her eyes closing briefly. "I hope you're right."

"*I am right,*" I assure her, pulling her close again. "*Rok is never wrong, unless Jus-teen says he is.*"

A chuckle goes through her, her body relaxing as I settle us both by the fire. I pull her into my lap, wrapping my arms around her to shield her from the chill of the cave.

As she drifts toward sleep, her thoughts growing fuzzy and disjointed, I allow myself to consider what she's told me. Not a daughter of Ain, she claims. Just a human female, lost and far from home.

And yet...I've felt the change in myself since finding her—the way my body has transformed, my thoughts have clarified, my stem has grown. These are not coincidences.

The stories speak of the wonder of the daughters of Ain. Their power. Their glory. Perhaps these beings, these humans, carry Ain's blessing without understanding it themselves.

I press my lips to her head fur, breathing in her unique scent. It doesn't matter what she calls herself. Daughter of Ain. Human. She is mine to protect now. Mine to cherish. And I will bring her safely to my clan, find her people, and ensure she never has reason to fear again.

CHAPTER 32
MY SUBCONSCIOUS: WAY AHEAD OF ME

JUSTINE

The revelation that I can now understand Rok without our foreheads touching is still spinning in my head. His voice had been like an actual caress—rough, deep, vibrating in places no sound should reach. Even thinking about it makes my clit jump, forcing me to stifle a gasp.

Can he—? Does he *know*?

My gaze shifts to him as we prepare to leave, only to find he's gone utterly still. My gaze slides down the taut muscles in his arms, the strong line of cords in his back. A fresh wave of heat floods through me.

Fuck.

This isn't lust. This is possession. And my traitorous body *welcomes* it.

I force myself to focus on preparing to leave the cave and not the humming in my veins. After two days of hiding out, the danger has apparently passed.

"*The sand serpent has moved on,*" Rok assures me, his thoughts flowing into mine with surprising clarity. "*We should continue our journey.*"

"It's still wild to me that I can hear you like this," I say, adjusting my pack. "No touchy-touchy required. Is that always how it works for your kind? Get intimate and suddenly you're in each other's heads?"

He gives me that now-familiar head tilt. "*Touchy...touchy?*"

"Never mind." I laugh, fighting the urge to press myself against him again. "Let's go."

As we exit the cave, I'm struck by a thought that's been nagging at me. The timing of this newfound telepathy isn't a coincidence. It's like the connection became complete after we...well, connected. After I took him into my body. After I swallowed—

Heat rushes to my cheeks at the memory, but I can't shake the suspicion. What if having sex with Rok is what triggered this? What if the wet dreams, the fever, the constant arousal— what if all of it was pushing me toward exactly what happened in that cave?

Like the universe, or the planet itself, wanted me to get on with it already.

And the moment I did—boom. Telepathy.

If I'd known alien sex came with superpowers, I would have signed up for NASA years ago.

What's more disturbing is how good I feel now. The fever that plagued me, gone. The headache? Gone. I feel stronger, clearer, more alert than I have since waking up on this dust ball. Like his touch has somehow changed me from the inside out, making me more adapted to this world. Making me more like him, perhaps.

But that's preposterous. Right?

Rok leads the way through the winding canyon, his powerful body moving with effortless grace. I follow, surprised to find that I'm keeping pace without struggling. Just days ago, I could barely walk an hour without needing to rest, my lungs burning, my limbs shaking with exhaustion.

But now? I feel like I could run a marathon. Well, maybe not a marathon, but definitely more than I should be capable of after nearly dying multiple times on this planet.

"*You are quiet,*" Rok's thought brushes against my mind. "*This is not like you. Does something trouble you?*"

"I'm just thinking about how weird all this is," I reply, gesturing vaguely between us. "This mind-reading thing. The fact that I'm suddenly feeling better than I have since I got here."

He glances back at me, his golden eyes assessing. "*Your body is adapting to the dust.*"

"Yeah, but why now? And why so suddenly?" I push my hair back from my face, frustrated. "It doesn't make sense."

Rok slows, falling into step beside me. "*Some things do not need to make sense, Jus-teen. They simply are.*"

"That's a very...alien way of looking at it," I mutter.

He tilts his head. "*Alien zen?*" The thought comes to me haltingly, like he's turning it over in his own head.

I snort. "No, just—wait, how do you even know the word 'zen'?"

His nostrils flare slightly. "*You thought it at me. With images.*" A pause. "*Small man with fur obscuring his mouth. Strange sitting pose.*" His claws flex. "*Why does he not fall over?*"

"Mother of—, you're literally inside my head watching my mental reruns of Kung Fu Panda?" My face burns. "Forget I said anything."

His amusement ripples through me anyway, warm as the

sunlight. After a few moments, he glances at me. *"Perhaps you are right, my light. Or perhaps you think too much."*

"Story of my life," I sigh, but I'm biting back a grin.

As we walk, I can't help but notice the way Rok positions himself—always slightly ahead of me, his massive body between me and any potential threat. He scans the landscape constantly, nostrils flaring as he scents the air, ears twitching at the slightest sound.

At first, I thought it was just caution—the same way he's been since he found me. But there's something different now. Something in the way his eyes track back to me every few seconds, as if he physically can't go too long without confirming I'm still there. The way he shifts his body whenever I move, maintaining a perfect shield between me and the open desert.

It reminds me of documentaries I've watched about certain animals after they mate—wolves, eagles, some big cats. The way they change, become attuned to their partners on a level that goes beyond simple attraction.

I remember what he said in the cave: *"As real as the pain I feel whenever you are not near. As if part of me is missing."* At the time, I thought it was just a romantic exaggeration. But what if it wasn't?

Rok isn't human. He's something else entirely—wild, beautiful, deadly. An alien creature with instincts and biology I can barely comprehend.

What if he's...what if he's imprinted on me?

He said he'd have killed me, but something stopped him.

A shiver goes down my spine at the thought that I came so close to dying and didn't even know.

And then there's the fact that his dick emerged, thick and perfect, just the way I like it.

Oh my God…this can't be real.

He turns at that moment, catching my gaze, and something in his golden eyes makes my breath stop in my throat. The intensity there…it's devotion. Something ancient and unshakeable.

"What?" I ask, feeling strangely vulnerable under that stare.

"*You are beautiful under Ain's glare,*" he replies simply, and the sincerity in his mental voice makes my heart flip.

Before I can respond, his entire demeanor suddenly changes. His head snaps up, nostrils flaring, muscles tensing. I freeze, recognizing the signs of danger.

"What is it?" I push through my thoughts as I scan the terrain for threats. "Rival clan again?"

Rok doesn't answer. His eyes narrow, focusing on something in the distance that I can't make out.

"Rok?" I reach for him, but he moves away, stepping in front of me, his posture shifting to something more aggressive.

"*Stay behind me,*" he growls in my mind.

I peer around his massive frame, trying to see what's got him so alarmed. The landscape appears empty—just rock formations and endless sand stretching toward the horizon.

And then I see it. Movement. Just a flicker at first, then a blur of motion so fast I can barely track it—a golden shape launching from a high rock, sailing through the air with impossible speed.

Before I can even cry out, the figure slams into Rok with bone-crushing force, sending them both crashing to the sand in a tangle of limbs and snarls.

"Rok!" I scream, my heart in my throat as I stumble backward.

The two forms roll across the ground, dust flying up

around them as they grapple. I catch glimpses of the attacker —golden skin like Rok's, but darker, more burnished. Broader shoulders. Longer, sharper fangs bared in a snarl.

Another male. One of Rok's kind, but clearly not friendly.

Panic surges through me. Is it one of the rival clan? Did they track us after all? I have to help him—but how? I have no weapons, no strength that could possibly match these beings.

My hands fumble, but all I'm carrying is my gourd of water. Not much of a weapon, but it's all I have.

I don't think. I just act.

Rushing forward, I raise the gourd high and bring it down with all my strength on the attacker's head. The container splits open with a crack, water splashing over the male's face and shoulders.

He freezes, shock evident in his suddenly wide eyes. His head swivels toward me, water dripping from his jaw, and a voice—not Rok's, deeper, rougher—thunders in my mind.

"WHAT IN THE NAME OF THE DUST?!"

The sheer force of his mental shout makes me stagger back. His amber eyes lock onto mine, rage and confusion warring in their depths.

*"Another male? You bring a rival male into our territory, Rok? One who **wastes precious water?**"* The voice in my head is accusing, furious.

Before I can process what's happening, the stranger lunges for me, a growl ripping from his throat. I flinch, throwing my arms up in a pathetic attempt to shield myself—but the impact never comes.

Rok slams into the attacker mid-leap, driving him into the ground with enough force to send sand spraying in all directions.

"SHE IS FEMALE!" Rok's mental shout is even louder than

the stranger's, filled with fury and...fear? *"STAND DOWN, THARN!"*

The name registers dimly in my panicked brain. Tharn. Not an enemy, then—at least, not from the rival clan. Someone Rok knows.

The two males separate, both crouched low, tense and ready to spring. I stay frozen, heart hammering against my ribs.

*"**Fe**-male?"* Tharn's mental voice is incredulous, his amber eyes narrowing as they sweep over me. *"That is not female."*

"She is," Rok insists, moving to stand between me and Tharn. *"From beyond the dust. A being from beyond."*

Tharn's eyes widen slightly, his attention fully on me now. I shift uncomfortably under his scrutiny, wishing I could somehow look more obviously female to avoid another battle.

But then Tharn's gaze suddenly shifts to Rok.

"What in the dust is on your being?" He asks suddenly, his gaze dropping to Rok's waist. *"You wear hides as trophies now?"*

I follow his gaze and have to stifle an inappropriate laugh. He's staring at Rok's loincloth—the one I fashioned for him after his...anatomical changes.

"It is not a trophy," Rok replies, his mental tone defensive. *"My female made it to cover my stem."*

*"**Your** female?"* Tharn snarls, his fangs looking decisively wicked. But then his face contorts in disbelief. *"**Lies**. Why would you need to do that? Your stem is always in your pouch."*

To my absolute horror—and secret fascination—Rok reaches down and grips himself through the loincloth, the shape of his impressive erection clearly outlined by the gesture.

"No," he says calmly. *"Not anymore."*

Tharn physically recoils, shock evident in every line of his body. His gaze darts between Rok's loincloth and my face, his expression a mix of disbelief and growing curiosity.

"*Let me see the male,*" he demands, trying to circle around Rok to get a better look at me.

Rok moves with him, keeping me firmly behind his bulk. "*Fe-male,*" he corrects. A growl rumbles low in his throat.

"*Impossible,*" Tharn scoffs.

"*Possible,*" Rok counters.

There's a long pause, the tension between them almost palpable. Then Tharn's mental voice comes again, quieter but no less intense.

"*A daughter of Ain?*"

Rok doesn't answer, but I feel a ripple of unease from him. The silence stretches. I could cut the tension with a steak knife.

I can't take it anymore. Ducking under Rok's arm, I step out from behind him, ignoring his growl of warning.

Tharn stares at me, his amber eyes widening a fraction. Up close, I can see the differences between him and Rok more clearly. He's bulkier, his features more angular, his skin a deeper golden bronze with patterns of darker markings across his shoulders.

Remembering how Rok had initially reacted to my voice, I decide to try this telepathy thing first. I focus on projecting my thoughts directly to Tharn, hoping he can hear me as clearly as Rok now can.

"I am female," I think firmly. "We...landed here. Rok helped me. He is no liar. I owe him my life."

Tharn's eyes narrow, his head tilting in a gesture so similar to Rok's that it makes my chest tighten with an unexpected wave of fondness.

"You claim to be female, yet look as a male does," he thinks back, his mental voice laced with skepticism. "Only smaller... softer..." His brow furrows, and I can almost see the confusion and disbelief warring with his stubbornness to not believe. "Why would Rok risk himself for an outsider? This does not make sense."

"Trust me," I respond dryly, "where I'm from, I'm definitely female. Though this is the first planet where my lack of curves has been mistaken for a different species rather than just bad genetics."

Tharn's gaze flicks to Rok, who stands tense beside me, ready to intervene at the slightest provocation.

"You claim this one is female?" Tharn asks Rok directly. "This small, pale thing?"

"I do not claim," Rok growls. "She is."

Tharn circles me slowly, his movements predatory. I stand my ground, refusing to show fear even as my heart races.

"She barely reaches my *chest*," Tharn observes. "The daughters of Ain were said to be like gods—females bigger than the males of our clan, bigger than any Drakav. While you..." He gestures at my slender form with something like disappointment. "You are small. Fragile."

He stops in front of me, nostrils flaring as he leans in slightly. "Though there is...something." Those golden pits fasten on me. "Something on you smells of Rok."

I feel heat rush to my cheeks and see the moment he rears back at the sight. Of course—I'm probably covered in Rok's scent after our activities in the cave. The thought is both embarrassing and oddly thrilling.

"She is my female," Rok states, the possessiveness in his thoughts unmistakable. "We are returning to clan grounds. She has others like her. Those we must find."

Tharn's head snaps up at this. "Others? More...females from the stars? More females like her?"

"Yes," I interject. "My sister and...many many others. They need our—your help."

Tharn stares at me for a long moment, then turns to Rok. "Kol sent search parties when you did not return many sols ago. I was tracking your scent when I found you." His gaze shifts back to me. "If there are indeed daughters of Ain fallen from the sky, he will want to know immediately."

"Aye," Rok nods and Tharn looks at him like he's suddenly a strange thing he's never seen before. I realize a little later it's because of the nod itself. That's something Rok learned from me.

"We will continue to clan grounds," he projects to Tharn. "Lead the way."

Tharn doesn't respond. Casting one more suspicious glance at me, he turns to head across the sand.

THANK THE GODS FOR THIS NEW STAMINA. I MANAGE TO KEEP THE PACE as we walk, though I know both males are going considerably slower than they are capable of. As we go, I notice how Tharn keeps pace not too far ahead, frequently glancing back at me with unconcealed interest. There's something in his gaze that makes me uneasy—not quite hostility, but a calculating intensity that has me instinctively moving closer to Rok.

"He doesn't believe I'm female," I whisper to Rok.

"*He will*," Rok replies, his mental voice tinged with grim determination. "*The clan has never seen beings like you. Their disbelief is natural.*"

"What if they all react like Tharn? What if they attack before asking questions?"

Rok's hand finds mine, his fingers intertwining with mine in a gesture so human it makes my throat tight. "*I will not let them harm you.*"

The promise is simple, but loaded with meaning. I glance

up at him, finding his golden eyes already on me, filled with that same fierce protectiveness I'm coming to recognize.

After about an hour of trekking through increasingly rocky terrain, Rok stops abruptly.

"*We must move faster,*" he says, turning to me. "*The clan grounds are still distant, and the dark will come soon.*"

Before I can respond, he sweeps me into his arms, cradling me against his chest.

"*I will carry you,*" he states, not a question but a declaration. "*It will be faster.*"

Tharn watches this exchange with narrowed eyes. "*The female cannot keep pace?*"

"*She is not of the dust,*" Rok snaps. "*Her strength is different.*"

Something flickers in Tharn's eyes—confusion, disbelief, and something else I can't quite identify. His gaze lingers on me for a moment too long, trailing over the way I'm nestled against Rok's chest, the way Rok's arms tighten around me possessively.

There's yearning there. Deep and unmistakable.

It sends a chill down my spine. Not fear, exactly, but a sudden awareness that Rok might not be the only one of his kind who could form this strange bond with a human woman.

"*We go,*" Rok's voice in my head is a growl, clearly noticing Tharn's stare. Without waiting for a response, he launches into a run, his powerful legs eating up the distance with astonishing speed.

Tharn follows, matching Rok's pace. His gaze keeps flicking to me, and each time it does, Rok's arms tighten fractionally around me.

As we race across the desert, the wind picking up around us, I find myself wondering what awaits us at the clan grounds. Will they all look at me the way Tharn does? With suspicion, disbelief, and that unsettling hint of desire?

And what happens when they discover I'm not what they expect—not a daughter of their sun god, but just a lost human woman trying to find her sister and a way home?

I press my face against Rok's chest, drawing comfort from his cool skin and the steady beat of his heart. Whatever comes next, I'm not facing it alone. I have Rok.

And as the landscape blurs around us, the wind growing stronger at our backs, I can only hope that's enough.

CHAPTER 33
JUST WHEN I THOUGHT IT COULDN'T GET WEIRDER

JUSTINE

The sun sinks toward the horizon as we approach the clan grounds, painting the rocky landscape in shades of amber and gold. Still cradled in Rok's arms, I feel his muscles tense beneath me, his heartbeat quickening against my ear. Ahead, dark silhouettes of massive stone formations rise against the darkening sky —a natural fortress of towering cliffs and hidden crevices.

"*We approach clan ground.*" Rok's thoughts brush against my mind, tentative and tense. "*Are you afraid?*"

The question surprises me. I've been so focused on the physical sensation of being carried by him—the powerful rhythm of his stride, the security of his arms around me—that I'd tried not to think about what awaits us.

"*Should I be?*" I counter, trying to mask my growing unease.

Rok slows his pace, allowing Tharn to pull ahead of us. When he responds, his mental voice is carefully measured. "*They have never seen a being like you. They will not understand.*"

"Like Tharn didn't understand," I say, watching the other male's muscular back as he leads us toward the cliffs.

"*Yes,*" Rok agrees, "*but many minds together can be...overwhelming.*"

I swallow hard, suddenly aware of what that might mean. If one skeptical Drakav nearly attacked me on sight, what will a whole clan of them do?

"*They will not harm you,*" Rok adds, obviously sensing my fear. "*I will not allow it.*"

There's a fierce certainty in his thoughts that should be comforting, but instead has me worried for him. What would happen if he had to defend me against his entire clan? What would that cost him?

Before I can voice these concerns, Tharn pauses ahead of us, raising his hand in a silent signal. The gesture is so human it momentarily throws me. These beings may look alien, but there's something fundamentally familiar in the way they move, communicate (well...kind of), and exist.

"*Kol awaits,*" Tharn projects, his mental voice carrying to both of us. "*He has sensed our approach.*"

"*How?*" I wonder, not realizing I've broadcasted the thought until both males look at me.

"*The clan bond,*" Rok explains. "*All males are connected. It is how we survive.*"

This new piece of information sends my brain into overdrive. They all talk to each other...*sense* each other...constantly? So together are they like a singular unit, deadly soldiers that don't even need to relay spoken commands because communication is like...instant?

"*Your female thinks very loudly,*" Tharn observes, interrupting my mental spiral.

Rok's chest rumbles with what might be a chuckle. "*She does.*"

"I'm right here," I protest, but there's no real annoyance behind it. In truth, their casual exchange has helped ease some of my tension.

As we approach the base of the tallest cliff, I notice openings scattered across its face—cave entrances, some clearly natural and others that appear to have been deliberately expanded. The setting sun casts them in deep shadow, making it impossible to see within, but I have the distinct feeling of being watched from those dark voids.

Tharn stops at the cliff base, his posture straightening as his eyes close in concentration. Though no sound passes his lips, I sense a powerful mental projection emanating from him —a silent call that seems to ripple through the air around us. The mental energy hangs for a long moment, then fades.

Silence follows, so complete, I can hear my own heartbeat.

Then, movement. Shadows detaching from shadows. Forms emerging from the caves above, scaling down the cliff face with inhuman grace. Others appearing from behind rock formations, rising from what I had thought was bare ground.

Within moments, we're surrounded by at least twenty Drakav males, their golden eyes gleaming in the fading light, their muscular bodies arranged in a loose circle around us. None approach, but their focus is like a heavy weight bearing down on me from all sides.

"They're beautiful," I think involuntarily, struck by the sight of them gathered together. Each one unique in the subtle variations of height and build, the color of their hair, their eyes —yet they're unmistakably of the same species.

There's an answering rumble in Rok's chest, his arms tightening around me in what is nothing but jealousy and possessiveness. I don't mind. I curl tighter against him, and not a moment too soon.

The circle parts, and a massive figure steps forward. Even

among these impressive beings, he stands out—taller than Rok by at least a head, his shoulders broader, his chest deeper. Intricate patterns swirl across his torso and face, more elaborate than those visible on the others.

"Kol," Rok acknowledges, inclining his head slightly but not bowing or kneeling as I might have expected. His arms remain firmly around me, holding me close to his chest rather than setting me down.

The leader's eyes fix on me with unnerving intensity. I feel the brush of his mind against mine—harder, rougher than Rok's gentle touch, like sandpaper compared to silk.

"What is this you bring to our grounds, Rok?" Kol's mental voice resonates with authority. "Why do you carry a strange male in your arms as if he were a hatchling?"

A ripple of curious thought-whispers moves through the gathered clan. I feel Rok's frustration spike, but his outward demeanor remains calm.

"Not male," he corrects firmly. "*Female*. Not from here. Not from the dust."

The mental whispers intensify, a buzz of disbelief and wonder that makes my temples throb. Kol steps closer, nostrils flaring as he scents the air around us.

"Set this creature down," he commands. "Let me see what you claim is female."

I feel Rok's reluctance as he slowly lowers me to my feet, but he keeps one arm around my shoulders, his body slightly angled to remain between me and Kol. The protective gesture isn't lost on the leader, whose face shifts in what might be surprise.

Standing on my own, I'm acutely aware of how small I am compared to these beings. The top of my head barely reaches Rok's chest, and Kol towers over me like a living mountain.

Fighting the urge to shrink back against Rok, I force myself to stand straight, meeting Kol's gaze directly.

"I am Justine," I project as clearly as I can, hoping my thoughts reach him. "I came from beyond the stars with others of my kind. Rok saved my life."

Something in Kol's eyes changes. Perhaps it's surprise. Perhaps he thinks I'm lying. He circles me slowly, reminding me how Rok appeared much like a predator assessing potential prey in those first moments when we met. I resist the urge to turn with him, keeping my gaze fixed forward, though every instinct screams to keep the threat in view.

"The daughters of Ain were mighty beings," Kol thinks, his mental voice dripping with skepticism. "Goddesses. This creature is small. Weak. It has no claws, no fangs." He reaches toward my face with one massive hand. "Its skin is thin, soft—"

Rok moves faster than I can track, his body suddenly between me and Kol's outstretched hand. He doesn't growl or bare his teeth, but his stance is unmistakably defensive.

"She is under my protection," Rok states, the thought carrying such force that I see several of the surrounding males flinch.

Instead of anger at this challenge, something like curiosity flickers across Kol's hard features. He withdraws his hand slowly, his gaze moving between Rok and me with fresh interest.

"You have changed, dust-son," he observes. "Your bearing. Your stance." His gaze drops pointedly to Rok's loincloth. "Your covering."

Several of the clan members shift closer, heads tilting in that now-familiar gesture of curiosity. I realize they're all noticing what Tharn had pointed out—the physical evidence of Rok's new anatomy, hidden beneath the crude garment I'd made for him.

"I have changed," Rok acknowledges simply. "She has changed me."

The admission sends another wave of mental murmurs through the gathered clan. I catch fragments of their thoughts —disbelief, fascination, jealousy, fear.

"—cannot be female—"

"—look how he guards it—"

"—never seen a male cover his pouch—"

"—what if it is true? What if—"

"—this strange male has many soft parts."

A lean Drakav pushes forward suddenly. "Let me see this creature," he demands, reaching for my arm.

Rok's response is immediate and terrifying. His body transforms before my eyes—muscles bunching, spine arching, a sound emerging from his throat that seems to vibrate the very air around us. It's not just a growl; it's a warning that transcends language, primal and absolute.

The male freezes, then slowly backs away, head lowered in submission.

"Enough," Kol commands, his mental voice cutting through the tension like a blade. His gaze shifts to Tharn. "What do you think of this creature—"

"*Jus-teen*," Rok corrects, his stance still rigid with protective fury.

Tharn straightens under Kol's attention, his amber eyes flicking briefly to me before returning to his leader's face. There's a moment of hesitation, then his thoughts project clearly through the gathering.

"I trust Rok's judgment," he states firmly. "If he says this one is female, then I believe him. Rok has never led the clan astray."

The declaration seems to carry weight, rippling through the gathered males. I feel Rok's surprise and appreciation beside me, though his protective stance doesn't waver.

Kol considers Tharn's words, his face unreadable. He takes so long to relay his judgment that I start to worry that he will turn me away. Finally, his voice booms in my mind. "Jus-teen," he pauses, his chin tilting slightly as he looks at me down the bridge of his nose, "will not be harmed or touched without consent."

For a moment, he simply stares at me, and I wish I could read his mind. Ha. I probably could, I just don't know how.

"You claim others of your kind are stranded. Where?" he projects.

Relief floods me at this change of subject. "Um, they're..." And then I realize I have no idea where they are. I don't know the direction or anything. "Where our ship crashed. We were... separated. We...meant no harm coming here."

"Ship..." Kol repeats thoughtfully. I feel him turn the thought over. Clearly, he has no idea what a ship is, and I'm not sure I should provide mental images to back up the word. "And how many of these...females...are stranded?"

"My sister," I project immediately. "And several other women—uh, females. Humans, we call ourselves."

"Humans," he echoes. The word comes off with a strange lilt in his thoughts. "We will search for these humans at first light."

My heart sinks. "First light? We need to go now. It's been days—more than I can count. What if they've encountered predators like the ones that attacked me and Rok? What if they're hurt or—" I cut myself off, unwilling to voice my deepest fear.

If it's even possible, Kol's expression hardens. "We do not travel when Ain does not bless us with her light. The creatures that hide from Ain's gaze are the deadliest. They hunt in the dark."

"But my sister—" I begin, desperation creeping into my voice.

"If your people stayed," Rok interjects, his thoughts so gentle they almost make my bravado crack, "near where I found you, then no creatures would go there."

But something in his tone makes a chill run down my spine. "Why not?"

I sense a ripple of unease pass through the gathered clan. Glances are exchanged. Bodies shift restlessly.

"They are in the Silent Valley." Rok's eyes search mine and I know there's more.

"Silent Valley?" I repeat. "Why do you call it that?"

"Silent Valley," Kol's voice booms in my head. "Where danger sleeps."

A heavy silence falls. Even the mental whispers cease, leaving an eerie quiet that seems to press against my eardrums.

It's Tharn who finally speaks, well, mind-talks. Mind-speaks? His thoughts carry a reverence far from how he sounded before. "The creature that lives there rests."

The words hang in the air, pregnant with meaning I can't fully grasp. Before I can ask for clarification, Kol turns to address the clan.

"Prepare for a journey at first light," he commands. "We seek the human females." His gaze returns to me. "Tonight, you will rest and tell us of your world beyond the stars... daughter of Ain."

Oh...shit.

The gathered males disperse at his command, though many cast lingering glances my way as they return to their cave dwellings. Only a few remain—Kol, Tharn, and three others whose names I don't yet know.

"Come," Kol directs, turning toward the largest cave opening. "You will share meal-offering with the clan."

As Rok guides me forward, his arm still protectively around my shoulders, I can't shake the ominous feeling left by their words.

Silent Valley. Where the creature sleeps.

And my sister—my only family—is right in the middle of it.

CHAPTER 34
THIS IS FINE. EVERYTHING IS FINE. I'M TOTALLY IN LOVE WITH AN ALIEN

JUSTINE

Hours later, I sit cross-legged beside a fire pit in the main cave dwelling. A fire, it seems, lit solely for my purpose as these Drakav don't appear to need its warmth. The dancing flames cast shifting shadows across the stone walls and the heat feels wonderful against my skin with the cold of the night creeping in. Despite the comfort of the fire, though, I can't relax. The weight of too many eyes follows my every movement.

The cave is massive—at least thirty feet high at its center, with a natural chimney that draws the smoke upward. The space is surprisingly orderly, with distinct areas that seem designated for specific purposes. Stone platforms line the walls —sleeping places, I assume. Various implements hang from pegs driven into the rock—tools, weapons, containers made from materials I don't recognize.

Kol sits across from me, his face illuminated by the firelight as he watches me with unrelenting intensity. Rok hasn't left my side since we arrived, his body a constant presence against mine, his hand frequently finding mine as if to reassure himself I'm still there.

The rest of the clan keeps a respectful distance, but their curiosity is palpable. Every few minutes, one approaches bearing some offering—a gourd of water, a portion of fresh meat, a strange fruit-like object with a hard shell. Each gift is presented with a careful glance at Rok, as if seeking permission to come near me.

Rok tolerates these approaches, but barely. His muscles remain tense, his breathing controlled. When a particularly bold clan member lingers too long, Rok's mental voice snaps out a warning that has the offender retreating hastily.

"Your protector is most vigilant," Kol observes after the fifth such incident, his thoughts tinged with something that might be amusement.

"He's always been protective," I reply, accepting a water gourd from a young male who immediately backs away from Rok's glare.

"No," Kol corrects, his face thoughtful. "This is different. This is..." He seems to search for the right concept. "Claiming."

Heat rises to my cheeks at the word, and Kol goes still at the visible change in my skin color. Several nearby clan members shift closer, fascinated by this new development.

"She changes color!" one thinks loudly enough for everyone to hear. "You have enraged her, dra-dam!"

Dra-dam? Leader, I suppose. Kol is leaning forward slightly, focus on my skin so intent, embarrassment makes me blush even harder.

"It's called blushing," I explain, taking care to remember to talk in my head while also wishing my face would cool. "It happens when humans are...embarrassed."

"Embarrassed?" The concept seems to confuse them.

"Uncomfortable with attention," I clarify. "Or when discussing certain topics."

"Such as claiming," Kol supplies.

My blush deepens. "Yes."

"I do not understand," Kol continues. It seems he's genuinely puzzled and I realize something I never noticed before. He, Rok, Tharn, the Drakav in general, do not seem to hide their emotions like humans do. Their minds are open. Their intentions clear.

Something warm develops in my chest as my gaze shifts to Rok. His intentions have always been clear to me. I've never had to guess.

"Claiming is simple." Kol projects, bringing me back to the present. "When a Drakav finds something useful in the dust— a tool, a water source, a hunting territory—he claims it for his use. It becomes his. Rok has claimed you as his useful thing."

My eyes widen as I realize the misunderstanding. He's talking about ownership, possession—not the intimate act my mind immediately jumped to. But it's too late; the memory of Rok's mouth between my thighs, his tongue exploring places no one has ever touched in so long, flashes vividly in my mind. The heat, the wetness, the way he drank from me as if dying of thirst—

A collective gasp echoes through the cave, not audible but mental—a wave of shock and confusion that makes me realize, to my absolute horror, that I've just accidentally broadcast that explicit memory to the entire clan.

The silence that follows is deafening. Every pair of golden eyes is fixed on me, expressions ranging from stunned to bewildered to intensely curious. Across the fire, Tharn's mouth has actually fallen open, a very human gesture of shock that would be comical under other circumstances.

Rok goes completely still beside me.

"What...was...that?" Kol finally asks, his mental voice careful, measured even, as if approaching something potentially dangerous.

I want to dissolve into the stone beneath me. Instead, I press my hands to my blazing face, unable to look at any of them.

"I'm sorry," I manage to think. "I didn't mean to show that. It was private."

"That was..." Someone's thoughts reach me, then stop, seemingly at a loss for words.

"Sharing water," Rok supplies calmly, though I can feel his discomfort rippling beneath the surface. "It is natural. As natural as breathing."

"Sharing water...from *there*?" Tharn asks incredulously, gesturing vaguely toward my lower body.

If possible, my face burns even hotter. I'm going to die of embarrassment right here in this cave, surrounded by confused alien males who've just gotten an unexpected glimpse of human sexuality.

"All females have water to share," Rok states, but his gaze darts to me for confirmation. Oh fuck. What should I even say? Cheeks blazing, I nod. Rok's shoulders straighten with even more confidence. "It is how bonds are strengthened."

The clan members exchange glances, a buzz of confused mental whispers passing between them.

"This is...claiming?" Kol asks, clearly trying to reconcile this new information with his understanding of the word.

"No," I hastily correct, the words coming from my lips. They all collectively wince. Shit. Closing my eyes, I take a deep breath and focus on saying everything in my head. "No. That's...something else. Something private."

"Private?" Kol does that thing again where I'm sure he's

turning the word over in his mind. They don't...they don't understand what I mean.

Pretty sure I'm digging myself a hole here.

"Private means it isn't shared with others. Only those we trust the most."

"I see," Kol says, though it's clear he doesn't see at all. "Your species has strange customs, star-daughter."

"Do all females allow this...water sharing?" Someone from the wider group projects directly at me. I don't know who it is until they lean forward, tilting their head at me. But before I can answer, Rok's growl fills my mind—a warning so potent I feel several of the gathered males recoil.

"My female's water is mine alone," he projects with unmistakable possessiveness. "As mine is hers."

This declaration seems to make sense to the clan in a way the act itself didn't. Territory, resources, possession—these are concepts they seem to understand well.

Kol raises a hand, silencing the murmurs that have broken out. "Enough," he commands. "The customs of star-daughters are not our concern. What matters is finding the others. At first light."

I've never been so grateful for a change of subject in my life. There's a hum now, one of anticipation and curiosity. Thoughts tickling my brain like being in a big crowd at the county fair and hearing all the voices at once.

A clan member with particularly elaborate markings across his chest approaches, bearing what appears to be one of those freshly killed lizard creatures. He presents it to me with a gesture that seems almost ceremonial.

"For the female's strength," he projects, his mental voice carrying an undercurrent of excitement. "The *dru-kii* gives greatest power."

I stare at the bloody offering. "Thank you," I manage. Rok

intervenes, taking the offering with a brief nod of acknowl-edgment.

"She requires food touched by flame," he explains, then turns to pierce the small carcass with a sharpened bone, holding it over the fire.

The male tilts his head, confused.

The gathered clan watches this process with fascination. I hear their mental murmurs—wondering at my strange dietary needs, at Rok's willingness to prepare food for me, at every-thing about this bizarre situation.

My gaze shifts to Rok. "Do you think they still believe I'm male like them?"

Rok's warm gaze shifts to me, so very different from the cold glares he's been sending his brothers. "No. If they thought you were a male from a rival clan, they would not be giving you offerings."

Well, that's a relief.

"Tell us of your world, star-daughter," Kol projects, diverting attention from the cooking meat. "Why did you return to our dust?"

All eyes turn to me expectantly. I take a deep breath, considering how to explain Earth and the fact that I'm not this...mythical daughter of the sun they think I am.

"I come from a world called Earth," I begin. "A planet—a... round ground in the sky—much like this one, but with more water. Our people have learned to travel among the stars, visiting other worlds to learn about them. But...we didn't come here. I am not the daughter of Ain you revere so much. I am simply a human. I and all the others females who need your help."

I take a deep breath, waiting for this revelation to come back and bite me in the ass. What's worse, Kol's face is unreadable. Even more than Rok's. I can see why he's the leader. Back on Earth, his poker game would be freaking marvelous.

"*Not* a daughter of Ain..." is all he says.

I take a breath.

"No," I shake my head. "I am not."

Kol leans forward. Everyone else is completely silent, not even their whispering thoughts reaching my mind. He inhales deeply, scenting me. "But you *are* female. In the image of Rok sharing your water, I saw that you had no pouch. No member."

Back to this again. I try not to blush, clearing my throat instead.

"You are correct." I take another deep breath. "Not a daughter of Ain, but female still."

A collective intake of breath that seems to draw the very air from the cave. The mental whispers suddenly intensify—a cacophony of wonder, disbelief, hope, and fear that makes my temples throb.

"I'm sorry." I close my eyes so I can focus my thoughts. "I'm sorry if that's disappointing. Sorry if that's not what you want to hear. But I beg, my sister and the others, the other women, the other females, they need your help. They will die out there if no one helps them."

I swallow hard, waiting for his response. When I finally open my eyes, Kol is studying me intently. As is everyone else in the cave except Rok. He's meeting each of their gazes in turn, tension radiating from his frame. As if should one of them make a move, he will tear their throat out.

"We..." Kol starts. "We will not let females die. That would go against everything passed down from generations of Drakav. You say you are no daughter of Ain, but you fell from Ain and landed in the dust. You are daughter enough to us."

The weight of his words settles over me. He doesn't have to spell it out. They will help us.

The relief I feel can't even be put into words or thought. Tears brim in my eyes, a single one running down my cheek.

The cave grows suddenly quiet—not a single thought coming through. Then all at once, every golden eye in the cave fixes on the teardrop trailing down my face.

"She...leaks water," comes Tharn's shocked exclamation, breaking the silence.

And suddenly the mental barrage intensifies, becoming a focused onslaught directed at me from all sides.

"—her face produces water!—"

"—is this how females share?—"

"—precious resource from her eye-holes—"

"—what does it taste like?—"

"—is she injured? Why does she leak?—"

"—can all females make water appear?—"

"—Rok must be powerful to bond with a water-maker—"

"—imagine never thirsting in the dust again—"

The onslaught is like a physical pressure against my mind, dozens of voices clamoring for attention. I press my hands to my temples, wincing as the mental noise grows louder, more insistent.

Rok notices immediately. Without hesitation, he shifts to face me, gently taking my face between his hands. Pressing his forehead to mine, he creates a bubble of quiet around my consciousness, blocking out the invasive thoughts.

"Focus on me," he instructs gently. "Only me. Build walls around your mind—strong, high. You control who enters."

I concentrate, visualizing the barrier as he describes. To my surprise, it works—the chaotic voices recede, becoming distant murmurs rather than shouting crowds.

"Yes," he encourages, his mental voice warm with pride. "Like that. You learn quickly, my Jus-teen."

The tenderness in his thoughts, the gentle care in his touch

—it overwhelms me with gratitude. Without thinking, I lean forward and press my lips to his in a brief, chaste kiss.

When I pull back, I become aware of the absolute silence that has fallen over the cave once more. Everyone's attention is fixed on us, expressions ranging from shock to fascination to something darker, hungrier.

"What was that joining?" Kol's voice booms in my head, absolutely cutting through the barrier I'd created. "What ritual is this?"

Heat floods my cheeks again. Oh fuck. This is like one of those alien movies where the clueless human accidentally marries the chieftain's son, starts an interplanetary war, and overthrows a thousand-year-old religious order all before dinner. At this rate, I'm going to single-handedly destroy their entire cultural foundation before bedtime.

"It's called a kiss," I explain reluctantly. "It's...a gesture of affection among my people."

"Affection," Kol repeats, as if tasting the word. "Like grooming?"

"Sort of," I hedge, not wanting to dive into the intricacies of human romance. "More intimate."

"Do all your females perform this type of water sharing, too?" Tharn asks, his voice carrying an undertone I can't quite identify.

"Well, yes," I admit. "With people they care about."

This revelation sends a ripple of excitement through the gathered clan. I can almost see the wheels turning in their heads, imagining a world full of females who might bestow such "affection" on them.

Oh god. What have I done?

"Enough," Rok growls, his arm encircling my shoulders. "My female needs rest."

Kol studies us for a long moment, his face unreadable.

Finally, he inclines his head. "Rest. At first light, we journey to find your lost ones."

Rok stands and offers me his hand. "Come," he projects softly. "You need rest."

I take his hand, grateful for the escape from the intense scrutiny. My legs ache from sitting cross-legged for so long, and exhaustion weighs on me like a physical burden. The events of the day have left me completely drained.

Rok leads me through a narrow passage branching off from the main cavern. The tunnel winds deeper into the cliff face, occasionally opening into smaller chambers.

"Here," Rok projects finally, gesturing to an opening in the stone wall.

He guides me into what is clearly his personal space—a modestly sized chamber carved into the living rock. The ceiling is low enough that he must duck slightly to enter, though there's enough room for me to stand comfortably.

Rok watches my face as I take in his dwelling. His chest is puffed slightly, but as he follows my gaze, his expression shifts to uncertainty, then something like embarrassment.

"This is my chamber," he explains. "I earned it when I became scout leader. Few have their own space."

I can tell he's seeing it through my eyes now, and finding it lacking. The chamber is Spartanly furnished—a pile of animal hides in one corner serves as bedding; various tools and weapons hang from pegs hammered into cracks in the stone; a small niche holds what appear to be personal items—a collection of unusual stones, a piece of metal that might be from a ship, and a few bone carvings.

Rok's brow furrows as he scans the bare rock walls. "It is... not much," he projects hesitantly. "Not worthy of a female."

I reach for his hand, squeezing it gently. "It's perfect," I tell him, and I'm being honest.

Because at this moment, it is. It's shelter, it's safety, and most importantly, it's away from dozens of curious eyes and probing minds. My legs feel ready to buckle beneath me, and my eyelids are growing heavier by the second.

Rok seems unconvinced by my assurance, his gaze still moving critically around the chamber. "Tomorrow I will make it better," he decides. "More comfortable for you."

"Tomorrow," I agree, though in my mind, tomorrow holds more pressing concerns—finding the others, making sure they're safe. The thought of Jacqui and the rest of the women alone in the wasteland sends a fresh spike of anxiety through me.

As if sensing my thoughts, Rok guides me to the pile of hides. "Rest now," he projects gently. "We will find your people when Ain rises. That is my oath."

I sink gratefully onto the surprisingly soft bedding, too exhausted to even remove my shoes. The hides smell of him. It's oddly comforting.

"Sleep," Rok projects, settling beside me, his body radiating warmth in the cool chamber. "I will keep watch."

As consciousness begins to slip away, my last coherent thought is of tomorrow—of traveling through the desert, of facing unknown dangers, of the hope and fear warring within me.

But for now, in this moment, sheltered in a cave with an alien warrior who's somehow become my protector, I feel something I've felt since only being in his presence.

I feel safe.

CHAPTER 35
EXPLAINING HUMANS: MORE DIFFICULT THAN HUNTING SAND SERPENTS

ROK

The first light of Ain has barely touched the sky when Tharn appears at the entrance of my chamber.

It is unusual. Tharn does not come to rouse me—not since we were younglings. He knows I wake before the light, my senses sharp and ever-watchful. Yet here he is, his broad form casting a shadow in the dim morning light, his golden eyes narrowed with curiosity.

I do not need to ask why. I know.

Jus-teen rests beside me, her small form curled in the pile of hides. Her pale skin glows faintly in the soft light creeping into the chamber, her loose mane spilling across the bedding like threads of Ain's own radiance. She is extraordinary. Even now, I can feel Tharn's mind brushing against mine, full of questions he does not yet push into my mindspace.

"She still rests," Tharn projects, his mental tone laced with amusement.

"She needs rest," I reply, my voice equally soft in his mind.

Tharn tilts his head, his focus shifting to her with unhidden curiosity. "I have never seen one rest so deeply. Does she not sense the light or the movement?"

"She is not Drakav," I remind him, annoyance flickering through my thoughts. "Her body does not respond as ours do."

I can sense he understands, but he still does not leave. Instead, he steps farther into the chamber, his gaze lingering on Jus-teen. I feel a low growl building in my chest, but I suppress it. Tharn means no harm. He is curious, as are all my brothers. They have never seen a female before, let alone one like her.

But she is mine.

Tharn stands at the entrance, his gaze lingering on her sleeping form. His curiosity is palpable, brushing against my mind like a persistent question waiting for an answer.

"She is unlike anything I have seen," Tharn projects, his tone cautious but probing. "Even her breathing is strange. Soft...uneven."

I grunt, unwilling to feed his curiosity. Jus-teen's breaths are soft, light, and melodic in a way I have come to find soothing. I watch her chest rise and fall, the faint warmth of her body radiating through the bedding.

"She is delicate," Tharn continues, tilting his head. "Not like us. Will she endure the journey to the Silent Valley?"

"She will," I say firmly. "She is stronger than she looks."

Tharn does not respond. Instead, he steps closer, his golden eyes narrowing as he studies her.

"What are you doing, Tharn?" I project a low growl, my brows tightening.

He glances at me, unperturbed. "Her skin changes color often. I have seen it. Is it...danger?"

"No," I reply. "It is her way."

Her flushed skin, her strange reactions—they are all part of her. At first, they puzzled me. Now, I find I look forward to them. They are signs of her emotions, her thoughts, and I notice them even when she tries to hide them.

"Strange," Tharn muses, stepping back. "But then, all of this is strange."

Before I can respond, Justine stirs. Her brow furrows slightly, and she shifts in the bedding, her hand reaching up to rub at her face. Her eyelids flutter open, and she blinks, her gaze finding mine almost immediately.

"Is it morning already?" she mumbles those words I cannot understand, the thoughts following her meaning shortly after.

Tharn flinches at the sound, his claws twitching at his sides as if preparing for an attack. His thoughts are sharp, unguarded: *What is this? What is she doing?*

I suppress a smirk, leaning closer to Jus-teen. "You are loud, light-bringer," I project gently into her mind.

She blinks, realization dawning as she sits up straighter, her cheeks flushing slightly. "Sorry," she thinks, her mental voice softer now. She turns to Tharn, offering him a small smile. "Good morning, Tharn."

Surprise flickers across Tharn's features—not just at her greeting, but at her casual use of his name, as if they are long-acquainted. Few address him so directly outside of Kol and me.

His thoughts ripple with confusion. "What were those sounds she made?"

"She vocalizes," I explain, the word forming clumsily in my mind. "It is her way of communicating."

Tharn tilts his head, his gaze flicking between her and me. "She speaks...with sound? Does it not disturb you?"

"No," I reply without hesitation. "She has spoken aloud many times in my presence, her strange human sounds startling and unfamiliar. But now, I find I like them. Her voice is soft, melodic, even when she is frustrated or amused. It is like water running over smooth stones—gentle, soothing, and alive."

"It is her way," I add simply.

Tharn steps back slightly, his gaze fixed on Jus-teen as if she is a puzzle he cannot quite solve.

Jus-teen shifts under his scrutiny, and I feel a surge of protectiveness rise within me. "We leave soon," I say, standing and moving to block Tharn's view of her. "Prepare the others."

Tharn hesitates, then inclines his head in the way we do, similar to Jus-teen's chin jerk. "As you say, scout-leader."

He lingers for a moment longer, his gaze flicking once more to Jus-teen before he turns and leaves the chamber.

Jus-teen exhales softly, her shoulders relaxing as the tension leaves the room. "He's...intense," she thinks, glancing at me.

"They are curious," I explain, sitting beside her once more. "You are the first they have seen. The first they have heard."

Her brow furrows. "I guess I'm going to have to get used to being the center of attention."

"You will," I assure her. "You are strong."

She bares her teeth at me, the expression soft and warm. "Thanks, Rok," she says aloud.

The sound of her voice tugs at something deep inside me, and I realize again how much I have come to treasure it. Her vocalizations are strange, yes, but they are hers. And every-thing about her—her voice, her scent, her thoughts—is precious to me.

I give her time to adjust before I take her to the cave's main chamber where the others are waiting, all ready with extra waterskins and pouches of fire bloom leaves strapped to their sides. Even under my brothers' annoying, but expected scru-tiny, Jus-teen does not flinch. She eats quickly and soon we are ready. We leave the clan's caves before long.

Ain is low on the horizon, casting long shadows across the dust as we set out. Jus-teen walks beside me, her pace slower than the rest of the group but steady. Ten of my brothers follow us, including Kol and Tharn, the others forced to stay and guard our territory.

The journey is uneventful at first; the landscape shifting from rolling dunes to jagged rock formations as we move steadily toward the Silent Valley. The air is cool, Ain's heat not yet oppressive, and the silence is broken only by the rhythmic crunch of sand beneath our feet.

But uneventful does not mean easy.

Solmarks into our journey, the strain begins to weigh on Jus-teen. Her steps falter more frequently now, the muscles of her smaller frame ill-suited to the relentless pace of the Drakav. She lags behind, and though I slow my stride to match hers, it does not seem to be helping.

The Drakav are built for this terrain. Our legs are long, our stamina unmatched, and we are accustomed to the grueling conditions of the dust. But my Jus-teen... she is soft. The dust does not welcome her as it does us. Yet she presses on, her jaw tight, her gaze fixed determinedly on the horizon.

The others do not mind her slower pace. They are too busy watching her, their curiosity palpable. Every movement she makes, every vocalization she speaks, draws their attention. I even notice they are not wincing as much when she forgets to use mindspeak. I do not know if I like that they are adapting to her, but I push the feeling back. I want them to welcome her. I want her to be happy. Comfortable.

Focus shifting back to her, I watch her stumble slightly, her foot catching on a loose stone, and my chest tightens.

"Let me carry you," I project into her mind.

She shakes her head, her lips pressing into a small, rueful smile. "Not yet," she thinks back.

"Why?" I press. I do not understand. "It would be easier for you."

She hesitates for a moment, her gaze flicking to the horizon. "You need to conserve your energy," she replies finally. "The others—the females—they'll need you more than I do when we find them."

The words catch me off guard, and I stare at her, uncomprehending. My energy? For the others?

"They might not be able to walk," she continues, a flicker of concern in her thoughts. "Or they might be hurt. You'll need your strength for them, Rok. I can manage for now."

Her reasoning is sound, but it does not sit well with me. She is *my* Jus-teen. My light. My duty is to her first.

"I will carry them if needed," I say simply. "But you come first."

She glances up at me, her cheeks flushing faintly, and I sense her gratitude even as she shakes her head. "I appreciate that," she thinks, "but I'll be fine. I promise. Let me do this on my own for now."

I do not argue further. I can feel the resolve in her mind, the quiet determination that has carried her through every challenge since she fell to this world. So I stay beside her, matching her stride, my presence a silent reassurance.

At one point, Tharn falls back to walk beside her. "Your water-sharing," he begins, his mental tone cautious. "Is it common among your kind?"

Jus-teen pushes a laugh through her nose as she glances at me, her cheeks coloring slightly. "It's...not something we talk about casually," she thinks, her voice hesitant.

Tharn tilts his head, clearly unsatisfied with her answer. "Strange," he says again, his favorite word for her.

I suppress a growl, my hand finding hers as I guide her forward. "Enough questions," I project firmly to Tharn.

He falls silent, but his curiosity lingers, a constant hum in the back of my mind.

"Go away, Tharn."

But he is not the only one.

Two sols pass. We are almost there. We continue on.

Jus-teen is the slowest among us, yet none complain or show impatience. They do not know her stamina has much improved, as if she has changed, too, as I have been. If anything, they seem content to match her pace, stealing glances when they think I am not watching.

I find myself reflecting on their fascination. They see only her femaleness, this rare thing they have heard of but never witnessed. They do not know how truly remarkable she is beyond this simple fact of her existence.

They did not see her face death without flinching.

They did not witness her attack Tharn to protect me.

They cannot comprehend the gift she gave in accepting me into herself, in sharing her water.

This last thought sends a wave of possessiveness through me so strong, it makes Tharn glance sharply in my direction. I know what most of my brothers are thinking. They wonder if they, too, might claim a female, if Jus-teen's arrival heralds a change in the endless sameness of our lives.

Kol has said nothing of how we will proceed once we find these other females. He is cautious, as a leader must be. But I can sense his curiosity, his calculations.

I am not certain these other females will be as receptive as my Jus-teen. I am not certain they should be. The thought of my brothers bonding with them brings a complexity of emotions I do not fully understand.

Each time we stop to rest, the others gather around Jus-teen, their questions coming fast and eager. She answers with patience I would not possess in her position, explaining concepts that must seem as foreign to them as our world must have once been to her.

"Do all females produce water from their eyes?"

"Why do you wear these different hide coverings?"

By the third rest period, I find myself wishing, with some guilt, that they might each find a female of their own—if only so they would leave mine in peace. The thought surprises me with its selfishness.

In the dark, when the temperature drops and Jus-teen curls against me for warmth, I can sense the weight of watching eyes. The interest of my brothers grows with each passing solmark, until our camp buzzes with anticipation like a hive of stinging mites.

Their questions become more specific, more personal.

"What did her water taste like?"

"How did you know she was yours to claim?"

"Will the others let us claim them, too?"

By the fourth sol, relief washes over me like cool water. We have arrived. We stop as a group, looking out over the dust. The Silent Valley—a vast area of dust that even the most fearsome predators do not tread.

And there, in the distance, something reflects Ain's rays back at us—a gleam of unnatural smoothness amid the rough terrain.

Jus-teen straightens beside me, her hand finding mine in an instinctive gesture.

"Oh my goodness...it's them," she vocalizes, her thoughts coming scattered, filled with relief and anxiety in equal measure. "It's the ship."

CHAPTER 36
JUST WHEN I THOUGHT THINGS WERE LOOKING UP

JUSTINE

The moment I see the glint of metal in the distance, something in me breaks loose. I'm moving before I can think, my feet carrying me forward in a stumbling run through the shifting sand.

"Jacqui!" I call out, my voice swallowed by the vastness of the desert. "Jacqui!"

Behind me, I sense hesitation from the Drakav, their confusion rippling across my mind like disturbed water. They didn't expect this sudden burst of movement, this desperate sprint toward the unknown. But I can't slow down. Not now. Not when I'm so close.

After a moment's pause, I sense them following. Rok's presence stands out most clearly in my mind, a mixture of concern and protectiveness washing over me.

"Be careful," his thoughts reach me. "This Valley holds much danger."

I don't slow. I can't. Every cell in my body is driving me

forward, toward that glint of metal, toward the hope that everyone is still alive.

As I run, a terrible thought grips me: What if I'm too late? What if the bus is empty, nothing but a metal coffin baking in the relentless sun? My imagination conjures the worst images—bodies withered from dehydration, or worse, nothing at all, just an abandoned shell with no clue as to what happened to the others.

My chest tightens, lungs burning both from exertion and from the fear squeezing my heart. The bus grows larger as I approach, but I still see no movement, no sign of life. The silence is oppressive, broken only by my labored breathing and the sound of my shoes pounding against the sand.

"Jacqui!" I call again, my voice cracking from strain and desperation. "Anyone! Can you hear me?"

Nothing.

I push myself harder, stumbling slightly as my shoe catches in a small depression. Rok's thoughts flare with alarm, but I right myself and keep moving. I'm close enough now to make out details—the bus sits just as I left it, half-buried in sand on one side. The drag chute still stands, creating that makeshift shelter extending from one side of the vehicle.

And then—movement.

A shadow shifts under the drag chute. Someone stands, one hand raised to shield their eyes from the sun's glare. Relief floods through me so intensely that I nearly collapse. I slow my pace, waving my arms frantically above my head.

"Hey!" I shout. "Over here! It's Justine!"

The figure freezes for a moment, then I see them turn and speak urgently to someone else. Another figure rises, then a third. They're moving now, scrambling toward the transport as if for protection. I watch as one of them disappears inside, only to emerge moments later with something in her hands.

As I draw closer, I can finally make out their features. Mikaela stands at the front, her dark braids pulled back in a tight ponytail, a high-heeled shoe clutched in one hand like a weapon. Next to her is Pam, the happy one, holding what appears to be a bag filled with sand, ready to swing it. Their faces are gaunt, skin reddened from sun exposure, but they're alive.

They're alive.

"*Justine?*" Mikaela calls out, uncertainty and hope warring in her voice. "Is that really you?"

"Yes!" I shout back, waving both arms now. "It's me! I'm here!"

I hear Mikaela's voice, pitched high with emotion, calling back into the transport. "Erika! Come quick! It's Justine! She's alive!"

Women begin emerging from the transport—first Erika, then Tina (the one who'd read through the manual), then Alex (the nurse), Mira (the med student) and others, faces I recognize but don't remember their names. They stand in a loose cluster, expressions ranging from disbelief to joy to caution as they watch my approach.

When I'm within twenty feet, Mikaela breaks rank and runs toward me. We collide in a fierce hug, her arms wrapping around me so tightly it knocks the breath from my lungs.

"*We thought you were dead,*" she sobs against my shoulder, her body trembling. "We thought you were gone forever."

"I almost was," I manage, my own tears flowing freely now. "But I'm here. I made it back."

More women approach, surrounding us in a circle of embraces and tearful exclamations. Hands reach out to touch me, as if confirming I'm real and not a mirage born of heat and desperation. I'm passed from one embrace to another, each woman offering some variation of relieved disbelief.

"How are you alive?" one of them asks.

"What happened to you?" asks another.

Their voices overlap, creating a cacophony of emotion that washes over me after days of the calm, measured mindspeak of the Drakav. It's overwhelming and beautiful all at once.

"You look…different," Alex says, stepping back to examine me. Her keen eyes take in my sun-darkened skin and probably the fact I don't look dehydrated or dying.

"I feel different," I admit, wiping at my tears.

It's then that I notice the hush falling over the group. One by one, the women's expressions shift from joy to uncertainty, their eyes fixing on something behind me. I feel a familiar tug in my chest, a presence in my mind that has become as natural as breathing.

I turn slowly to find Rok and his clan standing several yards away, maintaining a respectful distance. They've arranged themselves in a loose semicircle, with Rok standing just a few feet before them, his golden eyes fixed solely on me. The contrast between them and the human women couldn't be more stark—their tall, powerful frames, their alien features, the way they hold themselves completely still except for the slight tilt of their heads as they observe us.

"Holy shit," Mikaela breathes, her hand finding my arm in a tight grip. "What the actual fuck are those?"

"Who." I correct automatically, turning back to face the women. "Not what. Who."

"Fine," Erika says, her voice tight with fear and suspicion. "*Who* the fuck are those…people?"

I take a deep breath, trying to figure out how to explain everything that's happened—the connection I've formed with Rok, the clan's willingness to help us, the complex society they've built in this harsh environment. It all seems too much to convey in simple words.

"They're called the Drakav," I begin, keeping my voice calm. "They're native to this planet, and they've come to help us."

"Oh, thank God," Pam beams. "Thank God!"

But the others don't react the same.

"*Help* us?" Mikaela repeats. "They look like they want to eat us."

I glance over my shoulder to see several of the gathered Drakav snarling, fangs visible as they brace against the constant chatter that comes from my people. And I realise it must be like when I got overwhelmed by their mindspeak back in their cave. I give them a pleading look, hoping they'll understand.

"No." I shake my head. "They don't eat...I mean, they hunt, but not... Look, they're here to help. They saved my life. *He* saved my life."

I turn toward Rok, extending my hand in invitation. "*It's okay,*" I project to him. "*Come closer. Slowly. No sudden movements.*"

Rok hesitates, his gaze flicking between me and the cluster of women. I can feel his caution, his awareness of the fear radiating from the humans. But after a moment, he steps forward, his approach measured and non-threatening.

As he comes to stand beside me, I hear the collective intake of breath from the women. He towers over all of us, his golden eyes bright, his powerful frame casting a shadow over us.

"This is Rok," I say, reaching out to take his hand in mine. The gesture feels both natural and significant. "He found me in the desert after I left to find help. He kept me alive. Protected me."

I pause, suddenly aware that I've reached a moment of definition. What is Rok to me? What word can possibly encompass what we've become to each other in this short, intense time?

"He's my..." I pause. The word forms in my mind before I've fully acknowledged it. But it's...it's true. "He's my boyfr—." The word seems oddly wrong. As if it's lessening the gravity of our connection. "He's my mate."

The declaration sends a visible shock wave through the group of women. Mikaela's jaw drops open, and Erika takes an involuntary step backward.

"Your *what?*" Tina asks, eyes wide as they blink behind her glasses.

"Mate," I repeat, more firmly this time, squeezing Rok's hand. "We...bonded. Out there." I gesture vaguely toward the vast expanse of desert. Oh god, what am I saying? I can hear how it sounds. But it's the truth. And I'm not ashamed of it.

"You've been gone for like three weeks, Justine," Mikaela says slowly, as if explaining something to a child. "And you've...mated...with an alien?"

When she puts it that way, it does sound insane. But nothing about my experience has been normal or expected. How can I explain the intensity of survival, the depth of connection that forms when someone saves your life, learns your mind, accepts you completely?

"It's complicated," I say finally. "But he and his clan are here to help us. They know this planet. They can help us survive."

Rok's thoughts brush against mine. *"Tell them we mean no harm. We will protect them as I have protected you."*

I relay his message, watching as the women's expressions shift between disbelief, fear, and cautious hope.

"The others," I project to Rok. "They can come closer, too. Slowly."

Rok turns, making a gesture to the waiting clan members.

One by one, they begin to approach. Kol comes first, his face impassive but curious. Tharn follows, his gaze darting between the human women with barely contained fascination.

As they draw nearer, I notice something in the women's reactions—beyond the fear and uncertainty, there's a flicker of something else. A kind of stunned appreciation. For all their alienness, the Drakav are impressive—powerful, graceful, their eyes intelligent and observant.

"There are more of us inside," Erika says, her practical nature reasserting itself. "Some are too weak to come out. We've been surviving on emergency rations and some of us figured out how to harvest water from the ship's condensers. Mikaela even found some...uh...insects in the sand. We've been uh..." She swallows hard. "It's been hard. Between the headaches and fevers and nightmares, we thought...we never thought this day would come."

I pause. "Fevers and headaches...because of the heat and dehydration?"

Alex steps closer. "I think so."

Mikaela shakes her head. "I think it's something else entirely." She folds her arms. "But we agree to disagree."

I nod, suddenly noticing the gauntness in their faces, the way their clothes hang loosely on their frames. They've been barely surviving out here. And they've been having the same fever and headaches as I was.

It's strange, but too much for us to unpack right now.

"The Drakav know where to find water," I tell them. "They can help us gather food, too. We don't have to struggle anymore."

"That's all good. If they can help us till the Xyma arrive, we can probably make it," someone says. A sour feeling develops in the pit of my stomach. They're still hoping the Xyma will come? As my case shifts across the group, I realize it's not all of them that are hoping. Mikaela, for one, simply rolls her eyes when the woman speaks.

I don't know how I'm gonna break it to them, but I don't think the Xyma are coming and I believe the Drakav are our best bet. "The Drakav will help us," is all I say.

Relief washes over their faces, but I can see the questions still lingering in their eyes. What will this help cost? What does it mean to accept assistance from these alien beings?

Before they can voice these concerns, my heart drops. I've been so caught up in the reunion that I haven't registered the absence of the one person I was most desperate to see.

"Where's Jacqui?" I ask, scanning the group of women. "Where's my sister?"

A strange hush falls over the group. No one meets my eyes directly, and a cold dread begins pooling in my gut.

"Jacqui?" I call louder, stepping away from Rok and toward the bus. "Jacqui, why don't you come out? I thought you'd be happy to see me."

I move toward the vehicle, aware of Rok following close behind me. The interior of the transport is dim after the bright sunlight, and it takes a moment for my eyes to adjust. What I see makes my heart ache—makeshift bedding arranged on every available surface, personal items carefully organized to maximize space, evidence of their struggle to create some semblance of order and comfort in this harsh environment.

But no Jacqui.

I emerge from the transport, panic rising in my chest. My gaze sweeps across the group, wondering if I somehow missed her, before my eyes shift to the horizon, as if expecting to see her walking toward us from the endless expanse of sand.

"Where is she?" My voice rises. "Where is my sister?"

The women exchange glances, a silent communication that

sends ice through my veins. Finally, Erika steps forward, her face solemn, eyes filled with compassion and regret.

"Justine," she says softly, "your sister...she...I'm sorry."

The world seems to tilt beneath my feet. "What do you mean, you're sorry? Where's Jacqui?"

Erika swallows hard, unable to meet my gaze for more than a second. "She left about a week ago," she says finally. "She went to search for you."

Time stops.

I stagger backward, and would have fallen if not for Rok's arms suddenly around me, supporting my weight as my knees threaten to give way.

"What?" The word comes out as barely more than a whisper. "What are you saying?"

"We tried to stop her," Mikaela adds quickly, her face pinched with guilt. "When you didn't return, we told her it was suicide to go out there alone, but she wouldn't listen. She held back as long as she could. She said she couldn't just sit here and wait, not knowing if you were alive or dead. She said..." Mikaela's voice breaks. "She said she'd never forgive herself if she didn't try."

I shake my head, trying to deny the reality of what I'm hearing. My sister, my cautious, responsible sister, ventured alone into the desert to find me. Jacqui is alone out there.

"No." The word tears from my throat. My knees hit the sand before I realize I've fallen. "No, no, no—"

Someone says my name, but I don't hear it. The world narrows to a single, suffocating truth: Jacqui is gone. She went into that endless dust after me, alone, unprotected. And I wasn't there.

A violent sob claws its way out of me. My hands fist in the sand like I can dig through it, like I can tunnel back in time and stop her from leaving. "She wouldn't—I told her to stay. I—"

Strong arms wrap around me from behind, pulling me against a solid chest. His whole being encloses me as his chin rests on my head. He doesn't speak. Doesn't tell me it'll be okay. He just holds me, his grip unyielding, as if he can keep me from shattering completely.

I twist in his arms, pressing my face to his neck. My tears soak into his skin, and his growl vibrates through me. He isn't angry. This is something deeper. A promise. A vow.

Without understanding anything they just told me, he knows. As if he can feel my pain.

"*We will find her,*" he projects into my mind. "*I will tear apart every dune in the dust if I must. But I will bring your sister-female back to you.*"

I clutch him tighter, my fingers digging into his back. He doesn't flinch. Doesn't pull away. He just holds me harder, his mind brushing against mine. Steady. Unbreakable.

My rock.

After a few moments, I feel steady enough to take a breath and look over my shoulder at Mikaela. Everyone else averts their gazes from me as if guilty. As if they feel like I will blame them for letting her leave.

"Which direction?" I ask, my voice hollow. "Which way did she go?"

Mikaela opens her mouth to answer, but it's Pam who points toward those stone formations I'd set out to reach originally. "She followed your original route."

I turn to Rok, desperation clawing at my throat. "*We have to find her,*" I project, not caring if his brothers hear the frantic edge to my thoughts. "*Please, Rok. We have to find my sister.*"

Rok's expression remains calm, but I feel the surge of determination in his mind. "*We will find her,*" he projects firmly. "*If she lives, we will find her.*"

It's the "if" that breaks me. I collapse against him again.

The world narrows to a single, terrible thought: Jacqui is out there, alone, in a wasteland that nearly killed me despite having Rok's protection and knowledge.

As the gravity of the situation settles over me, I become aware of the Drakav clan and the human women watching us, two worlds suddenly thrust together by crisis and necessity. Whatever initial tensions existed between them seem temporarily suspended in the face of this new emergency.

But then Erika steps closer, arms crossed, but her shoulders are slumped. She looks defeated. "There's...there's something else."

The way she says it makes me stiffen. "What?" I whisper.

"It's...Hannah. She's gone too."

I ease off Rok and he helps me to stand, one powerful arm supporting me as I push back my tears and turn to face Erika.

"Gone?"

Erika sighs. "After Jacqui left and didn't return...she ventured off on her own. Said she couldn't sit here and wait to die."

Mikaela releases a sigh too, and slumps to the ground, crouching with her face in her hands. "Tried to stop her, too."

"Which way did she go? After Jaqs?"

Erika shakes her head. "No. She went that way." She points in the opposite direction to where the stone formation is. Oh shit.

My gaze shifts to Rok at my back. In about two seconds, I bring him up to speed.

"*Ain is high*," Kol projects, stepping forward. "*We should establish better shelter for these females and begin the search before Ain sets.*"

His practical approach cuts through my spiraling thoughts, giving me something to focus on beyond my fear. I nod.

Before I can respond further, Tharn steps forward, his golden eyes meeting mine with unexpected intensity.

"*I will go,*" he projects, firm and clear. "*I will find your sister-female.*"

I stare at him, surprised by his offer. Tharn, who had been so wary of me at first, now volunteering to search for Jacqui?

"*Tharn is our best tracker,*" Rok adds, his thoughts flowing smoothly into mine. "*If your sister-female is in the dust, he will find her.*"

I swallow hard, glancing at Rok.

"*I trust him with my life,*" Rok projects. "*I would trust him with yours.*"

Something in his certainty steadies me. I turn to Tharn, studying his face. There's a determination there, a steadiness I hadn't fully appreciated before.

"*I'm coming with you,*" I project. No way I'm staying here with the others.

Tharn tilts his head, considering me for a moment before inclining his head in a way that seems to suggest acceptance. Kol, however, looks less convinced.

"*I will send Sorn here to find the other lost female.*" He gestures to a male with a scarred face. He stands sideways, stiffly, and I realize he's keeping the scarred side away from facing the women. "*Will these other females follow us if you leave?*" Kol gestures to the women, who are watching our silent exchange with growing confusion. "*I can sense they do not trust us. But they will not survive much longer without our help.*"

He's right. They're all sunburned, tired, hungry, dehydrated. They've been surviving, but just barely. But they're also standing together in a protective huddle, watching the Drakav with curious but uncertain gazes.

I can just imagine how they feel. Trusting aliens is kind of what brought us here in the first place.

My gaze meets Erika's. I give her a nod. "They will follow you."

Kol's gaze shifts to her, his gaze so intense it's like it eats her up. I swear I see her cheeks darken. Or maybe I'm just noticing more sunburn.

Kol suddenly inclines his head, gaze shifting to the others of his group. Though no words are spoken aloud, I can sense the edges of their communication—Kol assigning duties, establishing guards. It happens with such swift efficiency that, within moments, the clan begins moving with purpose. Sorn, the male he sends after Hannah, sets off on a jog.

"What's happening?" Mikaela asks, stepping forward. "How do you know what they're doing when they haven't said a word?" Her eyes narrow as she catches several of the Drakav wincing as she speaks. Her voice rises, frown deepening. "And why do they keep doing that every time I talk?"

I sigh, realizing how much explaining I have ahead of me. "It's a long story, but they have a language—just not one you can hear. They communicate with their minds, and your voices...hurt their ears." I gesture toward the bus. "Let's get everyone settled, and I'll explain everything. I promise."

While I begin organizing the women, Rok and the others make themselves useful immediately. Three Drakav, including the one who offered me the lizard meat at the clan dwelling, set off in what looks to me like a random direction. But they know better than I do. They're hunting for food, I assume. Two others begin expertly adjusting the drag chute that's been serving as makeshift shelter, so it gives more shade. With their strength, they drape the heavy thing much better than any of us ever could.

Kol approaches the transport cautiously, his nostrils flaring as he takes in its scent. With careful movements, he begins to examine the structure, seemingly assessing its integrity and defensibility. His practicality reminds me of Jacqui, sending a fresh pang through my heart.

"*We leave as soon as they are settled,*" Tharn projects to me, his gaze fixed on the horizon in the direction Jacqui supposedly went. "*It is good we are in the calm season. We have many solmarks of Ain's light left to guide our way.*"

"*And we will leave this place shortly after. As soon as you depart. We head for the clan territory,*" Kol adds, his gaze shifting from the bus to the surroundings. "*It is not wise to tarry here, in the Silent Valley, for so long.*"

I nod, turning my attention back to helping the weakest women out of the transport and into the shade. The one with the broken arm, and the who had gotten the concussion look the worst.

"*They need water,*" I tell Rok. "*And food. Something gentle for their stomachs.*"

Rok understands immediately, retrieving water skins from the supplies they brought and demonstrating to the women how to use them. Some are hesitant, but when the first takes the leap and drinks, the relief on her face convinces the others. As they drink, it is painful to watch. How long have they been rationing themselves to the point of dehydration?

"You're communicating with them, aren't you?" Erika asks me quietly as I help distribute fire bloom leaves, showing and explaining to them how the plant has healing properties. "There's no way you all are just *moving* around each other intuitively like this."

"Yes, I am," I admit. There's no point in hiding it. "It's how they talk. It's how they...know each other."

"And you can do this *how?*" Mikaela crosses her arms, watching me.

"It's complicated," I say again, but I know the explanation is inadequate. "I'll tell you everything after we find Jacqui."

Erika nods, accepting the deflection for now. "She was so determined to find you," she says, her voice softening. "None of us could stop her."

My throat tightens. "That sounds like Jacqui. Always trying to protect me, even from myself."

As the camp slowly takes shape around us, I find myself continually drawn to that stone formation in the distance, my thoughts racing ahead to the search that's about to begin. Rok must sense my distraction because he approaches, gently placing a hand on my shoulder.

"Tharn will not fail," he projects, his faith in his fellow warrior absolute. *"And I will be with you."*

I lean into his touch, drawing strength from his certainty. *"Thank you,"* I project, hoping he can feel the depth of my gratitude.

By the time the camp is properly established, with water, food, and shelter secured for the women, Ain has moved noticeably across the sky. The hunters have returned with several of the desert creatures that have become familiar to me over the past days, and Rok is showing them how to cook them enough for human ingestion.

Mikaela approaches me as I gather the few supplies I'll need to go searching for Jaqs. A waterskin. Spare emergency blanket. "You're really going back out there?" she asks, concern evident in her voice.

"I have to," I tell her, checking the water skin Rok gave me. "She went looking for me, Mikaela. I can't just sit here knowing that."

She sighs, then surprises me by pulling me into a quick, fierce hug. "Be careful. We just got you back. Don't make us lose you again."

Touched by her concern, I hug her back. "I'll be careful. And I'm not alone this time."

Her gaze shifts to where Rok stands with Tharn, the two of them conferring in their silent way as they prepare for our departure. "No," she agrees, a hint of wonder in her voice. "You're definitely not alone." She bites her bottom lip and I can almost read the thoughts flying across her mind. "Are you sure about these guys?" She whispers low.

I take her hands in mine, forcing her to face me. "Yes." I say it with every ounce of assurance I can muster. "I do. Go with them. They'll keep you safe."

She swallows, still biting her lip before she sighs and nods. Another fierce hug before she releases me and heads over to help Erika divide the food.

By the time everyone is watered and fed, I am ready to start the search for Jaqs. Kol's insistence that they set out on their journey back to the clan grounds immediately makes some of the women unsure when I relay the message to them. But there is no other choice. Either go or stay in the desert waiting for the Xyma who may never come.

I explain the Drakav will be moving slower than usual, making the journey longer, but that they will ensure the women's safety. This seems to help, but there's still an under-lying tension. Even among the Drakav. Even though none of them mindspeak their unease, I can feel it in the way their gaze shifts over the suns around us. They do not like this place. This valley of silence, as they call it.

It's hard leaving the group when I've just found them again. But I need to. I bid my farewells and head toward Rok and Tharn. Kol intercepts me.

"We will guard these females. These daughters of Ain," he projects.

"I know you will, dra-dam...I put my trust in you."

I feel his brush of surprise at my use of his official title.

"You learn quickly, soft one," he projects. *"I have felt your*

thoughts. My brothers and I do not care if you are the true daughters or not. We will die for any one of these females anyway." I swallow down the lump of feeling that rises in my throat. His words feel like a vow. *"No harm will come to them while we draw breath."*

"Thank you." I give him a slight bow. *"They are my family. My clan."*

He inclines his head, accepting my designation. *"Find your sister-female. Bring her home to your clan."*

With that, he steps aside, and I join Rok and Tharn at the edge of the camp. *"Ready?"* Rok projects, his golden eyes searching mine. The urge to throw myself into his arms and just curl up and cry is almost overwhelming. His quiet support through all this has done more than he even knows.

I nod, casting one last glance back at the camp—at the human women tentatively putting their trust in the Drakav warriors as they prepare to head in the opposite direction.

"Let's find Jacqui," I say, turning to face the vast expanse of desert that swallowed my sister. "Let's bring her home."

CHAPTER 37
OKAY, DESERT. TRUCE?

JUSTINE

The stone formations grow larger as we approach, their jagged silhouettes stark against the darkening sky. We've been walking for hours, following the path Jacqui supposedly took, and my body aches with each step. I remember when I first took this journey. How I had to stop so many times. Now all I need is a swig from the waterskin and I keep going on. The heat is trying and the emergency blanket Alex gave me hardly feels like it's helping, but I can't stop. Won't stop. Not when my sister is out there somewhere.

By the time we reach the stone formation, I'm drained, but hopeful.

"Jaqs?" I call out. Only, there's no sign of Jacqui.

All that's left, all that's still there, is my message I left in the dust. The stones, now almost covered with sand, pointing toward the other stone formation in the distance.

Tharn releases a low rumble in his chest.

"In that direction lies our rivals. Territory we cannot cross."

I gulp hard. I've seen their rivals. I understand why they'd want to stay away. But it's my sister we're talking about here.

"We have to go. At least to the point where Rok caught up with me."

Tharn's gaze shifts to Rok. I can tell they're having an argument that Rok shields me from. Finally, Tharn's shoulders sag.

"We move with caution."

I swallow hard, nodding.

Tharn leads our small group, his powerful frame moving with surprising grace across the shifting sands. Every few minutes, he drops to a crouch, examining the ground with an intensity that gives me hope. Sometimes he lingers longer, head tilted as if listening to something I can't hear, before rising and adjusting our course slightly.

"Does he know where he's going?" I project to Rok, who walks beside me, his stride shortened to match mine.

"Tharn reads the dust like few others can," Rok replies, his mental voice confident. "Even traces that would be invisible to most leave marks he can follow."

I watch as Tharn pauses again, his clawed hand hovering just above the sand's surface. "What's he looking for, exactly?"

"Disturbances. Changes in how the sand settles. The dust remembers those who cross it, at least for a time."

The dust remembers. He's talking about tracking. It's such a poetic way to describe it and as I watch Tharn, there's something almost spiritual in how he approaches the task, as if communing with the desert itself.

"Your sister-female moved with purpose," Tharn projects suddenly, his thoughts directed at both of us. "Her path does not wander. She knew where she was going."

That sounds like Jacqui. Even lost in an alien desert, she would approach the task with her head on her shoulders. No panicked running in circles for my sister.

"Is that good?" I ask, hope fluttering in my chest.

"It means she conserved energy," Rok explains. "Used her water wisely. That improves her chances."

Her chances. The phrase sends a chill through me despite the lingering heat of the day. We're talking about her survival in terms of probability, and I hate it. I hate that we have to think this way.

As the sun, Ain, begins her descent toward the horizon, the stone formations that were my second destination loom before us. There's a small boulder that Tharn heads toward, gaze shifting from side to side now that we can see the stone formation that marks the rival clan's territory clearly.

"Justine." Rok's voice in my mind pulls me from my thoughts. "Come."

I turn to find him and Tharn standing a few yards from the boulder, both looking at something on the ground. My heart leaps into my throat as I hurry to join them. "Did you find something?"

Tharn gestures to the sand at our feet. At first, I see nothing unusual—just the endless grains that cover everything on this planet. But then, as I look more carefully, I notice a slight depression, a different texture to the surface.

"Someone rested here," Tharn projects. "Recently. Within the last two sols."

"Jacqui?" I can barely breathe around the hope swelling in my chest.

Tharn kneels, his long fingers hovering just above the impression. "The size matches what a being your size might leave."

I drop to my knees beside him, scanning the area desperately for any other sign. "But where did she go?" I lift my head, looking at the stone formations in the distance. If she went over there...

"There is...something else."

Tharn moves a few feet away, where the sand seems smoother, more deliberately arranged. Rok follows, crouching beside him, his head tilted in that curious way that reminds me he's not human, despite how comfortable I've become with him.

"What is it?" I ask out loud, joining them.

Rok looks up at me, his golden eyes reflecting the last of the sun's light. "Markings. In the dust."

I look down and my breath stops in my throat. There, etched into the surface, are lines and curves that I recognise immediately. Letters. English letters.

"J + J," I read aloud, my voice cracking. "4 EVER."

It's our childhood code, the one we used to carve into trees at summer camp, into the wooden bench at the park, even into the corner of my bedroom windowsill when I was twelve and Jacqui was eleven.

Tears spring to my eyes as I trace the letters with my fingertip. "It's from Jacqui," I whisper, then remember I need to use my thoughts. "She was here. She left this for me to find."

"What does it mean?" Rok asks, studying the markings.

I swallow hard against the lump in my throat. "It's her way of telling me she was here...and that she's okay."

"There is more," Tharn projects, moving a few feet to the right.

I follow him and find another set of markings, these bigger: "— H2O"

"Water," I translate. "She found water..." I look over the message, but the arrow has been erased by sand, leaving just part of a long line visible. I turn to the left and right, trying to spot where she might have gone.

Rok follows my gaze. "There are only two caves near here

where water collects," he projects. "We sheltered near one when—"

"When you saved me from the shadow creatures," I finish, the memory rushing back. That terrifying night when the predators had nearly caught me, when Rok had carried me up the steep side of a cliff to safety. "Could she have found the same place?"

Rok tilts his head. "Possible."

Hope surges through me, so strong it's almost painful. "How long could these markings last before the wind covers them?"

Tharn and Rok exchange a glance. "A sol," Tharn projects. "Two at most, if the wind is gentle."

"Then she was here yesterday, maybe the day before." I stand up, staring at the rock formations with renewed determination. "We need to go to the cave. Now."

Rok glances at Tharn.

"We must separate," Tharn unexpectedly suggests. "I will go to the farthest cave. You and Rok to the other closer one."

Rok considers this, then inclines his head in approval. "A wise plan."

I look between them, torn between gratitude for Tharn's offer and reluctance to split up. As the light dies, I know time is of the essence.

"Okay," I say out loud. With a deep breath, I reach up to my ear and take off my single remaining earring. I hand it to Tharn, taking his massive hand in mine as I press the little piece of jewelry into the center of his palm. He doesn't move, just stares at me and it.

"What is this?" He projects.

My fingers pause where I hold it there. The last thing I have from my mother. "It's something for Jacqui," I push my thoughts toward him. "So she will know I am safe. So she will know she can trust you."

Tharn gazes down at the earring as I finally take my hand away from it. I can tell by the way he closes his palm and holds it carefully that he senses the gravity of this little object. "I will make sure your sister-female sees it," he projects.

Before I can rethink it, I wrap my arms around Tharn in a hug.

He jerks, then goes impossibly still.

"What is the female doing, Rok?"

I chuckle, forcing a deep breath through my lungs. "It's called a hug." As I release him, he stands awkwardly, watching as I return to Rok's side. "Thank you, Tharn."

For a moment, he just blinks at me before inclining his head. Without another word, he turns and moves away from us, his form quickly blending with the gathering darkness.

"Come, my light," Rok projects. "We will reach the nearer cave before the dark." Lifting me into his arms, he takes off at a run, heading away from Tharn, the rival clan territory, and from the message Jacqui left.

I can only hope we're not too late.

CHAPTER 38
IS IT TOO EARLY TO SAY "I LOVE YOU"?
(ASKING FOR A FRIEND)

JUSTINE

As true darkness falls, Rok guides me into the cave. It's within a twisting rock face, the shadows cold. I hurry inside, heart in my throat.

"Jacqui?" But there's no answer.

It's clear it's empty. She's not here.

I can sense Rok's pain. It takes me a moment to realize it's because of me. Because tears are running down my face and *I'm* in pain. I wipe them away as he pulls me into his arms, settling on the ground, his body warming as if to provide heat to keep away the cold.

"Do you think she's okay?" I whisper, the question slipping out before I can stop it.

Rok's mind is quiet for a moment. "Your sister-female is resourceful," he projects finally. "She found water where most would find only dust. She did not go to the rival clan. She left markings for you to follow. These are the actions of one who means to survive."

It's not exactly the reassurance I was hoping for, but it's honest. And maybe that's what I need right now—not false comfort, but clear-eyed assessment.

"I should have never left her," I say, the guilt that's been building inside me finally spilling over. "I should have stayed with the bus. None of this would have happened if I hadn't been so stupidly stubborn about wanting to find help."

"Then you would not have found me," Rok points out gently. "Your people might still be slowly dying in the dust, with no hope of rescue."

"But Jacqui—"

"Made her choice," Rok interrupts, his mental voice firm. "As you made yours. Both choices came from the same place." He taps his chest, where a human heart would be.

Tears well up in my eyes at his simple wisdom.

"How did you get so wise?" I ask, attempting a smile through my tears.

"Not wise," Rok projects with a mental shrug, even as his fingers gently push away my tears, still clearly distressed by the sight of them. "Only existing for many cycles. One learns, or one does not survive the dust."

I move closer to him, seeking his warmth as the night chill begins to settle around us. He lifts his arm in silent invitation, and I tuck myself against his side, feeling the steady rhythm of his breathing. All along where our skin touches sends a nice comforting buzz through my veins.

"Tell me about your sister-female," Rok projects after a while.

The request surprises me, but as I begin telling him about Jacqui, of how brave she is and how happy I am that she's my sister, I realize it's exactly what I need—to remember Jacqui not as someone lost, but as someone whole and real and alive.

"She's my little sister." The memories flow more easily

than I expected. "Always been the responsible one. The planner. But fun, too. Jacqui is the type of girl who has her head on her shoulders but still knows how to loosen up and enjoy life."

Rok's confusion ripples through our link. "Head on shoulders? Where else would the head be?" A brief image flashes from his mind—some terrible creature with a misplaced head.

I can't help but laugh, the sound echoing off the cave walls. "It's just an expression. It means she's sensible. She thinks things through."

His mental voice carries a hint of amusement. "All Drakav keep their heads on their shoulders. Those who do not...do not live long."

I chuckle again before telling him more. Like about the time Jacqui dove into a lake to rescue me when I fell out of a canoe before we could swim properly and how we nearly drowned. The concept of so much water surprises him. I smile, continuing to tell him about the way Jacqui always, always put others before herself.

"She sounds like a good leader," Rok observes. "Like Kol."

The comparison startles another laugh from me. "Yeah, I guess she is. Practical. Reliable." I swallow hard. "Stubborn as hell once she sets her mind to something."

"Like you," Rok projects, amusement coloring his thoughts.

"Like me," I agree. "Though she'd hate to admit it."

As I talk, the weight on my chest seems to lighten somewhat. Not disappear—it won't until I know Jacqui is safe—but become more bearable. Rok listens with that intense focus I've come to cherish, his mind open to mine, absorbing every detail, every emotion.

"When we find her," I send the thought to him, "I think she will like you."

He grunts, and it makes me smile.

My very wild, unpredictable, dangerous alien.

Mine.

I stare at him now, the reality of it all coming down to settle around me.

"The Xyma," I project. "They're the beings that left us here. And...they haven't come looking for us. It's been weeks. Maybe they think we're dead, or maybe they just...decided we weren't worth the trouble."

The reality of our situation has been slowly crystallizing in my mind ever since we found the others. The transport isn't going anywhere. No rescue ships have appeared in the sky. We are stranded on this planet.

"If no one comes for us," I continue slowly, "we have to build a life here..." I stop, swallowing hard. "I want to stay with you."

Even as I say the words, something tugs at my chest. The thought of leaving without Rok...and then I realize, I hadn't really thought of leaving at all.

Rok shifts, turning to face me fully, his golden eyes intense as his glow pushes away the darkness.

"You are mine," he projects, the possessiveness in his mental voice sending a shiver down my spine. As if the thought never occurred to him that I wouldn't stay.

And I guess I'm not going anywhere.

I reach up to trace the contours of his face, memorizing each line, each angle. The first time I saw him, I thought him terrifying. Now, I see the beauty in his otherworldly features, in the strength and grace of his form.

The fear for Jacqui is a live wire under my skin, but Rok's arms are the only thing keeping me from unraveling. I need this. I need him. To remind me I'm not alone. My muscles unwind stitch by stitch, the heat of his body seeping into mine like sunlight against frost. For the first time since we left camp, my breath comes steady.

"Kiss me," I say in my mind.

His head tilts slightly, that now-familiar gesture of curiosity. "Water sharing, from the mouth."

"Yes," I whisper aloud, my voice barely audible even to my own ears.

Without hesitation, Rok leans down, his mouth brushing against mine, tentative at first, as if testing the waters. His lips are warm and firm, the press of them sending a shiver through me. I part my lips slightly, inviting him in, and the moment he deepens the kiss, all hesitation vanishes.

His hunger is raw, unrestrained, as if he's been waiting for this moment since the moment we met. His hand tangles in my hair, tilting my head back as his mouth claims mine completely. The kiss is not just a kiss—it's a declaration, a promise, a sealing of something unspoken between us.

And I kiss him back with equal fervor, my hands sliding up his chest, tracing the lines of his muscles, the heat of his skin against my palms. Every inch of him is strength and power, but beneath it, I feel the vulnerability he only shows me.

Rok pulls me closer, his massive arms wrapping around me as if to shield me from the rest of the world. His touch is every-where—his hands sliding down my back, gripping my hips, his claws careful but possessive. His body radiates a heat that seeps into me, igniting something deep in my core.

"Mine," he projects, his mental voice a low growl that resonates through me, sending a shockwave of need straight to my core.

"Yours," I whisper aloud, my voice trembling with the weight of the truth. "Always yours."

His glowing golden eyes meet mine, and for a moment, the world seems to stop. There's nothing but him and me, the space between us charged with an almost unbearable tension. Slowly, reverently, he lifts me into his arms and lays me down on the smooth rock. His gaze never leaves mine, his expression a mixture of awe. Desire.

Rok's hands move to the edges of my shirt, his claws careful as he peels the fabric away. His gaze darkens as each inch of skin is revealed, his breathing growing heavier. When I'm bare before him, his eyes roam over me, leaving a trail of heat in their wake.

"You are...like a ray of pure light," he projects. "Beautiful."

I feel a flush creep up my neck, but there's no time for embarrassment as he lowers himself over me, his mouth trailing a line of kisses down my neck, lingering at the hollow of my throat. His tongue flicks against my skin, teasing, tasting, and I gasp at the sensation.

His hands explore me with a surety that leaves me breathless, his touch both tender and possessive. He cups my breast, his thumb brushing over the sensitive peak, and I arch into his touch, a soft moan escaping my lips.

"Please," I whisper, voice trembling.

He growls softly in response; the sound vibrating against my skin as he takes my nipple into his mouth, his tongue swirling around it in a way that sends a jolt of pleasure straight through me. My hands find his shoulders, gripping him as he moves to the other breast, giving it the same attention, his teeth grazing just enough to make me gasp.

The ache between my thighs grows unbearable, and I shift beneath him, pressing my hips up against his. His loincloth does little to hide his arousal, the hard length of him pressing against me, and I whimper at the contact.

"Rok," I whisper, more insistently this time, my hands sliding down his back, urging him closer.

He pulls back slightly, his glowing eyes meeting mine, and the look in them steals what little breath I have left.

"Please," I whisper, and the last thread of his restraint

snaps. He claims my lips again, this time with a ferocity that makes my toes curl. His hands move to my hips, tugging away the last of the barriers between us. I shiver as the cool night air brushes against my heated skin, but the chill is quickly forgotten as Rok presses himself against me, his body radiating a warmth that sets me alight.

His hand slides between my thighs, his long fingers exploring me with a gentleness that belies his size. When he finds the sensitive bundle of nerves, I cry out; the sound disappearing into his mouth as my hips buck against his hand. He watches me intently, his eyes glowing brighter as he works me into a frenzy, his fingers teasing and stroking until I'm trembling beneath him.

"Now," I gasp, my hands clutching at his shoulders.

He growls softly, the sound sending a thrill through me, and positions himself at my entrance. He hesitates for only a moment, his gaze locking with mine, and then he pushes forward, slowly, carefully, until he's fully seated inside me.

I gasp at the sensation, the stretch of him almost too much, but the pleasure far outweighs the discomfort. Rok's breathing is ragged, his body trembling as he holds himself still, giving me time to adjust.

"You feel—" His thoughts stutter against mine, reverent. "Like fire and water combined. Impossible. Perfect."

His wonder floods through our connection, carrying images of the desert's cruel antagonism—the way life here exists between scorching heat and precious moisture, always at war. Yet with me, inside me, these opposing forces don't destroy. They ignite.

"My light," he growls, and the words vibrate through every point where we're joined, like a claim written in the oldest language. Of flesh. Of need.

I wrap my arms around his neck, pulling him down for a

kiss, and when I roll my hips against his, he takes it as permission to move. He starts slow, his thrusts deep, but as the tension builds between us, his control slips.

His pace quickens, each thrust sending a wave of pleasure crashing through me. I cling to him, my nails digging into his back as I meet each movement, our bodies moving in perfect sync.

"Mine," Rok growls again, his voice a low rumble that vibrates through my entire being.

"Yours," I whisper, my voice breaking as the pleasure builds to a peak. The word feels too small for what's between us now—what's been growing since he first carried me through the desert.

When my release finally comes, it's like a tidal wave, crashing over me with an intensity that leaves me shaking—not just from pleasure, but from the shocking truth that rises with it:

I love him.

Rok stills suddenly, his golden eyes widening. *"Why does your heart race? Are you dying?"* His mental voice is frantic, claws flexing against my hips like he's ready to fight death itself.

A breathless laugh escapes me. I press my forehead to his, our minds entwined as I whisper back, *"Worse. I'm in love."* I can't describe it. It's only a feeling. So I send that feeling to him, every ounce of it. The depth of it. The light of it.

For a moment, Rok's hips stutter. His growl vibrates through my bones, part triumph, part reverence. *"Love,"* he repeats, right before his glow suddenly swells. He seals the word with his lips on mine.

I love him.

This fierce, golden alien who learned to smile for me. Who fought monsters on my behalf without hesitation. Who changed himself to fit me better, yet never asks me to be anything but what I am.

Rok follows moments later, his powerful body shuddering against mine as he finds his own release, his mind wide open to mine, sharing every ounce of his pleasure and...and his love. The emotion pours into me, warm and certain as sunrise, and I clutch him tighter, my cheek pressed to his pounding chest.

We collapse together in a tangle of limbs, my revelation still humming through my veins. Rok cradles me against him, his arms wrapping around me like living armor. His skin glows faintly where it touches mine like our own private constellation, and my heart swells in my chest.

"Thank you," I whisper, but it's not just for this moment. It's for the water shared when I was thirsty. For carrying me when I couldn't walk. For seeing me—really seeing me—in a way no one ever has.

Rok's thumb brushes my lower lip. "We are one." His certainty vibrates through our connection. "Forever, Jus-teen."

And he's right. I know it with a bone-deep certainty. Messed up as my arrival was, I was meant to be here. He was meant to find me.

The knowledge settles in my bones as sleep pulls at me.

I am his.

He is mine.

And this desert that tried to kill us both?

It brought me home.

A sense of peace settles over me. Not complete—not with Jacqui still missing—but enough to quiet the worst of my fears.

"We will find your sister-kin," Rok projects, sensing the direction of my thoughts. "That is my oath to you, Jus-teen."

A smile crosses my lips.

I believe him.

EPILOGUE
THARN'S HUNT: BARBARIANS OF THE DUST:
BOOK 2

Hallucinations 101: Please take a seat

JACQUI

The desert holds twenty-seven ways to die. I've cataloged them all in my mind journal, a morbid habit that's somehow kept me sane during these endless days wandering this alien wasteland. Dehydration. Heat stroke. Predator attack. Starvation. Falling from heights. Quicksand. The list goes on.

Today, I'm fairly certain I've discovered number twenty-eight: hallucination-induced cliff diving.

I huddle in the shallow cave that has been my shelter for the past two nights, squinting at the figure moving across the sand below. Tall. Impossibly strong-looking. Golden-bronze skin that catches the last rays of the setting sun.

Not human.

I press myself deeper into the shadows, my heart

hammering against my ribs. After weeks alone in this desert, I've finally cracked. I'm seeing things. Have to be.

The figure stops, crouching to examine something on the ground. My tracks, probably. I'd been careful, but not careful enough. Not that it matters if this is just a hallucination.

But hallucinations don't kick up sand as they walk. They don't cast shadows. They don't pause, head tilting as if scenting the air.

My breath catches as the figure's head suddenly snaps up, golden eyes somehow finding mine despite the distance and shadows. Our gazes lock, and for a moment, time seems to suspend.

He's real.

I scramble backward, deeper into the cave, my hand automatically reaching for the makeshift weapon Mikaela had fashioned. Not that it will do much good against...whatever that is.

My mind races through possibilities. Another species dropped here by the Xyma? Natives? Somehow, the latter feels worse.

How happy would some barbarian be to find some tourist hanging out at his favorite lookout spot? Shit.

The smart move is to stay hidden, to wait until this creature moves on. But something about those eyes...there had been intelligence there. Awareness. And something else I don't want to pinpoint too clearly.

A sound outside—the soft slide of sand as something approaches the cave entrance. My fingers tighten around my weapon.

The creature appears in the entrance, his massive form blocking what little light remains. He makes no move to enter, simply stands there, watching me with those unsettling golden eyes.

My fingers tighten around the jagged metal in my grip—a piece torn from the bus wrapped in worn fabric. If this is a hallucination, it's the most detailed one yet—right down to the way the sand shifts under his feet. But hallucinations don't sniff the air so boldly I can sense the way it shifts. And they sure as hell don't look at me like they can see straight into my soul.

I don't wait for him to make the first move. Survival instinct takes over—I lunge forward, swinging my makeshift weapon with all the strength my exhausted body can muster.

He doesn't even flinch.

My weapon connects with his arm and bounces off like I've hit solid rock. He moves then, faster than anything his size should be capable of, catching my wrist in a grip that's firm but not crushing.

I thrash wildly, kicking, scratching, biting—using every dirty trick I've ever learned. He restrains me with insulting ease, eventually pinning me to the cave floor with my arms above my head, his weight carefully distributed so I can't move but can still breathe.

"Get off me!" I scream, knowing it's useless but unable to stop fighting. "Let me go!"

There's a grunt in his throat, a wince as he turns his head away from me, brow furrowed, as if I hurt him somehow. But he makes no other sound. Just watches me with those strange eyes, his expression unreadable. I'm about to scream again when something impossible happens.

Where his skin touches mine, light blooms.

It's subtle at first—a faint golden glow that pulses between us where his hands—no, fuck, those aren't just hands, they're claws—grip my wrists. Then it intensifies, spreading up his arms like liquid fire, not burning but warming, illuminating the cave with an otherworldly radiance.

He jerks back as if burned, releasing me and stumbling to his feet. His hand goes to his chest, clutching at it, his expression one of shock and something that looks strangely like pain. A low, guttural sound escapes him. Clearly distressed.

I scramble backward, too stunned to run. What just happened? What was that light? Why did he react that way?

As he recovers, something catches my eye—a small object that's fallen from him during our struggle. Something that glints in the fading light, familiar and impossible.

A butterfly earring. Golden and pink crystal. *Justine's* earring. The twin to the one currently burning a hole against my breastbone. Tucked away safe in my bra since the day I found it buried in the sand at that rock formation she was supposed to be, but never was.

The alien notices my gaze. Slowly, he retrieves the earring and places it on the ground between us. Not keeping it. Offering it.

My mind races with possibilities. He's killed her and taken it as a trophy. No—why would he come find me then? He's found her body. No—he wouldn't look so purposeful, so intent.

She's alive. Somehow, my sister is alive, and this creature knows where she is.

"Justine?" I whisper, my voice breaking on her name. "Is she alive?"

He doesn't speak—can't speak, maybe—but his head tilts slightly with a slight wince as he watches me. The gesture is so human, it steals my breath.

"You know where she is?"

No response.

My legs feel suddenly weak. I slide down the cave wall, eyes still fixed on the earring. After so long searching, waiting.

Of alternating between hope and despair. Of imagining the worst...

The alien crouches again, still keeping his distance, and points in a direction over his shoulder. The message is clear: She's that way. I can take you to her.

He reaches for something at his waist—some kind of pouch—and pulls out...is that a stomach? A dried animal bladder? It sloshes.

He extends it toward me carefully, like he's offering treasure instead of what looks like a grotesque science experiment. Water, then. It has to be. Nothing else would make that sound.

I don't care if it's a camel's recycled colon at this point. My fingers shake as I reach for it, the promise of liquid overriding every survival instinct screaming not to trust alien beverages. The moment coolness hits my lips, I'm gulping greedily, half-choking as it floods my parched throat.

The container smells faintly of herbs and something earthy, but the water itself tastes clean—better than the metallic tang of our emergency rations. When I finally come up for air, I'm lightheaded with relief.

When I hand it back, our fingers brush briefly. His entire body goes rigid as light erupts from the contact point, streaking up his arm toward his chest. He makes a sound like rocks grinding together—pained? Awed?—and stumbles back a step.

For three rapid heartbeats, we just stare at each other. His nostrils flare wide, and he inhales deeply, probably scenting me, his glowing eyes tracking every microexpression on my face. The intensity makes my skin prickle.

Something unreadable passes across his face.

I don't wait for whatever silent conversation he wants to have. Scrambling to my feet, I point at the earring, then toward the desert. "Take me to her. Now."

He moves faster than I can track, blocking the cave entrance with his massive body. When I try to push past, he doesn't yield, his skin like a light show as he points at the dying light outside.

I follow his gesture. The last sliver of sun vanishes below the dunes, plunging the world into violet twilight. A distant screech echoes across the sands—something hungry and hunting.

Understanding dawns with a chill.

"It's not safe," I murmur, shoulders slumping.

He makes a low sound in his throat and gestures to the back of the cave. An offer, I guess. Not an order.

I should argue. Should demand answers. But my legs wobble beneath me, my vision spotting with exhaustion. I haven't eaten anything proper in days. I'm tired. Hungry. Thirsty. For once, I listen to my body instead of my stubbornness.

As I slump against the cave wall, I find myself studying him—this alien being who's appeared out of nowhere with my sister's earring and water to share. Who somehow made light appear between us. Who wants to take me to Justine.

For the first time since I'd set out in this wasteland, hope warms me more effectively than any fire.

The desert holds twenty-seven ways to die. But as those golden eyes lock onto mine, I wonder—for the first time since I lost Justine—if it might also hold a way to survive.

AFTERWORD

❋☆❋☆❋

Dear Reader,

Well, hellooo. You made it.

First of all—*thank you.* The fact that you just spent hours wandering a death-desert with Justine, Rok, and a gang of feral creatures (shadowmaws and Drakav) means the world to me.

This book was born from three questions:

1 What if "enemies to lovers" but one of them is literally a glow-in-the-dark make-your-knees weak alien who's never seen a human before?

2 How fast would I personally perish if stranded on an alien planet? (Spoiler: Before lunch.)

3 And what if the universe... uh... **custom-designed** *the perfect partner?* (A custom-made D deserves its own fan club. I wonder what Jacqui will get :D)

Watching Justine and Rok crash into each other's lives—her sarcasm vs. his silent intensity, her human weirdness vs. his *"what is this tiny creature and why do I want to bite it"* energy—has been an absolute blast. And we're *just getting started.*

Because in Book 2:

✔ Jacqui is *done* with this desert (and her new grumpy alien shadow, Tharn).

✔ The Drakav are about to learn humans don't follow "silent hunter" rules. (We *will* scream about our feelings.)

✔ Someone's getting stabbed. Probably. (It's me. By my own outline.)

Want more?

• **Don't forget to join my newsletter.** Scan the QR code below for a hilarious bonus scene featuring Tharn's existential crisis.

• **Follow me on social media**. I **am** present on there. Pardon my introverted silence.

• **Leave a review** if you laughed, cried, or now side-eye deserts IRL. (Rok approves of territorial marking—but only in designated areas!! Like Justine's pus— ahem)

Most of all—thank you for trusting me to drag you through the sand. *The real treasure was the aliens we thirsted for along the way.*

See you in the Silent Valley,

🩶 A.G.

Tharn's Hunt

The desert holds twenty-seven ways to die. Today, I discover number twenty-eight: hallucination-induced cliff diving.

When a golden-eyed alien hunter tracks me to my cave, I assume I've finally cracked—until he throws me to the ground and *light* erupts where our skin touches.

He doesn't speak. Doesn't kill me.

Instead, he drops a butterfly earring—my missing sister's earring—between us like a challenge.

Now I have to choose:

1. Trust this glowing stranger who smells like desert storms and moves like a predator.

2. Stay here and let the creatures of the dark finish what the Xyma started.

Survival just got a hell of a lot more complicated.

(First-contact sci-fi romance with forced proximity, survival stakes, and a possessive alien hero who really doesn't like human screaming.)

Also By

Captured by Aliens

Xul

Crex

Yce

Kyris

Kyro

Riv's Sanctuary

Riv's Sanctuary

Sohut's Protection

Ka'Cit's Haven

The Restitution

Ajos

V'Alen

Akur

A New Home

An Alien for the Farm

An Alien for Her Heart

An Alien for the Future

Captured Earth

Arrival

Base Zero

Cataclysm

War

Rebirth

Fated Mates of the Atari

Claiming His Mate

Craving His Mate

Fighting for His Mate

Guarding His Mate

The Midnight Seven

Outlaw

Barbarians of the Dust

Rok's Captive

Tharn's Hunt

Scan the QR code to view all books

About the Author

A. G. Wilde is an avid reader, a gamer, a lover of all things space, alien, and sci-fi.

She is addicted to intense romance, irresistible heroes, and deliciously naughty things.

f facebook.com/agwilde

instagram.com/authoragwilde

tiktok.com/@authoragwilde

X x.com/authoragwilde

BB bookbub.com/profile/a-g-wilde

a amazon.com/author/agwilde

9 781915 772114